MAD AS HELL

MAD WORLD #2

HANNAH MCBRIDE

For my girl squad: Nicole, Tracy, & Katie
You three have kept me afloat when I was positive my life raft was defective.

AUTHOR'S NOTE

Hey, friend! If you're reading this, THANK YOU SO MUCH! But also, check this out:

Mad As Hell is a completely fictional story that deals with some very real world (and heavy) issues including substance abuse, sexual abuse, language, and has an alphahole that can be unsettling for some readers. If you're someone who might have a hard time with that, please stop here!

If you're one of my amazing family members here to support me... I love you, but you might want to consider stopping here. And by *might* I mean, **stop here.**

MAD AS HELL

MAD WORLD #2

By: Hannah McBride

CHAPTER 1

RYAN

The sounds from the party in the frat house next to ours were killing the buzz I was working on. I could hear girls squealing and shrieking, like that actually made a guy's dick hard. Hell, I'd fucked enough of them at parties to know that maybe they were on to something.

But tonight? Tonight I didn't care, and my dick was the last thing on my mind. All I wanted tonight was to get obliterated and forget about my shitshow of an engagement party the night before.

Maybe coming back to campus right away had been a bad call, but sitting around my house while Dad gloated at seeing his best friend's financial loss and total humiliation had settled like a lump of rotten sushi in my gut. When he'd suggested ordering me a companion to, and I quote, "Suck me out of that funk," I'd driven back to school.

At least my friends were here. Well, two of them. Who the fuck knew where Ash was, but at least Court and Linc were willing to jump on the pity train with me.

Court wasn't much of a surprise. Walking away from Bex—again—was fucking with his head, and I felt like an even bigger asshole because I'd brought her back into his world in the first place.

As for Linc… Shit, he had enough issues with women, and now the

1

two he'd actually started to open up to and gave a shit about had fucked us all. Maddie by betraying me, and Bex by taking her side.

Regret churned in my stomach, and I couldn't stop my thoughts from spiraling into *what ifs* and trying to see the signs I'd missed.

A bottle of Grey Goose dangled from my fingers as I contemplated going upstairs and hitting up Gordo's stash. He always had the best weed, and right now, I could use it to mellow out.

With a grunt, Linc leaned forward and snatched the bottle from my hand. He took a long drink and passed it to Court. "No."

"No, what?" I demanded, tracing my finger along the edge of the chair's arm.

"You know Coach drug tests," Linc shot back, his blue eyes dark and churning. "Last thing we need is your piss coming up positive."

Court nodded. "He's right. Especially with how shitty the games have been going lately."

Rage burned in my gut, and I lunged for the bottle and swallowed more of the fiery liquid. Dousing fire with fire probably wasn't the best idea, but what else did you do when the woman you loved fucked you over in front of everyone you knew?

Love.

I scoffed, hating that I'd lowered myself to even utter that word, let alone feel it.

Lifting the bottle into the air, I offered a toast. "To Madison. For fucking me *and* our shot at a championship."

Court grimaced. "She had us all fooled, man."

"Fuck her," Linc added coldly.

That stupid, fucking, weak-ass corner of my heart that she still ruled, even now, revolted at them talking shit about her. I took another drink, hoping to drown the fucker's voice. My heart needed to get it together: Madison Porter had played me. I had to lock down my emotions before she showed up at school.

I was Ryan motherfucking Cain. I wasn't the guy who got led around by his dick; I was the guy who set the tone. And it was time everyone, including Maddie, remembered that.

"What are you going to do?" Court smirked at me, probably

reading my expression. The guy was smart as hell and missed nothing. Considering his family, it wasn't a surprise. They'd probably drilled that shit into his head before the umbilical cord was cut.

I raised the bottle to my lips and smiled, feeling that familiar surge of darkness that had seemed to hover in the distance when Maddie had been near. Now it was back and hungry. The leash was gone, and I was ready for chaos.

"Maddie's fair game," I told them firmly before taking a sip of the vodka. "I might still have to marry her, but her happiness isn't my problem anymore."

Linc hesitated. "You sure, man? You know those academy douches will be brutal. And now knowing she sabotaged the team, too?"

"*Again,*" Court murmured. He clarified when we both looked at him, "They don't know Maddie isn't Lainey. So it looks like she betrayed the team *twice.* She made Ryan look like a joke *twice.*"

I rubbed my jaw thoughtfully. "You think lifting our order of protection isn't enough?"

He shrugged a massive shoulder. "I think we need to prove we're still in charge and no one's above us."

Linc sucked in a sharp breath between his teeth. "You realize it's not just Maddie that will affect, right? Bex seems to be staying by her side."

"Then it's her funeral, too," I answered coldly. I looked at two of my closest friends. "Can you both handle that?"

Linc grunted, his jaw clenching as he made up his mind. "She made her choice."

I stared at Court, knowing this would be harder for him, since he and Bex were the ones with history. It had rocked him when Dean threw Bex back into our orbit with that stunt at the beginning of the year, but I could see what I had known when we were kids: Bex got under his skin.

Cutting her out of his life one more time might be more than was fair to ask of one of my oldest friends.

"It is what it is," he finally replied, reaching for the bottle.

3

"Yo!" Ash yelled from somewhere in the house. "Where are you guys?"

"Out here!" Linc called, taking a drink and passing me the bottle once again.

Shit, at this rate we were going to need another one.

My head lolled back as I watched Ash walk out onto the deck, his laptop tucked under one arm.

Smirking, I extended the nearly empty bottle of vodka to him. "Come to join us?"

Linc shifted his sprawled legs up to give Ash a seat, but my best friend shook his head and waved us off.

"All right," I muttered, looking down into the bottle. "More for me." I lifted it to my lips.

Ash slapped it away, and the bottle shattered on the deck.

"Dude, what the fuck?" Linc whined. "That was a three-hundred-dollar bottle of—"

"Does it look like I give a shit?" Ash cut him off coolly, his green gaze focused on me.

My eyebrows lifted. The alcohol had settled like a blanket of indifference around me, but I could feel my anger scratching under the surface, begging to break free and spew havoc and pain on the world. "Clearly not. So fuck off and let us drink."

"You mean let you pout?" Ash corrected. "Because that's what it looks like your bitch-ass is doing."

I shoved myself to my feet so fast the chair I was in hit the wall behind me. Thankfully I didn't sway too much as I stared down my friend. "The fuck did you say?"

"I said you're out here pouting like a little bitch," he sneered, shaking his head in disgust. His gaze jumped past me to our friends. "And you two dipshits are cosigning on it."

Court frowned, and Linc started shaking his head.

"After the shit that went down?" Linc gave a low whistle. "I think Ryan's earned himself a fucking keg of whatever helps him forget what happened last night. We all have."

I clenched my jaw hard enough that I worried my teeth would

shatter. No amount of alcohol would help me forget the way Maddie had torn my heart out of my chest and used it as a soccer ball.

The alcohol just made the memories a little fuzzier and helped me settle on anger instead of letting the pain or the amazement that I had been played so totally settle in my heart.

No, anger was better.

I needed more to drink.

"Sit down," Ash ordered, like he knew I was about to bulldoze through his ass to find something else in the house to drink.

I let out a soft chuckle that would have most people backing away. "You gonna make me?"

"Depends," he said, not budging, "are you going to keep acting like a spoiled brat? Or are you ready for some truth?"

"What the fuck does that mean?" I spat. My head was spinning, and I was too irritated for word games. "If you didn't come out here to help me—"

"I did come out here to help," Ash cut me off, his green eyes flashing, "but not by letting you get blitzed."

"Then you're not fucking helping, *friend*," I hissed. I shoved him back a step and Court and Linc got up.

"Ry, man, chill," Court warned, his dark gaze snapping between the two of us.

"Ash needs to back off," I growled, dangerously close to decking my best friend.

With a snarl, Ash slapped my chest with his laptop. "It wasn't Maddie, you fucking idiot."

White-hot rage flushed through my body at her name. Rage and... fuck me. *Want.* My dick stirred to life, despite the copious amounts of alcohol that should have made me captain of the *S.S. Limp Dick.*

But of course, one mention of Maddie, and I could picture her sprawled out on my bed as I slammed my hips into her over and over. The glazed look in her eyes and the flush that ran from her cheeks across her perfect tits seconds before she came like a damn freight train beneath me.

I wiped a hand over my mouth as a bitter taste tinged my tongue.

5

I'd seen only a few seconds of her sex tape with Dean, but it was forever burned into my brain.

"Don't say her damn name," I seethed, my hands shaking with the need to break something or some*one*.

"Who? *Maddie*?" Ash smirked at me.

I lunged for him, but Court and Linc kept me back.

Barely.

"Jesus, Ryan, he played you," Ash snapped. "He played you, and you fucking let him, bro."

"What are you talking about?" Court demanded, grunting as my elbow landed on his ribs.

"Dean," Ash spat, shaking his head. "Dean fucking set Maddie up, and you fell for it."

His words penetrated the red fog around my brain and I slowly stopped fighting against my friends.

"What?"

Ash gave me a disgusted look and opened his laptop, flipping it around so I could see the screen frozen on Maddie riding Dean's dick.

I flinched away from the visual and glared at Ash.

"If you would've waited a fucking hour, I could have told you that the tape had been doctored," Ash informed me. "Whatever video he sent out? He slapped the timestamp on it, but all I had to do was look under one layer and see the *real* timestamp. Unless Madison was fucking Dean last fall? This isn't her in the video."

"It's Madelaine," Linc murmured, looking a little shell-shocked.

Court groaned. "Fuck me. Why didn't we think of that?"

Shock froze my system as I narrowed my gaze on the screen and noticed the *correct* time in the lower right corner. Ash was right; the video was from last year.

"But... she had the same sweater," I stammered. "And Josh said—"

"Josh said he saw her going into Dean's room, but how long was she in there? You think Dean isn't devious enough to set this shit up so Maddie happened to be in his room when a witness walked by?" Ash scoffed at me. "Wake the fuck up, Ryan."

My eyes drifted closed as the weight of what Ash was telling me sunk in.

No, no, no.

If he was right, then I'd fucked up bigger than I ever had in my entire life.

"Madison didn't cheat on you, asshole," he confirmed, but the bite was gone from his tone and replaced with something that reeked of pity. "She didn't do a damn thing, and you threw her to the wolves."

"The playbook," Court argued. "How the fuck did Dean get that unless Maddie gave it to him?"

With an aggravated sigh, Ash clicked onto another screen, and I recognized the hallway upstairs. Dean stood in his doorway, waiting as Maddie came out.

Whatever he said pissed her off, but when he grabbed her arm, I saw red. She managed to shake him off and leave...

And he walked right into my unlocked room. Moments later he was out, the playbook tucked under his arm, and then he ducked back into his room just as Maddie came upstairs and hurried to my room to lock the door.

Motherfucker.

She'd told me the truth.

I pinched the bridge of my nose and couldn't help but remember the betrayal and pain in her eyes, the way her voice shook.

If you leave, then I'm done.

Her last words echoed in my brain.

"I fucked up," I murmured, sucking in a sharp breath that made me dizzy.

"We all did," Linc muttered behind me.

Ash shot us a smug look. "I didn't. No one can fake the kind of innocence that girl had."

I scrubbed a hand down my face. "I need to find her. I need to talk to her."

It was after midnight and a two-hour drive to her house, but I needed to see her *now*. I had to make this right. Shit, she had every right to be pissed, but I refused to accept we were over.

"You're drunk, dude," Court pointed out. "Maybe not the best time to go driving up the coast."

I scowled at him. "Then I'll take a fucking Uber." I spun to leave, even as the space around me tilted precariously.

Fuck, I *was* too wasted to drive.

Ash clapped a hand on my shoulder. "I'll drive. You assholes get in the car."

It took longer than I would've liked for us to stumble out to Ash's Range Rover, and even longer for the nearly two-hour drive back up north to the Cabot estate.

My best friend drove like a little old lady, and I was going to punch him in the dick as soon as I was sober enough to get behind the wheel myself. Instead, I had to settle for glaring at him as he drove to Maddie's.

"It's dark," Court remarked from the backseat, leaning forward as Ash turned up the long drive to the massive mansion on a hill that Gary Cabot used to show the world how rich he was.

My heart thumped against my ribs as I stared at the dark house. It looked ominous with all the lights out. I would've thought the power was down if not for the fact that all the other houses had lights on.

"Something's not right," Ash muttered, squinting as he pulled up in front of the house and put the SUV in park.

I threw open the door and swore as the alcohol made me sluggish. I stumbled up the front steps, not really giving a shit what I looked like. I fumbled for my keys in my pocket, and it took three tries to find the right one.

Linc, Ash, and Court were at my back as I pushed open the front door of the house and was met with silence.

"If this was a horror movie," Linc whispered, "the killer would have us right where he wanted."

A smacking sound echoed in the hall as Ash slapped the back of his head. "Shut up."

"Jesus, you're grouchy when you're sober and acting morally superior," Linc groused.

"All of you shut the fuck up," I snapped, reaching over and turning on the lights in the front hall.

The sudden wash of brightness was blinding, and it took time for my eyes to adjust.

It was hard to believe that a little over twenty-four hours earlier, there had been a huge party here. Everything looked clean and sterile and… empty.

"Is anyone even here?" Court murmured, his dark eyes sweeping across the space suspiciously.

"I don't know," I replied in a clipped tone, my anxiety ratcheting up several notches. "See if you can find anyone down here. I'm going to find Maddie."

I didn't wait for them to respond as I ran up the stairs, taking them two at a time and not slowing my pace until I was outside Maddie's room. I shoved her door open.

"Maddie?" I called into the darkness as I stepped inside and flipped the light switch.

My breath caught as I realized she wasn't here. Her bed was made and clearly untouched. Everything looked normal and pristine, but it felt *wrong*.

I checked her bathroom and closet even though I knew it was pointless. By the time I came out of her room, Ash had made it upstairs, his expression grim.

"They're gone," he announced.

"No shit," I spat. "Where the fuck are they?"

"No idea," he admitted tersely. "I checked the security tapes, but they've been wiped."

I froze, panic clawing at my insides. "What do you mean, wiped?"

"I mean, someone erased everything," he replied. "The whole weekend is gone. The party, them leaving… It's gone."

I growled in frustration. "So, they're what? Fucking *gone*? They can't just vanish. That makes zero fucking sense."

Ash spread his arms wide. "I can't magically make them appear, Ry. Maddie's gone."

I clenched my fists, wanting to smash them into something.

No.

Into some*one*.

But right now, I needed to be smart. Think smart.

I rubbed the back of my neck, trying to ignore the way my head was starting to throb. "Okay, let's go."

"Go where?" Ash demanded as I pushed by him and hurried down the stairs.

Linc and Court were waiting by the front door.

"Call Bex," I ordered them as I kept going toward the car.

Linc frowned. "Bex?"

I glanced back over my shoulder as I yanked the door open. "She was the last one to see Maddie."

Linc and Court exchanged looks as Ash joined them.

"Dude, it's like three in the morning," Court objected. "Bex is probably asleep."

"Then wake her the fuck up," I demanded, getting into the car and slamming the door so hard the entire SUV shuddered.

I didn't care if Bex was asleep or not. I would raze the entire world until I found my girl, and God help anyone who got in my way.

CHAPTER 2

RYAN

L ights were on at the Whittier residence, but it was just security illumination around the perimeter since it was the middle of the night and people were clearly sleeping. The two-story brick monstrosity with manicured gardens was only a few streets away from Maddie's house, and it looked slightly out of place among the Tuscan-inspired homes of the gated community. Bex's mom had designed this house specifically to remind her of her East Coast roots.

Once Ash stopped the car, I opened the door, and his hand shot out to grab my arm. I stared back at him, annoyed at the interruption.

"What's our play here, Ryan?" he asked, the dim lighting of the SUV's interior casting shadows across his dark complexion. "It's the middle of the night. You really think Bex's parents are going to invite us inside so you can interrogate their daughter?"

I grimaced. He had a point. The Whittiers weren't like other parents I'd grown up around. They actually seemed to give a damn about their kid. Or her mom did, at least. Bex's dad wasn't quite as deep into shit as ours were, but he wasn't a saint by any means.

Court sighed from the back. "I can get you in," he muttered, pushing open his door.

Linc's brows shot up. "You still have a key? I would've thought Betty took that back after—"

Court glared at our friend, annoyed at the mention of Bex's mom. "She did. But since when has something like a locked door kept me out?"

I smirked and shook my head. Court's skill had come in handy, especially when he showed me the finer points of lock picking. It was how I had broken into Maddie's room that first day of school to surprise her.

Pain flared in my chest, and I fought back the wave of panic threatening to break over my head if I didn't find her soon.

"Want us to come, too?" Ash offered, drumming his fingers on the steering wheel.

Court eased his door shut so as not to attract too much noise. "No, it'll be easier with two of us than an entire group." He leaned in through my open door to look at Ash. "But, just to be on the safe side, you may want to hack into the surveillance cameras and erase us being here."

Ash nodded and reached for the laptop he had tucked between his seat and the consol. "On it."

"Court," Linc beckoned. He hesitated, wincing. "Fuck. Tell Bex..."

Court's lips pressed together in a flat line. "Yeah, I know, man."

"Seems like we're all buying tickets for the apology train," I muttered darkly.

Ash ticked up a finger, not pausing from where he was hacking into the Whittiers' security system. "Not me."

I shot him a glare. "Fine. Not you. Fucker," I added before closing the door more softly than I would've liked. I turned to Court.

He jerked his head toward the side of the house. "Their basement walkout is our best bet," he murmured as we started forward, sticking to the shadows. "Malcolm uses it to smoke at night, and he disabled the alarm so Betty wouldn't know."

"Maybe he gave up smoking," I remarked.

Court snorted softly. "I saw him ducking outside to light up at

12

your engagement party. I was kind of surprised to see them there, actually."

"Maddie mentioned that Gary's been trying to get Malcolm to help him with something," I admitted.

Court stopped cold, a calculating glint in his dark eyes. "Why am I just hearing about this now?"

"Because I've had other shit going on," I reminded him with a snarl.

His wide shoulders stiffened. "Ry, you know I like Maddie—"

I growled at whatever he was about to say.

"—but since you found out who she really is..." He trailed off with a grimace.

"What?" I whispered harshly. "Say it."

"You've been distracted," Court finished.

I folded my arms, annoyed that we were having this conversation now, in the shadows of the Whittier mansion. "And you haven't been?"

His eyes narrowed.

"You think I haven't seen the way you're constantly following Bex around?" I pointed out, knowing I'd hit the mark when the skin around his eyes tightened.

"And whose fault is that?" he hissed. "You're the one who had me carry her home that night Dean tried to..." His hands curled into massive fists, and I knew from experience that if one of them swung in my direction, it would hurt like a bitch.

"I didn't tell you to keep hanging around her," I pointed out like the asshole I was. I'd known it was a dick move, having him take Bex home that night, but I also knew their history, and no way would he have let anyone else do it.

"Fuck you," Court spat. "You knew exactly what you were doing. And none of us can afford a distraction right now."

"So, what? You want me to give up Maddie?" As I spoke them aloud, the words left a cold, hollow void in my chest.

His head tipped back as his jaw clenched. "No, of course not. I'm just saying, we need to be careful."

"Good," I snapped, "because Maddie is mine, and I'm not making the mistake of letting her go again."

His eyebrows lifted. "That's if you can convince her to take your sorry ass back."

My eyes narrowed. "She will."

"You sound pretty sure of yourself."

"That's because I am," I forced out, my irritation spiking. "Now can we go talk to Bex, or do we need to call the guys over for a circle-jerk while we discuss our feelings?"

Rolling his eyes, Court turned and kept going. Sure enough, the alarm on the glass doors of the basement walk-out had been disabled. We crept quietly to the house, sticking to the walls as we ascended to the top floor where the bedrooms were.

Court led the way, his steps sure even in the dark. Then again, he had practically grown up in this house before things went to shit between his family and the Whittiers.

"This one," he murmured, stopping at the last door in the hall.

I took the lights shining under the door as a good sign that Bex might be up.

Court hesitated.

"If you want me to do this alone—"

"No," he cut me off harshly. "I've got this." He lifted his hand and knocked softly.

It took a second, but the door cracked open and Bex's face appeared. Her hazel eyes went comically wide and her mouth dropped open to say something, but Court surged forward. He pushed the door open and grabbed her, pressing his hand over her mouth and walking her backward into the room by wrapping his other arm around her waist. I followed them inside and closed the door. I locked it for good measure.

"Can he let you go without you screaming?" I asked her.

She glared at me and then Court and then back to me. Finally, she gave a jerky nod.

"Let her go," I told him.

He lowered his hand but made no move to release her.

Bex slapped at his chest until his arm went slack and he stepped away, his face stony and unreadable.

"What the *hell* are you two doing here?" she demanded hotly. Her hair was twisted into a messy knot on top of her head, and her tiny shorts and tank top made it look like she was ready for bed. The glasses perched on her nose were an adorable touch. I'd forgotten she wore contacts.

"Looking for Maddie," I replied.

Her cheeks flushed with anger, pink suffusing the porcelain skin of her face. "Like I would tell *you*."

It took everything in me not to grab her and demand she tell me what she knew. I was still working on controlling my tone when Court spoke up.

"Becca, come on," he said softly.

Her jaw dropped a little in surprise. "Don't call me that," she ordered, her tone quivering. "We're not friends, remember? You made that perfectly clear years ago."

"You know things have changed," he reminded her, speaking gently like she was a deer that might startle and run.

Her brows lifted and she folded her arms. "Bullshit."

"We don't have time for this," I snapped, getting between the two of them and using my height to tower over Bex. If I needed to intimidate the little mouse to get my answers, I would. "Where is Maddie?"

Her jaw set in a mulish line. "Why would I tell you anything? You broke her heart when she needed you the most."

I bit back an angry retort. "Because I know I was wrong. I know Dean set her up and everything was faked, okay? I feel like shit."

"You should," she muttered.

"Rebecca, please," I tried, the word tasting strange on my tongue. I was Ryan Cain; I didn't beg for anyone or anything.

Except the girl who had stolen my fucking heart.

"I went to her house tonight and it was empty. No one's there."

Her eyes widened with... fear?

"Oh no," she whispered, her hand drifting up to cover her lips. "No, no, no. Are you sure?"

"What's wrong?" Court demanded, coming to stand at my side as he peered down at a rapidly freaking out Bex. "Hey, *breathe*, Becca."

She sucked in a hiccupping gasp, not bothering to correct the name. It was what he had called her the entire time we were growing up. The name he still called her when he was alone with his friends and had too much to drink.

"You have to find her," Bex told me.

"I'm trying to," I reminded her, something dangerously like fear tried to mix into my blood. "But I have no idea where she is."

Her tongue darted out to wet her lips nervously. "After you left... Jesus, Ryan, why did you leave her?"

God, I wished I had an answer other than because I was a freaking idiot.

"What happened?" Court asked, obviously trying to stay calm.

Tears gathered in her eyes as she looked at us. "Gary lost it. Like, *really* lost it."

I winced. "I'm sure. He was pissed as fuck. I'm sure he said some nasty shit."

"No, Ryan," she said, starting to shake her head. "He beat the hell out of her."

My world stopped.

It ground to a jarring halt as everything froze in some weird suspended limbo. I could hear the soft hum of the HVAC system in the house as it pumped air through the ducts. I could hear the ragged breathing from Bex, and Court's knuckles popping as his hands balled into fists.

"He did *what?*" The three words were barely a ghost of a whisper on my lips.

Because no *way* did she say what I thought she'd said.

Bex blinked and the tears rolled free, sliding down her cheeks until Court reached out and framed her face with his hands, swiping at the tears with his thumbs.

"Tell us everything," he told her quietly.

She sniffled a little. "I went upstairs to check on her after you guys left."

Fuck.

I'd *left* her. I'd left her, and she'd been... That motherfucker had...

I swallowed the bile burning up the back of my throat and focused on now. I couldn't change what had happened, but I could find Maddie now and fix it.

Starting with Gary. He was a fucking dead man.

"She was in the hallway," Bex went on, her eyes locked on Court's as she spoke, like he was keeping her anchored right now. "Her face was bruised and her ribs... I helped her get changed and we left. We were going to the bus station."

"She got on a bus?" I reached for my phone, ready to tell Ash to look at all the terminals and figure out where the hell Maddie had gone.

The idea of her getting on a bus, scared and alone, was like having acid dumped on my heart and pumped through my veins. The pain was unbearable and caustic, eating me alive with fear and worry. Even bruises wouldn't hide how gorgeous my girl was, and I knew all too well how many sick fucks out there could take advantage of her.

All because I didn't protect her. Because I fucking ran at the first sign of trouble.

Fury and self-loathing mixed in a toxic cocktail that made me physically ill. What had I done?

"No," Bex told me sharply. "She wanted to see Madelaine first. I took her to the cemetery. She went inside their family's mausoleum, and the next thing I knew, these guys were there. One grabbed me—"

Court went eerily still. "Did he hurt you?"

"No," she assured him. "The other two grabbed Maddie inside the crypt and took her back to their car. I recognized them as part of Gary's security team. I'd seen them at the party earlier. The guy who grabbed me drove me back home. I've been trying to call Maddie ever since, but her phone is going straight to voicemail."

She stepped back and scuffed a toe into the carpet. "And I guess Gary called and said something to my parents, because they've basically kept me on lockdown here since last night. I tried to leave. I was thinking of trying to sneak out tonight, but the security cameras are everywhere." She paused, her nose wrinkling. "How did you two get in here?"

"Ash hacked the cameras," I answered with an indifferent shrug.

"Of course he did," she muttered. "Look, I thought Maddie was still at Gary's. If she's not there…"

My heart sank like a fucking rock to the bottom of the ocean.

Where the hell was my girl?

CHAPTER 3

MADDIE

By the morning of the third day in my cell, the bruising around my jaw didn't hurt quite so much. I was still on a soft-food-only diet, courtesy of my father's fist, but at least pain wasn't the first thing on my mind when I woke up.

The sun was already bright in the sky, rising above the mountains in wherever-the-hell-we-were. I still had no idea. The remote, almost rustic cabin that Gary had brought me to, the morning after his goons dragged me back to his house, was isolated, as far as I could tell. I wasn't sure what the house even looked like, or how big it was, since I'd been drugged when I was brought here.

After crying myself to sleep, I'd woken up in Madelaine's room at the mansion to hands holding me down and a needle pressing into my arm. Everything had gone fuzzy and dark, and then I had woken up in *this* room.

The view outside my window—locked of course—gave me only a glimpse of an endless series of hills and valleys with trees just starting to change with the season.

I got up from the bed and walked to the window on the other side of the room, pressing my hands to the chilly glass that was my only view to the world outside. The first day, I'd considered breaking the glass and jumping, but I wasn't an idiot. Even if I survived the fall to the ground from the second story without breaking anything, there was no way to tell if I was a mile or a hundred from civilization.

And there was also the fact that my mother was being held captive by my psycho father.

My fingers curled into fists at my sides as I turned from the window and looked around the sparsely decorated room.

A queen-size bed dominated the space with simple white linens and a gray duvet. There was a chair next to a bookcase with no books on it. Anything that might have been in the room before my arrival had been removed, including the TV that I assumed had been mounted on the wall. Now only a cable cord dangled from it.

The bedside table was empty, save for a simple digital clock that at least let me know what time it was. An empty dresser was pushed against a wall to the left of the bed, and there was a closet, which I'd found disturbingly stocked with clothes in my size like Gary had been waiting for when I'd inevitably fuck up and he'd bring me here.

The tiny attached bathroom had a shower stall, a toilet, and a sink. The mirror had been removed from the wall, which sucked, because I could've smashed it and used the broken glass as a weapon.

Actually, that was probably why it had been removed.

Twice a day, meals were brought to my room by a woman I didn't recognize. I tried talking to her at first. Then pleading, and finally screaming.

Nothing worked.

At eight a.m. on the dot, the lock on my door clicked and it opened. But this time, instead of the slight woman who normally brought my food, Gary was there with a tray in his hand.

He gave me a wide smile and kicked the door shut with his foot but didn't lock it.

I weighed the idea of rushing him and making a break for it... and realized that the odds weren't in my favor.

"Smart girl," he remarked, as if seeing the decision I'd made internally. He set down the tray, another bland breakfast of scrambled egg whites and plain yogurt, on the bedside table.

"Would you like to talk or eat first?" He posed the question like he was doing me a favor.

I snorted and crossed my arms. "I want answers."

His gaze sharpened. "Watch your tone."

I gritted my teeth and swallowed a retort. *"Please."*

He nodded approvingly. "That's better." He crossed the room and sat in the armchair. "Have a seat."

Keeping my expression as neutral as possible, I went and sat at the foot of my unmade bed.

"First, I would like to apologize," he began, surprising me when I hadn't thought it was possible for him to do that anymore. He waved a hand in my general direction. "My outburst was reckless, and I know better than to physically assault your face."

Just my face, huh? So places where bruises were easy to hide were fair game. Good to know.

"I also realize now that you were telling the truth," he went on conversationally, "and that Lainey was to blame for that unfortunate tape."

My eyes narrowed, and my nails bit into the flesh of my palms.

"Your sister always was a spiteful little bitch," he concluded with a shake of his head.

"I thought you said you two were *so* close." Disdain dripped from my words.

He smiled benignly at me. "Well, you wouldn't have agreed to stay if I'd told you the truth, right? If I had told you that your sister was a constant thorn in my side? Or that her untimely death was one of the best things that could have happened to me?"

I flinched at his words. "You're a fucking monster."

"And you're a naive idiot," he sneered. "I can't help it if your need to have a daddy overrode common sense. At least your sister had that much. That, and whatever liquid gold between her legs made every male in the vicinity turn into a bumbling fool."

"That's your *daughter*," I cried, horrified.

"Not by choice," he replied nonchalantly. He smiled again and exhaled. "It's so nice not to have these pretenses anymore, isn't it? We can just be us."

"You really had me fooled," I admitted, steeling myself against the sting of tears threatening to break free. "I thought you cared about Madelaine. About *me*."

"I cared about my investment, which is all you two ever have been." He glanced at his nails. "My mother—your grandmother, may she rest in hell—fancied herself an actress. She was always bringing me to auditions. Guess I picked up a few things."

"Lucky you." I wondered if my teeth would crack from how hard I was clenching them together.

He snorted. "You bought it, didn't you? The dad you always wanted, who plucked you from your piss-poor life in the slums? You took it all, Madison. The fancy education, the new clothes... I didn't see you complaining."

"You never gave a shit about me. About Lainey." I swallowed hard around the realization that it had all been a lie. A calculated lie, from the tears in his office when he'd said Lainey was dead, to the gifts and the compliments.

"It's hard to care about something you never wanted," he admitted. "Hopefully you can be managed a little bit better than your sister. If you think this place is hell? You have no idea what I can really do. It took your sister a few years to figure that out before she came to heel."

"She still ran away from you," I pointed out smugly.

The corner of his mouth hooked up. "And now she's ashes in a box. So, who really won this game, Madison?"

"Is she?" I challenged. I thought back to the mausoleum and the name inscribed on my twin's final resting place. "Pretty sure it was *my* name on that marker."

He smiled cruelly. "I couldn't very well have you running back to your former life, now could I? Consider your old life gone, and now you've been reborn."

"All I have to do is go to the police and tell them the truth." I meant it as a threat, but he laughed like the idea was absurd.

"Please do. I filed all the necessary paperwork for the death of Madison Porter. Go and tell anyone you want that you're her. I'll have no problem convincing people that my deeply disturbed daughter has lost her mind. I know more than a few judges and psychologists who would happily sign off on your mentally unstable status." He chuckled and shook his head, seeming genuinely amused that I would consider going against him.

He was right. I had no way to prove I was really Madison. I didn't have a driver's license or any kind of proof that I was me. In fact, the opposite was true. All the credit cards and identification I had were in Madelaine's name.

"So, what do you want?" I demanded flatly, trying to suppress a shudder of revulsion. "And where's my mom?"

"Safe. For now," he added as an afterthought. "Whether or not she remains that way is entirely on your shoulders."

I closed my eyes, bracing for whatever came next.

"You will, of course, be returning to Pacific Cross. Once you've healed, obviously. If I thought I could sell Ryan doing that damage to you, I would, but honestly it's more drama than I need right now."

"Of course," I agreed, sarcasm thick in my tone.

"You'll still marry Ryan, and once the nuptials are finalized, you'll sign over your inheritance to me, and me alone."

"I thought you and Beckett were splitting it," I muttered.

"Things change."

I lifted a brow. "Won't my darling husband have something to say about that?"

He shrugged, the picture of indifference. "Not my problem. I have plans that no longer include the Cain family. Beckett should've considered all he had to lose before insulting me with the petty addition to our arrangement. I hope the ten million is worth it."

"Why are you even telling me this? What's to stop me from making another deal with Ryan or Beckett?" I challenged. But we both knew the answer to that question.

He crossed one leg over the other like he had all the time in the world. "It would be most unfortunate for them to learn of my plans, Maddie. Your mother would be… well, she'd be absolutely *sick* over it. In fact, so sick she might not recover."

I sucked in a ragged breath.

"Or, I know a few men in Indonesia who would like a permanent toy. I can't promise they would keep her flying high for what they have in mind. Truthfully, they love it when their toys scream and fight back."

I shuddered, bile burning as it crawled up my throat.

"You betray me? And your mother will pay. *You* will pay. Fuck, I might even arrange for the Whittier brat to take a trip overseas herself." He leaned forward, a maniacal glint in his eyes. "You think she's still a virgin? I could get top-dollar if she is. Pretty little innocent American girl?"

"Enough!" I tried to shout the word, but it came out strangled. "I'll do it. Whatever you want, okay? Just… leave my mom and Bex alone."

He wagged a finger at me with a grin. "See? This is why you're so much easier than Madelaine. Little cunt only thought about herself. But you? No, Madison, you *care*. You actually love people, and that means you can be controlled."

I hated him, but he was right. I knew it and couldn't do a damn thing about it, unless there was a magical way to shut off my emotions.

"Once you get back to school, I'll expect you to repair things with Ryan. I'll need an insider's point-of-view on what he and Beckett have going on." Gary stood up and tugged down the cuffs of his shirt.

"How the hell am I supposed to do that? Ryan made it pretty clear that he hates me." Not only that, but the idea of being anywhere near the guy who had emotionally eviscerated me was about as appealing as chewing glass.

"I'm sure you'll think of something. Besides, you'll have plenty of time to focus on Ryan. I've made the decision to clear your schedule so you can focus on your studies and what's really important."

"Meaning what?"

"No more cheerleading, for starters," he answered.

My jaw dropped. "What? But... I'm the *captain*."

"And now you're not," he replied icily. "While we're talking about changes to your life, I'm sure you've noticed the food being brought to you? Consider this your new diet. I've already told the school that, with your allergy to consider, we're taking extra care and I've arranged all your meals."

"So, you're going to tell me what I can eat now?"

"Little girl, I'll tell you when you can shit if I want to," he snarled, his cheeks flushing. His gaze raked over me in disgust. "At least your sister knew how to keep up appearances. You're all muscle and bulk. You need to look like my heir. And my heir isn't a fat cow."

Hate rolled through me like a thunderstorm. Lightning flashed in my veins at his comments. Yeah, I had tits and an ass, and I was *healthy*.

He paused at the door. "I'm leaving to go out of town now. Adam will be here to make sure you get back to school safely."

I went rigid at the idea of being alone in a house with the demon who had been abusing my twin for years. "Do you even know what he did to Madelaine?"

"You mean their little dalliance?" Gary snickered and rolled his eyes. "Adam always has liked them young, and Madelaine was a needy little thing. Always throwing herself at whoever she thought might save her."

"He started going into her room when she was *thirteen*," I hissed, getting to my feet. "She was a *child*."

He stilled and stared at me. "How could you possibly know that?"

Shit. If he didn't know about Madelaine's app and the files, I wasn't telling him.

"She told Bex, and Bex told me," I replied, hoping he bought it.

His eyes narrowed. "Interesting."

I didn't move—hell, I barely *breathed* in case he was watching for a crack in my armor.

"I'll make you a deal," he said softly. "Adam won't touch you unless you become a problem. Do as you're told, and I'll make sure he knows you're off-limits."

"Fine." I wrapped my arms around myself as a chill rippled down my spine.

Gary smirked at me. "That's my girl."

CHAPTER 4

MADDIE

It took over a week for the bruises to fade. I spent every day in my little room with nothing to do and no company, save for the silent woman who delivered my meals. It made me long for the days when Mrs. Delancey would make me food while I sat in the kitchen chatting with her.

The only sign my keeper could hear me was when I'd asked for something to read. Anything to break up the monotony.

The next day I'd gotten a copy of the Bible and *Hustler*.

Fucking hysterical.

My window to the world became my only source of entertainment. I counted how many animals I spotted scampering through the woods—eighteen deer, thirty squirrels, and three foxes.

As the sun set each day, I wondered if anyone knew I was gone. Hell, if they cared.

Bex probably did, but she might be the only one. Maybe Mrs. Delancey? She had been at the mansion when everything had blown up. For that matter, there'd been a lot of staff around for the party. Someone had to have cleaned up the blood in the hallway, and I had a feeling that wasn't Gary's first time getting violent.

On the twelfth day of my prison term, Adam showed up. His

bulky frame paused in the doorway, his beady eyes raking over me in a way that made my skin feel like hundreds of ants were scurrying across it.

I forced myself not to jump up from where I had dragged the only chair in the room to the window. I gave him a cursory glance before looking away, like he wasn't worth the effort.

In reality, the window gave me a blurry reflection of whatever he planned to do next. But much like running from an attacking dog would only get you bitten, I knew showing any sort of fear from his presence would be something for him to pounce on.

"Amazing," he murmured, leaning a shoulder against the frame.

I didn't bother answering. He wasn't worth my words.

Undeterred by my silence, he stepped into the room. "The resemblance is absolutely uncanny."

So Gary had told him who I was. Great.

"I mean, you're a little curvier, but I don't mind that." Another step. "Your father said I wasn't allowed to touch, which, I have to admit, is disappointing. You seem like you'd be a lot harder to break than your sister."

It took everything in me to keep my expression placid while inside I was raging at this disgusting pig who had violated and abused my twin.

He moved closer, and the pungent stench of his aftershave filled my nostrils. "But your sister was always good at keeping secrets, so maybe you can be, too? I could make your life a lot easier."

I turned as he reached for me, glaring at him with all the hate I could muster. "Touch me, and I'll cut your dick off."

He paused, and I stupidly let myself think my threat was enough of a deterrent.

But then he lunged forward and grabbed a fistful of my hair, and then wrenched my neck back.

"You ungrateful little cunt," he hissed, spittle hitting my face.

My eyes watered as pain seared across my scalp. I choked on a gasp, trying not to show any emotion, but holy shit, it freaking *hurt*.

"Mr. Kindell!" a sharp voice snapped from the open door.

I managed to peer around him to see Mrs. Delancey standing there, her expression grave.

Adam released me and stepped back. "I was just checking on our little bird. It doesn't look like her father broke her wings too badly."

Mrs. Delancey's gaze flicked to me. "I'm here to assess her to see if she can return to school. You can go."

Adam's eyes narrowed, his cheeks flushing. "Don't forget who you work for."

"I work for Mr. Cabot," she asserted coolly, unimpressed by his warning. "And he instructed me to prepare Madison for her return to Pacific Cross."

Her words settled in my brain as Adam huffed a breath and stomped across the room. He glared at Mrs. Delancey, who didn't seem the slightest bit concerned, before he pushed past her.

She entered the room and closed the door before clasping her hands in front of her and looking me over.

"You know who I am?" I swallowed nervously.

She gave a curt nod. "I should have seen it from the beginning. Lord knows, maybe I did and I just didn't want to consider it."

"So, you knew I existed?" I whispered.

"I was there when your mother gave birth to you both. I brought Madelaine home and raised her until a nanny was brought in when she began school. Yes, I knew you existed. I also knew that, even with that wildcard of a mother, you got the better end of the deal." Her lips pressed together in a flat line.

I slowly got up from the chair. "You have to help me get out of here."

"And go where?" She seemed genuinely curious. "Where do you think you could run that Gary Cabot couldn't reach?"

"I have no idea," I answered, frustration heavy in my tone. "I'll figure it out on the way. I just need to grab my mother—"

"Your mother should be the least of your concerns now." She cut me off with a shake of her head. "No, your chances at a normal life went out the window the second you stepped on that plane to come here."

My eyes narrowed. "Normal went out the window the first time my mom overdosed in front of me. Are you really not going to help me?"

"Do you think you're the only one with something to lose?" She barely lifted a brow, but the chilly tone of her voice spoke volumes.

"He has something on you, too," I muttered, running a hand through my long hair. It fell in loose waves down my back, and I wished like hell that someone had at least left me a hair-tie in the bathroom so I could pull it up. Though I supposed I was lucky I had a brush.

"My son has special needs. He requires round-the-clock supervision and care, and he gets both at the best facility in the world. Mr. Cabot arranges for me to visit monthly."

"In exchange for your warden services?" I snarked, unable to help myself.

She barely blinked. "In exchange for whatever he needs. Raising his daughter, supervising his house, and any other tasks he requires that keep my son happy and safe."

"Sorry," I grumbled, knowing she wasn't really the bad guy here. She was just as stuck as I was. Her son's life, much like my mother's, depended on making Gary Cabot happy.

"How are you feeling?" she asked.

"You mean other than scared and angry?"

"I meant your injuries." Her gaze moved across my face and exposed skin. "I don't see any lingering bruises. Not visible ones, anyway. How are your ribs?"

"Still aching, but better." The first few days, it had been hell just trying to breathe. The kick Gary had delivered had likely cracked a couple.

"Your face looks... Well, you look like you," she finished, but seemed satisfied.

"I wouldn't know," I muttered.

Regret shadowed her eyes. "Yes, well, your father didn't want to take chances by leaving a mirror in the room for you to break. Not after Madelaine..."

"Tried to kill herself?" I snorted. "I'm not suicidal. Though if I'd had one to break, I might've used a shard on him or Adam."

"You're a fighter," she said. "Good. You'll need that for what's to come."

"I'm going to stop him," I declared.

Mrs. Delancey gave me a small, sad smile. "I believe that you'll try. I also know that you'll fail. Madelaine spent a lifetime learning her father's moves, studying his ways, and ultimately not even she could escape."

"Maybe she did. Maybe she was smart enough to fake her death and get out. Maybe I was just the idiot she tricked into taking her place." A bitter taste flooded my mouth and soured my thoughts.

"She's dead." Her soft words barely penetrated.

I glanced up to see real grief in her eyes.

"Do you honestly believe that your father would simply let her get away? Let her get the best of him?" She shook her head. "He would have used every dollar just to teach her the lesson that he can't be crossed. It's why his companies are in so much debt—he lets his emotions get the best of him."

My hand lifted to my jaw, remembering how swollen it had been after he'd hit me. "I'm well aware of his anger-management issues."

"Then you also need to accept that your sister is dead. There is no alternative here, Madison. There's no reality where you escape the future he's laid out for you, and there's no way to save yourself." Pity glistened in her eyes. "All you can do now is try to protect your mother."

My chin lifted, the last lingering traces of defiance still simmering in my blood. "And how do I do that?"

"Play his games and accept what's going to happen next. Do as he commands." She forced a smile. "If you can prove that you're an asset, he might be more lenient with you. When Madelaine played along, she wanted for nothing. He gave her whatever she asked for and then some."

Dread coiled in my stomach. "And when she didn't play along?"

Mrs. Delancey looked away. "Let's just say that her death wasn't the worst consequence her actions ever had."

~

I t was dark as the town car rolled through the gates of Pacific Cross. On a random Thursday night in the middle of the semester, no one was around as we drove over the winding road to the academy dorms.

Adam turned to me, a smile on his face. "Want me to walk you up and tuck you in?"

My hands balled into fists on my lap. "I've got it from here."

I felt oily and gross after riding in a car with Adam Kindell for the last four hours. My muscles ached from being locked up and tense as I prepared for an attack that never came. Adam would occasionally flash me a smile, loving when I flinched away from his leering smirk.

I still wasn't sure where I'd been for the past week. A cabin, I assumed, considering the forest, mountains, and polished wood siding I'd managed to glimpse as I was escorted to the car.

When Adam had climbed in beside me, I'd plastered myself to my side of the car and clutched the small purse Mrs. Delancey had given me. It had my keys, a new cell phone, and my ID. Well, Madelaine's ID.

Once she'd handed me the purse, she'd ushered in a new woman, who'd waxed me within an inch of my life before giving me a facial and deep conditioning treatment for my hair.

The skin and hair treatments I understood, but the waxing felt like overkill. And when I'd opened my mouth to ask Mrs. Delancey *what the fuck*, the look she gave let me know I didn't want the answer.

If I was going back to school, I needed to look the part of the Cabot heiress. And apparently that extended to my pussy. Shaving was for peasants.

The roads we'd traveled had been dark and unfamiliar, and by the time we arrived at Pacific City, I realized we were driving into the town limits from a completely different direction than I was used to.

"Your father asked me to remind you to be a good girl," Adam said softly, his words a teasing purr that made my stomach twist. He reached out a hand and toyed with the ends of my ash-blonde hair. "Personally, I'm hoping you're naughty. With him out of town, I'll be the one who has to bring you to heel."

"I thought your orders were to look, not touch," I snapped, jerking my head away and glaring at him as my hand settled on the handle.

He glared at me but brought his hand back to his side.

I shoved the door open and got out before glancing back inside the dimly lit interior of the car. "Good dog."

I slammed the door on his ruddy face and turned toward my dorm. I gave myself only a moment to look up at the mostly dark building before following the lighted path to the front door.

I withdrew the keys from my purse and used the fob to open the door, which auto-locked at ten p.m. to protect students.

Snorting, I pushed through the doors and went to the elevators. I rode in silence, ascending to the top floor, where the doors opened quietly. My room was at the end of the hall to the right, and I made my way to it as quietly as possible.

I opened the door and quickly shut it, locking it behind me and finally exhaling a long breath as I leaned my back against the door.

My insides trembled as I tried to gather my thoughts. Everything was so jumbled and out of control. Part of me wanted to go for a run to burn off the jitters. I hadn't been able to exercise beyond sit-ups and push-ups in my room at the cabin.

But more than that? I was starving.

I pushed away from the door and stalked to the kitchenette area before yanking open the fridge.

"Dammit," I swore, seeing that all the snacks and sodas I had stashed in there were gone and had been replaced with bottles of water and a baggy of raw carrots and celery.

I slammed the door shut hard enough that it bounced back open. I kicked it with another curse and leaned against the counter to catch my breath.

A sob threatened to rip from my chest as I closed my eyes and buried my face in my hands.

I could do this.

I *had* to do this.

First, I needed a shower, and then I would go to bed. I had class in the morning, and I would already be behind after missing almost two weeks for an unnamed illness. That was the excuse Gary had given the school.

Of course, after the engagement party, everyone probably just assumed I was too embarrassed to return.

There was no way Dean had stopped at sharing that video with just the people at the party. By now it had probably gone viral and been uploaded to a porn site, where some guy in his parents' basement was currently jerking off to it.

A shudder of revulsion rippled down my spine as I moved through the dark suite and into my bedroom. I flipped the light switch, and my heart tugged at seeing Sir Trunks-a-lot propped up against the pillows. The ratty, stuffed elephant was one of the few things I had brought from my old life into this world, and it looked just as out of place amongst the thousand-dollar-sheets as I felt.

I stripped out of my clothes as I went to the bathroom and was down to my underwear when I stepped onto the cool tiles and hit the switch.

The extreme brightness in the illuminated mirror over the sink space blinded me for a second before I adjusted and got my first look at myself in nearly two weeks.

I moved toward the mirror as if in a trance, barely recognizing the girl looking back.

My eyes were flat and my skin, already pale, looked even more translucent as all color had leached from my cheeks. The bruising and swelling around my face were gone. The only trace of Gary's attack was the faint yellowish-green marks around my ribs.

I tentatively touched the skin and hissed at the ache that blossomed across my side. There wasn't much left between my skin and my bones as I prodded my ribs. I had lost weight over the last two weeks.

That unnamed illness excuse wasn't that much of a stretch; I looked like I was sick.

I twisted away from the mirror and finished getting undressed before knotting my hair into a messy bun and stepping into the glass shower.

The initial cold spray was a shock to my system that quickly bled away as I turned the hot water on full blast. My skin turned red as I let the hot water sluice over me and tried to scrub away the past two weeks. The feel of the cabin and the stale, oppressive air. Even the lingering, heavily fragranced scent of the aftercare lotion the waxer had used tasted cloying on my tongue.

I felt used and dirty and craved being clean. The water rained down my body, swirling around the drain to rinse away the feel of strange hands and beady eyes from my flesh.

Hell, the last several months could go down the drain, too, as far as I was concerned.

I lost track of time as I stood under the water, taking the time to scour every inch of my body before I shut off the shower.

The bathroom was one giant cloud of steam as I towel-dried off. I wrapped the towel around my chest and knotted it and then shook my hair loose before going to my bedroom to grab pajamas.

I stumbled to a stop with a gasp when I realized I wasn't alone.

Ryan slowly stood up from where he'd been sitting on the edge of my bed. His expression gave nothing away even as his blue gaze swept the length of my body before meeting my eyes. "Hey, Maddie."

CHAPTER 5

MADDIE

There was a special sort of agony reserved for seeing someone you loved who had betrayed you.

After the shitty two weeks I'd just had, my first instinct at seeing Ryan was to run and bury myself against his chest. I knew he could help shoulder the weight that was threatening to crush me.

But then it all went to hell when I remembered that *he* was the reason I was so broken. He hadn't just turned his back on me. No, first he had ripped out my heart and stomped on it before leaving me in the dust.

"Get out," I whispered, barely able to move my lips.

He flinched. "Mads—"

"Get *out!*" I screamed the words as I felt my heart crack wide open.

Gary hadn't broken me, but Ryan would. I hadn't shed a tear yet, but now I could feel them threatening to drown me.

His lips pressed together, his face pained. "Baby, you need to listen to me."

I clutched the knot in my towel. "Get out. Get out. *Get out!*" I chanted the words like I could invoke some magic to make him vanish.

His eyes narrowed and his jaw clenched. I knew that determined look in his eyes meant he wasn't going anywhere.

"I don't want you here. Get *the fuck* out of my room and out of my life!" I was bordering on hysterical now, but this was too much.

Ryan Cain was too much for me to handle.

He held up his hands and stayed where he was. "Maddie, I need to know if you're okay. Bex said—"

"I don't care what Bex said!" I resisted the urge to slap my hands over my ears and hum a Christmas song.

He sucked in a deep breath. "Calm down, Mads."

"Don't tell me to fucking calm down, Ryan!" I snarled as my heart thundered in my chest. I blinked and—dammit all to hell—tears fell from my eyes and dripped down my cheeks.

He closed his eyes like the sight of me crying was too much for him to bear.

Not fucking likely.

He was probably relishing this. Loved seeing me broken down and defeated.

I felt exposed and vulnerable, and it had nothing to do with the fact that I was naked under my towel.

Surprisingly, he took a step back and his shoulders hunched in... defeat? "I'll go, okay? I didn't mean to upset you."

My head was spinning, and I realized that my breathing was ragged and choppy. I was actually hyperventilating.

"Just... *shit*. Let me call Bex first, okay? I can't leave you alone like this, Maddie."

Darkness blurred the edges of my vision as my knees wobbled. I managed to brace a hand on the wall before squeezing my eyes shut and focusing on my breathing.

I was dimly aware of Ryan's voice as he barked orders at someone. Minutes bled together as I sank deeper and deeper into a pit that was going to swallow me whole. A hand brushed my shoulder, pushing my hair from my face and I shuddered because I *knew* that touch.

That touch had been my everything once. And now it was a blistering reminder of all I'd lost.

With a cry, I wrenched myself away from Ryan and tumbled into the bathroom. My back slammed against the counter as I slipped on the slick tiles and went down.

Firm hands grabbed my arms long enough to deposit me on the floor without any more injury, but immediately the hands were gone and I was alone. So endlessly *alone*.

I curled up, bringing my knees to my chest and wrapping my arms around my shins as I rocked and tried to stop crying.

A soft voice entered the room next before someone else was dropping down beside me.

"Maddie? Maddie, hey. It's me, Bex." She started to reach for me and then stopped. "I'm going to hold your hand, okay? It's just me."

Gentle fingers slowly pried one of my hands from my leg.

"Can you try taking a deep breath?" Bex encouraged, her quiet voice steadying me with its kindness.

I managed a trembling breath that rushed out in a small whimper.

"Bex—"

"Get out, Ryan." I'd never heard her voice sound so cold and brittle. "Haven't you done enough damage?"

A low growl filled the space. "I didn't do this."

"What did you expect would happen if you showed up and surprised her?" Bex demanded, fiercely protective as she crouched between us. I didn't have to look up to know she was glaring at him.

"I just needed to make sure she was okay," he answered roughly. "I can't... Fuck, Bex, I know I messed up."

"And now you're making it worse," she snapped. "So, go. Leave us alone."

Ryan didn't move, and I could practically hear him thinking, working over the situation in his head and trying to figure out his next move.

"Fine," he agreed in a low voice. "But tell her—"

"I'm not telling her shit," Bex spat. "If you want to try and beg forgiveness, don't use me to do it. If it were up to me? Maddie would never have to see you again."

A soft laugh came from Ryan, totally void of humor. "I'm glad she has you."

Bex's hand tightened around mine. "She does. Now *leave*."

"I'll be back, Mads. We're not done," he said gently, and it felt like a promise more than a threat.

I didn't lift my head until I heard the front door close. Then I peered up at Bex through a tangled mess of blonde hair.

Her hazel eyes were wet with unshed tears as she held my hand with one of hers and used the other to stroke my head like I was a scared puppy.

I started to open my mouth, but the words got stuck.

Her eyes narrowed. "I swear, Madison, if you're about to apologize, I'll... Well, I don't know *what* exactly, but think of something bad, and it'll be *that*."

I choked on an unexpected laugh, and she smiled.

"I'm okay," I finally managed to get out.

She snorted in disbelief. "Sure you are. That's why you're sitting on the floor in a towel with your coochie hanging out and snot on your face. That's the definition of *okay*."

Another laugh bubbled out of me, and I tried to adjust my legs so I wasn't flashing her.

"Ready to get off the floor?" She kept the question light and airy so as not to pressure me, a fact I was grateful for. "I mean, I'm also good to hang out down here, but it's a little chilly."

I nodded and, with her help, got up. Once on my feet, I leaned my ass against the counter. I was utterly drained.

"How about if I grab you some clothes?' Bex flashed me a smile and left me before I could answer. I heard her rummaging through my drawers before she came back with a soft flannel pair of bottoms and a t-shirt.

I dropped my towel and changed. At this point, my modesty was buried somewhere with my pride.

"We need... ice cream," she decided. "I'll raid the kitchen and grab all the carbs and sugar—"

"Don't bother," I cut her off in a tired voice. "There's only water and rabbit snacks."

"Huh?"

I gave her a self-deprecating smirk. "Gary thinks I need to go on a diet."

Her jaw dropped open, and I used the momentary surprise to slip past her and go into my bedroom. My eyes were automatically drawn to the wrinkled spot where Ryan had been sitting.

I dragged my lower lip through my teeth as I shoved the image out of my head.

"What do you mean by diet? You're, like, one of the most in-shape people I know." Bex had found her voice and, *damn*, she sounded pissed.

I loved that she was so protective.

I grabbed my hair brush from the dresser and started ripping it through the mess. I really couldn't bring myself to give a shit about split ends or whatever damage I might be doing. My scalp burned as I yanked on my hair.

Bex came up behind me and extracted the brush from my hand. "Sit and explain," she ordered, pointing to the stool in front of my vanity.

I shuffled over to it and dropped down so Bex could brush my hair.

"It doesn't matter," I muttered, picking at a loose thread on my pants.

"Maddie—"

"What happened to you after those guys took me?" I twisted around to see her, but she simply glared at me before turning my head back around.

"They took me home," she answered after I had done as she wanted. She gently worked on a knot, her soft touch not pulling at my scalp at all. "My parents were pissed. Well, Mom was pissed. Dad was drinking, but that's nothing new."

I stiffened. "I didn't know your dad drank."

"I don't really talk about it. And it's only when he's home. He and my mom hate each other. Like, sleep in different bedrooms and arrange all social activities through their assistants kind of hate. Your engage—I mean, the party, was the first time I'd seen them together without fighting in over a year. And that was just for show."

"Why don't they just get a divorce?" I asked.

She hummed under her breath. "I asked my mom that once. She told me that I would understand when I was an adult."

"Maybe try asking her now that you're *almost* an adult?"

Bex scoffed. "I asked her that a few months ago, Mads."

"Oh."

"Dad travels a lot for work, so honestly, it's not that big a deal." She finished with my hair and set the brush aside. "Maddie, I'm so sorry for what happened that night."

Now I turned and shook my head. "Bex, *none* of that was your fault."

"It wasn't yours either," she pointed out, looking down at me. Her hazel eyes were wide as she sighed. "I could *punch* Ryan—"

"I don't want to talk about Ryan," I interrupted, feeling my heart start to race at the mention of him.

"Right. Sorry." She made a face. "I tried to come and find you, but my mom had me on lockdown after Gary threatened to file charges for grand theft auto."

I groaned, but she waved it away.

"It's fine. Mom was pissed, but she's *always* pissed about something. The idea of me ruining my collegiate future because of *that girl*." She paused and gave me a look. "Mom's not your biggest fan."

"My twin made your life hell for years." I felt my returning smile crack around the edges. "I have no idea why she'd hate me."

Bex rolled her eyes. "I wish I could just tell her the truth."

"It won't do any good." I really didn't want to dive into the fact that I was legally *dead*.

"I tried calling, but your phone just went to voicemail."

"He took my phone," I muttered. "I have a new one. New number and everything. It's in my purse."

"Wow. New phone, new diet, new... you."

41

"No," I said flatly. "The same me. Or the me I'm supposed to be. The dutiful daughter that Gary can manipulate."

She smiled. "Then he doesn't know you very well."

I glanced down at my lap. "He took my mom."

She stilled and then took a step back. "What?"

I looked up at her and tried to swallow the wave of panic. "He took her out of rehab, I guess. He has her at the house, totally drugged up."

"She's at Gary's house?" Bex demanded.

I nodded.

"No, she can't be there. She wasn't there the night..." She trailed off and gave me a guilty look.

"The night what?" I prodded.

She backed up and sat across from me on the edge of my bed. "I'm only bringing *him* up because it pertains to your mother."

Well, the only *he* that she would hesitate to bring up would be the guy who'd mutilated my heart.

I braced myself for whatever came next.

"He went looking for you the night after the engagement party. He went to your house with the guys."

I snorted and shook my head. "Why? So they could all jump me? Find a way to add to my humiliation?"

"No. Because they figured out it wasn't you in the tape, that it was Madelaine." Her shoulders drooped and she rubbed her temples.

All I could get out was a strangled, "What?"

"Ash figured it out," Bex added softly, almost reluctant to meet my gaze. "He figured out that it was your sister with Dean. He also found proof of Dean going into Ryan's room and grabbing the playbook before you locked the door."

Time seemed to freeze around me as I processed what she was saying.

"Ryan knows you didn't betray him."

A piece of me wanted to sob in relief.

But the quiet storm of fury brewing in my chest quickly smothered it.

"He should have known that when I *told him*," I seethed. "Not because his best friend had to show him a damn tape. He should have *believed me.*"

"I'm not arguing, nor am I saying you should forgive him. I just thought you should know." Bex gave me a steady look. "I've got your back, Mads. Those guys fucked up."

"Damn right they did." I shot her a look. "How do you know this?"

"Because when Ryan couldn't find you, he came to *my* house," Bex admitted with a grimace.

"Bet your mother loved that."

"Oh, no she didn't know they were there. He and Court broke in."

I jerked in surprise. "They what?"

She nodded. "Yup. Showed up in my bedroom at, like, three in the morning. Ash disabled our security system and... yeah."

"What is it with these guys just breaking into girls' rooms?" I asked, throwing my hands up.

"I wish I knew," she said wryly, shaking her head. "But Ryan figured I knew where you were and..." She flashed me a guilty look.

"What?"

"I might've let it slip that Gary attacked you," she replied, ducking her head.

I let out a heavy breath.

"*Are* you okay?" She leaned forward a bit. "I mean, I don't see any bruises."

"My ribs are still a little banged up, but I'm fine." I pasted a fake smile on my face. "Can't have Madelaine Cabot returning to school looking less than flawless."

"I wish flawless would be enough," Bex murmured. "Mads, everyone at the school knows. They're *pissed*. I'd like to say you could fly under the radar, but..."

"I don't care," I answered woodenly. "There's nothing these assholes can do to me that's worse than what's happening outside of this place. I'll play Gary's game while I figure out how to get my mom free."

"What about you?"

I met her gaze and held it. "I don't care if I have to go down in flames, too, but I'm going to stop Gary."

Her eyes widened. "And Ryan?"

I scoffed. The blistering rage from earlier had burned away to a charred shell of emptiness that echoed in my soul. "Ryan Cain better stay out of my way, or I'll take him down, too."

CHAPTER 6

MADDIE

If I'd had any kind of luck left, I wouldn't have been dropped off at Pacific Cross on a Thursday night. Not that there would have ever been a *good* day to restart classes, but I wasn't looking forward to rejoining my classes Friday morning.

I glared at the clock as the minutes ticked by, wondering if almost two weeks away had dimmed everyone's memories of the engagement party or the video, which Bex had confirmed everyone knew about.

"Maybe you could take a sick day?" Bex suggested from the other side of the room.

Like the awesome friend she was, she'd spent the night. I'd been able to get some sleep with her by my side. There was something comforting about not being alone, and Bex was the only person I had left who actually gave a shit about me.

I shook my head, forcing myself to keep moving. "No. Gary made it pretty clear that I need to toe the line or my mom suffers."

She frowned but didn't argue, just waited as I finished getting ready.

I swiped on a layer of mascara and gave myself a hard look in the mirror. Lainey would've been proud of the makeup application I'd nailed today. This was as close to armor as I was going to get.

Slowly I stood from the vanity, smoothing down my blue and white plaid skirt before reaching for the matching blue blazer to pull over my white button-up. Bex handed me a pair of black pumps, which I slipped onto my feet.

My stomach churned but not from hunger. Anxiety was crushing me as I realized that, before I could enter the horror that was high school, I first had to endure the cafeteria.

"I can just run in and grab our food," Bex offered softly. "We can eat outside."

The southern California air was still warm despite it being well into fall. I was used to Michigan, where frost would ice over the grass and leaves. Eating outside was an option, but Bex couldn't pick up my *specially prepared meals*.

I just knew that, if Gary thought I was finding a way around his ridiculous diet, there would be hell to pay. Odds were, it would be my mom who paid that price, so no, thank you.

I squared my shoulders. "Let's get it over with."

She gave me a tight nod and led the way out of my room. The hall was empty when we stepped into it—unsurprising, since I was on the top floor where there were only a handful of other rooms.

We got onto the elevator, and the quiet ended when the doors opened on the floor below mine and three girls got into the car with us.

I didn't know them, but they clearly knew me. The glares they tossed me didn't hide their disdain at all. And if that wasn't enough, there was the not-so-subtle "whore" that one coughed. The other two giggled.

Bex's pinky looped around mine in a silent show of support, but I was glad she didn't try to defend me. I was already worried about the target being painted on her back at being seen with me. I didn't want to add to her trouble.

Two floors later more girls joined us. I moved into a back corner, but someone made a point to crush my toes beneath her heel.

"Oops," she muttered as her friends started to cackle. She flipped her long, dark hair so it slapped me in the face. "Totally didn't see you there."

"You might not have seen her," one of her friends said, snark heavy in her voice as she eyed me from behind a pair of black glasses, "but I don't know how you could miss the rank smell of skank in the morning."

Another round of laughter.

I clenched my jaw and forced myself to keep my head up. I wouldn't cave or crack because of the school's resident mean girls.

Bex shot me a sympathetic look.

Hair-Flip shook out her tresses, and I moved to avoid being hit again.

We dropped to another floor and the doors opened once more. I barely bit back a groan because, *come on.*

I was taking the stairs from here on out. Or maybe just jumping off my balcony.

The doors opened with a soft *whoosh* to reveal Brylee, flanked by Kayleigh and Hayley.

Seriously? Who had I accidentally killed in a past life to have this shit happening?

Brylee eyed the occupants of the elevator with a cold assessment before snapping her fingers. "Out."

Like trained dogs, all the girls scampered from the car until Bex and I were the only ones left. The doors started to close, but Brylee planted a foot in the opening to keep them from shutting.

Her eyes narrowed on Bex. "I said *out.* Or are you as stupid as you are irrelevant, Becky?"

"Back off," I snapped.

Brylee's gaze snapped to mine, surprise lurking when she realized I was taking up for Bex. Did she think I was going to stand here like a meek little mouse and take her shit?

"If you have a problem with me? Fine. Don't be a bitch to her just because you can." I glared at her with all the hate I could muster.

Which, considering it was Brylee, was a fucking lot.

"Pretty big talk for someone who has zero pull around here."

Brylee sneered at me, her lip curling. "Honestly, I'm shocked you even came back."

"Well, I just *live* to surprise you," I drawled, rolling my eyes.

Bex snorted, which unfortunately drew Brylee's attention.

"What the fuck are you still doing here, Vapors? Fucking disappear like the useless waste of space you are."

Bex flushed, and I took that as my cue to step forward.

"You need to walk away," I ordered her flatly, refusing to budge when her eyes flashed with warning.

"And you need to remember your place," she spat back at me. She eyed me up and down. "I'm going to really enjoy what happens next."

If Brylee thought I was afraid of her, she was terribly mistaken. Was she an annoying bitch who could make my life hell? Sure. But she was ultimately a spoiled princess in Prada, and I had spent years standing up to girls who carried actual guns and knives.

The urge to punch her was tempered only by the reminder that my actions could have a direct impact on things that happened to my mom.

Or, I realized with a horror that was like waking up in bed with a snake, Bex.

My heart was thundering in my chest, but I swallowed my nerves and dipped them in steel. The worst thing I could do was show any signs of weakness. Especially if I couldn't even back up my bark with a decent bite.

Brylee sniffed delicately and stepped back. "Let's wait for the next elevator, ladies. This one is full of trash."

The doors slid closed and I turned to Bex. "I'm so sorry."

She waved me off, but I could see she had gone a little pale. "It's fine, Maddie. I'm used to Brylee's bitchiness. It's been getting worse since… Well, you know."

I flinched. I couldn't help myself. The reminder of that night evoked a visceral reaction every single time.

The doors opened on the ground floor, and we hurried from the elevator and out the front doors, starting down the winding path to the dining hall.

Bex didn't speak until we were a few yards from the building. "He may not be here." She barely lifted her voice as she spoke.

I paused and looked at her.

She gave a small shrug. "The team has been meeting in the mornings, coming up with new plays since the playbook was... compromised."

I barely bit back a groan. "Well, at least I won't have to worry about where to sit." Ryan couldn't make me sit with him if he wasn't here.

"Definitely a plus," she murmured, but there was something in her gaze that snagged my attention.

"What?" I demanded, stepping to the side and into the grass as a group of people came up behind us.

More glares were shot my way.

Awesome.

Bex huffed a laugh and moved into the grass with me. "It's not you. It's just... the guys have been pretty relentless since they realized they messed up."

I could feel my brows climbing. "I guess that realizing they were actually wrong about something would be pretty cataclysmic for them."

She smiled. "Yeah. Court and Linc have been apologizing like crazy."

"But?" I prompted when she hesitated.

That fierce glint returned in her eyes. "But they acted like jerks, and I'm not so sure I'm ready to forgive them. Are you?"

"No," I said bluntly. "I know that I'll have to talk to Ryan at some point because Gary ordered me to fix this mess. I guess it'll be easier since Ryan knows that I didn't really set him up, but that doesn't change the fact that he broke my heart. I'm not going to give him a chance to do it again."

"For what it's worth, I think he really is sorry," she said quietly. "Like, genuinely sorry."

"He should be," I retorted flatly. "But I've got enough to deal with right now. His regrets and his sorries aren't my cross to bear."

49

"Right." She nibbled on her bottom lip, looking unsure.

"Bex, just because *I'm* mad doesn't mean you have to be, too," I pointed out gently. "You don't have to—"

"Maddie, I love you, but please don't tell me what I do or don't *have* to do." Bex cut me off with more heat than I'd expected. "Remember how you just said you wouldn't give Ryan the chance to break your heart again?"

I nodded slowly.

"I gave... I gave them the chance to break *my* heart again, and they did." Her mouth set in a stubborn line, but the slight tremble on her bottom lip gave her away. "I should've known it was too good to be true. That they would just be my friends again."

"Bex, you know they weren't faking that. Especially Linc and Court."

She winced when I said Court's name. "I don't care. Not anymore."

She was lying, but I wasn't going to be the one to call her on it, because I knew exactly how she felt.

I could tell myself and everyone until I was out of oxygen that I was done with Ryan Cain, but the scary truth was, I wasn't entirely sure that was true. I wasn't totally certain that my heart was really done with the guy who had put it in a blender and force-fed it back to me.

How messed up was that?

For now, though, we were both willing to live with the half-truth as we went into the dining hall.

Class started in thirty minutes, so the room was full of people who were trying to eat before first period. I used the chaos to slip into line with Bex and get my food. Upon seeing me, one of the women working the line disappeared into the back and came back with a plate just for me.

Two egg whites and a plain yogurt.

"Seriously?" Bex whisper-hissed at me, eyeing my plate. She requested extra bacon and cheesy eggs in return, and I didn't have the heart to tell her not to bother.

My stomach rumbled unhappily as we found an empty table near the edge of the room. I sank down into my chair, ignoring the stares being tossed my way.

Yeah, I was definitely public enemy number one.

Bex sat down across from me and started to move some of her food to my plate.

"Don't." The word came out sharper than I'd intended, and I mentally slapped myself at the hurt in her eyes. "If I break the rules, he'll know. I can't risk it."

Her mouth turned down, and she took a reluctant bite of bacon that I swore I could taste through scent alone.

My mouth watered, and disappointment flooded my system as I swallowed a bland bite of egg. I eyed the salt and pepper shakers in the center of the table. Did they have too many calories?

Unwilling to take a chance, I turned away from them and tucked into my food.

I was pretty much sulking when a tray set down beside mine and the chair was pulled back.

I blinked in surprise at the newcomer. "What are you doing?"

Charles Winthrope the Fourth grinned at me as he sat down. "Eating, of course." The teasing lilt in his British accent coupled with the roguish glint in his eye would melt many a panty.

Mine, however, were drier than the Sahara.

Bex's guarded gaze watched him warily.

"Rebecca, right?" Charles didn't seem phased by our reluctance. He tapped his temple. "Shit, sorry. *Bex*, yes? That's the name you prefer?"

She nodded.

"Seriously," I said, pulling his gaze back to me. "What are you doing here?"

"Eating." He barely blinked at me as he replied. "Was this seat taken?"

"No," I managed, still confused, "but in case you hadn't heard? I'm the town pariah now."

He snorted and shook his head as he started cutting up his massive stack of pancakes. "I'd heard a rumor about such. Saw the video, too."

All the food I'd swallowed congealed into a sticky, cold slime in the pit of my stomach.

"Personally I say good for you." He gave me an approving smile. "You put that wanker in his place. I'm not sure that Dean O'Shea is a much better bedfellow, but I suppose anyone is better than Cain."

My jaw dropped. "Excuse me?"

Charles waved a fork. "I was truly concerned by the way he treated you. Like you were a piece of property. Good on you for being smart enough to out-play him."

"I didn't... That wasn't..." I shot Bex a surprised look, but she was clearly as dumbfounded as I was.

"Is that really what you think?" Bex found her voice first.

Charles nodded, looking back and forth between us. "I'm not the only one. Not everyone here is as awed by the Cain prince as you might think." A grimace flashed across his face. "Although, that being said, most of the people have been rallying to his defense."

"So, you're here because you think I set Ryan up?" I asked stiffly, setting my fork down since my appetite was gone.

"I'm sitting here because I like you," Charles replied.

"You don't know me."

He shrugged. "Then how about because your prat of a fiancé— pardon, your *ex*-fiancé—deserves to be knocked down a bit. I like your moxie, Madelaine."

"My *moxie*?" I echoed.

He grinned. "You're also one of the most beautiful girls I've ever seen."

"Well, you've also seen me naked," I muttered, blushing at the memory of Madelaine completely nude in that video.

"I swear I only looked at your eyes. They're positively hypnotic. Have you had your ancestry tested in one of those things to see if you're part celestial being?"

An unexpected laugh burst out of me. "Does that line usually work?"

His grin turned sheepish. "Better than you'd expect from Americans," he admitted.

"Well, thank you," I mumbled, ducking my head as my cheeks heated. "But honestly—"

I broke off in a ragged gasp as something thick and cold splashed over my head and slid down my back. Bex's face reflected my shock, and Charles shoved his chair out of the way to avoid being splattered.

Wetness slipped under the collar of my shirt and down my spine. Glancing down, I saw chunks of what looked like a smoothie clinging to my chest and splattered over what was left of my breakfast. But whatever was in this smoothie wasn't the usual Pac Cross fare; this stunk like rotten fish and old cheese. It was a grayish white with chunks, and I was already gagging at the stench.

"Oops," a soft voice said from behind me with a giggle. "Didn't see you there."

"Maddie." Bex started to stand up, but I shook my head and—oh, gross—a glop of something splatted on the floor.

Charles tried to hand me a napkin, but I ignored him as I slowly pushed away from the table and stood up to see a girl behind me with an empty cup in her hand.

"What the *fuck?*" I seethed through clenched teeth.

She smirked at me with big blue eyes and a wrinkled nose. She was a good five inches shorter than me, and I didn't recognize her, but that didn't stop her from pointing a pastel blue nail at me. "You might want to clean that up, honey."

My hands balled into fists at my sides as everyone in the dining hall watched the exchange, their eyes bright as they scented blood in the water. At the center table, I could see Brylee and the cheer team watching with avid interest.

The girl in front of me swung around and began walking away. She set the now-empty cup down on Brylee's table with a knowing grin before she kept going back to her own table.

"Maddie, don't," Bex warned, but I ignored her and stormed over to Brylee's table.

The bitch's smirk only deepened as she watched me approach. "Rough day, Lainey?"

Several girls on the team cackled. A few snapped photos.

53

"Seriously?" I hissed, flinging out a hand as the liquid dripped down my arm.

Hayley squealed as a droplet hit her. "Watch it, slut."

Brylee simply arched a brow as she eyed me. "I thought you'd be used to being covered in sticky white substances by now."

"Cum bucket," Kayleigh added with a snort.

Humiliation crawled up my neck as a wave of laughter swept the room.

"Maybe next time you should wrap it up," Brylee suggested. She reached into her pocket and flicked a foil square at me.

A condom.

Like it was the first shot in a war, foil packets were launched at me from every direction as people threw condoms like confetti at me.

Awesome.

I was the leader of the Slutty Parade.

Tears pricked my eyes and I whirled before they could fall. In my haste to get away, I slipped on a condom-smoothie blob and went down. My knees cracked against the floor.

More laughter. More flashes from phone cameras. Someone actually bent down, videoing my literal downfall.

I shoved to my feet and did the only thing I could.

I fled.

CHAPTER 7

RYAN

"Cain!" Coach's voice barked across the clearing as we started heading inside. I paused, glancing over my shoulder more out of curiosity than respect, even if Coach was one of the few men who had actually earned my respect at this school.

Most of the teachers were terrified of the students and acquiesced to whatever we wanted. Not that I didn't use that to my advantage at every turn, but it was hard to respect a teacher who couldn't even summon the balls to look me in the eyes when I asked a question.

Coach wasn't afraid to push or call us on our shit, and I appreciated that.

Except when it was crucial I get to my girl.

I felt my friends pause near me, but I waved them on with a heavy sigh.

Morning practice had been brutal, and the new plays were like trying to relearn muscle memory. Our playbook had been set since the beginning of summer. Now it was all shot to shit, thanks to Dean.

Fucker.

But I knew today was Maddie's first official day back, and I needed to see her before she was swallowed up by her schedule. Even if she didn't see *me*, I would stalk her sexy ass like a perv just to make sure she was really okay.

Last night had been an absolute clusterfuck. I hadn't expected her to be happy to see me, but the way she'd flipped out?

Even now, a sick feeling opened up a pit in my stomach, leaving me nauseated and worried. I needed to see Maddie and make sure she was functioning.

My jaw clenched as I waited for Coach to walk over to me. My helmet dangled loosely from my fingers, and it was only years of conditioning that kept me from tossing it around anxiously. My father had drilled it into my head to lock down all emotions, even when dealing with someone as benign to my existence as my coach.

Coach McGrath was a few inches shorter than me but still in great shape. The former NFL running back still looked imposing, even with silver coloring his temples before fading to a shock of dark hair. His dark eyes missed nothing... unless it was his assistant QB coach selling out our team last year while fucking my former fiancée. But hell, we'd all missed that.

"How are you, son?" he asked gruffly, clearly as uncomfortable with feelings and shit as I was. He was one of two men who called me *son*, but he was the only one who didn't make me feel like punching something when he used the term.

"Fine," I replied, keeping my tone even and clipped. It took all my control not to glance at my watch to see the time. Fuck, at this rate, I was going to miss seeing Maddie.

That bothered me a lot more than it probably should've, but that girl... Dammit. That girl fucking *owned* me. Last night had been brutal, and I would likely never get over the betrayed look in her eyes or the way she'd started sobbing.

I swallowed the sudden wave of emotions, shoving them back into the corner of my heart they'd escaped from as I focused on my coach.

He sighed and rubbed his jaw. "I know things have been rough on you lately."

Everything *rough* hung unspoken between us. The team, the play-book, my fiancée.

As far as the school knew, Maddie was *Madelaine*, who had betrayed me yet again. I was still trying to work out how to undo *that* mess. Dad was pissed, and demanding I prove that the Cabots weren't above the wrath of the Cain family. He was as aware as I was that we needed Maddie to go through with the marriage, but he wanted her crawling back to me in the most public way possible.

Personally, I didn't give a fuck what my father thought, but I knew he could make Corinne's life hell, so I had to tread carefully while I worked out how to get my girl back for real without setting off my father on my sister.

"I'm focused," I replied honestly. I *was* focused: on making things right with Madison, making Dean pay, finding a way to shut my father down for good, and helping my team recover from the setback of having our plays leaked.

I was so fucking tired of this shit.

Coach's lips pressed together in a thin line. "Ryan, you're one of the best quarterbacks I've ever seen."

I smirked a little at that, the praise feeling good even if it was useless. As much as I loved the sport, football wasn't my end game. It didn't matter how many scouts Coach could call in favors to come and watch me when my path was already determined. I was destined for a boardroom, not the gridiron.

"I know you've got plans that don't lead to me watching you on my television on Sundays," he added with a disappointed shake of his head, "but I worry about you. You've got a good head on your shoulders, that dickwad of a father of yours notwithstanding."

I let out a sharp laugh. Coach had made it abundantly clear he didn't give a damn who my father was or how much money there was in my bank account. It was one of the reasons I respected him. I was all too aware that a group of spoiled rich pricks could get a teacher or coach fired with one mediocre donation to the alumni fund, but Coach didn't care. He told it like it was to whoever he wanted.

"I'm also more than aware of why we're learning a whole new set of plays." His gaze caught mine. "*Again.*"

The smile fell from my lips. "It's complicated, sir."

"I'm sure it is," he muttered. "Which is why I'm going to give you some advice."

I tilted my head and waited.

"There's more to life than the expectations of others," he said quietly. "I'm well aware of who you are and how easily you command this school like it's an extension of this team. People look up to you, respect you. And I see how you put up a wall of not giving a fuck, but being vulnerable doesn't make you weak. Loving someone doesn't make you weak."

I nodded slowly. "Thanks, Coach."

He slapped my shoulder with his ever present clipboard. "Hit the showers. You smell like ass."

I grinned and turned to jog back to the locker room. Most of the team was almost done in the showers by the time I started mine. I let the hot water pelt my shoulders as I quickly scrubbed myself clean.

I wrapped a towel around my waist before stepping out and walking to my locker. When I realized my friends were gathered in front of it, I slowed.

"What?" I demanded, my gaze flicking between them as the sounds of the team leaving echoed in the room.

Ash grimaced. "Something happened at breakfast."

My heart sank like a fucking stone. "Maddie."

Linc gave a terse nod, looking ready to rip someone's head off. "Brylee started shit."

"It's not good," Court added grimly, his dark hair still wet and curling around his collar.

"You need to handle this," Ash finished, passing me his phone.

I tapped the screen and started the video. "Fuck," I swore when I saw Maddie, helpless and humiliated, as something dripped off her hand a second before everyone started hurling shit at her.

I squinted. "Are those…"

"Condoms," Ash confirmed, taking his phone back before I could snap it in half. He pocketed it and gave me a sharp look. "Handle this."

I glared at him, well aware that he was feeling morally superior for being the only one of us who hadn't immediately written Maddie off.

"I plan to," I snarled, shoving him aside to open my locker. I yanked my clothes out and started dressing.

Court leaned a shoulder against the wall of blue metal beside me, his eyes on his phone. "Bex won't answer me."

"Are you surprised?" Ash scoffed.

I slammed my locker shut hard enough for it to bounce back open as I rounded on my best friend. "Are you fucking done?"

"No," he spat, eyes flashing as he squared his shoulders. "This whole mess could've been avoided if you'd just stopped to fucking think." He glared past me to Court and Linc. "*All* of you. What happened two weeks ago is *nothing* compared to what we're up against next."

My jaw dropped open, and shock was the only thing keeping me from wrapping my hands around his throat. "Nothing? You think what happened is *nothing*?"

"No, dumbass," he snapped. "I'm saying that if you can't handle your emotions for a single fucking night, then we're fucked before we even get started."

"I get it," I hissed, shoving him back a step. "I fucked up."

"And what are you doing to fix it?" he demanded, stepping up to me once again, challenging me.

Linc eased between us, his dark blue eyes looking around at the guys still lingering who were taking too avid an interest in our argument. "Chill, guys. We all want the same thing here."

I glared at our remaining teammates until they scurried away, leaving me with the only real friends I had.

Ash sighed and glanced down before lowering his voice. "You've been saying you'll handle it, Ry, but it isn't being handled. It's blowing back on the girl you claim to love."

"I *do* love her," I retorted, running a hand through my wet hair.

"Then how do we fix it?" he countered. "Because Dean is running around the house like he won, and Brylee is out of fucking control. You know we have your back, but this shit needs to be settled. If we can't handle schoolyard bully shit, how are we supposed to handle everything else?"

I pinched the bridge of my nose and nodded. I'd been stagnant for too long, and I realized now that had been a mistake. I was done sitting on my ass, and if that bumped up our timeline, then I'd deal with the fallout. "Get Dean into the dining hall at noon."

Linc's brows rose. "Do I even want to know what you have planned?"

I grinned, knowing it probably came off a little feral. "No. Can you guys take care of it?"

"Of course," Court said with a nod.

I looked at Ash. "Get Maddie excused from her morning classes, okay? I'm going to see if she's okay."

"She won't want to see you," Ash pointed out, but most of the hostility had been replaced with curiosity.

"Good thing I'm not asking permission." I glanced at Court and Linc. "I want a full house at lunch, got it?"

Linc smiled. "Absolutely." He turned, Court following, to spread the word that lunch wasn't a time to miss. Odds were, people would be expecting me to one-up Brylee's crusade against Maddie. If there was one thing the assholes around here loved, it was fresh blood in the water.

I hung back and looked at Ash. "You still have all the files?"

He nodded slowly, realization dawning in his green eyes.

"Good. I want you to send them where we talked about," I informed him.

"Shit. Are you sure? That's setting this whole thing in motion, Ry. There's no going back," he warned me. "When I said to handle it, I didn't mean like *that*."

I clapped a hand on his shoulder. "I'm sure."

"She's worth it?"

I pressed my lips together. "She's worth everything."

His lips pulled back in a slow smirk. "It's about fucking time you pulled your head out of your ass. Go get your girl, man."

I snorted and turned away to do just that.

CHAPTER 8

MADDIE

I didn't actually break down until I made it to my room and was in the shower. I stepped under the spray, still fully clothed, and tried to wash the gunk down the drain as best as I could before stripping and dropping my ruined clothes in a corner of the shower stall.

They were going in the trash; I wasn't going to even bother getting them cleaned.

I stood in the shower for as long as possible, already having decided that I was giving myself a pass for morning classes. If Gary had a problem with it... I would deal with that later.

Right now, I needed to get my head on straight.

It's not like I was a stranger to bullying. Being an awkward preteen with a junkie mom hadn't exactly curried favor with my Michigan classmates. I was used to the name calling, the jeers, and even being pushed around. In the past I'd kept my head down and focused on moving through the day until the bullies found a more reactive person to torment.

Somehow I didn't think that approach would work at Pacific Cross. I had a feeling that if I tried to ignore Brylee, she would only take it as a challenge and up her antics. The kids here had been taught torment and hell in a master class. I was just now starting to realize that I'd been in the remedial version my whole life.

I twisted the shower knob to off and reached for one of my ridiculously soft towels to start drying off. I went through the motions on autopilot, letting my mind go blank as I re-dressed and then toweling my wet hair.

Maybe I could trick myself into being an emotionless void so whatever they had planned next wouldn't hurt as much.

I jumped as someone knocked on my door.

It was probably Bex. She'd been texting me nonstop since I'd run from the dining hall. I'd ignored all the notifications as she blew up my phone.

Sighing, I crossed to the door and jerked it open. "I'm fine, Bex."

My breath caught as ice blue eyes stared back at me.

"Ryan." My heart tumbled into a chaotic rhythm as I drank him in. I hated that even now I still wanted to throw my arms around his broad shoulders and bury my face against the firm muscles of his chest.

The tears I thought had dried up threatened to spill over, and I barely managed to blink them back. "Go away."

Ryan's hand flew out and slapped against the wood as I started to close the door on his beautiful, somber face. "Can we talk?"

I yanked the door open a couple of inches and wedged my body into the small opening. It was pointless. We both knew he could be inside this room in seconds if he wanted to. The thick, defined muscles he was barely hiding under his casual t-shirt and jeans weren't just for show. The fact that he was actually pausing and asking for permission instead of storming in showed just how far we had come.

Or how far we'd fallen.

"No," I said stubbornly, my pride refusing to let me give an inch. It might have been a few weeks, but the pain and humiliation of that night was fresh and raw. An exposed wound that was still festering and bleeding.

His blue eyes softened, the gentle expression on his face almost undoing my resolve. "Maddie."

I flinched away from the door, physically jolting at my name. "Don't."

He leaned slightly into the open space I'd created, the warm, almost hypnotic, notes of his cologne mixed with a fresh scent that was completely *Ryan* making me dizzy. "Mads. Let me explain."

I stared at him mulishly, forcing myself to remember how he'd humiliated me. How he'd *destroyed* me. Just when I thought I'd figured things out, Ryan Cain had gone and ruined me in ways I'd never expected.

The memory of that night was more than enough ammunition to fortify myself. "We're done, Ryan."

His eyes flashed with warning, but there was no anger in it. Almost like my words were a challenge and he couldn't wait to engage. "Mads."

"Stop calling me that," I gritted out through clenched teeth.

"I fucked up," he continued quietly, shame coloring his words.

"No," I replied scathingly. "You fucked *me*."

Now he winced, and a tiny streak of triumph shot through me at seeing his regret.

A muscle in his jaw ticked as he reined in a retort dancing on the tip of his wicked tongue. He was trying, that much was obvious. "Can I just explain? Can we talk?"

"Why?" I demanded. "Why, Ryan? Because you feel bad?"

"I *do* feel bad," he insisted. "I feel like shit."

"You should," I shot back. "And if you feel some need to unburden your conscience to make yourself feel better, then that's your problem. Not mine. I'm done hearing your lies, and I'm done playing your games."

"You're still my fiancée," he pointed out grimly, loading that last, fatal bullet in the chamber of his emotional arsenal.

I held up my ringless left hand. "I'm not your anything." Okay, so that was technically a lie, since Gary was definitely holding me to this unholy alliance, but right now, I was pissed.

"Fine," he agreed, his tone deceptively calm. The kindness in his eyes slowly swirled to calculating ice. It was a look I knew too well.

A thrill shot through my chest that echoed between my thighs.

I needed fucking therapy.

His breath fanned across my face as he leaned in closer. "I get that you need to sulk and lick your wounds, baby. But I'm not going anywhere."

My eyes narrowed and my breathing grew shaky. "This has nothing to do with sulking. I'm not some petulant child who got her feelings hurt. What you did to me? It's unforgivable, Ryan. So, go away. Get on with your life. A life that doesn't involve *me*. Maybe if you really push it, we can just be done with each other for good."

His blue eyes glittered like twin diamonds as he stared down at me. "I messed up, and I'll own that. I'll put in the time to make it up to you, but it changes nothing between us. You're mine."

"Fine. Whatever. Are we done here? I still have to go to class so I can get something else dumped on my head."

He flinched. "I heard about what happened. Are you okay?"

I stared at him as if he'd grown another head. "Fabulous. I'm thinking of starting every day with a smoothie scalp treatment. Think Brylee would give me the recipe? It smelled like sour milk and tuna, but it might've been halibut."

His jaw clenched. "Can you just stop with the attitude for a fucking minute, Mads?"

I draped a hand over my chest in mock surprise. "I'm *so* sorry. Is my tenuous grip on not losing my shit offensive to you? How would *you* like me to handle being made a fool of, Ryan? How can I possibly make this whole situation easier for *you?*"

He rubbed the back of his neck. "That's not what I meant."

"Then what did you mean?"

He grunted and pressed his lips into a flat line. "Can I come in?"

"No."

"Maddie, we need to talk about what's going on," he argued, bracing his hands on the doorframe. He glanced pointedly at my hand. "And we both know that, ring or not, there's no getting out of this deal."

Fuck him. No, seriously. Fuck Ryan Cain.

And I hated that he was right.

As if on cue, my phone started ringing and my blood chilled. I'd given Gary a different ringtone so I'd know when he was the one calling.

I spun away from the door and stomped to the table where I'd dropped my backpack and phone.

My free hand curled into a fist as I answered the call, lifting it to my ear. "Yes?"

"You're not in class." Gary's cold voice sent chills down my spine. "Do I need to remind you what's at stake?"

"There was an incident," I muttered through clenched teeth.

"Do you think I give a shit?"

I closed my eyes to keep from screaming. "I know. I'm handling it."

The door snicked shut and I looked over to see that Ryan was now *in* my room.

Awesome.

Actually…

"I have to go. Ryan's here. We're trying to talk things out." I barely managed to get the half-truth past my lips.

Ryan gave me a curious look.

Gary chuckled in my ear, the sound not exactly warm but definitely not as cold as a moment earlier. "Well, then. Carry on. Consider your absence excused for today."

I was still gritting my teeth as he hung up on me. It took everything not to throw my phone against the wall.

"Maddie?"

Ryan's soft voice was almost too much to handle.

I held up a hand. "Just… don't."

He stayed quiet. In fact, he didn't move from where he stood just inside the room. His brows were drawn low as he frowned at me.

But he didn't actually speak.

I dropped my phone back onto the table with a clatter.

Gary wanted me with Ryan. I guess I should have counted it a blessing that I didn't have to fight Gary *and* Ryan. Ryan was totally on board with us reconciling, but I wasn't ready to risk my heart again.

"I want a schedule," I said slowly, finally looking at him. "Like before."

His frown turned into a scowl. "Mads, that's not what I want. I—"

"I really can't say this enough, Ryan. I don't *care* what you want." I channeled all my fury and hurt and helplessness into a glare that I leveled at him. "The only reason I'm here is because I *have* to be. Whatever was between us is over."

"You don't believe that. Don't tell me you don't feel this pull between us."

"The only pull I feel when you're around is to the nearest bathroom so I can throw up," I retorted icily. I crossed my arms and gave what I hoped was an indifferent shrug.

The corner of his mouth hooked up. "You're lying, baby. Your right eye does this cute little twitching thing when you're not telling the truth." He held up his hands. "But I'll play it your way. For now."

I dragged in a shaky breath, watching warily as he walked to the couch and sat down. He gave me a pointed look and patted the cushion beside him.

"Sit down so we can work out our *schedule.*"

Ugh.

I dragged myself over to where he was but took the armchair opposite instead of sitting on the couch. I flashed him a triumphant smirk when he frowned.

"You realize you're going to have to act like we're a couple in public if you want to sell this to Gary," he pointed out. His eyes practically glittered. "You'll have to act like you enjoy it when I touch you. Hold you. *Kiss* you."

I felt my cheeks heat.

"Or maybe you won't be pretending," he murmured, watching my reaction.

"Clearly I'm attracted to you," I spat, pushing past my unease. "Being attracted to you isn't the problem. Trusting you is."

He sobered quickly. "I know, Maddie. I'm sorry. I should have trusted you."

"Yeah, you should have," I snapped, not ready to give a freaking inch. "Bex told me that it was Ash who figured it out. If he hadn't, would you still think it was me in the video?"

He was quiet for a long time. "Honestly? Yeah, I probably would."

Hurt sliced through my heart. So much for the emotionless void I was going for.

"But that speaks volumes about how fucked up I am, Maddie," he continued, his brilliantly clear blue eyes locked on me. "I don't trust people easily, and you…"

"And I *what?*" I demanded. "What did *I* do to make you believe you couldn't trust me?"

"You were too good to be true," he admitted hoarsely. "I was looking for a way to sabotage it, because there was no way someone like *you* could love someone like *me*. You're… good and pure."

I scoffed under my breath, shaking my head.

"It's why I know Gary has to have something big over your head to get you to come back here," he added.

My gaze snapped to him, wondering if he knew the threats Gary had thrown my way to force me to cooperate.

"I wish you'd tell me what it is." He swallowed roughly. "I can't help you if I don't know."

I mashed my lips into a line, not trusting myself to speak.

"But I know I betrayed you. It's going to take time to win back your trust." He dug into his pocket and pulled out the ring he'd given me the night of the party. His grandmother's ring.

It was hilariously less ostentatious than the one he'd given Madelaine, but I knew the meaning behind it. That alone made it priceless in my eyes.

He gently set it on the coffee table between us. "This is yours."

I cleared my throat. It physically hurt to look at that ring now. "No, it isn't."

He caught my gaze and held it. "Yes, it is. There's no other woman

I'll ever offer it to. That ring is yours, Mads, whether you wear it or not."

"I'm not going to put it on," I said, snatching it off the table and pressing it into his hand. I jolted at the current that sizzled between us when I touched him, and quickly scrambled back a step. "I brought the other one. I'll wear *that*."

Ryan inclined his head toward me, his fist closing around the ring before he shoved it into his pocket. "Whatever you want, Maddie. Whatever makes you comfortable."

I would rather wear the six-carat rock worth more than I could ever pay back than something so precious.

He leaned back on the couch. "Can we talk about what happened earlier? Are you okay?"

"Peachy," I replied in a clipped tone, looking away.

He sighed softly. "I'm going to make things right."

"How can you do that? Tell everyone who I really am?"

"I'll stand up and admit the truth about who you are to everyone if that will make you happy," he countered.

"No!" I could only imagine the hell Gary would rain down on me—and my mother—if I spilled the truth. Besides, it didn't matter now. Not since I was technically dead.

"Then tell me what will make you happy, Mads. What can I do to prove that I'm with you?" The raw edge of desperation in his voice was matched by the worry deep in his eyes.

"I don't know!" I exploded out of the chair. "There's not a manual for how to un-break a heart, Ryan!"

His head dropped, his shoulders heaving with the effort to breathe.

"Don't you think I *want* to trust you?" Tears colored my tone, cracking it like brittle ice. "Do you know that every time he hit me, I knew that pain didn't hold a fucking candle to what *you* did to me?"

A shudder rippled down his large frame, his hands curling into fists at his temples as he stared at the floor.

"I would rather have Gary kick my ass every single day than give you the chance to break my heart again." I finished my tirade by choking on a sob. I swiped at my eyes, but it was useless; the tears were falling completely unchecked.

Ryan shot up, his face red and eyes furious. "I won't let him touch you again, Madison."

A strangled laugh hiccuped out of me. "*That's* what you got out of this? That I need you to protect me? I needed you to protect my *heart*, Ryan. That's it. All you had to do was *trust me*."

He stormed around the table and grabbed my shoulders. His touch was like being zapped by electric wires. I felt the charge down to my toes.

"Maddie, I want to fix this," he insisted, blue eyes wild.

I twisted out of his hold with a cry. "You *can't*. You broke my heart. You broke… Fuck, Ryan, you broke *me*." I slapped a hand to my chest, the sting barely an echo of the agony I felt in my heart.

He looked as devastated as I felt and as utterly helpless as to how we moved on from here. We were both stuck.

So for the second time that day, I ran away from my problems.

I turned on my heel and practically sprinted into my bedroom, slamming the door behind me. I leaned against it and slid down to the floor before drawing my knees to my chest and letting myself cry.

CHAPTER 9

MADDIE

I never finished breakfast. Between that and bawling my eyes out all morning, my stomach was rumbling unhappily by lunchtime. I wondered at my odds of showing up during the last five minutes of the lunch hour to grab my food and not being seen.

Yeah, they sucked.

But unless I wanted to gnaw on the raw carrots in my mini fridge, I needed to go get actual food. Or whatever Gary deemed to be actual food.

I opened my bedroom door and came up short when I saw Ryan, still sitting on my couch. His phone was out, and he seemed to be comfortable as hell as he scrolled through social media while waiting for me.

"Why are you still here?" I blurted out.

He didn't look up. "Because we have shit to work out."

I leaned against the doorframe with a heavy sigh, my heart feeling like it had been put through a blender at high speed. "Ryan, can we not do this again?"

"You said you wanted a schedule," he replied evenly. "Let's work out a schedule. Sit." He jerked his chin at the chair.

I walked slowly to the chair before sinking down into it.

His gaze came up, assessing me critically. "You look like shit."

"Thanks," I muttered sarcastically, rolling my eyes.

He gave me a half-hearted shrug. "Would you rather I lie to you?"

I blinked slowly at him. "No, thanks. You've lied to me enough for one lifetime."

He sucked in a sharp breath between his teeth. "I never lied to you."

I snapped my fingers. "That's right. You thought *I* was the one who was lying."

With a growl of frustration, Ryan massaged his temples. "Can we not do this? I'm trying here, Maddie. You wanted a schedule, so let's make it happen."

I hated when he made sense. "Fine."

He tossed my phone at me. "I programmed my number into this one, since it's new. You really should use a password. Also, I told Bex you were okay, since she was threatening to come over herself." A ghost of a smile played on his full lips. "She might've threatened to string me up by my nuts if I fuck this up again."

I didn't bother adding that Bex would have to get in line behind me for that privilege. Not that I was actually going to give him a second chance. But it was good for me to file that memo away in case he disappointed me in a *non*-romantic way.

Yeah, that sounded like bullshit even as I thought it.

"Games are easy enough," Ryan went on, opening the calendar app on his phone. "I already synced my schedule with yours, but you'll have to let me know which games you won't make, since you'll be traveling with the academy."

"I won't," I murmured. A pang of regret rippled through me as I mourned the loss of one of my favorite things to do. Not that I expected the squad to welcome me back, especially not after this morning.

Ryan shot me a questioning look.

"Gary told me no more cheer," I added bitterly, running a hand through my hair. "One of his many new rules designed to keep me in line."

Ryan gave me his full attention then, his forehead creasing. "What other *rules* has Gary laid down?"

I barely held in a laugh, because the new spindles on my gilded cage were barbed and designed to inflict maximum damage. One wrong move, and I'd be sliced to ribbons. Or, worse yet, someone I cared about would pay the price.

"Nothing you need to worry about," I finally replied, keeping my tone as even as possible.

He stared at me for a beat. "This is ridiculous. Maddie, you have to—"

"Trust you?" The mocking edge in my tone chilled the very air in the room. I cocked my head. "I don't think so, Ryan. I'll tell you what *you* need to know. If that doesn't work… tell your daddy you want a new fiancée."

He raked a hand through his hair as if barely resisting the urge to yank it out at the roots. "Fine. Is there anything I *need to know?*"

"No missing class." I gave him a long look. "That's why Gary called a few minutes ago. I got a generous pass today on account of working things out with you. Oh, that's another condition. I'm supposed to win you back."

A faint smile tipped up the edges of his mouth. "So, he still has no idea that I know you're *you?*"

I shook my head. "No, and we should keep it that way. As far as he needs to know, you're giving me a second shot because my blow job skills are the best in the state."

"Fact." His eyes glittered as he watched me. Instead of offering a smile or a retort, I looked away with a blank expression.

"Okay." He gritted out the word through clenched teeth. "Anything else?"

He's holding my mom captive and drugged up to keep me in line. Oh, and I'm pretty sure he wants me to spy on you and your dad.

"That's pretty much it," I lied. I glanced down and picked at a loose thread on my skirt. "I'm either in class or in my room if I'm not with you."

The smile he flashed made my pulse race. "In other words, I'm the key to your freedom?"

I knew he meant it in a joking way, but his words rang true. The realization soured my stomach, and I clenched my jaw.

"Sorry. I didn't mean… Fuck." He looked pissed at himself now.

"Whatever," I mumbled. "Honestly, after today? I have zero problem staying in my room and ignoring all of *that*." I waved a hand in the direction of the door.

"*That* won't be a problem after today," Ryan said, the hard edge in his tone making me pause.

Unease trickled through my blood. "What are you talking about?"

"Do you trust me?"

The unexpected question rocked me. "*Me* trusting *you* was never the issue, Ryan. Not until you stabbed me in the back."

Hurt flared in his eyes for a second before he got up and held out a hand to me. "Let's go."

I glanced dubiously at his hand like it was a viper. "No, thanks."

He sighed impatiently. "Maddie, it's lunchtime. You need to eat." He frowned slightly. "Have you lost weight?"

Oh, was *that* supposed to entice me to get up?

Yeah… no.

"Way to make a girl feel good," I snapped, bristling.

"That's not what I—"

I leaned back in my chair and crossed my legs. "Whatever. I'm good here." He sucked in a deep breath through his teeth, like I was dangerously close to pushing him over the edge. "I'm trying really hard to give you the option to make the right choice, but I have no problem carrying you there myself." The hard look in his eye let me know he wasn't bluffing.

"Why?" I spat. "Why would you ever think I would go back there? Didn't you hear about what happened?"

He winced a little, and my bullshit radar went wild.

"What?" I demanded.

"I saw it. There's a video," he admitted quietly.

I let that sink in before a hollow laugh crawled out of my gut. "Of fucking course there is. I'm sure Brylee already made it go viral."

"Ash actually pulled it down," he replied, still looking down at me. "He put out a program that identifies the video and scrubs it anytime it goes public."

And to think, Ash was the guy who had seemed the most stand-offish of the four. As it turned out, he was the only one who really had my back.

"As great as that is, I'm not jonesing for a repeat performance."

Ryan's eyes narrowed. "Brylee won't fucking touch you when you're with me, and pretty soon, the entire school will realize you're off limits."

"Another decree from King Ryan?" I drawled, tilting my head back to eye him.

"Just get up, Maddie," he muttered, holding out his hand again. "Or don't. I have no problem throwing your sexy ass over my shoulder and carrying you there. But considering that skirt, everyone might be filming you for a new reason."

I blushed and shot to my feet, because the last thing I needed was an indecent exposure video making the rounds. I pointedly ignored his hand and sidestepped him.

He made a soft, almost disappointed, sound in his throat as I stalked back to my room to grab my shoes. I caught a glimpse of myself in the mirror and winced, realizing I *did* look like shit.

Whatever. I wasn't here to impress anyone, so they could all suck it.

I found another pair of shoes, since my originals were still splattered with whatever the hell Brylee had her fangirl dump over my head. I took my time putting them on, dreading going into the other room and joining Ryan.

Finally, when I couldn't realistically stall any longer, I got up and went to the door. "Let's get this over with."

He smiled tightly. "Words every guy wants to hear."

I cocked an eyebrow. "You should be lucky I'm speaking to you at all. Personally I'd just as soon grab a sledgehammer and beat the shit out of you."

He looked offended and hurt. "Mads, you don't mean that."

I smiled up at him, baring my teeth. "Find me a sledgehammer and watch me go."

"Nah. We both know you can't resist me," he teased, opening the door for me.

"Oh, I'm *full* of resistance," I snarled, stalking past him and striding to the elevator.

He followed me into the car and pressed the button for the main level, then crowded against my back so that his chest brushed me as he breathed. "I could always fill you up with something else."

"Pass," I muttered even as I tried not to clench my thighs together at the memories of him doing just that.

He chuckled softly, and I knew if he leaned forward an inch, his mouth would touch the shell of my ear.

"I've missed this," he said quietly.

I focused on the digital counter above the elevator doors ticking away the floors. "Missed, what? Having a girl hate your very existence?"

"You're sexy when you're feisty," he told me as if I hadn't replied. I could hear the smile in his voice.

Ryan Cain is the devil. Ryan Cain is your enemy.

My hair shifted as he leaned forward and sniffed me. "God, you smell fucking delicious."

Fuck me.

Thankfully the doors opened, and I scrambled out of the elevator before I could do something really stupid, like lean against him.

Sucking in an indignant breath, I whirled around before he could step off. "Stop. We're not together, we aren't *friends.* Just… stop."

His head angled to the side. "Why? Afraid you won't be able to resist my charms much longer?"

"I hate you," I hissed.

His eyes narrowed. "If I actually thought you meant that, I might back off." He inched closer. "But I know you really don't. Eventually you'll accept what I already know."

"And what's that?" I asked through clenched teeth, because the freaking nerve of this guy.

"That you're the girl for me, Madison Porter," he answered simply, as if that sentence held all the truth in the universe.

Except one thing.

Madison Porter was dead.

I swallowed and stepped back. "Let's just go, okay?"

Luckily Ryan was willing to let it go, even though I'm sure he saw the pain flash across my face at the mention of my name.

I reluctantly followed Ryan outside and down the path to the dining hall. My stomach twisted into a pretzel as we drew closer to the building. People were *everywhere*. Had the student body always been this big? Did all the teachers usually hang out here during their lunch?

As if sensing my hesitance, Ryan reached back and grabbed my hand, linking our fingers.

I started to squeeze his hand, grateful for the support, when I remembered I was supposed to hate him.

I mean, that I *did* hate him.

Dammit. Why did he make everything so complicated?

I tried to pull away, but he shot me a severe look.

"Optics, Maddie," he murmured, looking pointedly at our joined hands. "Happy couple, remember?"

I gritted my teeth, keeping my eyes focused ahead. In my periphery I still saw the heads swing to look at us as we walked by. Once we were inside, Ryan let go of my hand long enough to wrap an arm around my shoulders.

It was hard not to absorb the warmth he offered. My blood had turned to ice water since we'd walked inside, and now that we were almost to the football table, the glares were accompanied by a hushed silence that fell across the room. Brylee's dark gaze landed on me from her usual table.

My jaw dropped a bit as I saw a pissed-off Bex standing near Court. He seemed to be holding her backpack hostage so she couldn't storm away from his side.

"Looks like everyone's here," Ryan murmured with a nod.

Dread trickled into my numb system. "What?"

He looked back at me with an unreadable expression. "Time for the show."

"Sh-show?" I repeated, my voice barely above a whisper.

Ryan smiled at me, but there was something dark in his eyes. Something that promised hurt and pain and... vengeance.

"Ryan, I want to leave," I whispered, trying to move away, but his arm was like cement glued to me. Short of me throwing an actual fit, I wasn't leaving his side. And even then, people around here would probably just laugh as I struggled against their prince.

"You can't leave yet," he told me. A line creased the space between his eyes. "I set this up for you, babe."

Oh, God. Oh, shit.

Panic started to claw at my throat. Honest-to-God panic that made me want to run away. Whatever was about to happen would be bad. Horrific, even.

I noticed Brylee started to smile, smelling blood in the water.

My blood.

There were teachers in here. If I started screaming, then surely *someone* would—

The doors to the dining hall slammed open like a scene from an actual movie. They banged against the walls of the silent room with a crash that made me flinch and a few girls shrieked.

Linc and Ash strode in, yanking Dean between them. The frat president looked angry and terrified at the same time. His face was ashen under the mottled red of his cheeks. He struggled between them, trying to pull away.

Linc grinned, practically feral, as he hauled Dean forward. Ash didn't give away anything on his impassive face. When Dean was in front of us, they pushed him to his knees before letting go of his arms and taking a step back, still flanking him.

"Hey, brother," Ryan greeted in a tone that was anything but welcoming. His blue eyes had hardened into chips of ice and his voice was just as arctic.

Dean glared at him and struggled to his feet. "What the *fuck*, Cain?"

Ryan released me and stepped in front of Dean, folding his arms across his wide chest. "I just wanted to clear a few things up."

Dean's gaze bounced around the room, looking for an ally and finding no one. He swallowed, his Adam's apple bobbing, as he looked at me and then Ryan. "What?"

Ryan laughed, the sound deep and throaty. "Maybe he needs a reminder about a certain video?"

A wave of whispers swirled around the room, and Dean blanched before he tried to school his features.

Tried... and failed.

"A video where you made it look like you were sleeping with my fiancée?" Ryan prompted, eliciting another round of gasps and hushed words.

Dean's eyes narrowed, a sneer curling his lip. "I should think you'd be thanking me for helping you realize what a slut you were letting into your bed. Not to mention the fact that she's a fucking traitor."

"Traitor bitch!" Someone shouted across the room. More comments quickly followed.

"Fucking whore!"

"Slut!"

"Cum bucket!"

Ryan held up a hand and, like the trained puppets they were, everyone quieted.

"It was a good story," Ryan admitted, rubbing his jaw as he spoke to Dean. "You almost had me convinced."

Dean glared back. "Almost? Please. You ran out of your engagement party like someone kicked your puppy. Never knew you to be pussy whipped, Cain."

Ryan smirked. "Clearly you've never had good pussy."

My cheeks flushed red at the insinuation while several people started laughing.

"I had your girl's," Dean remarked smugly.

"Did you? Because Ash checked out that video and, I don't think you had my girl that night." Ryan tapped his temple. "In fact, I think that video was close to a year old, bro. When Maddie was still underage."

Dean paled.

"I mean, putting a phony timestamp on there was pretty stupid," Ryan went on, almost congenial. "Did you really think we wouldn't figure it out? And stealing the playbook from my room to frame her? Did you forget we have security cameras upstairs?"

"Fuck you, Cain," Dean hissed. He glared at me. "And fuck you, Madelaine." He literally spat at the ground by my feet.

"The only one fucked here is *you*, Dean," Ryan replied with a soft laugh.

Like he had timed it, the doors opened once more, but instead of teachers or students coming into the dining hall, people in dark blue jackets stalked inside. *FBI* was emblazoned on their chests in gold letters as they easily walked through the crowd.

"Dean O'Shea?" The woman leading the charge stopped in front of the guy in question. "We have a warrant for your arrest."

"On what charges?" he spluttered as another agent moved forward to yank his arms behind his back.

The woman glanced at the folded paper in her hand. "Dissemination of child pornography, attempted rape, drugging a victim with the intent to commit a felony, statutory rape, and endangering a minor." She closed the paper and gave him a savage smile. "And multiple counts on each of those charges, too. Aren't you the overachiever?"

"I want a lawyer!" he cried as they started to pull him from the room.

She nodded. "You'll definitely need one of those. You have the right to remain silent..." Her words trailed off as they pulled Dean back out the doors they'd just entered through.

There was a momentary lapse of time where no one in the room seemed to even breathe, and then it exploded into chaos as people started talking.

A sharp whistle from Court, loud enough that my ears rang, silenced them once more.

"And just so we're clear," Ryan announced to the room, turning in a slow circle to see everyone before leveling his gaze on Brylee, "the next time someone attacks my fiancée, I'm taking it personally."

CHAPTER 10

MADDIE

Ryan's hand on the small of my back spurred me into moving. He guided me to a vacant chair at the center of the football table as the whispers in the dining hall rose to a new crescendo. I sat in the chair he held out for me, trying to wrap my head around what the hell had just happened.

A tray of food appeared in front of me as everyone else took their seats. Ash and Ryan bracketed me while Court pulled Bex into the seat between him and Linc across the table.

Bex's wide brown eyes found mine, looking just as shocked and maybe even a little mortified.

A hand on my thigh made me jump, and I spun to see Ryan giving me a curious look.

"It's food, Mads," he teased softly, so only I could hear. "You're supposed to eat it."

I looked down at the food. Two slices of pepperoni pizza with extra cheese waited for me, and *dammit*, I wanted to devour them. My stomach grumbled, cramping painfully at the reminder that it was uncomfortably empty.

I shoved the tray back like it was poisoned. "I can't eat this."

Ryan frowned. "It's your favorite."

"And I can't—" I cut myself off, snapping my mouth shut and breathing hard through my nose to steady the rising tide of panic.

Bex shoved her seat back. "It's okay, Maddie. I'll go get your food."

Court looked ready to argue, but Bex managed to slip away before he could reach for her. With a huff, he pushed back and followed her.

"Maddie, what's wrong?" Ryan demanded, keeping his voice soft enough, but I could tell we were still attracting way too much attention.

Pizza definitely was *not* part of my diet. Gary would flip his shit at the notion of this much grease and carbs in the vicinity of my mouth. And if he found out...

My stomach cramped again for a whole new reason.

Who knew *what* he would do to Mom if I disobeyed? I wasn't ready to find out.

"Get it away," I hissed, glaring at the pizza like it had personally offended me.

Ryan's brows slammed together. "Maddie—"

Ash's dark-skinned hand lashed out and moved my tray in front of his. He grabbed one of the slices and took a huge bite, giving me a steady look.

I exhaled a shaky breath. "Thank you."

He gave me a curt nod, his jade-colored eyes bright and curious as he watched me. "No problem." He swallowed and glanced past me to Ryan and then back. "You forgive him yet?"

I shook my head.

Ash smirked. "Good. Fucker doesn't deserve it."

My jaw dropped open as Ryan growled beside me.

"You're supposed to be *my* friend, dipshit," he muttered at Ash.

Ash barely blinked. "I am your friend, which is why I'll tell you when you're being an asshole, asshole."

Ryan rubbed his forehead, looking like he was torn between storming away and punching Ash.

Bex appeared then in front of me, sliding a tray of—what else?— salad with no dressing and two thin slices of grilled chicken before me. Her pinched mouth conveyed what she thought of my meal. She sat down, and Court joined her, frowning at my plate.

Trying not to make a big deal out of it, I stabbed a piece of chicken and forked it into my mouth. It was bland and unseasoned as I chewed, the act of eating more mechanical than anything else as I tried to work through the shock of seeing Dean hauled away by federal agents.

"What is *that*?" Linc demanded, clearly not having a problem drawing attention to me.

I glared at him and swallowed before taking a drink of water. "Food."

"Rabbit food," he muttered, waving a fork at my plate. "Since when are you a salad only girl?"

I could feel Ryan's gaze on me, curious and probing as he wondered the same thing.

A brittle smile pulled at the corners of my mouth as I looked at Linc. "I guess I'm just being more cautious since I almost died eating something around you guys."

Linc flinched at the memory and turned to his plate of lasagna with a stunned expression.

Rage churned in my stomach, gnawing away at the hunger until all I felt was helpless and furious. I shoved my tray away, the silverware clattering noisily, and then I stood up with a sharp scrape of the chair legs.

"Maddie?" Bex lifted worried eyes to me.

I shook my head. "I just need to go. I'm okay, Bex." I started to leave the table.

"Sit down," Ryan ordered in a low voice, grabbing my wrist.

I glared down at where he was touching me. "Let. Go."

His gaze hardened and his fingers tightened, not enough to bruise but enough to let me know I wasn't going *anywhere* without his permission.

God, I was so *sick* of being manhandled and told what to do.

Unfortunately for me, Ryan was about to see my least favorite trait: angry crying. When I got truly pissed off, like beyond reason pissed off? I cried. Not like some simpering beauty in a movie, but full-on swollen eyes, red face, snotty crying.

After this morning I didn't think I had any tears left, but apparently there was no end to the well of pitiful sorrow and rage my soul lived in.

"You're making a scene," he reminded me coldly, but something else lingered in his eyes.

If this had been Ryan from a few weeks ago, I wouldn't have even noticed it. I would have just assumed he was being his usual dictatorial asshole self by ordering me around.

But now that I *knew* him? I could see the genuine worry in his gaze. I was freaking him out.

I gritted my teeth and leaned down. "Unless you want the entire school to watch your fiancée have a full-blown meltdown, I suggest you let me the fuck go."

His eyes narrowed, that piercing blue seeing too much.

"Ry, let her go," Ash murmured.

Ryan drew in a long, slow breath, as if he was trying to get himself under control. His hold on me loosened, but only enough to slide his fingers down to mine and tangle them together as he stood up.

Bex looked ready to get up, too.

"I'm fine," I assured her.

She didn't look convinced. "I'm supposed to go to the doctor—"

"Why?" Court demanded.

Bex stiffened, barely sparing him a glance. "None of your business." She looked at me. "I can cancel it and hang out with you."

"Are you okay?" I asked softly, my gaze sweeping her. I noticed the guys were watching her closely, too. Like they were looking for signs something was wrong.

Bex's cheeks tinged pink at the attention. "Just a routine checkup. No big deal."

"I'm good," I assured her. "I just need some space." I turned and gave Ryan a pointed look that he blatantly ignored.

"Let's go, baby." He smiled stiffly at me and cocked an eyebrow.

Clenching my jaw to keep from screaming, I jerked my hand out of his and started marching toward the door.

But *of course* someone would step into our path.

I recognized the guy as one of the defensive lineman from Ryan's team.

"Pascal," Ryan drawled, clearly not wanting to talk but feeling obligated to stop.

Pascal looked at me. "Glad your girl wasn't a traitor." He smirked, and I wanted to slap him. "Again."

Ryan smiled back, something darkly chilling passing across his face as he took my hand once more. "Yeah, we worked out our shit. Sorry about you and your girl, though."

Pascal frowned. "What?"

Ryan's expression turned cold and calculating. "She's out back sucking Hanson's dick." He leaned forward. *"Again."*

Pascal's complexion turned red, and his beady brown eyes looked around the room desperately. His face went purple, I assumed when he realized neither his girlfriend nor the Hanson guy were in the room.

Ryan clapped a hand on his teammate's shoulder with more force than necessary, if Pascal's grunt and wince was any indication.

"Worry about your own girl," he growled, the threat clear as freaking crystal as he held me against his side. "If I see you near mine again, I'll make sure you're benched the rest of the season. It'd be a shame if one of your drug tests came up positive with all those scouts looking at you this year."

Pascal's eyes went a little wide and he nodded jerkily as Ryan released him.

"It's pretty fucking cliché, but check under the bleachers," Ryan added with a smug look. "That's usually where Hanson takes her."

With a scowl, Pascal stormed by, but he didn't give me another glance.

"My hero," I muttered, shaking my head in disgust.

Ryan shot me a surprised look that quickly darkened into a frown. "Fine. Let's get this over with."

I snorted in response but kept up as he walked us out of the dining hall and a little ways down the path. He veered off toward an old oak tree and didn't stop until we were under it. A quick glance around showed everyone was still inside and we were alone. Only then did I rip my hand free of his.

He threw his hands in the air. "What now, Maddie?"

I stared up at him. "Are you honestly asking me that right now? Like, you're serious?"

His blue eyes went cold. "I would think that you'd be thanking me right now."

"*Thanking* you?" I echoed incredulously. "For *what*?"

"For setting the record straight?" He stabbed his fingers through his already mussed hair. "For making sure the entire school didn't think you were cheating on me?"

"You think I give a flying fuck about what the entitled assholes at this school think of me?"

"Considering the state I found you in when I came to your room? Yeah, I do," he snapped back.

I folded my arms across my chest. "You asshole. You have *no idea* what I'm going through. You have no idea if you're making it better or making it worse. You're just..."

"Just what?" he demanded in a cold, detached tone.

"You're Ryan *fucking* Cain," I spat, using his name like the curse it was. "You think you can just snap your fingers and take back what you gave away. Like standing up for me, even though I was *innocent*, will make me just forget everything that happened?"

His jaw clenched, a muscle popping out. "I'm trying here, Maddie."

"Oh, you're *trying*!" I clapped my hands together. "Well as long as you're trying, that's all that matters, Ryan. Lucky, lucky me to have a guy who is so willing to defend my honor except when it really counts."

He exhaled hard and planted his hands on his hips. "I know I messed up, Mads. I've apolo—"

I scoffed and rolled my eyes. "Okay then. Sure. Bygones, and all that shit. We're totally even."

"What the *fuck* do you want from me?" He roared, slamming his fist into the trunk of the tree with enough force that pieces of bark went flying and the skin across his knuckles split. "Tell me, and I'll do it!"

"Why now?" I asked slowly. "Why would you out Dean *now*?"

He stared at me like I'd grown a third boob. "Seriously?"

"You did it to help me, right?" I went on.

"Obviously," he retorted in exasperation.

I gave a singular nod. "Got it. So, you'll do that to help *me*, but not anyone else?"

His forehead wrinkled in confusion.

"Dean tried to *rape* Bex last month," I pointed out, my voice trembling with fury. "I wanted her to go to the cops, and you told me she couldn't. What changed now, Ry? You'll do the right thing, but only if it scores you brownie points?"

"I shouldn't have done what I did," he admitted, his jaw tight enough that I worried his teeth might shatter.

"No, you shouldn't have. You should've driven Bex to the police station that night," I whispered, angry tears spilling down my face. "You're not a good guy, Ryan. I think I deluded myself into believing you were—that you could be better than men like Gary and Beckett. But at the end of the day, unless you're getting something out of it, then morality is just a fucking inconvenience to you."

"I meant, I shouldn't have done what I did to Dean *today*," he corrected in a soft tone. "What I did today, *for you*, fucked up more than you'll ever know." He dug into the pocket of the jeans and pulled out his phone, which must have been on silent. He flashed the screen at me so I could see the eleven missed calls from his father.

"You're right, Maddie," he added, putting the phone away as it started to vibrate again with an incoming call. "I'm not a good guy. I've never claimed to be. And, yeah, I'm an asshole for not encouraging Bex to go to the police. There's a reason I didn't, and one I'll tell you about when I don't think you'll use my secrets to blow up everything I've spent the last *decade* working on."

I blinked in surprise.

He stepped closer to me, the proximity of his body making mine hum with awareness.

"And, yes, I exposed Dean today for *you*. Because I might be willing to let this entire world go to hell, but I won't let you burn with it." His eyes glittered as he watched me. "Maybe that makes me an asshole or a dick, but you're my priority. Not Bex, not my father, not even my own fucking agenda."

My breath caught, the intense storm in his eyes sucking me in and rooting me to the place I stood.

His hand lifted to my face and gently traced the curve of my jaw until his fingers slid through my hair. "I'm choosing you, Madison. Today, tomorrow, and every other day."

I swallowed hard. "Too bad you didn't make that same decision two weeks ago."

Regret burned in his eyes. "No one regrets that more than me, baby. Just... Dammit, Maddie, let me *in*." His hand fisted my hair at the base of my skull as his forehead dropped to mine.

I let my eyes close as I inhaled him, filling my lungs with the air he breathed.

"I know something else is going on, but I can't fix it unless you trust me." His voice was soft and practically begging me to knock down the wall between us. "Just give me another chance, baby. Please."

A strangled sob wrenched from my chest a second before his lips found mine. I reacted on instinct, lifting to my toes and wrapping my arms around his neck as I kissed him back.

He poured everything into his kiss. Regret, love, desperation, and hope. I tasted it on his lips and felt it in his touch.

Ryan might have betrayed me, but I still loved him.

I was such a freaking idiot.

His mouth moved to my cheek, kissing away another tear. "Madison, *please*. Let me in."

I opened my eyes, and the raw emotion in his gaze almost made my knees buckle. My hand drifted to his mouth of its own accord, tracing the fullness of his bottom lip.

I gave him a sad smile. "No."

And then I walked away from the man I loved.

CHAPTER 11

RYAN

I watched Maddie walk away, barely resisting the urge to chase her down, throw her over my shoulder, and kidnap her to some remote location where she'd be forced to give me another shot. Hell, I was even okay with Stockholm Syndrome at this point, if it meant she wouldn't look at me that way.

Like I'd betrayed her.

Which, yeah, I fucking had.

"Dammit!" I hissed, punching the tree again. I glanced down at the smear of blood on the trunk and then at my mangled knuckles. Coach would have a bitch fit if I damaged my hand.

I flexed my fingers gingerly, testing them. I could feel one of the bones grinding against another as I grimaced around the pain. I'd probably fractured one, but I'd played through worse.

Our next game was against Havenshire, and my backup could beat their team hungover with explosive diarrhea. A bruised and slightly broken hand wouldn't keep me from throwing enough passes to demolish their pansy asses.

"Didn't go well, huh?"

I turned to glare at Ash. My best friend was like a damn ninja the way he could sneak up on anyone.

He gave me a benign smile. "I'm shocked."

I flipped him off with a sigh as my phone started ringing *again*. Tension knotted the muscles around my neck as I let out an aggravated sigh. "I don't get it. I thought Maddie would've been happy that I set shit straight."

"I think we've all learned by now that Maddie isn't just another fangirl who's going to drop her panties because you smile at her, dipshit," he told me.

Irritation spiked in my blood. "Don't fucking talk about my girl's panties. Ever. Best friend or not, I'll knock you out."

Ash's brows lifted in amusement. "I'd like to see you try." But he didn't say anything else about Madison. "Anyway, I came out here because we've got shit to handle."

"I know." I scrubbed a hand over my face. "My dad's blowing up my phone."

"That," Ash agreed, "and the frat is losing their minds. You'd think this was their first scandal."

I scowled at him, not for the first time annoyed at my *brothers*. This frat was a fucking joke, and I'd only pledged because I was a legacy and it was expected. It was easier than fighting Dad.

Okay, and it had also given me an inside position to make a lot of moves that benefitted me and my friends.

"I'm so sick of holding their hands through shit," I muttered, falling into step with Ash to head toward the house. Blowing off English for a day wouldn't tank my GPA, and Mrs. Reedsy was obsessed with the team. All I had to do was smile, and she'd give me whatever grade I wanted.

It was actually a little pathetic how easily the teachers and staff around here could be bought or cajoled into doing whatever we wanted. And it wasn't just me and my friends; it was the majority of the student body. Because our bank accounts had a few—okay, a *lot*—of extra zeroes, they let us get away with murder.

Case in point? Linc and Ash had literally dragged Dean's ass across campus and into the dining hall without being stopped or questioned.

The staff were here for their paycheck and a show, not necessarily in that order.

It was why no one had intervened when Brylee pulled that shit on Maddie earlier.

That reminded me...

"Where are we with the cuntasaurus?" I snarled, looking at Ash.

His lips twitched into a smirk. "Going a little slower than I would like, but I think we'll pull it off without much of an issue."

"Good. She's paying for what she did to Maddie."

"And what about you?" Ash inquired quietly.

I jerked to a stop, staring at him because I wasn't sure I'd heard him right.

"Fuck did you say?" I demanded.

He met my gaze levelly. "What are you doing to pay for what *you* did to her? Because people might argue that you fucked her over more than anyone else, bro."

I spread my arms wide. "I'm making shit right. Dean is going away—"

"A plan we already had," he cut me off with a sharp shake of his head. "Dean was never riding off into the sunset. We just bumped up the timeline. But that shit was in motion before Maddie ever came here."

My jaw clenched, and I wanted to throttle my best friend. I hated that he was even asking me this shit, but he was the only one who would. Even Court and Linc would back me without question. They'd done that the night of the engagement party by turning their backs on Maddie and Bex.

Ash questioned things. He was inquisitive and like a fucking pit bull until he learned the truth. He challenged me to look at the world through the same lens, and I had tried.

Until Maddie.

I exhaled a hard breath, my hands on my hips. "I don't know. I don't know how to fix this. I thought turning Dean in would be a start, but—"

"—but she isn't rolling over that easy?" Ash grinned. "I knew I liked that girl."

"That's really fucking helpful," I drawled, shaking my head in exasperation.

"It actually is," Ash retorted, shoving my shoulder. "Ryan, I know you better than anyone else, and you *need* someone like Madison, but only if you're willing to put in the work. She isn't going to forgive you because you gave her a gift, even if it was a would-be-rapist in handcuffs."

I rolled my eyes. "She basically said it was too little, too late."

"She's right," Ash replied bluntly.

"You know why we couldn't move on O'Shea before today," I reminded him. "His father is a shoe-in for the next Supreme Court Justice. Or was until today. I'm not sure even Judge Reginald O'Shea can sweep away a rapist for a son."

"Ry, we've been playing defense for so long, planning and plotting, and where has it gotten us?" Ash's brows raised. "Dean wasn't even the worst guy on our hit list. We've let shit slide for years because we're waiting for the stars to fucking align."

"We show our cards early and everything will fall apart," I snapped, rubbing the back of my neck as irritation prickled up my spine. "We all agreed to that when we started Phoenix years ago."

"And I think we made the wrong call," he replied. "I think we've been sticking to the shadows because it always gave us an out."

"An *out?*" I repeated. "What does that even mean?"

"It means that until today, we could've closed the doors on Phoenix and the whole plan. *Someday* was never going to happen. There would always be a reason not to pull the trigger." His expression softened. "Until Maddie. She's the pivot point—the reason we decided to move. She's the one person who was able to get through to you."

I rubbed at my chest, as though that would make the ache go away. "Your point?"

"Today meant that we're all in, even if we go down in flames, and it's about fucking time." He reached over and clapped a hand on my shoulder. "It's time we went on offense, bro."

I snorted and pressed my lips together. "Maybe you're right."

A brow lifted. *"Maybe?"*

"All you're getting is a *maybe,* you smug bastard," I replied, pushing him back with a smile. "Let's go deal with these asshats so I can focus on my girl."

"You know, the easiest way to get her back might be to just tell her the truth. Loop her in on it all," Ash told me as we started walking again.

I looked at him sharply, my heart slamming in my chest at the thought. "No. No way."

"Ry—"

"I'm not dragging Madison any deeper into our world than she needs to be." The idea of her knowing even more details of the world I came from—the *family* I came from—was enough to make me shudder in revulsion. I could only imagine how fast it would send her running.

Call me a selfish asshole, but I wasn't prepared to lose her further than I already had. Especially not if I could help it. "Maddie isn't going to be touched by any more of this shit than she already has been."

He gave me a long look. "You really think more secrets are the best plan?"

"I think I would burn the world to the ground if it meant I could keep her safe," I replied in a hard tone. My hands balled into fists, the barely closed scrapes on my knuckles splitting open anew with a blaze of pain that radiated up my arm.

I embraced it, letting the fire licking through my veins burn away my doubts.

It could all burn, and I wouldn't care as long as Maddie was protected. Because even if I burned with it, she and I were the endgame.

Not even the total destruction of my world and all the people in it would keep me from Madison.

I would rise from the ashes just like a fucking phoenix and reclaim her every single time.

92

CHAPTER 12

MADDIE

*P*arty *at 8 at the frat. Look sexy AF unless you'd like me to strip you down and dress you myself. I'm hoping you pick option #2.*

I stared—for, like, the twelfth time—at the text Ryan had sent me an hour ago.

After stalking off, I'd gone back to my room and taken a nap. I'd been emotionally drained and had wanted nothing more than to crawl into my bed and forget the fucking world.

So I had.

Gary had given me a pass for today, and since it was Friday, I'd planned on hanging out with Bex all weekend and laying low.

But apparently the best way to celebrate your frat president being hauled away by the FBI was with a party.

I mean, honestly, I didn't have a problem celebrating Dean's incarcerated status. I might even send him a gift.

Like soap.

On a rope.

A twisted smirk of satisfaction crawled across my lips as I thought about Dean getting back everything he'd dished out over the past few years. Maybe I'd been spending too much time in this cutthroat world, because I couldn't even dredge up a single scrap of a fuck to give that Dean would be spending the foreseeable future as the bitch he was.

When someone knocked on my door, I crossed my room. Even though I knew it was probably Bex, I still checked the peephole. Once I confirmed it was my only friend in the freaking world, I opened the door.

Bex frowned at me, holding up her phone. "I got your message. What's the emergency?"

I groaned and let her inside. "Ryan."

Her lips pinched together in annoyance. "What *now?*"

"Apparently my presence has been requested at a party tonight," I deadpanned as I shut the door after Bex and locked it.

"Seriously?"

I passed her my phone so she could read Ryan's message. Her nose wrinkled when she'd finished. "And you're going?"

"I don't want to," I grumbled, dropping onto the couch and picking at a piece of lint on my yoga pants. Skin-tight yoga pants were as comfortable as my new Gary-approved wardrobe allowed.

"Maybe you can fake the flu?" Bex suggested. A wicked glint stole into her eyes. "Or tell him you've got your period? That usually sends guys running."

My stomach cramped with a memory of when I'd been riding the crimson wave, and Ryan had snuggled me in his arms all freaking night. He was better than pain relievers and heating pads combined.

No, no, no.

I quickly changed my train of thought before wallowing led to more tears. I wasn't sure how I had anything left at this point.

"So, what's the plan then?" Bex asked me.

I cut my gaze to hers. "I plan to look as hot as humanly possible to show Ryan exactly what he threw away." As I spoke the words, the plot forming in my mind sparked life into my chest.

Bex's hazel eyes glittered. "I'm guessing you won't be sharing that hotness with him?"

I gave an indifferent shrug. "He can watch all he likes, but I'm moving on. Emotionally, if not physically, anyway."

Her brows slowly, and not at all subtly, inched higher. "Oh, really?"

My head dropped back, and I stared at the ceiling. "When you say it like that, I get the feeling you don't believe me."

"I mean..." She spread her hands wide on her lap. "Am I wrong?"

"No," I muttered. "I wish I could turn my feelings on and off like a light switch."

"Yeah," Bex breathed, "that would be awesome."

I cast her a long look. "Are you okay? I mean, we didn't really talk about you and Court and Linc. I know you were getting close to them."

A grimace twisted her features. "And now I'm not. I guess I'm someone who needed to learn that lesson twice." Bitterness laced her words like acid.

I pulled my legs onto the sofa and faced her. "Bex, come on. I know it meant something to you. And I think it meant something to them, too."

"Not enough," she replied tartly. "And I'm the idiot who fell for it." She wiggled two fingers. "Again: *twice*."

"You fell for it? Or him?" The question escaped before I could censor it.

Bex glared at me, but there was little heat behind it.

"Sorry," I apologized.

She waved a dismissive hand. "It's fine. And both, I guess. I mean, the Linc thing was new, but Court... I'm so stupid, Maddie."

I reached over and linked our fingers, giving hers a sympathetic squeeze.

Her head tipped back as she blinked away tears. "It just felt *real*, you know?"

I nodded morosely, because I could absolutely relate.

She used her free hand to swipe at her eyes. "Shit. I forgot how much I liked just being with him. With all of them."

"What went wrong?" I asked. Bex had mentioned that she'd grown up with Court, Linc, Ryan, and Ash. Her family and Court's had been extremely close at one point, until it all fell apart.

"I wish I knew," she muttered. "One day, Court was my best friend, and the next, he stopped talking to me." She gave me a pointed look. "I guess I have that effect on people."

I winced, because my sister had done the same thing.

"Maybe I just naturally repel people," she joked, but I got the impression she was only half teasing.

"Not me," I said emphatically. "You're the only person I can trust. I think I'd be suicidal if you weren't—" I snapped my mouth shut as what I'd said ricocheted through me like lightning.

Bex's face went a little ashen.

I dropped her hand, mine suddenly feeling cold and clammy. I drew my knees to my chest and wrapped my arms around them. "I didn't mean that."

"Okay," she said slowly, her eyes unreadable.

Not, *Of course you didn't, Maddie.*

"I'm not suicidal," I said quickly. I wasn't. I hated my circumstances, but I was still ready to fight, no matter how weary I was.

"But if Madelaine spent *years* feeling as trapped as I have for the last two weeks..." I trailed off and looked away. "I don't know, Bex."

"I wish she'd told me," she murmured. "About Adam, about Gary, about everything. Maybe I could've helped."

I was eighteen and couldn't see a way out of this nightmare, so I could only imagine the toll it had taken on a thirteen-year-old. Especially one being abused and manipulated by the adults who were supposed to protect her.

Anger rolled through me, leaving an icy numbness in its wake.

"They're going to pay," I forced out through clenched teeth. "I'm going to *make* them pay."

"How?"

"Gary gave me a new phone, but Ash still has my old one. I wonder if he got anything else from the app. Maybe Madelaine had a plan to get out from under them. One that I can use."

Bex sighed. "I guess that means we're going to a party?"

I smirked a little. "Of course we are. And we'll look like walking sin when we do."

~

The pledge who picked us up a few hours later introduced himself as, "Five." Because pledges got numbers, not names. He was a perfect gentleman as he opened the back door of his Range Rover to let us in before slipping behind the wheel and driving us across campus to Greek Row.

To be fair, Five seemed pretty sweet, and the way his gaze kept snagging on my exposed legs as I got into the car boosted my confidence.

I'd picked the black leather miniskirt and red halter top for maximum skin exposure. The sexy-as-fuck black Louboutins made my long legs look even longer. I'd left my hair loose and down and used minimal makeup, just a coat of mascara and a ruby shade of lipstick to finish the effect.

Bex hadn't gone quite as extreme as me, but the slinky green dress with a high neck and an open back made her vibrant eyes pop and accented the green-and-blue-dyed strands of her dark hair.

If the way Five occasionally had to swerve back onto the road when his gaze lingered too long in the rearview mirror was any indication, we'd nailed the *sexy AF* requirement of Ryan's message.

Five pulled into the circular drive of the frat, parking in a reserved spot before leaping from the vehicle and opening the back door for us.

I awkwardly turned my legs, careful not to flash him a view of the pink lace thong I was wearing under my skirt because the effect of this outfit would've been ruined by panty lines. And also? Sometimes a girl just needed some sexy underwear to boost her confidence, even if she was the only one who knew it was there.

Five hesitated, shooting us a nervous glance. "Want me to walk you in?"

I glanced around the front of the house. The party was in full-swing, with people gathered on the lawn and music pumping from the speakers in the massive, three-story brick monstrosity of a house. Almost every light in the place was on, and I could see silhouettes of

97

people inside. Splashes from the back signaled people were taking advantage of the warm California night to use the pool.

"We're good," I said coolly.

Five gave a slow nod, his eyes already on a girl who was giving him some serious fuck-me eyes as she peered at him over the top of her cup. He walked away from us without another word, headed in her direction.

I dragged in a slow breath, turning my attention to the house and squaring my shoulders as butterflies flapped in my stomach. "Okay."

Bex grabbed my wrist and stared at me with wide eyes that took in my outfit. "I don't know about this, Maddie."

I frowned a little as I looked at her, glancing down at my outfit. "Is my skirt too short?"

She nibbled on her lower lip. "I mean, not *really*—"

With a smirk, I reached down and tugged the hem up, exposing another inch of skin and making a mental note to avoid bending over. Or sitting. Honestly, I might flash an ass cheek if I walked too fast.

It wasn't much different from the way half the girls here were dressed. I looked ready to party.

Or work a corner.

Eat your heart out, Ryan.

Bex groaned softly and shook her head. "Seriously, Maddie. Ryan's going to flip when you walk in, and probably not in a good way. He won't take this lying down."

I met her eyes and couldn't help but smirk. "I don't care if he takes it lying down, standing up, or bent over. Ryan can suck it."

"That's what I was afraid you were going to say," Bex muttered behind me as I started walking to the front door.

"Besides, he's the one who told me to dress sexy," I reminded her with a wink.

She blew out a breath and muttered, "Not what I think he had in mind."

I kept my focus solely on walking, because cobblestones and heels were a deadly combination, and the effect of my outfit would be ruined if I face planted in front of everyone outside. I missed someone coming up behind me until it was almost too late.

"Maddie." A hand touched my elbow, and my heart leapt as I turned quickly. Too quickly. My ankle started to roll, and I flung my arms out to steady myself.

Charles laughed as his hands steadied me. "Sorry. I didn't mean to scare you. I thought you heard me."

Bex stared at me, wide-eyed, behind Charles.

"I was lost in my own world," I replied, letting him go.

His gaze traveled down the length of me, warming appreciatively but not in a creepy, undressing-me-with-his-eyes way. "Wow."

My smile felt a little brittle. "Thanks."

His gaze snapped to my eyes and didn't drop below my chin. "Perhaps I can escort you inside? We can't have you falling, now, can we?"

Bex made a slightly distressed sound in the back of her throat, and I knew why. Walking into the house on the arm of a guy who *wasn't* my fiancée? Yeah. It wasn't a good look, and I knew it would piss Ryan off.

And as furious as I was with Ryan, something in me recoiled at the idea of touching another guy.

So much for my *moving on emotionally* speech to Bex.

My heart, in all its annoying traitorous loyalty, was still firmly Team Ryan.

"I'm surprised you're here," I blurted out. My cheeks heated when I realized how accusatory and rude that had sounded.

Charles simply lifted his brows. "It was an open invitation, or so I was led to believe. Most of my teammates were coming, so I decided to join them."

"Right," I muttered, running a hand through my hair. "How's your season going?"

"Soccer isn't football, well at least not here in America, but the team is quite good," he answered with a smile.

"That's great." I really tried to be enthusiastic, because he was my friend and I should be supportive. But my gaze was already wandering, searching for the guy I should be avoiding.

"I was hoping you would be here," he admitted, his cheeks pinking a little in an adorably innocent way. He glanced back ruefully at Bex. "And I've completely lost all sense of manners. Apologies, Bex. How are you?"

"Fabulous," she replied in a tone that suggested she was anything but. She gave me another look.

I grimaced as I looked at Charles. "I think I need to—"

"Oh," he said with a soft sigh and a regretful smile. "I know that look. The it's-not-you-it's-me look, right?"

"Ryan and I are still engaged," I replied carefully. "It's... complicated."

He gave me a tight-lipped smile in response. "Things usually are when it comes to matters of the heart. But I'm assuming he doesn't have a leash on your friendships?"

"No," I answered slowly.

"Then as your friend, may I offer some advice?" His tone dropped and he edged a little closer.

Amused, I nodded back.

"What happened between you two is all over school, and while your name has been cleared, it's also blatantly obvious to anyone paying attention that your fiancée was a little late to the realization that you were innocent of all accusations." He gave me a knowing look.

Discomfort squirmed in my chest at the reminder. "You're not wrong."

"I'm also guessing that you're not too keen on letting his lack of support slide?" A smile started to appear on his face.

"Maybe," I hedged.

He offered his arm. "Then allow me to escort you inside. Perhaps seeing what he's at risk of losing will give him the kick in the arse he needs to behave."

I almost snorted at the idea of Ryan *behaving*, but a part of me kind of liked the idea of rubbing it in his face that I *could* move on. Even if it was totally for show.

"Why?" Bex asked, eyeing Charles with a frown.

"Honestly? I've known men like Ryan Cain my whole life. Arrogant, entitled, think they own the world."

"Said the duke," Bex deadpanned with an arched brow.

He chuckled at that. "True, but I'd like to think I'm a little more evolved than the world I was born into." He winked at Bex. "And technically, my father is a duke, not me. Not yet, anyhow."

I exchanged looks with my best friend before giving my attention back to Charles. "Just as long as we're clear that this is nothing more than a friend helping a friend."

He held up his hands with an innocent smile. "Absolutely."

"Okay, then," I agreed, slipping my arm into his.

Bex huffed behind me. "This really isn't going to end well."

She was probably right, but the thrill that shot through my veins lit me up with anticipation. I couldn't wait to see the look on Ryan's face when another guy led me into *his* house.

Game on, Ryan.

CHAPTER 13

MADDIE

The noise inside was almost deafening. People were everywhere, except on the stairs, which I noted were blocked by two bored-as-hell looking pledges. A game of strip beer pong was happening in the dining room to the left, and the twelve-foot table was covered in cups and spilled beer as half naked coeds cheered whenever someone landed a shot. I turned away before a girl who was down to her underwear could whip off her bra.

The living room to the right looked like one big orgy as people took advantage of any and every surface to hook up. Most still had their clothes on, but several were naked. The hairy ass of a guy I recognized from the frat started twerking for a girl on the sectional. I whirled away, but not before I got an eyeful of his swinging kibbles and bits.

But the most surprising sight was the banner hanging in the middle of the foyer with a mugshot of Dean that proclaimed, "Ding-dong, the bitch is DEAD!"

And—*holy shit*—more mugshots had been taped to a wall and people were playing darts.

"Wow," Charles murmured next to me.

My hand tightened reflexively on his arm as a girl in a bikini ran by, knocking against my shoulder.

"Sorry, Madelaine!" she chirped, rushing past us. A second later, a guy from the football team chased after her with a whoop.

I stepped aside to avoid being flattened by Ryan's offensive tackle.

"Friend of yours?" Charles asked dryly.

"Never met her in my life," I murmured, taking in the unholy amount of chaos and debauchery. I knew some of the parties around here could get crazy, but this was a whole new level.

Bex moved to my side, her eyes wide and alarmed as she looked around. "This is insanity."

I shook my head, barely able to think. I was on sensory overload. "Let's go out back," I suggested in a voice that was more yelling than anything.

Charles nodded and used his larger frame to move people out of the way as we walked down the hallway toward the back of the house. Bex linked her fingers with mine so we didn't get separated threading our way through the packed kitchen and out the back door.

I jerked to a stop, staring at all the naked bodies in the pool playing volleyball. People danced on the lawn under strings of Chinese lanterns hanging from tree branches. A DJ had been set up in the far corner with massive speakers pouring out music.

"Oh, this is much better," Bex muttered, rolling her eyes.

My gaze roved around as a prickle of awareness tingled up my spine. I could feel eyes on me, and I knew whose they were before I found the owner.

Like a king amongst his subjects, Ryan was seated in the middle of the large group of people around the fire pit. The flames reflected in his crystal blue eyes, and I swallowed when he stood up and moved toward us.

"Oh, shit," Bex muttered, casting me a nervous glance.

I hated that my body immediately reacted to seeing Ryan. My mouth practically watered at the sight of his wide shoulders encased in a tight-fitting white t-shirt that hugged his biceps and clung to his chest before tapering into a waist where I knew he was rocking more than a six-pack. A shudder rippled down my spine as anticipation sang in my blood.

If he had come up and pulled me into his arms, I would've gone willingly. Wantonly. I would've climbed him like a monkey and wrapped my arms around his waist before—

"What the fuck is this?" Ryan growled, snapping me out of my rapidly devolving fantasy. He glared at where my arm was tucked inside of Charles's before turning his hateful look to the guy in question. Like Charles had super-glued my hand to his elbow without my consent or knowledge.

I mean, I guess that was progress from Ryan outright accusing *me*, but still.

Pushing Charles aside a bit, I returned Ryan's glare with one of my own. "Charles offered to escort me in."

Ryan's gaze ripped to me. "Really."

My eyes narrowed in defiance. *"Really."*

He forced a grimace as he turned back to Charles. "Well, thanks for seeing my girl in. I'll take it from here, Chucky."

Charles, to his credit, barely blinked. "We're good, thanks, mate." He looked at me. "Care to dance, love?"

Ryan's hand shot out and grabbed my free hand. "Can we talk?"

I gave him a benign smile. "I was invited to dance."

Ryan's jaw clenched, and I had a feeling that I was treading the line of too far. A thrill shot through me at seeing him lose it a bit. But on the heels of that, a tiny thread of guilt twisted around my heart.

I knew Ryan was sorry for what had happened, and I knew he genuinely loved me, even if it was in a way I would never fully understand or be able to accept.

"Give me a sec," I murmured to Charles, letting him go so Ryan could pull me out of earshot. I caught sight of Bex hiding a grin as we moved aside.

"Maddie." Ryan's voice was full of a heavy emotion that made my insides tangle. "Seriously?"

I arched a brow. "What? I can't hang out with a guy unless he's on your pre-approved lackey list?"

"I sent Ben—"

"Ben?" I interrupted.

He smirked. "Five. I sent him to get you because I had to handle shit here. Dean's arrest meant we needed a new president."

"Let me guess," I drawled, giving him a long look. "You're the next president?"

He grinned smugly. "Was there ever a doubt?"

"Glad to see you've benefited from Dean's disgusting practices," I muttered, shaking my head. "Then again, why would I be surprised? Do you do *anything* that doesn't directly benefit you?"

"Not as a general rule, no," he replied. There wasn't even arrogance in his tone. He simply meant that he didn't lift a finger if it didn't help his own cause in some way or another.

I willed my hormones to lock it down as I took a step back. "Right."

Ryan's hands shot out, grabbing me by the hips and tugging my closer. "Maddie, I'm trying."

"Are you?" I lifted my gaze with a challenge, not bothering to move away from him. Ryan Cain was my own personal center of gravity, and I was helpless to stop from falling into his orbit.

"Yes," he insisted, his blue eyes flashing as he glanced over my shoulder. "But bringing that douche canoe here isn't helping us."

I sucked in a sharp breath. "Maybe it's helping *me*, Ryan. Did you ever think about that?"

His forehead wrinkled in confusion. "What does that even mean?"

I placed my hands on his forearms and gently pushed them down so he wasn't touching me. "It *means* I want my own friends."

"You have friends," he argued stubbornly. "You have Bex and the guys."

"Bex is *my* friend," I agreed, nodding, "but the guys? Hell no. They're loyal to you first."

"Debatable," he muttered.

I frowned. "What?"

"Nothing." He gave me a tight smile. "I just don't think Charlie-boy is the friend you need."

"I don't think you get to tell me *what* my needs are anymore," I snapped back.

His gaze heated as he thumbed his lower lip. "Even if I still know what you need?"

God, that *look*. It was all I could do not to press my thighs together in a shallow attempt to relieve the sharp ache between them.

The dimple that flashed as his smile grew only confirmed he knew exactly where my brain had gone.

I needed therapy. So much therapy.

"No," I blurted out.

His head tilted to the side in amusement. "No?"

I cleared my throat. "No, you don't know what I need."

Except that he just might.

Shit.

He made a low sound in the back of his throat that sent all sorts of flashbacks zipping through my head.

"Stop looking at me like that," I snapped, his gaze feeling like a caress as it stroked over my heated skin.

"Stop looking so gorgeous," he returned, licking his lips.

"I'm going to dance," I announced, flustered and thrown off my original game plan. "With Charles."

All amusement vanished from his face, replaced with a scowl. "Seriously, Mads?"

"Yes, seriously," I replied coolly. "Charles is a friend. I can dance with my friends."

"Dance with Bex then," he replied, shaking his head. "Not that walking condom."

An unexpected laugh burst from me. "What?"

"Calling him a dick would be insulting to dicks," Ryan explained with an indifferent shrug.

"You don't even know him." I wasn't entirely sure why I was pushing this issue so hard. Maybe because I wanted to prove that Ryan didn't control me. Maybe to get back at him in the only way I could.

Maybe because I was a total masochist.

If Ryan ground his teeth any harder, he would need dentures before the night was over. I took a sick sense of smug satisfaction in knowing that I was driving him nuts.

"Goddamn it, Maddie," he seethed, eyes flashing again with warning.

I was tap dancing across his nerves and loving every second of it. Even if he looked ready to snap.

Swallowing my growing unease, I lifted a brow. "What's the matter, Ryan? Don't you *trust me?*"

He sucked in a sharp breath through his teeth as I threw that gauntlet down. A second later, his eyes narrowed. "You're playing with fire, baby."

I glanced down at my skimpy outfit. "I *am* a little cold. Fire might be what I need to warm up."

He simply stared at me, the darkness in his eyes a bottomless void of some emotion I couldn't name.

"So?" I prompted. "What's it gonna be?"

He gave a slow, almost imperceptible nod. "I trust you."

Any sense of triumph I felt was quickly squashed when he snaked an arm around my waist and pulled my front flush to his. I damn near swallowed my tongue at the hard length pressed against my stomach.

Ryan lowered his mouth to the shell of my ear. "I don't trust *him.*" He inclined his head to where Charles was still waiting with Bex. "Just remember, Maddie, I'll be watching. And soccer players don't need *hands* to play."

He pressed a hard, fast kiss to the corner of my mouth, like he was claiming me in front of everyone, before letting me go. I rocked back on my heels, my legs a little wobbly, as he stalked back to his seat and sank down.

Meanwhile, I was still standing like a thunderstruck idiot, my lips tingling where his had touched them. I was seconds away from lifting my fingers to my lips to make sure they were still there when Ryan met my gaze.

He reached down and grabbed his beer, lifting it casually in a way that screamed, *your move.*

His friends were all looking at me, in addition to half the people outside. Ryan and I were prime material for these gossiping assholes, and we were definitely giving them a show. All eyes were firmly fixed on us for the foreseeable future.

I pivoted and walked back to Bex and Charles.

"That looked like it went… well," Bex said lamely.

"Are we dancing?" Charles asked.

I swallowed, feeling Ryan's gaze pressing on my back. "No. We're drinking."

CHAPTER 14

RYAN

My girl was wasted.

I took another sip of my beer as I watched Maddie toss her head back and laugh at something that English twat said. Irritation licked through my blood as I contemplated walking over and smashing my bottle against the side of his head.

This had been going on for more than two hours now. I'd watched Maddie toss back drink after drink, Bex meeting her almost one-for-one. Charles, to his credit, had stopped after two and had taken to watching them.

It might have even been a cool move if I didn't know for a fact he would happily take my rightful place in Maddie's life—and between her perfect thighs—in a heartbeat.

Fucker.

I'd been forced to sit on the edges and watch as Madison got drunk. Uncharacteristic for her, or at least I assumed. Nothing chafed more than realizing all the ways I *didn't* know her, but in the weeks that we'd known each other, I'd never seen her have more than two drinks in as many hours.

Now? Now she was the life of the fucking party, and I had a front row seat to the spectacle as she shook her ass in that barely there skirt while dancing with Bex. Wisely, she'd decided not to call my bluff and hadn't danced with the Duke of Douches.

Just then she stumbled in her heels, and Charles reached out to steady her by grabbing her elbow.

There was nothing sexual in the move, and I could admit Charles Fuckington the Fourth or whatever hadn't been anything more than platonic in his actions, but he was still touching *my* girl.

Fuck that.

My *fiancée*.

I dropped the bottle into the grass and started to push myself up.

Ash slapped a hand across my chest. "Don't."

I glared at him, beyond annoyed.

He inclined his head toward Maddie. "She's happy right now, bro. And he isn't being a perv or doing anything sketchy. Let it play out."

My teeth clenched together.

Ash leaned forward in his chair so I could hear his low tone even over the music. "Do you really think going over there and swinging your dick around is going to make Maddie forgive you?"

I smirked at him. "I wasn't aware you'd been checking out my dick."

He gave me a bland look. "Only because I wasn't aware they came that small."

My fist shot out and clipped his shoulder with enough force to bruise. He didn't even flinch.

"Seriously, Ry. Let Maddie do her thing. If anyone has earned a night of drunken shenanigans, it's that girl. And this is as safe a space as any for her to let loose. None of us will let anything happen to her." Ash lifted his own drink to his lips and took a long sip.

I released a slow breath and tried to look at Maddie with objective eyes, but it was pointless.

She wasn't just a girl having fun at one of our parties.

She was *my fucking girl*, and I could see the stress tightening the skin around her eyes even as she swayed unsteadily to the music. The halter top and tiny skirt weren't something she would have normally worn, and while I appreciated the way those heels made her legs look impossibly long, I also knew she was probably off balance as hell.

My eyes narrowed as she threw an arm around an equally intoxicated Bex. Charles managed to catch them both before they toppled over into a heap on the lawn.

Regret ate at my insides like acid, burning through my gut and twisting up what was left.

I had done that to her. To both of them.

I'd backed Maddie into my world without a second thought. Hell, I'd thought I'd struck the fucking lottery when I realized that Madelaine was gone and I was left with a more pliant, less bitchy fiancée.

A smirk worked across my mouth as I realized that, in a lot of ways, Maddie was even more of a challenge than Lainey had been. Probably because I never gave a shit about what Lainey wanted or felt.

But Maddie...

Dammit, this girl was in my blood. Somewhere along the lines of playing my father's games, I'd fallen for her.

I shoved a hand into my pocket, feeling the cool metal of her engagement ring. I hadn't been able to stop carrying it around like some fucked up sap.

Jean-clad legs blocked my vision a second before Court threw himself into the seat on my other side, a scowl on his face that I knew matched my own as he stared at Bex.

"One phone call and pretty boy could be gone for good," he murmured, rubbing his jaw absently.

I didn't bother holding back a dark chuckle. "Ash already said I can't maim the prick, so I'm guessing homicide is out, too."

"Or maybe I'll let you both go down for his murder and take Phoenix for myself," Ash countered softly with a snort.

At the mention of Phoenix, my smile dissipated. "I talked to my father. He expects me home next weekend. Apparently he's concerned that things are getting out of hand."

Court's spine stiffened and his dark eyes cut to me. "What does he know?"

"More than I'd like," I admitted, an uneasy feeling tingling up my spine. "But he's still way off about a lot. We'd hoped to have more time to set things up, but—"

"But you went rogue?" Linc interrupted as he came up behind us. He punched my shoulder lightly before sitting down next to Ash. "For something that's supposed to be a secret, you might wanna lower your voice, man."

I glared at him. "Do you see anyone paying attention?" I waved a hand at the party raging around us.

We'd carved out a spot in the center and easily chased off the people who tried to sit with us with a few curt words and lethal glares. We were fucking royalty at this school, and people knew to respect the boundaries we set.

Other than the occasional wasted girl who was looking for a bed to warm, no one had approached us. No one would dare. Even the team knew better than to come over when we purposefully separated ourselves from everyone else.

Linc rolled his eyes before passing me another beer. I twisted the top off but didn't drink. Maddie was drunk enough for the both of us, and someone needed to stay sober.

Besides, my odds of punching out Charles increased drastically with alcohol in the mix.

"What are you going to say to your dad?" Ash demanded, bringing my attention back to the topic I was trying to avoid.

I shrugged. "I'll figure it out." Then I looked at Linc. "And you were the one dragging O'Shea's ass into the dining hall. If you had an issue, you should've spoken up."

Linc raised his hands. "I didn't have a problem. Shit he did to Bex was fucked. Messing with Maddie was the final nail in the mother-fucker's coffin. That was long overdue."

Court let out a low growl beside me. "I still think you should've given me five minutes in a room alone with him before we dumped him on the cops."

"There's a lot we should've done," I murmured to no one really, but my friends nodded along in commiseration anyway.

The song changed to some overly synthesized version of a pop song that was blowing up on every radio station, and a cheer rose from the crowd. A second later, Maddie kicked off her heels and —*fucking hell*—started climbing onto a nearby table as Bex walked back inside.

I was on my feet before Charles even put a hand on her hip to try to get her back down.

People cleared a path for me as I stalked to where Maddie was raising her hands above her head and starting to dance.

A new chorus of cheers rose, but this time they were mostly male as guys fixed their eyes on the gorgeous girl putting on a show.

I elbowed Charles out of the way before reaching up and grabbing Maddie's ankle. "Maddie, come on. You're done."

She looked down at me, her blue eyes unfocused and bright. "No. Go away, Ryan. I'm *dancing*."

"Yeah, Ryan," a voice called behind me. "Let her dance!"

I turned and glared at the guy—a random douche whose name I'd never bothered to learn. His leering smile slipped, and he damn near tripped over his feet backing away.

Fucking pansy-ass.

That problem settled, I looked up at Maddie. My teeth ground together when I realized I could see up her skirt to the lacy pink panties.

Which meant *everyone* around the table could see them, giving these assholes spank bank material until they OD'd on Viagra in their nursing home.

"Maddie, get down!" I snapped, my voice harsher than it probably should've been.

"I tried to stop her," Charles muttered from next to me.

I shot him a scathing look. "Congratu-fucking-lations, dipshit. You failed."

His eyes narrowed. "Somehow I have a feeling she wouldn't be up there if it wasn't for something *you* did."

A shot of anger heated my blood along with a chaser of guilt, because I knew he was right.

"Why don't you fuck off?" I growled. I couldn't take my frustrations out on Maddie, but this guy would be an awesome substitute. I was thinking of all the ways I could rearrange his face when Maddie's foot slipped on a wet napkin and she started to go down.

I caught her as she fell, anchoring an arm around her waist and under her legs as I held her to my chest.

She blinked sluggishly up at me and then frowned. "How did I get here?"

"You fell," I replied dryly. "I think it's time for bed, Mads."

Her nose wrinkled. "But I was dancing."

"And now it's time for sleeping," I corrected as gently as I could.

"I can take her home," Charles cut in.

I stared at him, wondering if it would be a complete violation of dude-code to kick him in the nuts, since punching was currently out of the question. Maddie required both hands on her—which, conveniently, was where I liked my hands to be.

"Walk away while you can," I ordered instead with as much coldness as I could infuse into those five words.

His shoulders straightened. "No. Maddie's my friend, and I know she wouldn't want to go anywhere with you."

I looked down at Maddie, who had snuggled against my chest like a sleepy kitten. "Baby, you ready to take a nap?"

She gave a slow nod. "I love naps. I even have a t-shirt that says I'm the nap queen." Her forehead crinkled. "Or I did. I think he threw all my stuff away. I hate him. But I think he hates me, too, doesn't he?"

Worry prickled at my spine as I realized she was talking about Gary. Drunk Maddie might turn into chatty Maddie, and that could be dangerous for everyone. "You can sleep it off in my room."

"Not fucking happening," Charles snapped, blocking my way. "She's in no shape to be making any decisions. I would've thought this frat learned their lesson about trying to assault unconscious women, but I guess the tradition is carried from president to president."

"The only reason you're still standing right now is because my *fiancée* is in no shape to stand up herself. A fact *you* aided in by letting her down shot after shot," I pointed out. "I would never hurt Maddie. Ever."

Charles arched a brow. "Funny, I seem to recall a recent engagement party where you did just that."

"*That*," I forced out, "was a misunderstanding. One I'm working on correcting. For whatever reason, Maddie seems to like you, and I'd really rather not have to justify beating the shit out of you on top of the other shit I've heaped on her. So, be a fucking pal and step off, your royal dickishness, okay?"

Something like grudging respect flickered in his eyes. "Fine. But if Maddie tells me tomorrow that you did anything untoward—"

I snorted. "We'll duel at dawn or whatever the fuck it is you Brits do to avenge a maiden's honor. Got it."

With a sigh, I pushed past him and went into the house. I spotted Bex and was relieved to see that she was with Court. Judging by the angry slant of her brows as she talked, things weren't going that great, but I didn't have to worry about her passing out and no one seeing. Court would take care of her the way he always should have been able to.

I glanced down at the now-docile girl in my arms, and a wave of gratitude swept over me.

Yeah, Maddie and I had problems, but they weren't as convoluted and deep as the ones Bex and Court had.

"Ryan?"

My heart practically stopped as I looked down at her. "Yeah?"

"Am I going home now?" she asked in a small voice.

I wanted to tell her that I was her home, but I knew we weren't back in that place.

Yet.

Determination fueled my steps as I maneuvered us through the party and up the stairs to my room. I bypassed Dean's old room. The door now hung open, and the furniture had been stripped and sterilized. Technically it was the biggest room and, as the new president of the frat, mine. But I didn't want it.

I didn't want anything that the prick might've touched.

It took a little finagling, but I managed to unlock my door without dropping Maddie. Once inside, I kicked it shut, and the sounds of the party below were immediately muted.

"It smells good. Like you're everywhere in here," Maddie murmured, her eyes closed.

I tried not to smile. "Probably because it's *my* room, baby."

One eye popped open as I settled her on the bed. She blinked owlishly as she looked around. "Oh, yeah."

With a chuckle, I turned and went to the mini-fridge I kept stocked with drinks. I grabbed her one with extra electrolytes.

"Ryan?"

I glanced back to see she was sitting in the middle of my bed with her legs crossed, the angle pulling her skirt up higher. I bit back a smile as I tried not to focus on her barely covered pussy.

I seriously deserved a medal for being able to look anywhere except at that perfection between her legs.

"Yeah, babe?"

Her mouth turned down unhappily. "It's a mess. We're a mess. And I don't think we can fix it."

I handed her the bottle before sitting down beside her. Everything in me ached to pull her back into my arms, but this was the closest thing we'd had to an actual conversation in days, and I knew we needed to talk if we were ever going to be right again.

"I'll fix it, Maddie," I vowed, meaning it with everything I had. "I promise."

She shook her head, her blonde hair falling around her face. "You broke my heart." Her lower lip wobbled and tears clung to her lashes.

And *that* broke *my* heart.

"I know," I managed to get out around the ball of emotion in my throat. I reached for her hand and tangled our fingers together. "I'm so sorry, Maddie."

Her nose scrunched up as she looked at our hands. "I hate you."

"I know," I repeated, her words shredding what was left of my heart. All I could do was raise her hand to my lips and press a kiss to it. I didn't have any more words to fix what I'd broken between us. Not tonight anyway.

A calculating glint entered her eyes and, before I could figure it out, she pitched forward and pressed her mouth to mine.

I kissed her back instantly. My body knew no other option than to return what she gave and then some. My hand came up to cradle her head as I deepened the kiss. My tongue swept inside the hot cavern of her mouth as I took control while her tiny hands fisted the cotton of my t-shirt.

Great. I was going to have to fucking duel Charlie-boy at dawn, because no way could I stop kissing her now.

In the back of her throat she made a soft little noise that made my cock go from hard to granite. Then she was climbing onto my lap, her skirt around her hips as she pressed her pussy against me.

Which was, of course, when my conscience made an appearance.

"Fuck," I whispered, pulling my mouth from hers with a groan. "Maddie, stop. We can't."

Not like this. Not when I knew she would hate herself—and me—in the morning. The hole I was trying to dig out of was already deep enough.

"Ryan, *please*," she begged in a breathy voice that had my dick ready to punch through the zipper of my jeans.

I circled her wrists with my hands and firmly held her. "Not tonight, Madison."

"You don't want me?" A tremor of hurt rippled through her voice.

I lifted my hips, grinding them against her center as I gritted my teeth. "Does this feel like I don't want you?"

She pressed against me once more with a throaty moan that made my cock jerk. "I want you. Now. *Please*."

"I want you, too," I replied, fisting a hand in her hair and holding her head back so I could look into those beautiful eyes. "But tonight neither of us is ready for that. And the next time I'm inside you? You'll want me there as much as I want it."

"I want it *now*," she whined, but her eyes were already starting to droop. They were bleary and unfocused.

A sad smile touched my lips as I eased her off my lap. "Me, too, but not like this. Not while you hate me."

She swallowed and slowly got off the bed. "Can I use the bathroom? I need to pee."

I nodded. "Want me to get you something to sleep in?"

Her nose wrinkled. "I can't sleep here."

"You can, and you are," I replied, not willing to give an inch on that. She was too wasted to sleep on her own. I'd tie her to the bed if I had to.

Huh. Not the *worst* idea. But probably not the best way to get us back on track.

She hesitated at the door, her fingers tracing the edge of the frame. "I lied."

I barely caught her whispered confession. "Lied about what, Mads?"

She looked back at me, her blue eyes soft and sad. "I don't hate you. I still love you. *That's* what I hate. That even after you hurt me so much... I still love you."

I rocked back at the confession, but she disappeared into the bathroom and closed the door before I could recover.

I dropped back onto the mattress and stared up at the ceiling. A tiny kernel of hope settled somewhere in the vicinity of my heart.

Maybe I hadn't completely fucked this up.

CHAPTER 15

MADDIE

Years ago I had taken it upon myself to clean out the trailer. Mom had been at rehab in yet another failed attempt at getting sober, and I'd wanted her to come home to a clean place.

So I went to the store, used a bunch of coupons to buy a name-brand cleaner—because it had to be better than the dollar store generic if it cost five times as much—and scrubbed every surface until my fingers were red.

In hindsight, I should've used the dollar-store cleaner and splurged on a pair of rubber gloves for my raw hands.

I'd saved Mom's room for last, because I wasn't sure if she would want me in her personal space. Inevitably I gave in and tackled her room, starting with the closet.

Buried under a mountain of dirty clothes and towels that were growing moldy was a single sock that had become cemented to the floor by a noxious combination of sweat, old water, and some other substances I refused to acknowledge to this day. But what I remembered was the smell. The old, crusty, moldy smell of mothballs and death.

That was the taste I woke up to in my mouth.

The only thing worse was the blindingly painful headache that threatened to split my skull in half.

I made some sort of half-groan, half-dying cow whine as I rolled over to hide my face from the brutal rays of the sun. The world tilted, and with it, my stomach.

Sweat broke out in places I didn't know it could as I tried not to vomit all over myself.

I was vaguely aware of a door opening somewhere in the room, but I was too busy trying to extricate from the tilt-a-whirl in my head to really pay attention.

"Shit," Ryan's low voice said with a healthy dose of sympathy. "Can you sit up, Maddie?"

"Depends," I mumbled, face against the mattress. "How much do you care if I throw up all over your bed?"

"I mean, it wouldn't be the worst thing the pledges have cleaned up in the last twenty-four hours," he admitted with a laugh that still made my tummy flip.

Or maybe I was just going to throw up.

Yeah, I was gonna go with that excuse.

His hand settled on my back and rubbed slow, soothing circles into my muscles. As much as I hated it, I felt myself relaxing and my body feeling less like it needed to perform a self-induced exorcism.

"I can't believe I drank that much," I muttered, more to myself than to the guy I should be running away from.

Ryan gave a soft snort. "You were knocking them back pretty good. I think you out-drank half the guys."

"That good old Porter metabolism," I deadpanned. "It's why we make such excellent addicts."

Ryan's fingers stilled for a second before starting up again.

"It's why I don't drink like that," I admitted, not sure why I felt the need to keep confessing. "Mom started with alcohol and kept going. I never wanted to live that life."

And yet... here I was.

Nursing a bitch of a hangover, in the bed of a guy I should hate, and essentially whoring myself out. Maybe not for a fix, but I was going along with Gary's shit all the same. My body was the price tag I was willing to pay.

Way to break the fucking cycle, Maddie.

"One night of partying doesn't make you your mom, Mads," Ryan told me in what I'm sure would have been a helpful, sweet tone if I wasn't currently ass-deep in a downward psychological spiral about how screwed up my life had become.

I snorted and instantly regretted the action. Groaning, I squeezed my eyes shut and willed the piercing pains away.

"Think you can handle some painkillers and water?" he asked, taking care to keep his voice soft.

"Yeah," I muttered, weakly lifting my head and letting Ryan gently maneuver me into a sitting position against the headboard. I kept my eyes closed and focused on breathing in the clean scent of soap from his shower.

Two pills were pressed into my palm, and I threw them back before reaching for the bottle of water he had readily available. I downed half of it, needing something to wash the ick out of my mouth. Once I was able to stand on my own two feet, I planned to march into the bathroom and guzzle a bottle of mouthwash.

I finished drinking the water and took a deep breath, relieved that the pounding in my head was less like a freight train and more like a jackhammer.

Progress.

Only then did I crack an eye open to see he was sitting next to me on his bed in nothing but a towel slung deliciously low on his hips. His tanned skin was damp from his shower, and a bead of water had the freaking audacity to glide down the ridges of his abs. His blonde hair was dark from being wet and had curled around the edges of his face in an almost boyish way.

Shit, I wasn't supposed to be checking him out. I lifted my eyes and caught his smug ass smirk.

"What?" I demanded flatly. I waved a hand in his general direction. "We both know you're hot, Ryan. I'm not going to apologize for looking at what you're offering."

"Look away," he chuckled. He stood and rested a hand on the precariously loose knot of the towel. "I can give you an unobstructed view if you want. Hell, I'll even give you a demonstration of how certain parts work."

I sighed heavily, the teasing banter souring in my stomach. "I've had that view plenty of times. It's not the view that's the issue, or the equipment. It's the man behind it."

His jaw clenched for a second, his gaze hardening, and then he turned away to his dresser. I watched the phoenix tattoo on his shoulders writhe and move with each flex of his muscles. The mythical bird rippled as though it would take flight from his skin at any second.

Until he caged it by covering it with a black shirt that clung to his biceps in a way that was a gift to all women. Hell, forget gender norms. Anyone with a pulse would look at him.

A tight black shirt and frayed jeans were the uniform of every bad boy, and Ryan Cain could be their front man.

"How are you feeling?" he asked in a gruff tone, reaching for the watch on his dresser and clasping it around his wrist.

"Like shit," I muttered, unable to muster anything even halfway witty. I pulled my knees to my chest and ran a hand through my hair. I frowned, the memories of last night a little blurry. "I don't usually drink that much."

"I've noticed," he replied while coming back to the bed and sitting at the foot of it. The space between us felt so wrong and uncomfortable. "I'm sorry."

My brows lifted. "What did you do this time?"

"I'm guessing I had something to do with the drinking." He winced and shook his head.

I snorted. "I make my own decisions, Ryan. Not everything I say or do is because of you."

Honestly, of all the crap I was dealing with at the moment, Ryan being a semi-decent human wasn't even cracking the top five.

He hissed out a breath through clenched teeth. "Dammit, Maddie, I'm trying here."

"Do you want an award?" I stared at him incredulously as that same yawning pit of betrayal gaping between us was ripped open again. "What? You think because you did the right thing *for once* with Dean that you get a pass? That it erases every other shitty decision you've made? That it changes the fact that you turned your fucking back on me when I needed you most?"

His hands balled into fists, the veins on his forearms popping out. "Madison, I know I messed up."

"I know that you know," I shot back. "And you know what else I know? I don't care. The only reason I'm at this school is because I have to be. The only reason I haven't run out of this room screaming is because I *have to be here.*"

He flinched like I'd landed a physical blow. A muscle in his jaw ticked. "Then leave. I won't stop you. I won't force you to come back."

"Until the next party, right?" I sneered, disgust welling up in me. "Until the next time your dad or Gary demand you parade me out like a pretty little show pony for the world to look at. *Then* I can go back to my room and wait like a good girl for the next time I'm needed."

Ryan stared at me for a beat. "Maddie, I want to find a middle ground here. At least until you can accept my apology as truth and we can move on."

"Fine. Apology accepted. I believe you're truly sorry that you jumped to conclusions that ended what we had. Let's move on," I huffed, tugging the sheets up to my neck like that would somehow make me feel less exposed in front of the one person who had been able to see past my bullshit.

He stabbed his fingers through his hair. "Tell me what I can do to fix this, Mads. I mean really fix it."

"You can build a time machine and go back to the moment you fucked me," I spat, my heart clenching.

"I know I blew it at the engagement party—"

"No," I cut in sharply, balling my hands into fists so tight my nails cut into the flesh of my palms. I welcomed the sting, embraced it as a way to guard my heart. "I meant the night you literally *fucked me.* I wish I'd never let you in, Ryan. *That* is my biggest regret. Not the crap at our engagement party, but the night I fell in love with you." My voice cracked and—*dammit*—I was crying again.

Ryan made a soft, pained noise and started to reach for me, but froze when I flinched away.

"I'm well aware that we have to continue acting like we're a happy couple or whatever, but don't you dare expect me to do it behind closed doors. Consider this just another business arrangement. I'll play the part you all want in public, but I want everyone to leave me the *fuck* alone otherwise." A ragged sob ripped from my chest and I squeezed my eyes shut like that could block out the pain.

My already throbbing head pulsed with every cry, every tear. I covered my face with my hands, feeling utterly hopeless. I was trapped. Completely and totally trapped in this nightmare. I wanted to wake up in that stupid, dirty trailer and see Mom chain-smoking away her morning while watching some shitty soap opera on our stained couch.

I wanted to go back to my high school, with its metal detectors and barred windows. At least there I could be invisible and fade away. I wanted Marge and all of her ridiculous stories as we closed down the library together.

But those days were well and truly gone. My life was over.

Madison Porter really was dead.

CHAPTER 16

MADDIE

I t was pretty much an unwritten rule that the majority of the male population would run at the first sign of a crying woman.

Ryan, to his credit, stuck it out for a little while, but when he realized I wasn't going to let him comfort me and considered he might be the cause of my tears, he reluctantly left me alone.

Props to him for hanging in there for a change.

Once he exited and closed the door to his bedroom, I let myself cry for a few more minutes. At this point, I figured I had earned a solid pity-party.

But sitting here in Ryan's bed, in his shirt, wouldn't solve any of my problems. It wouldn't get me or my mom out from under Gary's thumb, so I forced myself to get to my feet and go into Ryan's bathroom.

It was bittersweet, the way it looked like I still belonged there.

The brand of shampoo, conditioner, and body wash I used was still on a shelf in the massive shower stall. My toothbrush and toothpaste were still in the top-right drawer of the vanity along with my hairbrush and a few elastic bands.

When I exited the bathroom, there was still a drawer where Ryan had encouraged me to stash some clothes and underwear. Although, as I picked up a pair of lacy blue panties, I remembered him trying to not-so-discreetly hide them. He'd argued I didn't need underwear in his room.

I closed the drawer before I could fall too far down memory lane.

How had it been only a couple weeks since we were... us?

I dressed quickly, frowning when my jeans hung too loose on my hips. I swapped them out for a pair of leggings and winced when I saw myself in the mirror.

I looked like Madelaine.

My stomach was flatter, but so was my chest, for that matter. Seriously, why did women always lose weight in their boobs first? My cheeks were more angular, any last traces of baby fat having burned away. And my eyes?

Jesus.

They looked lifeless and utterly hopeless. Just the way hers had, when I'd stopped to look close enough beneath the sparkle of her makeup and glam.

I turned away from the image in disgust as someone knocked at the door.

I frowned, because I kind of doubted Ryan would bother.

"Come in?" I called hesitantly.

The door pushed open, and Ash's face appeared. His dark complexion contrasted starkly against the white shirt he wore. His green eyes were narrowed and emanating concern.

"Hey. Can I come in?"

I nodded. Unsure what to do, I pulled out the chair at Ryan's desk and sat.

Ash came into the room only enough to close the door and lean against it. "I wanted to see how you were."

"Fantastic," I replied with obviously forced enthusiasm.

He gave me a small smile. "Yeah, I guess that sounds about right."

"Here to plead your best friend's case?" I asked.

"Hell no," he answered with a snort. "Ryan fucked up. He's got to dig himself out of this mess. I told him to take a minute and think, but..."

"But he didn't," I finished softly. "Thanks for trying."

"You're good for him, Maddie," Ash added. "Probably too good for him. Hell, all of us. I get you were dealt a shitty hand growing up, but your sister was a bitch for dropping you into this world without more of a heads up."

"It was only supposed to be for the summer," I mumbled, still feeling some deep need to defend her actions. Maybe I understood her a little better now. After barely two weeks of seeing Gary's true colors, as much as I wanted to believe that I wouldn't sacrifice someone else to take my place right now, if I'd had seventeen years of this? My morals might not be so black and white.

"No offense, Maddie, but that's bullshit." Ash shook his head. "I didn't know your sister all that well, but I don't believe for a second that she didn't plan on using you as her escape hatch."

An uneasy sensation prickled up my spine. "What are you saying?"

"I'm saying, have you actually *seen* a body? Are you sure Madelaine's dead?" Ash's flat voice rocked me to the core.

I clasped my hands together in my lap and tried to keep my expression neutral. "Gary had her remains brought over."

"Remains," Ash said almost carefully. His gaze shuttered. "So there wasn't an actual body to identify?"

"Well, no." My pulse pounded in my veins as I considered what he was saying.

No. No *way*. It wasn't possible.

Was it?

Gary would have known if something shady went down with Madelaine. After everything that had happened, I was painfully aware of how much he knew.

He'd known what Adam was doing to her. He wasn't the type to miss a damn thing. Hell, he'd known who I was all along. Why would he let Madelaine just disappear?

The truth made me queasy.

Because Madelaine had proven over and over that she wouldn't be controlled. And I could be. Gary had trotted out my doped-up mother, and I'd immediately backed down. He'd threatened Bex, and I'd shut up instantly.

I could be manipulated in a way that she couldn't.

Ash sighed and rubbed the back of his neck. "Look, I can check it out, if you want."

I nodded numbly. It had been one thing to consider that my twin had died before she could come back and save me.

But believing that my sister would have set me up and left me to carry on her miserable life? That was unfathomable. With all the many faults I'd unearthed about my twin, I just couldn't picture her setting me up so heartlessly.

As far as I was concerned, Madelaine's death in the fire would remain a tragic accident.

"I also unlocked more stuff on your phone," he added, sensing it was time to change the topic. He pulled it out of his back pocket and handed it to me.

I studied the dark screen for a moment. "Anything worth knowing?"

He shrugged. "Don't know. I didn't look."

I frowned at him as my fingers tightened around the case. "You didn't?"

"It's your business, Maddie," he told me firmly. "I mean, technically it was your sister's, but now it's yours. I think you've had your privacy and shit violated enough lately, don't you?"

"Thanks," I murmured, touched by his consideration.

"For whatever it's worth, I think you should consider if you really want to know more. That shit you saw with your sister as a kid? I'm sure that's not the only thing Madelaine kept hidden. You're already dealing with a lot. Think about whether or not you want to shoulder any more of her fucked up history before you open the app, okay?" Ash pressed his lips together, his brow furrowed with concern.

"I will," I replied.

"I mean, it doesn't have to be Ryan, but…"

I sighed. "Just say it, Ash."

"He loves you. He knows he messed up. He'd want to be there for you." He gave me a small half-smile.

"So much for not pleading his case, huh?" I smirked and shook my head, not upset. It was hard to be angry at Ash for looking out for his best friend.

"He's my brother in every way that matters," Ash admitted. "I've seen him at his highest highs and lowest lows. I know shit about him no one else does, which is why I know I've *never* seen him like this. He's a fucking mess, Maddie, but you make him better."

I glanced down, unable to maintain eye contact anymore. "He hurt me, Ash. And what happened after..." I shuddered at the memory. At Gary's fist connecting with my face. At Adam's leering gaze as he drove me to school. At the way my mom sagged between the men who had held her, her glassy eyes vacant.

"If you want to talk about what happened, I'm here. I know I'm not Ryan or Bex, but I can keep a secret, and I won't judge." His simple offer almost made me break the promise I'd made to myself that I was done crying over all of this.

Instead, I just nodded and swallowed around the uncomfortable lump in my throat.

Ash clapped his hands together. "Great, so we're done with the emotional shit for now, right?"

A laugh bubbled out of me and I nodded, grateful for the change in topic. "Definitely."

"Hungry?"

My stomach growled in response, and I hesitated. The last thing I needed was my mom suffering because I ate a rogue piece of bacon.

Ash's eyes narrowed. "We can eat here. I'm not the best cook, but I can handle breakfast. Bex spent the night, too, so she's probably hungry."

My brows flew up. "Bex spent the night?"

Ash laughed. "Yeah. In *my* room. I slept on the floor. She mentioned castrating Linc or Court if they tried sleeping near her, and she wasn't leaving without you. Even with Dean gone and the guys in the house on notice, I wasn't leaving her on a couch downstairs."

"Look at you being the good guy," I teased with a smile.

He grimaced and shook his head. "Look, if you want to help me out? Sort shit out with Ryan. Or convince Bex to sort shit out with Court and Linc. My back can't handle sleeping on that floor again."

I snorted a laugh. "Noted, but I'm not promising anything."

"Fine." He rolled his eyes. "So, breakfast? Or brunch, I guess it is now?"

"I should go to the cafeteria," I hedged carefully.

"Don't take this the wrong way, Maddie, but you look like shit."

I flinched, even though his tone was calm and even.

"If I notice, you bet your ass that Ryan's noticed. He probably thinks it's something he did, but I have a feeling there's something else going on here, Maddie. Something that has me worried." His unyielding gaze was somehow kind and hard at the same time.

I drew in a slow, shaky breath. "I can't talk about it, Ash." Part of me wanted to. Ash might even be able to give me some insight, but I was also aware that he was Ryan's best friend. That loyalty would probably always come first.

He closed his eyes for a brief second. "Okay. But if it gets to be too much, promise me you'll come to one of us. I don't care who, but..." He hesitated for a second before going on. "Maddie, you're one of us now. Not just Ryan's... whatever. You're my friend. Or at least, I'd like to think you are."

"I'd like to think that, too," I confessed quietly, the barbed wire wrapped around my heart loosening a tiny amount.

He gave a short, concise nod. "Then as your friend? I'm here for you. So are those other idiots. And Bex loves you to pieces. You aren't alone."

I nodded back even as I knew he was wrong.

I *was* alone. The only person who could save me now was me. But first I needed a plan, and for that?

For that, I needed the devil.

"Instead of making breakfast, can you ask Ryan to come up here?

Maybe he'll want to go out and grab something. I think I could use a change of scenery."

Ash grinned, and I hated that he was probably thinking I was going to give his bestie a chance. "I'll go grab him."

"Thanks," I murmured, watching as he went. I tucked Madelaine's old phone in the waistband of my leggings and mentally started building the walls around my heart that I would need to survive a date with Ryan.

CHAPTER 17

MADDIE

I n another life, texting my father to say I was going out to brunch with a guy might have been normal. But when you were texting to essentially ask permission to eat with a guy he expected you to marry for money, it was a little less normal.

I tried not to grit my teeth when his text reply was: *Behave.*

But I must have done a poor job of hiding my frustration, because when Ryan entered the room, his brows immediately shot up. His icy blue eyes flashed to the phone in my hands. "What's wrong?"

I sighed, trying to censor my aggression a bit. If I wanted to figure this mess out, I needed to stop reacting and start thinking. "Nothing. Just… It's nothing."

He looked like he wanted to press the issue, but he didn't. "Ash said you wanted to go out?"

"Yeah. I think it would be a good idea to figure out schedules and everything to make this as easy as possible on us both. I figured a neutral place would be best," I added.

"Sounds good," he agreed with a faint smile. "Ready now?"

I nodded back and stood up before grabbing my purse and shoving both phones into it.

"Ash give you that?" Ryan's cool gaze lingered on my purse.

My fingers tightened reflexively around the fabric. "Yeah."

He looked like he wanted to say more, but ultimately he sighed and crossed the room to grab his keys from the dresser. Giving me a tight smile, he opened the door and waited for me to walk out before leaving and locking the door behind us.

I hesitated and opened the purse once more before fishing out the piece of metal I was looking for. Without a word, I held out the key to him.

He stared at my hand, confusion wrinkling his forehead.

"Take it," I finally said, shaking my hand emphatically.

His gaze lifted to mine. "No."

I sighed. "Ryan—"

He shoved his hands into his pockets and squeezed by me in the hallway, his shoulder brushing mine. "No, Maddie. It's yours. Keep it."

"I don't want it," I said, digging in stubbornly. "Take it."

"No." His clear blue eyes were calm.

I was seconds away from stomping my foot like a petulant child. "Ryan, stop being an idiot."

His voice lowered and he stepped closer to me, eviscerating the small space between us. "Maddie," he began in a low voice that made shivers dance up my spine, "I don't know what's going on, but keep it. In case you need a safe space, you can come here."

I glanced at the door to my left. Could I feel safe in that space again?

Yes.

A tiny piece of my mind whispered the last truth I wanted to hear.

With everything currently stacked against me, I knew in my gut that Ryan wasn't a threat to anything but my heart.

I believed he was truly sorry for not trusting me, even if it was only after his best friend had shown him that he'd been wrong. And Ryan definitely wasn't to blame for Gary beating the hell out of me and locking me in a room for two weeks. He wasn't to blame for the shit Dean and Brylee had done.

I could even admit that a lot of my current animosity toward him had more to do with Gary and the fact that Ryan was the only outlet for my pain right now.

Yeah, he had messed up majorly. But he was also trying to atone for his betrayal.

Maybe I could somehow separate my head and my heart enough to let him help me. Maybe we could even be... friends.

Sighing, I put the key back in my purse and zipped it shut with a quiet, "Okay."

His expression softened and he held out a hand. Without thinking, I took it. Instinct seemed to override sense.

"Optics," I said, needing to cover up my knee-jerk reaction to hold his hand.

"Of course," he replied, a small hint of the cocky asshole he was shining through even as he lifted his eyebrows innocently. "Why else?"

"Smart-ass," I muttered, shaking my head as he guided me down the staircase. At the landing, I was surprised to see Bex waiting. Her arms were folded, and she was standing a solid three feet away from a noticeably annoyed Court.

"Everything okay?" I asked slowly, my gaze bouncing between them. I pulled away from Ryan as soon as we reached the bottom. He frowned but let me go without complaint.

Bex turned, angling her body so she didn't have to see Court. "Peachy. I just wanted to make sure that this whole breakfast-with-my-mortal-enemy thing wasn't another kidnapping."

I winced as Ryan glared at Bex.

Bex's eyes widened slightly. "I mean, I wanted to make sure that this really is *your* idea."

"It is," I said quickly, needing to push past the kidnapping comment because I didn't want to draw attention to my weeks in hell at Gary's cabin. The only way to protect Mom was to make sure it seemed like I was the good little Stepford daughter.

If Ryan knew what had really happened to me over the last two weeks? He would lose his shit and likely blow up at Gary, which would blow up my life.

Well, more than it already was.

I didn't know how things could get worse, but I knew that adding Ryan's explosive tendencies to the nuclear fallout already wrecking my world was a recipe for full-scale disaster.

I needed to keep things calm until I could find a way to outmaneuver Gary. And Beckett. And maybe Ryan.

My head was throbbing again, and this time it wasn't from the amount of alcohol I'd consumed the night before.

"Are you good?" I asked Bex, my gaze flicking to Court for a second.

He snorted and rolled his eyes. "Oh, princess is great."

"I'll be great when you leave me the fuck alone," Bex growled, glaring at him.

My brows shot up. I mean, I knew Bex was mad at the guys, but damn. Apparently she was embracing her inner tigress.

"Gladly. Feel free to skip your ass back to your own bed," he snarled, waving a large hand at the door.

"Mads, if you're okay, then I'll be going," Bex seethed, turning to face me with a tight smile.

"Uh, I'm good," I replied. "Do you want—"

She whirled and stormed out of the front door, slamming it for good measure.

I flinched at the sound as the blood in my temples seemed to pulse. Rubbing my forehead absently, I looked over and saw Linc wandering into the hallway, shirtless and eating a pancake with one hand.

"What'd I miss?" he asked.

"Fucking nothing," Court hissed before stomping to the front door and yanking it open.

Ryan snorted, but it sounded more like a laugh. "Where are you going?"

"To make sure Bex actually makes it back to her room without anyone giving her shit," he replied curtly before closing the door, thankfully a lot more softly than my best friend had.

"I don't think she wants company." I frowned at the door, imagining Bex yelling at him when he caught up.

Linc smirked and leaned against the wall. "She won't notice. She never has before."

I turned and stared at him.

"He's been doing this shit since…" He seemed to hesitate and look at Ryan before speaking in a quieter tone. "Since Madelaine really started laying into Bex and he found out about it last year. He's kind of been her shadow around campus. He's still pissed he missed Dean drugging her, but, to be fair, he had seen her change into her pajamas and get ready for bed that night. He didn't know she'd showed up at the party."

My brows shot up. "He's been *stalking* her?"

"More like guarding her without her knowledge," Ryan corrected with a grin.

"Stalking," I reaffirmed. "She has to know."

"No, she doesn't," Linc said quickly, shaking his head. "Look, Bex and Court are… complicated. He feels like he failed her twice now."

"There's a lot of that going around," Ryan murmured.

My heart clenched a little, but I ignored him.

Linc rubbed the back of his neck with the hand not holding a pancake like a taco. "Court won't hurt Bex, Maddie. I promise."

"Oh, well, if you *promise*," I said in a voice thick with sarcasm. As much as I was trying not to be bitter about that night, apparently the mental chat I'd had with my heart about letting my brain do the thinking about Ryan hadn't immediately extended to his friends.

He sighed and shook his head while walking closer to me. "Maddie, I'm sorry. I sided with Ryan, and I should have remembered you were my friend, too. I should have given you a chance to explain."

I nodded and let my shoulders relax a bit. "Thank you for apologizing."

"Cool." He flashed me a quick smile before shoving the rest of the pancake into his mouth.

"Did you even consider a plate?" I stared at him.

He finished swallowing. "For what?"

"You know what? Never mind." I turned to Ryan. "Ready?"

He smiled at me in a way that quickened my pulse and turned my bones to jelly.

I mentally groaned at myself, because that definitely wasn't how I was supposed to feel when a *friend* smiled at me.

T he cafe in town that Ryan drove us to had a line curled around the brick exterior. I almost hesitated when Ryan pulled us to the front of the line, but ultimately let him do what he wanted, because it was easier than arguing about it. He pulled open the glass door with the word *Monica's* engraved on it in a sweeping script.

Inside, the place was packed. People waited on benches near the hostess station, and Ryan bypassed them all to walk up to the flustered girl furiously checking a laminated floor map of the tables. She grabbed the phone that started ringing with a forced, but chipper, "Monica's" before turning to the messy map in her hands with a frown.

"I think we might want to go somewhere else," I murmured, kind of glad he was once again holding my hand as we navigated the crush of people.

He shot me an amused smile. "You're adorable."

I frowned, not entirely sure what he meant by that, but I had a feeling he was patronizing me.

"Wait's an hour," the hostess announced, barely glancing up as she hung up the phone.

"Actually, we'll take a table in the back," Ryan replied smoothly, giving her a grin that I'd seen him flash countless people. His this-will-be-going-my-way smile.

I sighed and shook my head, because sometimes he was so out of touch with reality it was ridiculous. Maybe back in Los Angeles he could ask for a private table or whatever, but this was Pacific City, and *city* was putting it loosely. It had more of a small-town, Hallmark movie vibe with some extra-fancy stores and a steakhouse thrown in for the rich elite at Pacific Cross.

The hostess looked up and her expression went a little pale. "Of course. Right this way." She grabbed two menus from under the stand, and I noticed that they weren't the laminated ones everyone else had as she led us past the main dining room and down a hall.

When we reached a staircase, I vaguely wondered if I should be concerned, but we followed her to the second floor and what looked like a second restaurant.

Instead of basic wooden chairs and tables like downstairs, here there were crisp, white linens on each table. The chairs were wooden but had details carved into the gleaming, polished surfaces. Instead of inches between tables, there were feet here separating diners.

The room was only half full, and I vaguely recognized a few students as we were led to a table near the middle of the room.

"We'll take that table." Ryan pointed to one in a far corner away from the other diners.

"Of course," the hostess said smoothly, carrying the menus to the table he'd requested and waiting for us to sit before handing us the menus and hurrying away. Two glasses of water already waited for us, and in the middle of the table was a freaking lit candle.

I glanced around before leaning in with a hushed, "What the hell is this?"

Ryan chuckled softly. "This is what happens when you have a small town with a percentage of clientele who can't mix with the townies."

My brows shot up. "Can't?"

He grimaced. "Won't."

"Are you serious?" I gaped at him.

"This used to be Monica's apartment. The Monica who owns this place." He reached for his water. "When some parents came to town, they bitched about having to wait for tables. One of them approached Monica about turning the top floor into a secondary dining room that was a bit more... upscale."

I rolled my eyes. "But there're other restaurants in town."

"After all the shit you've seen, you think this is too much? Rich people throwing their checkbook around to prove a point?" Ryan shook his head. "So, he convinced her to flip this into a place where there's a Michelin-starred chef to cater to people willing to pay a base cost of a grand for a table."

I could feel my eyes bug out. "A thousand dollars just for a *table?*"

He nodded, still bemused by my reaction.

I leaned forward. "You mean *this table* cost a thousand freaking dollars?"

He looked a little uncomfortable, like maybe he'd realized he'd gone too far. "Yes."

"That's insane," I spluttered.

"Not to Monica. She lives in a million-dollar mansion at the edge of town now." Ryan shrugged. "Money talks, Mads."

I scowled, annoyed on principle. "This is everything that's wrong with the world."

"It is?"

"Yes." I flushed, my frustration rearing up once more. "People thinking that they can throw money at everything and just snap their fingers to make it happen. Or thinking that, because they have money, the world and everyone in it should bend the freaking knee or some other archaic bullshit."

Ryan nodded slowly, his expression neutral and controlled. "Is that what happened?"

I stopped in confusion, a frown tugging at my lips. "Huh?"

His lips pressed together in a tight line. "I'm talking about what happened with you and your dad, Maddie. I think it's time you told me everything that happened that night after I left."

CHAPTER 18

MADDIE

"He's *not* my dad," I blurted out with more venom than I probably should have.

Ryan winced. "Maddie—"

I held up a hand. "No. He's *not* my dad, Ryan. He's Gary." It was crucial I made that line in the sand as clear as possible.

"Okay, baby," he said softly, his tone cajoling, like he was talking down a spooked horse. I didn't even bristle at the term of endearment.

The freaking **Behave** text was burned in my mind.

For a second, I played out the fantasy of standing up and screaming. Of hurling my purse and both the phones out the picture window before hitchhiking to the nearest airport.

And then all the oxygen rushed out of me as I imagined Gary turning on Mom. Maybe the police would find her body dumped in some remote ditch in a few days.

Or maybe Bex would go missing and end up in some sadist's home overseas where she would be...

Oh, God. I shouldn't have gone there, but now it was all I could picture. Mom dead and Bex hurting. And it would be all my fault.

Panic began to spiral in my chest, coiling so tight that spots began to dance in my vision.

I jolted as Ryan's hand covered mine.

"Breathe, Maddie," he added, his gaze concerned as a waiter stepped up to our table. Ryan didn't stop looking at me as he said, "We need a minute."

The waiter slipped away with practiced ease.

I struggled for breath and slowly pulled in air as I looked into his crystalline blue eyes.

"Breathe, baby," he encouraged. "In and out."

The air came through my lips in shaky pants as I did as he instructed.

"Sorry," I mumbled when my numb lips could form words again.

"I think that's my line," he teased gently before squeezing my hand. "Maddie, I think we should talk about what happened with Gary."

I stiffened and tried to pull away. "No."

His fingers tightened around mine, but not to the point of pain. "I know that he hit you, and Bex made it sound pretty bad." Ryan swallowed, his gaze darkening before he locked down whatever demon was rattling the bars of the cage he was keeping it locked up in. "What happened after I left?"

"He hit me," I said in a detached voice, simply echoing what Bex had said. I tried pulling away again, but Ryan wouldn't let me go.

"Maddie, come on." He was practically pleading, or as close to pleading as Ryan Cain could get. "I can't help you if you don't tell me."

I finally managed to free myself. "What are you going to do to help, Ryan? Magically undo the last two weeks? Maybe yell at Gary for hitting me?"

His eyes flashed. "More like break his arms. Or at least make sure all his bruises match your old ones, and then some."

"Don't," I snapped, my tone sharp enough to cut diamonds. "Just leave it alone. Let me handle Gary. You've done enough."

He reared back like I'd slapped him, but then his hands balled into fists on the table before he discreetly tucked them under the tablecloth. "Maddie, I'm *sorry*. I fucked up. I want to fix this."

"God, don't you get it?" I hissed, slapping my palm on the table and making the water splash. "You *can't* fix this. You can't throw money at it, or sexy smiles, or beat it into submission. Not this time. You left me standing there. *Alone.* You can't undo that, or what happened next."

"Then tell me how we move on," he retorted quietly, his eyes flashing. "You wanted us to come here and sort shit out."

"No, Ryan." I pressed my fingers against my temples. "I came here so we could work out a schedule to make things as easy as possible. I just need to know where and when you expect me to be so I can plan my life accordingly."

He frowned and began shaking his head. "Maddie, you can do whatever you want. Go back to practice—"

"Cheerleading is off the table, remember? So, forget it." I cut him off as fast as I could, ignoring the pang of regret at giving up something I loved.

Then again, staring across the table at Ryan, I realized there were more important things that I'd loved and lost recently.

"You love it," he replied, his eyes narrowed. "I can talk to Gary—"

"Please don't." I shook my head, resigned. "It's not worth the fight. Besides, he wants me to focus on the wedding."

"Is there going to be a wedding?" he asked carefully.

I held up my left hand, where that obscenely large diamond glittered. I hated this ring and all it represented. "Of course."

Ryan looked down. "I don't expect you to still marry me, Maddie."

"What about Cori?" I asked softly. His sister's future hinged on us getting married and pregnant.

His jaw clenched. "Cori isn't your problem. She's mine, and I'll figure it out."

I sighed. "It's not up to either of us. We're just playing the hands we've been dealt, right? You do what Beckett wants, I do what Gary wants. Let's just keep it simple. We're getting married in June, just like they want."

His expression turned furious for a second before he pushed it down. "Fine. Next weekend I have to go home. Since we're *together again*, my father will expect to see you there as well."

I nodded, my stomach shriveling at the idea of seeing Beckett again. "Okay."

"I have a game Friday. Even if you aren't cheering, we're engaged. If we're really selling this blissed-out couple thing to the masses, then you need to be in the stands and waiting for me after."

I licked my dry lips. "Okay."

His eyes narrowed, and I could practically see the calculating wheels turning in his brain. "You might as well spend the night Friday."

Immediately, I wanted to say no, because it was easier to keep my emotions locked down when Ryan wasn't so close to me. When I wasn't staring face to face with what I could have had. At least in my room, I could mope around in peace.

"Optics, baby." The slightly mocking note in his tone hung between us. "Besides, we'll leave first thing Saturday morning to make it back home for dinner that night."

"Okay." My entire vocabulary had been reduced to this word.

The snark dissipated from his eyes as he leaned back and studied me for a second. Like he was waiting for me to say something else, or attack him.

But I was tired. So damn tired and overwhelmed. I wanted to go back to my room and nap for the rest of the day.

With a soft sigh, Ryan turned his attention behind me and signaled the waiter over.

"What can I get you both?" the young man asked.

"Maddie?" Ryan prompted.

I opened the menu reluctantly and scanned it quickly. Immediately I craved a Belgian waffle and every kind of meat they offered.

My fingers curled, my nails digging into the side of the leatherbound menu as I struggled to make a decision. I even missed Ryan covering for how long I was taking by ordering for himself first.

Finally I muttered that I wanted an egg-white omelet with my usual side of yogurt. I couldn't look at Ryan. This was embarrassing, and I knew my cheeks were pink as I passed my menu to the waiter and he disappeared.

Ryan cleared his throat, and I braced myself for whatever comment or question came next.

"We have practice in the mornings now, but you shouldn't have any more issues in the cafeteria."

My head snapped up, stunned that he wasn't pressing me about the sudden change in my diet. There wasn't a trace of sympathy or judgment in his eyes as he watched me.

I jerked my head up and down unsteadily, watching him with what I was certain were big eyes.

"Lunch and dinner we should spend together. Are you good with that?"

"Yes," I said softly, hoping he caught the note of gratitude.

"Brylee should be done giving you shit, but if things change, tell me and I'll handle it," he told me seriously. "I mean it, Maddie. I don't want you taking on the fucking school by yourself."

"You can't protect me all the time," I reminded him.

His gaze sharpened. "The fuck I can't. Watch me."

Agreeing was easier than fighting him, so I just gave another quiet, "Okay."

"Okay, you're trying to shut me up? Or okay, you'll do what I said?" He smirked at me across the table.

I laughed a little because he knew me too well. "Okay to both? But mainly the first one."

He rolled his eyes. "Fine. But with Dean gone, things should be easier."

I squirmed in my seat. "I appreciate you doing that. I know I kind of jumped down your throat—"

"You were right," he said, shaking his head to stop me. "Dean should've been handled before then. Maybe we wouldn't be sitting here if I'd done something sooner."

He could be right. But if that was true, then I also probably wouldn't know what a snake Gary really was. I wasn't sure if being ignorant of just how cruel my sperm donor was would be a blessing or a curse.

"We can't change what happened," I replied, selecting my words as kindly as I could. "But why didn't you do something? I mean, you were so emphatic that Bex not go to the police when Dean drugged her."

His eyes drifted shut for a moment. "I thought I knew what I was doing. I thought I had everything under control."

"What changed?"

His electric blue gaze caught mine and held with an intensity that stole my breath. "The girl I love got hurt. That changed everything."

My pulse pounded as my heart thundered in my chest. All I could do was stare at him, my insides shaking as what he was saying registered in my head.

"What are you doing if you won't be cheering?" Ryan quickly changed the subject to something less emotionally charged.

My nose wrinkled as I shook off the weight of the previous topic. Instead of throwing walls up, I tried taking one down. "Studying and planning our wedding? Worshiping you?"

The corner of his mouth hooked up with his smirk. "Well, obviously. Just so we're clear, I'm expecting something huge and elaborate."

"Didn't peg you as a groomzilla," I teased, letting some of the tension leach from my body as I fell back into our natural banter.

He snorted. "I expect to be the main focus of our big day."

"Of course," I agreed with a small smile. "I was thinking of wearing something like a potato sack to make sure no one pays attention to me."

His eyes warmed considerably. "Baby, if you think burlap is going to dim your beauty, you've clearly not been looking in any mirrors."

I bit my lower lip as my face heated. Two weeks ago, the look in his eyes would've had me dragging him into the nearest bathroom for a quickie.

He blinked and the look vanished. "Can I say something without completely pissing you off?"

Slowly, I nodded.

"I've missed you," he confessed. "I miss *this*. Talking to you and seeing you smile. I know I sound like a broken record at this point, but I'm going to make it up to you, Maddie."

It wasn't the first time he'd said as much in the past two days, but something about this moment made the words land a little different. Maybe because my back wasn't completely against the wall…or maybe because I felt the same way.

A sad smile crept across my face. "I've missed you, too."

CHAPTER 19

MADDIE

After Ryan dropped me off in front of my dorm, I took the stairs to Bex's room on the fifth floor. Judging by how winded I was when I reached the landing, the last two weeks without cheering had killed some of my stamina. Maybe I should start running again.

Not that I really had any extra calories to burn, but I needed *something*.

I knocked and waited for Bex. The door was wrenched open a second later and revealed my still visibly annoyed bestie.

"Not a good time?" I gave her a small smile.

She let out a groan and waved me inside. "No, come in. Sorry. I'm still just so freaking done with... everything."

I entered and closed the door behind me. Her room was standard for an academy student, which meant it was a third the size of my suite and she shared it with a roommate who never seemed to be around.

Bex's side of the room was messy. Papers and books lay in piles on her desk, effectively burying her laptop. Despite Bex sleeping in Ash's room last night, her bed was unmade. Her closet doors were open, and I could see a pile of clothes at the bottom.

"Stop looking at my mess," she ordered playfully, pushing my shoulder a little. "You're such a neat-freak, Mads."

My eyebrows lifted. "Yeah, well, when you come from a place that is never clean, you like being able to control it once you're free."

Ha. *Free.* That was such a joke. I was more caged now than I'd ever been.

I tried to change the subject. "Heard you slept with Ash."

She whirled, her jaw dropping open until she saw I was barely holding in my laughter. She threw a pillow at me. "Jerk."

I tossed it back. "Sorry. Couldn't resist." After a pause I added, "Ash unlocked more stuff on Madelaine's phone."

Her eyes widened. "What's on it?"

I shrugged. "I don't know. Honestly, I don't even know if I can stomach seeing any more than I have." I could feel my intestines twisting into knots.

Bex watched me carefully, as if trying to get a read on my head space. Ultimately, she opted to change the subject. "How was brunch? Is Ryan still being an ass?" She turned around and yanked up the covers to messily make her bed, then tossed the pillows on top.

"Bittersweet?" I frowned, remembering how Ryan had tried to give me some of his breakfast when he'd seen me picking at mine. The bland food felt gelatinous when I tried to swallow, and I'd nearly gagged. He knew something was off, something beyond my hurt feelings, but he wasn't pressing the issue.

Yet.

I knew eventually I would have to come clean. Ryan wasn't the type of man to let something slide, especially when he knew it was upsetting me.

Bex sat at the head of her bed and thumped the mattress. "Come sit. Unless you want to go hang out in your room?"

I shook my head. After dropping my purse by the door, I crossed the room and crawled onto the foot of her bed. I kicked off my shoes and pulled my legs to my chest, wrapping my arms around my shins and resting my chin on my knees as I looked at her.

"I have snacks," she offered, pity and concern shining in her eyes.

I shook my head. My stomach was upset, and I was getting disturbingly used to not having food again. It had been years since I'd let my hunger turn to numbness. As soon as I'd been old enough to hold down a job, I'd made sure I got food. Usually it was from the places I'd worked, because it was free or heavily discounted. But over the past few months, I had gotten used to living in a world where excellent food was available at the ready.

"Okay," Bex murmured, "what happened with Ryan? Did you tell him more about what went down with Gary?"

"No." I sighed a little and glanced away. "I don't know what a difference it would make, and I'm not sure I trust Ryan. Today was just about figuring out a schedule so I know when and where I'm expected."

She pressed her lips into a thin line. "And you did that?"

Nodding, I picked at a stray piece of lint on my leggings. "Yeah. I need to keep Gary happy while I try to figure out my next move."

Bex reached out and grabbed my hand. "You're not alone, Maddie. Remember that."

I slowly pulled my hand from hers. "Actually? I think we should talk about how involved in my life you want to be, Bex."

Her eyes narrowed. "Meaning what?"

"Meaning that it isn't just my mom that he's holding over my head." I met her gaze levelly. "He threatened you, too."

Bex's eyes rounded as she squeaked out, "Me?"

"Yeah. You know, if it was just my mom, I might say fuck it. She's never been much of a mom, you know? And God knows I'm probably better off on my own." I pushed my toe into the mattress of her bed. "I think that's why he mentioned you. He knew threatening you had a better chance at keeping me in line long term."

"Threaten me *how*?" Her soft face was visibly pale, her hazel eyes wide and scared.

Dammit. This was all my fault.

His threats echoed in my ears, turning my stomach over. "He threatened to take you."

She ran a shaky hand through her hair. "I mean, Maddie—"

"Jesus, Bex, he threatened to sell you overseas. Mentioned how much money you'd make him." I whispered the last part, horrified and ashamed that I'd dragged her into this.

Bex gasped, her head snapping back in shock. "Holy shit."

"I'd say tell your parents, but..." I shrugged, knowing that Gary would spin it. He was a pillar of the community and, given their perception of Madelaine, Bex's parents would probably think it was *me* threatening their daughter.

"Did you tell Ryan?"

My forehead wrinkled. "No. I don't want to talk to him about Gary."

She licked her lips nervously. "Maybe you should."

"You want me to tell Ryan?" The incredulity in my tone bordered on slightly hysterical.

Bex shrugged helplessly. "I don't know, Maddie. I've never been threatened with human trafficking before. What's the correct response?"

I flinched. "I think the correct response would be ending our friendship in a public spectacle so Gary thinks you mean nothing to me."

"No way." She shot down the idea so fast that I'd barely had time to say it. Her eyes narrowed like she was seconds away from slapping me. "Maddie, you are *not* doing this on your own."

"Are you not hearing what I just said? Gary could—"

"I'm well aware of what Gary could do," she interrupted, holding up a hand. "Which is why I'm scared shitless for us both. But there's no way I'm going to leave you to fend for yourself. You're... Maddie. You're my best friend."

Tears sprang to my eyes as I watched Bex huff and roll her eyes, but I could see the same moisture glistening in them as she tried to play it off.

"I know, okay? We've only known each other for a little while, and I probably sound like that needy kid who never had any friends growing up—"

I lunged across the space between us and wrapped my arms

around her, cutting her off. She let out a laugh and hugged me back, not caring that I'd basically jumped into her lap.

After a long moment, I pulled away and wiped my eyes. "I'm sorry. I just... *I* was that kid, too. I never had a best friend. Not until you."

Bex smiled and tucked a lock of dark hair behind her ear. "Well, it's been a few years for me, but I can tell you now that besties are always there for each other. No matter what. And I'm not abandoning you because your asshole of a father threatened me."

I nibbled on my lower lip. "Yeah, but this isn't a normal threat, Bex. He's not trying to get you expelled or in trouble. He's threatening to sell you to another human being to become a sex slave. And the scariest part is, I believe him."

"So do I," she answered seriously, her eyes somber. "Which is why we might want to consider outside help."

"Like?"

"I'm guessing the police or FBI are out?"

I snorted and nodded. "Yeah. I'm pretty sure he could buy them off, if he hasn't already. It's like I'm living in some twisted soap opera. Evil twin and everything."

"I don't know if Madelaine was *evil*," Bex wheedled, trying to be considerate.

I gave her a flat look. "She tortured you for years. She *drugged* you. Are you really defending her?"

"I mean, she's your twin." Another helpless shrug. "I don't want to speak ill of the dead."

Sighing, I turned my body so I could lean against the wall while looking at her. "About that."

She groaned and dropped her head back onto the headboard. "There's *more?*"

"You know how I told you Mrs. Delancey thinks Gary might have killed Madelaine?" I waited for her to nod. "Ash said he thinks Madelaine may have faked her own death and left me here to be her."

Bex winced and looked away. "I mean, it's not outside the realm of possible. Lainey was twisted *and* she was pretty damn brilliant. As much as I'd want to think she wouldn't be *that* heinous, I could see her doing it."

"Great," I muttered. "All I know is…my old life is gone. Gary literally killed me."

"There's people from your old life who remember you, right? Would they defend you?" Bex suggested.

"I considered it. But there are only a few, and as soon as Gary plays the twin card, they wouldn't know which I was. And Gary said he'd have me labeled as crazy or something." I shook my head. "Bex, I'm screwed. I've been trying to figure a way out of this, and I just don't see it."

She let out a heavy breath and eyed me closely. "I don't want to beat a dead horse, but have you considered telling Ryan all this?"

I frowned. "I don't *trust* him. Do you?"

She hesitated for a second. "He broke your heart, Maddie. No one is denying that. But I think Ryan really loves you. And while I'm in no way advocating you two picking up where you left off, I do think he could keep you safe."

"I've considered it, but I just don't know. Part of me is waiting for Ryan to find something else to get tripped up on and break my heart. Again." I bit the inside of my cheek. The idea of opening up to him only to have my emotions trampled on one more time seemed impossible.

Keeping things calm between us was one thing. But stepping back into a world where I trusted him was something else. I was barely holding on at this point. I didn't have the emotional capacity to deal with Ryan turning his back on me again.

"I'll think about it, okay? But if you want to tell Court, or—"

"No." She slammed that door shut with cold finality. "Court and I are not even worth mentioning in the same sentence."

"Except that you just did," I pointed out with a soft laugh.

She glared at me. "Court's an asshole. You think you and Ryan have issues? We're like the freaking *Titanic*. We were doomed before we even left the dock."

"I told Ryan I would sit with him at lunch and dinner." I made a face. "If you don't want to sit with us, I understand."

"If I can handle Gary threatening me, I can sit at a table with Court. But I draw the line at talking to him."

I nudged her with my toe. "You keep mentioning how sorry Ryan is—you don't think Court is sorry?"

She scoffed. "Oh, I *know* he is. But I also know he's *always* sorry. And I just want to move on." She straightened her shoulders, a wicked gleam in her eyes. "Think Charles is available?"

I considered telling her the truth about how Court followed her around to make sure she was safe, but honestly, I was okay with him hovering, since Gary had threatened her. Court wouldn't let anything happen to Bex.

That being said, I wasn't entirely sure my best friend was ready for the fallout of openly hitting on another guy in front of him. Ryan hadn't handled it well, and Court seemed wound up tighter than Ryan in a lot of ways.

Ryan could turn on the Prince Charming with ease, but there was a darkness that always seemed to linger around Court. I could see the appeal to a lot of the girls around campus. There was something in a lot of women, including myself, that wanted to be the one to tame the bad boy.

Bex, though, didn't seem to care that emotions swirled around him like storm clouds about to be swallowed by a black hole.

Then again, the darkness seemed to dissipate when he was around her.

"I think you should consider how you'd feel if Court was trying to rub another girl in *your* face." I tried to pick my words carefully, but apparently I'd said the wrong thing.

With a soft hiss, Bex got off the bed and stormed to her closet. She started hurling the clothes on the floor into the empty hamper.

"What did I say?" I asked, slipping off the bed but hanging back.

She shook her head but didn't turn around. "Nothing. It's nothing. He's just... Court Woods. I guess I should just accept that, in some way or another, he's always going to be in my life. Even if it's just in the regrets I can't seem to kick out of my brain."

"Bex, I'm sorry." The compulsion to apologize was overwhelming. I'd bitch-slapped some kind of nerve, but I didn't know what, or how to fix it.

She spun, and the defeat on her face broke my heart. "It's not you. It's just ancient history."

"Wanna talk about it?" I offered.

She shook her head. "No. Not now, anyway. But you're right. Hurting him won't make me hurt any less."

Ooof. Those words hit a little harder than I liked.

She was right.

Me hurting Ryan wasn't making me feel better. If anything, it made me feel worse. And what was the point of that?

"I hate it when you make sense," I muttered. The only thing that would happen by dragging Charles into this mess would be Ryan getting furious, me getting sadder, and Charles probably visiting an emergency room.

I'd have to find another way to make Ryan hurt the way I did. Because he totally deserved that.

At least, that's what I was trying to convince myself.

CHAPTER 20

MADDIE

When I walked through the cafeteria doors later that evening for dinner, my back ached from the tension I carried in my spine. It wasn't my imagination that the room quieted considerably as soon as I crossed the threshold.

The only thing that kept me from turning back was Bex at my side. She looped her arm through mine and pressed against me. "You've got this, Mads."

I scanned the room, and my eyes widened when I saw Ryan stand up from his table in the center with the rest of the football team. His long legs ate up the distance between us as a devastating smile broke out across his face.

"Hey, baby." That was the only warning I got before his hand slipped into my hair and his mouth crashed onto mine.

It was like being struck by lightning; the feel of his mouth as his body pressed against mine while he pulled me away from Bex in one effortless move. Shivers danced down my spine, curling my toes, as I eagerly met his kiss in response. One hand cradled my head, angling my lips just where he wanted me, while the other landed on my hip before slipping around to squeeze my ass like he owned me.

I'd missed this. His taste, his touch, his possession... his everything.

And then I remembered we weren't really together. Reality crashed around me, and pain ricocheted through my chest with enough force to make me gasp.

As if he could sense the change in me, he ended the kiss but didn't stop smiling as he took my hand and led me to the table.

The room was completely silent as people watched and openly stared.

Unease curdled in my stomach, and I squeezed his hand harder.

Ryan turned and arched a brow at the gawkers.

That was all it took. One look, and they immediately stopped staring and started talking. Because that was the power of Ryan Cain.

Another shiver zipped across my skin, leaving goose bumps in its wake.

Ryan pulled out the empty seat next to him so I could sit down. Thankfully there was another open seat for Bex, between me and Ash.

"I'm going to grab some food," Bex told me.

Ash gave her a tight smile and stood. "I'll go with you."

No need for me to go; I could see one of the staff coming toward me with a tray of something leafy and green.

I gritted my teeth as I sat down, keeping my eyes on the table even as my salad was set in front of me. I caught Ryan staring hard at my plate, but he shrugged it off as he turned to the teammate beside him and started talking about their upcoming game.

I knew him from the other times I'd sat at the table. Everyone called him Bubba, but I had no clue why. The massive defensive tackle had always been nice enough to me, but he seemed uncomfortable talking to me. Judging by the flush in his cheeks when he did stammer out a few words to me or Bex, I think it had less to do with my sister's reputation and more about his unease talking to girls.

Trying to tune everything out, I lifted my fork and stabbed a slice of cucumber.

Linc joined in their conversation with a laugh. "I mean, you're right, bro. The Homecoming game was epic."

Homecoming.

I'd missed it. Which meant I'd missed the cheer routine I'd choreographed for the game, a collaboration between the academy and the university. I had felt honored that my coach had asked me to create it.

Bubba grinned back, clapping a hand on Ryan's shoulder. "That's because our boy was unstoppable."

I glanced at Ryan.

"I had a lot of rage to take out," he admitted, his gaze cutting to me for a second. The tight smile he gave me spoke volumes.

I nodded and took my time chewing my food so I wouldn't have to speak. Instead, I shifted my gaze to wander around the room, which was when I saw Brylee and her entourage walk in like the dining hall was a freaking runway.

Brylee paused just inside the doorway, flicking back the silky curtain of her dark hair as she let her fans absorb the gift of her presence.

Barely muffling my snort, I reached for my water and took a drink.

Ryan's head lifted and his eyes narrowed. "Showtime."

Curious, I looked at him, but his eyes were on Brylee. In fact, with matching smirks, Court and Linc turned to watch from the other side of the table.

I looked around, and my eyes widened when I realized the table where Brylee and her friends usually sat had been replaced by a tiny table and chairs that looked like they were made for kindergartners.

Brylee seemed to notice the switch when her friends did, but while Hayley's head tilted in confusion, Brylee's expression turned murderous and shifted to... me.

Great. I set my fork down with a sigh.

The room dwindled into silence again as Brylee stomped toward me, her heels click-clacking across the floor with annoying resonance.

As she got closer, Ryan draped an arm across the back of my seat.

"This is childish," Brylee spat, glaring at him as she stopped in front of Court and Linc. She sneered at them. "After she makes you all look like pussy-whipped losers, *this* is what you do?"

"Hey, Court," Linc started loudly, ignoring the venomous snake at his feet as he turned to his friend.

Court's head lolled to the side to look at Linc with a grunt.

"Do you think Brylee knew her boyfriend was a rapist?" Linc asked, his voice carrying across the room.

Court shrugged and seemed to consider it. "I mean, maybe? She definitely helped him set up Maddie for something she didn't do. Pretty childish shit."

Linc snapped his fingers. "Yes. *Childish*. That's exactly the word I'd use, too." He peered around Brylee intently to the children's furniture that sat where her table had been.

"Hysterical," she snapped, her focus narrowing on Ryan. "Are you really this dense?"

"Are you?" Ryan let out a low chuckle while his fingertips played with the ends of my hair. "Because from where I'm sitting, *you're* the one who fucked with my fiancée yet again."

She glared at him and popped her hip, planting a hand on it. "You should be thanking me for trying to save you."

"*Save* me?" Ryan's fingers slid to the hair at the base of my neck and tightened. He turned my head toward his, his eyes searching mine. "Think I need to be saved from you, babe?"

I swallowed my confusion and played the part, starting with a smile that slowly spread across my lips. "Maybe? I mean, we both know who the boss is in our relationship."

His fingers flexed, jerking my head back. The small yelp that escaped my mouth was entirely natural. As was the hot rush that shot through me. Ryan's gaze simmered as he watched me react to him.

He knew my body too freaking well.

Holding my gaze, his fingers relaxed and went from clenching to stroking my hair like I was his favorite pet. Which, to these people, I might as well have been. He had just proven who was the alpha in this relationship.

My teeth snagged on my bottom lip, scraping across it as Ryan watched, and his eyes darkened. With a soft groan, he pulled me to him and kissed me. The bruising force of our kiss scorched my nerve endings and fried my brain.

I gasped, and his tongue swept into my mouth. He dominated the kiss, and I could feel myself softening and surrendering because I wanted this. I *needed* this.

The fact that we were doing this for Brylee's benefit and in a room full of people completely fled my mind as I kissed him back. My tongue stroked against his, and I sank into his kiss as my hand lifted to cradle his jaw.

The rough kiss softened, his lips turning gentle as he moved them across mine. He licked into my mouth, sipping and taking while giving.

"Get a fucking room," Brylee snarled, breaking the magic of the moment.

I jerked back, but when I turned my head, I couldn't help shooting her a smug smile.

"We have a room," Ryan reminded her. "Trust me—we use it often."

"She slept with Dean!" Brylee practically shrieked.

Ryan gave an indifferent shrug. "Last year. Things change."

I glanced down at my half-eaten salad and then back up at the girl melting down in front of me. "Do you want this, Bry?"

Startled, her lip curled up. "Why would I want your fucking salad?"

I lifted my shoulder insolently. "You seem to like going after what I've already had. I was just trying to make it easier."

Linc's loud laughter spurred the rest of the room to join him. Someone whisper-yelled, "Burn!" and Brylee's face turned crimson.

"You stupid *slut*," she seethed, taking a step toward me like she would vault over the table to wrap her fingers around my throat.

"And now you're done," Ryan said with a grim smile. He snapped his fingers. Literally *snapped his fingers,* and people left their tables to collect the kiddie furniture and take it away.

"Here are your choices," he went on in a cold voice as he held up one finger. "You can leave and figure out where the fuck you're eating the rest of the year, because it sure as shit isn't in here if you can't stop insulting Maddie."

Brylee went still as she seemed to grasp the gravity of the situation.

Ryan ticked up a second finger. "Option two, apologize to Maddie and beg forgiveness. Then you can sit on the floor like the bitch you are and eat. Maybe one day, if you behave, we'll give your table back." His gaze drifted over her shoulder. "That goes for your friends, too."

She stepped back, her face pale. "You can't be serious. Do you know who my father is?"

"The coke-addicted CEO of a company in multiple violations of the S.E.C. who's too busy screwing his eighteen-year-old mistress to come home to your mom every night? Or to see that his partner's embezzled millions over the past five years?" Ryan's grin was evil. "I'm well fucking aware. The question is, are the feds?"

Holy shit.

"You better pray your daddy gets caught up on his bills before someone comes to repo that shit nose job you got over the summer," Court added with a dark chuckle.

Hands clenched at her sides, Brylee turned to me. Hate sparkled in her eyes. "I'm so sorry, Madelaine."

I glanced up as Bex and Ash joined us. Bex stared in amazement as she lowered herself to the seat beside me.

"Apologize to Bex," I ordered.

Brylee looked like she was swallowing shards of glass. "I'm sorry."

"Didn't seem sincere," Linc mused, rubbing his jaw.

"Probably because it wasn't," Court agreed. "Maybe she should beg on her knees."

"Not a bad idea," Ryan chimed in, still grinning.

Brylee's jaw dropped, and I noticed her friends were trying to edge as far away as possible. As if that could stop them from being included in her punishment.

"M-my knees?" Her voice came out as an astonished squeak.

One of the guys farther down the table laughed. "Don't act like you haven't spent a lot of time there."

A ripple of giggles spread through the room, and I actually started to feel kind of bad for her.

Then I remembered the smoothie she'd had dumped on me. The condoms. Harassing Bex and countless other people she deemed beneath her.

"I'd do what they say," I chimed in, folding my arms and giving her a bland smile. "Unless you want to make things even worse."

I wasn't sure how they could get worse, but Ryan's brain was twisted, and clearly his friends shared the same mindset. Testing their creativity wasn't high on my list of things to do.

Brylee must have come to the same conclusion, because she slowly lowered herself to her knees, an act that took some work, since she was wearing a tiny brown skirt. Cell phones appeared as people started to record the event.

Tears gleamed in her eyes as her gaze met mine. "I'm so sorry, Madelaine, for what I did to you."

I arched a brow.

"And I'm sorry for being a bitch to you, Re—Bex," she amended quickly. The hate in her dark eyes was nearly dulled to something that looked like defeat.

Ryan gave a perfunctory nod. "Just so we're clear, if anything else happens to Maddie *or* Bex, I'm coming for you."

Her eyes widened with comical innocence. "I wouldn't, Ryan."

The ice in his glare was enough to freeze the fires of hell. "I mean, if *anyone* else, including you, does something, I'll know, and *you'll* pay."

Brylee's forehead wrinkled. "I can't control what other people do."

Ah. There was the loophole she'd been planning to exploit. And Ryan had just tied it into a neat little bow.

Or a noose to slip around her skinny neck.

"If Maddie trips on air in the hallway, you better be ready to throw a pillow under her to make sure she doesn't scratch her knees. I see *any shit* happen to my girl or her friend, and I'm holding you responsible. Am. I. Clear?" He ground out the last few words.

"Yes," she whispered, her shoulders slumping in defeat.

Ryan stood slowly, his hand on my shoulder as he addressed the room. "That goes for everyone in here. This campaign against my fiancée ends *now*. If you come for her, you're coming for me."

More than a few people looked like they were going to piss themselves.

"Oh, my God," Bex breathed beside me, her eyes wide.

I nodded, not sure what else I could add. What Ryan was doing was...

He was making sure that I was untouchable. At least at school.

Some of the tension knotting my back relaxed, and I felt like I could actually take a deep breath.

Ryan sat down beside me and waved a hand. "Get them their food." The people who had removed the table and chairs stood up and headed for the food line.

Brylee stood up on shaky legs before looking around dumbly. "Can we have our chairs?"

Ryan simply glared at her.

"P-please?" she stammered.

He shook his head. "You haven't earned them back yet. But, I did arrange for you and your friends to have a special dinner."

The people who'd gone to the line came back with cups.

I frowned. "What are you doing?"

He turned and smiled at me. "Giving them a taste of their own medicine."

Ash chuckled beside Bex. "Literally."

Still confused, I turned to see the cups being passed out to Brylee and her friends. When Brylee tentatively removed the lid, I got a whiff of the contents. Even from several feet away, it was impossible to miss that vomit-inducing scent.

It was like the disgusting smoothie she'd poured over my head, but somehow *worse*. I'd smelled garbage dumpsters in the middle of summer that seemed more appetizing.

"Ew!"

"Gross!"

"I'm going to be sick."

People turned away and covered their noses and mouths from the sight of the prettiest girls in the academy holding a concoction of the nastiest shit they'd ever smelled.

"I can't... What..." Sweat broke out on Brylee's forehead as she held the cup away from her body with a trembling hand. One of the girls behind her turned and started gagging.

"Tell you what," Ryan said in a generously teasing tone, "I'll give your friends a choice. Either they all take a drink from their cups, or they can vote to have you drink your *entire* cup while they watch."

Linc started laughing and glanced back at Ryan. "That's fucked up, man."

Ryan shrugged. "Let's see if she actually has any friends." His brows raised as he looked to the girls behind Brylee. "Any takers?"

"W-what's in it?" Kayleigh asked hesitantly, eyeing the cup with contempt.

"Nothing that will kill you," Court promised savagely. "Pureed pig brains, some pickle juice, a few fish eyes, spoiled milk, and grasshoppers for a little added crunch. And a shit ton of the world's hottest hot sauce."

I pushed my plate away, sure I would be sick, too.

"Should we vote?" Ash drawled, waving his fork. "I'd like to eat *my* dinner."

"All in favor of sharing a toast with Brylee?" Ryan called.

No one lifted a single hand. In fact, they all stared at the floor like it held the answers to the world.

Ryan laughed. "All in favor of Brylee drinking the whole thing?"

One by one, hands from her so-called friends lifted. To their credit, Haley and Kayleigh were last.

In one brutal move, Ryan had cut off Brylee from her friends and the only safety net she had at this school. She was as alone as I had been when I'd first stepped foot in Pacific Cross.

"No!" Brylee shook her head wildly. "I won't do it."

"You will," Ryan informed her coldly, "or I'll end you and your family. By the time I'm done, instead of that shit, you'll be sucking dick on a corner to earn enough change for the dollar menu at some fast-food shithole."

"Shouldn't be too hard," Linc chimed in. "I mean, you've got years of practice under your belt."

"Jesus Christ, you selfish little bitch." Her older sister, Molly, got up from the table where she was sitting at with her sorority sisters, her face a mottled red. "Just fucking do it before you ruin everything!"

"It's good advice," Court offered ruthlessly. "Molly's dick-sucking skills are better than yours, so you'd have some serious competition if you want to make a living on that corner."

Molly, clearly smarter than her sister, gritted her teeth and kept her head down.

Beside me, though, Bex made a soft, pained sound.

Dammit, Court.

"Bottoms up," Ryan prompted, smiling as though he'd given her a shot of tequila instead of... whatever the hell that was.

With a shaking hand and teary eyes, Brylee lifted the cup and took a drink.

CHAPTER 21

MADDIE

B rylee had barely swallowed the first sip when she started to gag. She nearly dropped the cup as she doubled over and made a retching sound.

"Don't you dare throw up in here," Court warned, shaking his head. "Go outside and finish if you're going to be sick."

Brylee turned and walked stiffly out of the room. Her friends by the doors scattered to clear the way for her. Once she left, they turned in unison to Ryan.

He shrugged. "Throw your cups away and go get your food. You can eat on the floor." Then he turned away, effectively dismissing them.

"Did that actually just happen?" I murmured.

Ryan turned to me and seized my chin between his thumb and index finger. "Damn right it did, baby. I told you, things are different now. You're safe."

I drew in a shuddering breath. "Thanks."

His gaze softened as his index finger traced my bottom lip. I had the insane urge to bite his finger, wanting to see his eyes widen with need.

Instead, I flashed him a weak smile and turned back to my salad.

When I noticed Bex wasn't eating beside me, I nudged her leg under the table with mine.

She gave me a shrug. "I'm okay."

Across from us, Linc and Court exchanged frustrated looks but didn't say anything.

"Bex," I said softly, noting the small tremor in her hand.

She dropped her fork with a clatter and pushed her chair back in the same motion. "Actually, I'm not that hungry, and I need to work on my paper for English. Can we catch up later?"

I nodded slowly. "Want me to come with you?"

She shook her head. "No. I just need to finish some stuff."

Court tossed down his half-eaten slice of pizza. "I'm done, too. I'll walk you to your dorm."

She scowled at him. "I don't need—"

I squeezed her hand and gave her an imploring look. Yeah, I knew that Court would probably follow her no matter what, but *she* didn't. And until I knew I was solidly in Gary's good graces, I was a little scared to let Bex out of my sight or leave her alone.

Sighing, she nodded. "Fine. Whatever. Let's go."

"I can come, too," Linc offered, his expression hopeful.

Bex shot him a withering look. "I only need one asshole to escort me around. You two can rock-paper-scissors for it."

Looking glum, Linc sat back with a sigh until the guy on his other side chuckled. Then Linc nailed him with a solid punch to the arm.

"Fuck, dude," the guy bitched, rubbing his arm.

Court shot him a sympathetic look and stood up to follow Bex. I watched them leave and then went back to picking at my food.

Ash moved over to Bex's seat. "Did you have a chance to look?"

I shook my head slightly. "No. I'm not sure I want to."

He nodded thoughtfully. "I get that. But the not knowing might be worse. And if there's anything that can help give you closure or answers..."

"I have a pretty good feeling the only thing I'll see is more stuff to keep my nightmares in business," I replied rather curtly.

Ryan's hand settled on my thigh, the unthinkingly possessive move making me freeze. If he noticed, he didn't care. "We can check it out for you. See if there's anything you need to know."

"No," I replied softly. "She's my sister. I'll watch it eventually. Just... not now."

Not when my mindset was as stable as a sculpture made of pudding.

Linc sighed heavily and we all looked at him. "If you guys are going to whisper, can I at least come sit over there, too?"

"No," Ash said bluntly before chucking a green bean at his head.

Somehow Linc caught it in his mouth. He grinned while chewing. "Does this at least mean we're all friends again?"

Ryan inhaled sharply beside me.

Across the table, I met Linc's gaze. "No."

"Damn," he muttered, shaking his head. "What else do we need to do? What other dragons can we slay for you, m'lady?" He dramatically placed a hand over his heart in some invisible pledge. His voice dropped. "Need us to go visit dear old daddy?"

"No!" I blurted the word out loud enough that our private conversation turned a few heads.

There was a thump under the table, and Linc groaned, bending to grab his leg as he glared at Ryan. "The fuck, bro? That *hurt*."

"It was supposed to," Ryan snarled. "Shut up."

Linc looked wounded as he rubbed his leg where Ryan had kicked him.

I glanced down, my appetite completely and utterly *gone*.

"I think I'm going back to my room," I mumbled.

Linc looked stricken. "Shit, Mads, I didn't mean to upset you. I was kidding. I mean, sort of. Not really, because we can absolutely—"

Another thump, and the table actually shifted with the force of Ryan's kick. Linc winced and hissed a pained breath through his teeth.

"Stop," I ordered, grabbing his wrist. My fingers barely reached more than halfway around. Ryan had always made me feel small but protected. I'd loved laying my palm against his and scrutinizing the size differences while we lay in bed together.

Now I just felt *small*. Insignificant, except for whatever value could be bartered out of me.

A wave of nausea swept through my system, and my back broke into a cold sweat.

Ryan's gaze met mine and held, pinning me in place. I was too tired to keep my emotions controlled, so I knew he saw it all—hurt, frustration, and fear.

"I'll walk you to your room, okay?" He posed it as a question, but I knew I was getting an escort to my room whether I agreed or not.

I simply nodded and watched Ryan stand before offering me his hand. I slipped mine into his, hoping he didn't notice how icy my fingers felt. My steps naturally matched his as he led me from the dining hall. Once we were outside, the doors closed behind us and the background noise of chairs scraping, people laughing, and utensils clacking disappeared.

Drawing in a deep breath, I forced myself to relax.

"Do you want to talk about it?" Ryan's soft voice cut through the white noise buzzing in my brain.

"No," I muttered, hoping he would leave it at that.

He gave a slight nod, but his fingers tightened even more around mine.

Content with the silence, I glanced around the sprawling campus of Pacific Cross. Even though it was mid-October, the California sun-drenched lawns and trees were still vibrant shades of green. There was no chill in the air to indicate a cold snap was coming. I kind of missed the crazy colors the leaves changed back in Michigan.

Everything here looked just as picturesque as the website advertised.

But looks could be deceiving in so many devastating ways.

We made it to the front of my building, and Ryan pulled me to a stop.

"Thanks for walking me," I mumbled, tugging my hand free of his grip.

"Maddie." His hands came up to frame my face. He gave me no

option but to look into his eyes. They searched mine for a long, desperate moment.

"I can't help you if I don't know who I'm fighting, baby," he whispered, a note of pain in his voice that almost made me want to break.

I tried to shake my head. "There's no one."

"Liar," he rebuked gently. "Look, I'll give you a week, okay?"

I frowned. "A week for what?"

"Lick your wounds, keep your secrets," he explained. "After that, you're letting me in or I'm bulldozing my way."

I choked out a strangled laugh. "Good luck with that."

"You think I won't?" The darkness in his voice made me shiver. "Don't test me."

I swallowed around a lump of emotion and rallied the last of my reserves. "You think that's going to, what? Score points with me?"

He scoffed, his blue eyes alight with a fire that would consume us both. "I don't give a fuck about scoring points if something's wrong with you, which I'm guessing it is."

I pressed my lips together, refusing to speak.

He smirked, the corner of his mouth hooking up. "I'm giving you a chance to come to me, sweetheart. Take it. Don't make this harder than it has to be."

I tried stepping back, but he still had my face in his massive hands. Unless I was planning to decapitate myself, I wasn't going anywhere.

"Let go," I ordered, struggling.

"You first," he challenged. "Let go of that pride of yours that's keeping me from helping you."

"*My* pride? Oh, that's rich." A cold, brittle laugh rattled in my chest. "God, you're such an asshole." Finally, I wrenched free and staggered back a step.

"Fine. I'm an asshole," he agreed, shrugging as he shoved his hands into the pockets of his jeans. "But I'd rather you be pissed at me for being an asshole if it means you're not hurting."

"You're the one hurting me!" I snapped.

He stepped closer, staring down at me hard. "I hurt you, yes. But I'm not the reason you're jumpy and look like you haven't eaten in a fucking month. You're not just scared, Maddie, you're *terrified*. I can see it in your eyes."

Biting the insides of my cheeks, I didn't speak.

He snorted and rolled his eyes. "Yeah, that's what I thought. Keep quiet, baby. I have no problem digging into every single facet of your life until I find out what's wrong."

"Can't you just leave me alone?" I asked, suddenly exhausted and wanting my bed.

He shook his head. "No. I love you, and that means I'm going to fix whatever's wrong."

"You can't fix everything!" I cried. "Don't you get that? You just *can't.*"

"Agree to disagree," he replied firmly. "We're on the same side. I'm going to help you, whether you like it or not."

"I hate you," I hissed, frustrated and *over* the way he thought he could make everyone and every*thing* bend to his will.

"No, you don't," he answered with another annoying smirk. "You talk a lot when you're drunk. It's cute."

I don't hate you. I love you.

Ugh. I was never drinking again. Ever.

"Good *night*, Ryan," I snapped, whirling away and stalking to the entrance.

"Sleep well, baby!" he yelled in an obnoxiously loud voice that had people outside turning to look.

I hunched my shoulders and opened the doors. Since almost everyone was at dinner still—and Ryan's scene earlier had pretty much guaranteed I would be left alone—I took the elevator up to my floor.

Still pissed off, I shoved the key into the lock and twisted it hard enough to almost break the damn knob. I kicked it shut with a shout into the dark room before slapping my palm against the wall to find the light switch.

As soon as the lights turned on, I stopped dead.

People always talked about how there were two responses to fear: fight or flight. They never seemed to mention the third option.

Freeze.

And that's exactly what I did. My feet froze to the floor as all the air was sucked from my lungs. Because Adam was sitting on my couch waiting for me, and the leering grin on his face told me whatever happened next, I was going to hate it.

CHAPTER 22

MADDIE

A dam stood up from the couch, and that finally seemed to help my brain reconnect with my body. Unfortunately, it was too late. I turned and had barely laid my hand on the doorknob before he slapped a meaty palm across the door near my head. Instead of trying to wrestle control of the door from him, I ducked away before he could pin me.

I managed to get a few feet of space between us. But my pulse was thundering, and blood roared in my ears as I stared at him.

"Calm down, you fickle bitch," he groused, looking annoyed and turned on at the same time. "I'm not here to hurt you."

"Right, because guys frequently break into women's places intending just to chat," I muttered, shaking my head as my phone began to ring in my purse. "Why the hell are you here?"

"Answer the phone," Adam prompted like I was a stupid child.

Frowning, I unzipped my purse and fished out my phone while keeping my eyes on him to make sure this wasn't some kind of trick. Worry swirled in my gut when I realized the caller was Gary.

"Hello?" I whispered into the phone when I answered.

"Adam will be arriving at your room. I expect you to behave yourself." Gary's clipped voice was cold and unfeeling as he told me.

I barely resisted rolling my eyes. "He's already here. And I've *been* behaving myself. Why is he here?"

"I've hired a designer for your wedding dress," he informed me. "She's in Milan, so you'll need to video call her for your measurements. Adam will assist with taking measurements."

"No way," I shot back quickly, glaring at Adam while he smiled.

"I wasn't asking," Gary ground out. "He can either assist you in your room, or he can go down to the fifth floor and assist me in finding the measurements we'll need for the box they'll bury your friend in."

My blood ran cold and I wanted to throw up. I could taste acid and bile even as my mouth dried up.

Adam, clearly knowing where this was going, went as far as to open my door and prepare to walk out.

"I'll do it," I managed to get out.

Triumphant, Adam closed the door and flipped the lock.

"Good. Now, since I'm feeling generous, I'll give you an extra present while he sets up."

I warily watched Adam go back to the couch and lift up a computer case I hadn't noticed. He pulled out a laptop and began turning on lights, chasing away any shadows where my pride might have gone to hide.

On the other end of the phone, I could hear mumbles and then a low moan.

"Hello?"

I'd know that slurred voice anywhere.

Tears sprang to my eyes. "Hi, Mom. Are you okay?"

"Maddie?" She hiccuped. "Wh-where are you?"

"At school," I replied, wishing I could see her in person. I needed to make sure she was really okay. Or as okay as someone hooked on who-knew-what could be.

"Mmm." The noncommittal noise was encouraging and dismissive. "Your father's here. I forgot how... how lovely he is."

My eyes closed and a tear squeezed free. "Mom, you can't trust him."

"Ungrateful girl," Mom spat, her stupor turning to ire in a heart-beat. "Always mouthing off."

Before I could figure out what to say, Gary took the phone back.

"See? You listen, and I reward," he said smugly. "Keep this up, Madison, and things might be a little more bearable for you. Now, I expect to hear you obeyed Adam. He's been instructed to keep things professional. I expect you to do the same."

Translation: *Don't fuck this up, little girl.*

"Got it," I uttered quietly.

He hung up without another word, and I let the phone slip from my fingers as the world spun around me. I kept my eyes closed, praying I wouldn't topple over.

A thick finger traced the path of my tear and my eyes snapped open to see Adam lift his pudgy finger to his lips and suck the tear into his mouth.

"Tastes better than your sister's," he murmured absently.

I reared back and almost tripped over the chair behind my legs.

Adam turned back to the laptop he had set up on a shelf. He tapped a few keys, and then a voice with a heavy Italian accent came on the line.

"Where is the bride?" the woman snapped.

Adam shifted out of the way so I was facing the screen. A painfully thin woman with dark hair pulled back in a severe bun at the base of her skull stared at me with scrutiny. The light in the room wherever she was caught the sharp angles of her face. Variations of white fabric lined the wall behind her.

"Come closer," she ordered me, waving a hand holding a pen.

I shuffled closer, my gaze hesitantly tracking where Adam was.

"Decent body," she mused, looking down and writing notes. "Good complexion. Your father says that you're willing to let me have full control over the dress?"

I nodded mutely.

Her dark eyes narrowed. "I don't want one of those bitchy little American brides who thinks she knows what couture is and then tries to tell me how to do my job."

I cleared my throat. "I promise I truly don't care what this dress looks like."

Adam's eyes narrowed dangerously.

"I trust you and my fa-father," I added quickly.

She huffed and leaned back in her seat. "We'll see. Strip."

My heart juddered, and I, once again, froze.

Another annoyed huff escaped her thin, red lips. "Is there a problem?"

I looked at Adam, my stomach roiling at the greedy way he licked his lips. His eyebrows arched, prompting me to follow her orders.

But I couldn't.

My muscles and joints had frozen to ice and stone. I couldn't get them to move.

Adam chuckled. "She's shy, Marietta. If you'll indulge us for a moment, she has a friend a few floors down. I can go get her and persuade her to assist us. Rebecca, right?"

Bex's name on his disgusting mouth kicked me into action.

"No," I practically snarled. "Bex is busy. I'm fine."

"I do have more appointments," Marietta reminded me with a loud sigh. "Can we please hurry up? I swear, your father promised you would be more agreeable."

Fuck.

I kept my eyes on the computer screen as I slowly stripped down to my underwear. I looked only at the woman behind the screen as everything inside me shriveled up.

"Height," Marietta barked.

Adam moved behind me, a tape measure in his hands. He hooked the bottom under my bare foot and slowly stood, his fingertips caressing the backs of my legs and my butt as he went upward.

I didn't move. I let my mind blank out as I separated it from my body.

This isn't real.

"One hundred and seventy-five centimeters," Adam reported, stepping back finally.

Marietta wrote that down off camera. "Hips."

175

I repressed a shudder as his arms wrapped around me from behind and the tape measure circled me. His fingers skirted the edge of my panties.

"Eighty-eight point one."

"Waist."

The tape measure lifted a bit higher.

"Sixty-one point five."

Marietta nodded. "Bust."

I'm a statue, I reminded myself, staring straight ahead as Adam repositioned the tape measure.

He fit it across my breasts, and then suddenly, it slipped, and his hand darted out to catch it. Instead, he grabbed a palmful of my left tit and squeezed.

"Sorry," he apologized with a laugh as he moved the measuring tape back into position across my chest. "Ninety-one centimeters."

I tuned them out as Marietta got more detailed in what she needed —neck length, shoulder width, and even the circumference of my damn head.

"Hmm," Marietta murmured toward what had to be the end of this torture session. "Let's do inseam in case I opt for a drop waist."

Adam immediately knelt in front of me, his back blocking most of the view Marietta would have, as he once again tucked the edge of the tape measure under my foot and ran it up the inside of my leg. He stopped when his knuckles grazed my underwear.

I kept my jaw locked as he rubbed the back of his hand between my legs and made a soft grunt. My hands curled into impotent fists at my sides.

A finger dipped into the bottom of my panties and touched my slit. Unable to help it, I jerked back.

"Eighty-two centimeters," Adam breathed, his cheeks ruddy as he slowly stood. His eyes met mine, his back still to Marietta, as he reached down and adjusted himself between us with a soft moan that I knew the laptop didn't pick up.

"That's everything I need for now," Marietta called. "I'll be contacting you again if I have questions, Madelaine. Oh, and congratulations." The offhand comment was all I got before she signed off and I was left alone, in my underwear, with Adam.

I stared into his feverish eyes, knowing mine were dead and flat. I refused to move. I wasn't going to cower and hide. What was the point now? He'd seen it all.

A small smirk quirked up the corner of his mouth. "I'm not supposed to hurt you. But if you say yes… I can be gentle."

I ground my teeth together, waiting for the enamel to crack.

"Fine. I'll see myself out," he murmured, his gaze sweeping down me once more appreciatively before stepping back. "Mind if I use your bathroom first?"

He didn't wait for me to reply before walking through my bedroom to my en suite instead of using the powder room out here.

I quickly bent and pulled on my clothes before retreating to the kitchenette. I grabbed a knife from one of the drawers and waited.

Adam exited my room and glanced at me, then laughed when he saw the knife. He started collecting the laptop. "No need for that, sweet thing."

"Just like you have no need for your balls?" I commented coldly, touching the tip of my finger to the knife. I didn't even feel the prick of it as blood beaded from the small cut I'd given myself.

Another laugh. "Cut them off, little girl. If you think all I need is a cock and balls to fuck you, then clearly Cain isn't that creative." His eyes lit up. "Your sister, though…" He rubbed his mouth, salivating at some memory. "She was usually up for anything. You'd be amazed at how much a cunt can stretch and what it can hold. I know I was."

"Get out," I hissed.

He smiled. "Fine. I'll be seeing you around, Maddie girl." He lifted the laptop case and walked out of the room. I waited for the door to close before lunging across the room and locking the deadbolt and regular lock.

My body started shaking uncontrollably, and the knife clattered uselessly to the floor. A sob tore from my throat as my knees gave out and I crashed down.

With numb fingers, I fumbled for my purse and pulled out the second phone—the copy of my old phone. I pulled up the text messages and sent out the only word I could.

Help.

CHAPTER 23

MADDIE

The key sliding into the first lock sent lightning bolts of fear through my chest. With a gasp, I jerked my head up and scrambled backward until my back hit the couch. I was shaking so hard that my teeth were clacking together when the second lock was disengaged, and then the door pushed open.

"Maddie? What the *fuck?*" Ryan demanded, rushing to me and kneeling at my side. He'd left the door open.

"C-c-close it," I forced out, staring at the open doorway, expecting my nightmare to come back.

Ryan frowned, his gaze darting around to check for whatever had freaked me out so bad. "Baby—"

"Close the goddamn door!" I shrieked, fear leaching out of every pore in my body. I couldn't get past the irrational fear that Adam would be back, his lecherous body appearing in the doorway ready to...

A shudder rolled through me so hard that I almost threw up my dinner.

Ryan turned and slammed the door before turning all the locks. Only then did I lower my forehead, pressing it against my trembling knees.

"Madison, what happened?" Ryan was by my side again, but he didn't touch me. His fingers twitched like he wanted to but was holding himself back.

Thank God.

I needed a shower. My skin was crawling, coated in some invisible, oily substance that I couldn't shake. I needed the hottest water possible and maybe a gallon of bleach to scrub the feel of Adam's touch off.

"Shower," I managed, lifting my eyes to see confusion swirling in his cerulean eyes.

His mouth flattened. "Okay. Can I help you up?"

I nodded, knowing I'd need his help to stand. My legs wouldn't hold my weight, especially not the way I was trembling.

Ryan held out his hands, and I set mine in them. His gaze narrowed as he helped me rise, swiftly grabbing me around the waist when my knees failed me.

"Easy, baby," he whispered, pressing a kiss to the side of my head.

I flinched away, remembering Adam's fingers stroking my hair. I didn't want Ryan tainted by that.

"Sorry," he muttered, misinterpreting my reaction. He helped guide me into my bathroom. He hit the light switch and I startled.

He hissed out a breath. "Sorry," he apologized once more.

I stepped away from him, locking my knees and bracing my hands on the counter of the sink. Ryan stood uselessly in the doorway, looking like he wanted to punch someone, but he wasn't sure who.

"Maddie, talk to me," he implored, meeting my gaze in the mirror. "What happened?"

I shook my head, humiliated and overwhelmed. Fabric brushed my fingertips and I glanced down, frowning when I saw one of the hand towels wasn't on the rack where it belonged.

Curious, I picked it up tentatively. When my fingers touched something white and sticky, I dropped it with a cry.

"What?" Ryan picked the towel up from the floor and inspected it. Disgust curled his lips. "Is that..."

Well, now I knew why Adam had used *my* bathroom.

The fucker had marked it like a pissing dog.

Spinning around, I turned the water on the tap as hot as it would get and pumped soap into my palm. I shoved my fingers under the stream, flinching as it scalded me.

"Madison." Ryan's low voice caught my attention, the hint of murder in it somehow making me feel safer.

I was so messed up.

He reached around me to turn off the water, worry in his eyes. "Maddie, your hands."

I licked my lips and turned to lean on the counter. "Adam was here."

His eyes went wide for a fraction of a second before he went fucking nuclear.

With a roar, he slammed a fist into the doorframe hard enough to crack the wood. I winced, wondering if this place had a security deposit.

As fast as his rage flared, it dimmed to a simmer and he stepped into the bathroom. His blue eyes were like the base of a flame burning as he looked at me. "Can you tell me what happened?"

"Wedding dress fitting," I explained. When he frowned, I added, "Gary hired some Italian designer for the dress. She needed measurements, so Gary sent Adam to get them."

"Motherfucker," Ryan seethed. "Did he... Are you..."

"Majorly grossed out? Yeah. He didn't do much more than cop a few feels, but it scared me," I confessed.

"I'm going to break his fingers off one by one and shove them up his ass," Ryan vowed.

A soft, dry chuckle slipped from my lips. "Do me a favor and let me watch, okay?"

"I'm so sorry," Ryan murmured, shaking his head. "I should've been here to protect you. I should have—"

Surprising us both, I reached out and covered his lips with my fingers. "Don't. This wasn't your fault."

He kissed the pads of my fingers before grabbing my hand with his, his touch gentle, like I was the most delicate china that would shatter any second. "This *is* my fault." His head tipped back as he left out a frustrated breath. "Is this what you wouldn't tell me before? Has Adam been bothering you?"

Fear lingered in his eyes as he studied me.

I shook my head. "No. And I probably shouldn't have texted you, but I was scared and…"

"And?" His hand cradled the side of my face.

I let my eyes drift closed as I leaned into the warmth of his touch. "And you make me feel safe."

His arms came around me, soft and hesitant at first until my arms wrapped around his waist and I clung to him. When he realized I wasn't shying away, he crushed me to his chest with a groan.

Finally, I felt the ice in my veins start to melt. Here in Ryan's arms, nothing could hurt me.

I knew I was supposed to keep him at arm's length, but after Adam had slinked away, smug and satisfied, I'd needed a safe harbor. I needed to feel like my room—the one place on this campus I should have been able to escape to—hadn't been violated.

His large hand rubbed slow circles across my back. My tense muscles slowly relaxed, but my back still ached from shivering for the past ten minutes straight. Now that my adrenaline was crashing, I was painfully aware of how gross and tight my leggings and shirt were. I needed them off.

A whole new wave of panic set off a cascade of impulses. I lurched back from Ryan with a gasp, my hands going to my shirt and ripping it over my head.

Ryan's eyes flared wide in a surprised way that would've been comical any other time. "Mads."

"I need a shower," I snapped, spinning around. I yanked off my clothes in fast, jerky movements. The sound of fabric tearing as I pulled my leggings off echoed in the silent bathroom. I didn't stop until I'd peeled off my underwear and kicked them as far away from me as possible.

It didn't even register that I was *naked* and Ryan was *right freaking there* as I stepped into the shower stall and turned the hot water on as high as it would go.

The initial spray of cold water before it heated was a shock to my system. The air in my lungs evaporated, and I was dimly aware of Ryan collecting my clothes from the floor and taking that goddamn towel with him.

I reached for the bar of peppermint scented soap I adored as he left the bathroom. My heart juddered at the sight of his retreating back, and I almost yelled for him to come back.

Instead, I clamped my teeth together and focused on scrubbing every surface I could. He would be back. I knew it in my gut.

It was why I had called him. I'd known on some primal level that Ryan would come through for me.

He returned a moment later and went into the linen closet to pull out fresh towels for me. For a second, his eyes met mine through the steamed-up glass, and I could see he was still conflicted. He wanted to be there for me, but he also wanted to find Adam and beat the shit out of him.

I forced a small smile onto my lips, but his frown only deepened. With a heavy sigh that I read in the rise and fall of his shoulders, he turned and left the room. He pulled the door halfway shut, probably in case I needed him again.

Longing surged in my veins.

I always needed him.

It was a hard, ugly fact that I'd been avoiding. Now that the initial shock of Adam being here and *touching me* was starting to fade a bit, I was left with that bone-deep truth.

I shut off the water, my skin red and glowing. My scalp tingled from the tea-tree-infused shampoo and conditioner I'd used. I wrapped my hair up in one towel and used the other to dry myself before knotting it around my chest.

Once I'd finished towel-drying my hair so it wasn't dripping down my back, I tossed that towel in the hamper. I hesitated by the door before pulling it open, unsure of what I'd see.

Ryan was perched on the edge of my bed, phone in hand, tapping out a message. He hit send and turned off the screen before setting it down, his blue eyes dark and fathomless as he stared at me.

I worried my lower lip between my teeth, trying to figure out what to say.

"What do you need?" The rough, gravelly tone in his voice betrayed how stressed he was. His hands hung limply between his spread legs as he looked up at me.

Too tired to keep up the fight, I padded forward barefoot until I stood between his legs.

His head tipped back, and he looked up at me while one hand settled lightly on my hip. "Maddie?"

"You," I answered softly, reaching out to run my fingers through his soft hair. The dark blonde was almost brown at the roots, fading to a perfectly sunkissed paleness at the tips. Women paid hundreds for what God and nature had blessed him with. "I just need you."

It was kind of freeing to admit that. To acknowledge what my soul still craved. It was a hunger that would never go away, even if I wanted it to.

His eyes closed, his features tightening. "Maddie…"

My fingers trailed down to his jaw, scratching against the stubble left over from a long day. My head tilted as I watched him, his throat worked as the hand not on me flexed at his side. There was something seriously sexy about a muscular forearm contracting.

His eyes snapped open. "Baby, I think we need to talk about what happened."

I shook my head. "I don't want to talk about it. I lived it. That was enough."

He released a frustrated growl. "I'm trying here, Maddie."

My eyes narrowed. I could still feel the ghost of Adam's touch on my skin. I wanted it gone and replaced with something else. Some*one* else.

Not giving myself time to overthink, I lifted a leg and straddled him before easing down onto his lap.

"Fuck," he breathed with a soft groan. "You're not fighting fair, baby."

I looped my arms loosely around his neck. "Maybe I don't want to fight at all." I rocked my hips against him, my bare pussy finding the friction I needed against the hardening length in his jeans. I gasped as my nerve endings flared to life. Heat suffused my body, warming me from the inside.

His hands landed on my hips and tightened. "Maddie, stop."

I paused, arching a brow. "You don't want this?"

He snorted. "Of *course* I want this."

I smiled and ground against him again with a soft moan.

The hands on my hips stilled me before I could repeat the motion. "No, Madison."

The bite in his tone made me stop instantly. All at once, this was too much. His eyes were peering into mine too intensely. He was seeing too much.

Using my hands on his shoulders as leverage, I tried pushing off. Instead, he rolled us, laying me flat on my back against the mattress while he loomed over me. His arms caged me in. Unable to bear the humiliation of rejection, I looked away.

"Look at me," he demanded softly.

When I didn't respond, a hand went to my throat and forced my chin up. "Madison," he growled, the warning note in his tone making me finally lift my eyes.

The corner of his mouth kicked up as his thumb rubbed under my chin. "Good girl, baby."

Fuck, if those three words didn't still send my ovaries into overdrive.

"I'm not fucking you tonight," Ryan informed me, his blunt tone softened by the affection in his eyes. "I'm not sure exactly what happened, but I don't think sex is the answer."

"Since when?" The bratty comment slipped out before I could sensor it.

He took it in stride with a mild smirk. "Since I realized I was playing the long game to win you back, and I'm not about to set us back by sleeping with you to erase another man. You'd hate me in the morning, and I'm not losing any more ground with you."

Unexpected tears welled in my eyes. "You're right."

"Can you say that again so I can record it?"

I punched his rock-hard abs lightly. "Ass."

He released my throat and snagged my hand before drawing it to his lips and kissing my knuckles. "Easy, bruiser. I have a game next week."

I rolled my eyes, thankful that he could put me at ease so effortlessly. "Can I get up and get dressed?"

His gaze dipped to where the towel was starting to gape open. With a ragged groan, he pushed up and walked to the balcony doors. "I can't believe I actually shut you down."

Now it was my turn to smile as I turned away and pulled out a set of pajamas from my dresser. With a rueful look, I turned back and gestured to the bathroom. "I'll just... Yeah." I ducked into the bathroom and closed the door.

I dressed and brushed my teeth before I attacked the wet, tangled mess of my hair. When I was done, I stared at my reflection in the mirror. The lingering flush in my cheeks was undeniable, but I could feel the cold beginning to seep in again at the realization that Ryan would be leaving, and I would be left alone.

Stomach in knots, I turned off the light and exited the bathroom. Ryan wasn't in the room, and my heart sank before I realized I could hear voices in the front room.

Curious, I moved silently through my bedroom and paused in the doorway when I saw Ryan in front of the open door, talking to Ash.

Ash's green eyes, serious and sparking with anger, moved to me. "Hey, Maddie. You okay?"

I nodded and wrapped my arms around my waist. "Yeah. Uh, what are you doing here?"

Ryan held up a duffel bag I hadn't noticed before turning to Ash. "I'll catch you later, okay?"

Ash nodded. "Yeah. I'll let you know if anything turns up."

Ryan dipped his head in acknowledgment.

"What's going on?" I asked softly, my eyes tracking back and forth between them.

"Nothing," Ash said with an easy smile. "See you later, Mads."

Ryan shut the door behind him, then looked at me while locking up.

"Do I get an explanation now?" I pressed.

"Nope," he replied, brushing past me to enter the bedroom. He dropped the bag at the foot of my bed and stripped off his shirt.

Once I'd stopped swallowing my tongue and found my voice, I managed to get out, "What are you doing?"

Ryan turned to face me, giving me a glorious view of his sculpted chest and stomach. Hours on the gridiron and in the gym had honed his body to perfection.

"I'm getting ready for bed." He jerked his chin at the bag. "Ash brought me some stuff."

"You're… staying?" The hesitance in my tone was fueled by hope. Some of the knots in my stomach untangled a bit.

"Of course I am."

Relief coursed through me so hard and fast that I almost sagged against the door.

His smile turned soft, intimate. "Get in bed, Maddie." He grabbed the bag and headed into the bathroom, kicking the door shut.

I didn't hesitate to follow that order. I had barely gotten settled on my side of the bed when Ryan came back out in gray sweatpants that hung deliciously low on his narrow hips.

He paused at his side of the bed. "Put your tongue back in your mouth before I change my mind and put it where it belongs."

I giggled, burrowing into my pillow. "And where does it belong?"

He finished turning off the lights until his silhouette was all that remained in the dark. Then he was sliding between the sheets. A hand reached out, snagging me around the waist and hauling me to his side. I abandoned my pillow to rest my head in the divot between his shoulder and chest. My hand curled against his heart as I snuggled into his side.

"If you don't know where your tongue belongs," he said in a mild voice while reaching down to hitch my leg up, "then I'm happy to remind you." My thigh brushed against his erection.

His lips pressed against my hair. "Go to sleep, baby."

Another command I was happy to obey.

CHAPTER 24

MADDIE

Fingers brushed my hair from my face as a soft voice said, "Wake up, baby."

Disoriented, I fluttered open my eyes, and a sleepy smile stole across my face. Ryan gazed back from the pillow opposite me, his hair mussed and his eyes bright.

Then I realized *Ryan was in bed next to me.* That was quickly followed by *why* he was in my bed. What had happened the night before crashed into my barely conscious brain. A cold sweat broke out across my back.

Ryan's hand settled possessively on my hip. "Breathe, Maddie. It's fine. You're fine."

I nodded, taking a quick inventory of myself until I came to the same conclusion he'd offered; I was okay.

"Sorry," I whispered, and licked my lips. I hated the knee-jerk compulsion to apologize for having a momentary freak out.

"Don't be." His thumb stroked the bare skin above my hip from where my shirt had ridden up. "How do you feel?"

"Okay," I said after a beat. "You?"

He smiled slowly, his gaze dipping to where my top had gone askew and part of my boob was hanging out. "Never better."

Rolling my eyes, I huffed but didn't move to fix myself. It wasn't anything he hadn't seen before. Besides, something had shifted last night. I wasn't ready to say we were back to normal—far from it—but I also didn't feel the same burning need to put space between us that I had before.

"What's got you thinking so hard?" he asked.

"You," I confessed.

His brows shot up. "Uh oh."

I curled my hand under my chin, tucking it against my chest. "You know, when Adam left, I just wanted to feel safe." I met his eyes. "You make me feel safe. Even with everything so complicated between us, I knew you'd come through for me."

"Good," he murmured. "I'm not going to let you down again, Mads. I promise."

A frown pulled at my mouth. Thinking about the engagement party just made me sad. "It's a little soon to be making promises."

"Not for me," he replied. "Not for us. I know what I want. It took royally fucking up to see it, and I'm sorry you paid that price."

My gaze skirted away.

"Do you think you'll ever tell me what happened that night? Or where you were for almost two weeks after?"

"I don't know," I admitted. "Part of me doesn't want to think about it."

Resignation darkened his gaze. "I guess I deserve that."

"It's not about *deserve*, Ryan," I responded gently. "I just... A lot happened. A lot changed. I can't go back to the person I was before that night." God, I wished I could. I'd been so blissfully ignorant. I thought I had won the lottery. I had a dad, my mom was getting better, college and beyond was secure, I had friends, and I had Ryan.

Then everything had blown up in the span of a minute-long video.

"So, how do we move on?"

Not *can we*; Ryan had already decided we were going to work. And honestly, I was running out of energy to fight both him and myself. I was totally going to be *that girl*. The one who stupidly went back to the guy who had pulverized her heart.

190

"I don't know," I replied with a tiny shake of my head. "I'm still making it up as I go along."

"How about we start with you packing some of your stuff and coming to stay with me?" he suggested. "I don't want you here by yourself."

I almost agreed, but then I realized Bex would truly be alone here. "No. I can't."

His eyes narrowed. "Fine. I'll grab more of my stuff and move in *here*."

"You can't!" I squeaked. "I mean, there are rules—"

"Which we've broken many times," he pointed out with a chuckle. "I've spent the night here before."

"If we get caught, I don't want anyone to get in trouble."

He shot me an amused look. "Baby, you're aware of who we are, right? I mean, the combined power of our families means we could commit mass homicide on the quad and the alumni would pay off the president to make it go away."

And that was why Gary got away with all the shit he did. Why my mom was locked up somewhere, strung out on who-knew-what while his staff turned a blind eye.

"I was kidding," Ryan added when he saw my expression harden.

"I know," I muttered, trying to shake the lingering anger. I turned over to see the clock on my nightstand, partly because I was curious about the time, but mostly to avoid looking at Ryan.

Which he must've known, because he hauled me across the bed until my back was flush to his chest. He buried his face in my neck. "I'm sorry."

"Do you even know what you're apologizing for?"

He hesitated. "Whatever made you upset?"

I snorted and rolled my eyes.

He smiled against my shoulder and cuddled me closer. "Isn't that what our entire life together will be? Me endlessly apologizing for shit I did that pissed you off and I didn't even know it?"

I glanced over my shoulder, my heart pounding when I saw how close his face was to mine. "I mean, am I that bad?"

"No, but I am." His wolfish grin made me laugh. "I need to go. I have practice in a couple hours, but first we have a fucking house meeting."

"Aren't you the president now? Don't you set those up?"

"I didn't anticipate being in bed with you when I did," he groused, nuzzling into my hair with a groan. "I'd have cleared my whole schedule, but there's still some stuff we need to handle. Everything's a little chaotic."

"Did you mean it?" I asked, my voice hesitant. I rolled onto my back to look at him. "About moving in here?"

He nodded slowly. "Yeah. If you're okay with that?"

The air in my lungs rushed out as I breathed, "Yes, please."

His gaze heated and drifted to my lips. "I really want to kiss you."

I couldn't help but hesitate. The only other kisses we'd had lately were for show, because I was drunk, or because my adrenaline was crashing. This would be just for us.

Ryan smiled, sadness tinging the edges of it. He leaned in and brushed a kiss against my cheek. "Don't worry about it, Maddie." He let me go and slid out of the bed.

Regret instantly hit. "I… I'm sorry."

"You don't have to explain or be sorry, baby," he told me. "I plan on kissing you for the rest of our lives, so I can wait a little while longer."

"Okay, when did you swallow a Hallmark store?" I demanded, shaking my head as I sat up. I ran my fingers through the knots in my hair.

He rolled his eyes. "Mind if I use your shower?"

"Of course not." I yawned and leaned against the headboard, wondering if I wanted to get up or sleep in for a few more hours. Undecided, I grabbed the TV remote from the drawer in my bedside table while Ryan went into the bathroom.

I flipped through the channels mindlessly, finally stopping on a rerun of a sitcom that had aired a decade earlier. As the shower turned on, I snuggled under the covers and did my best to pay attention to the storyline and not the naked man in my bathroom.

When a commercial came on, my mind wandered and I flipped to another channel to distract myself before I did something stupid like join him.

"The collision on interstate one-oh-five last night took hours for rescuers to clear. Sadly, the driver was pronounced dead on scene. Channel six news has since learned that it is believed he was heavily intoxicated at the time of the single-vehicle accident. Due to the driver's reckless speeds, the car veered off the road and collided with a concrete barrier wall before it exploded into flames. The unusually dry November conditions led to a small fire that spread into the trees, but was ultimately contained by firefighters."

Damn. I winced as the camera panned from the woman with dark hair and a perfectly schooled expression of grim horror to a destroyed black car. Pieces of it were strewn across the road, and the grass around the area was charred from where it had been on fire.

The screen returned to the news anchors, both who looked simultaneously bored and energetic. "Linda, any word on the identity of the driver?"

It cut back to the field reporter, Linda, who nodded gravely. "Yes, Pam, he's been identified as Adam Kindell, long-time business partner to Cabot Industries CEO Gary Cabot."

The room spun a little as I felt all the color leached from my face.

Holy fucking shit.

Adam was dead.

That mangled, burned-out husk of what used to be a car had been his. He'd probably been heading back from here when...

"Ryan!" I shouted, and a second later the water turned off.

He made it to the doorway, dripping, with a towel barely wrapped around his waist. "What's wrong?"

I pointed at the screen.

He looked and frowned. "A car accident?"

"It's Adam's car," I choked out. I expected Ryan to react with the same surprise I felt. To say something like, *Damn, Maddie. It's what he deserved.*

Instead he just murmured, "Huh."

I watched him closely, from the way he assessed the grisly scene with almost clinical indifference before looking at me.

"You don't seem surprised," I said slowly. A feeling I couldn't place niggled at the back of my mind. "Why don't you seem surprised?"

"Accidents happen all the time," he replied, his expression giving nothing away.

"Ryan—" I cut myself off because no. No *way*. I was being crazy.

"What?" Ryan pressed, a thread of steel in his tone that hadn't been there a second ago. His gaze sharpened as he watched me.

"Did you do this?" I whispered.

He might as well have been carved from slate for all the emotion he was giving. "Did I do what?"

I swallowed uneasily. "Did you... Did you kill Adam?"

His brows lifted slowly. "It looks like Adam killed Adam."

"That's not what I asked." I could feel my heart pounding in my chest. I fisted the comforter in my hands, desperately needing something to hold on to.

Ryan gave me a careful look. "Maddie, I need you to think about what you're asking me. And then ask if you really want the answer, because I don't want to lie to you." He held up a finger when my eyes went wide. "I mean it—Adam killed Adam. His choices sealed his fate."

I couldn't miss the double meaning. To the world, Adam had sealed his fate when he got behind the wheel drunk, or whatever excuse they were giving this.

But Adam had chosen to hurt me, and in Ryan's mind, that had sealed his fate, too.

I looked back at the TV. The news had moved on to a segment about adopting puppies. A bulldog was chewing on the visibly annoyed anchor's fingers while he emphatically told everyone how sweet the pup was.

"Maddie?" Ryan prompted. He gave me a pointed look, still waiting for my response.

This was it. The moment I would look back on and know everything had changed. When I was either all in, or I would forever linger on the fringes.

I'd always known what Ryan was capable of, hadn't I? He wasn't a guy who was all talk and no action.

I smiled at him genuinely, my shoulders relaxing as I leaned back in bed once more. "What time is your meeting? Maybe we have time to grab breakfast first."

CHAPTER 25

MADDIE

I t took less than a week to establish a normal, almost domestic way of living with Ryan. By Tuesday, I knew he liked to get up early to run, and I decided to go with him. After I got a little lightheaded the first time, he told me next time I could join him only if I first had one of the chocolate and peanut butter energy bars he had on hand.

The added boost of calories helped, and chocolate, was never a bad idea. I figured the run would burn off what I'd consumed. And if Gary asked, I'd tell him Ryan had insisted, which wasn't a lie.

At night, we sat at my table and studied. Well, I studied. Missing two weeks at Pacific Cross had set me behind, and I was struggling to catch up on top of my already heavy course-load. Ryan, freaking gorgeous genius that he was, seemed to read something once and remember it verbatim. He switched to helping me study when he noticed I was frustrated.

I saw him like clockwork at lunch and dinner, and Bex always sat with us. She'd thawed toward Linc but was still stubbornly holding Court at arm's length. Okay, maybe more like at a football field's length. My best friend was holding tight to that grudge, and she wasn't sharing her reasons with me.

She'd understood Ryan moving in, and she'd even given her

blessing when I'd explained that Adam was the motive. Granted, Adam was dead, but neither Ryan nor I seemed to care about that point.

Gary never said anything about Adam. In fact, he hadn't said anything to me at all. Maybe he'd had an unfortunate car accident, too.

By Friday afternoon, I was exhausted, and not just from finally getting caught up on school.

It was amazing how exhausting ignoring things could be.

Like when Ryan would brush by me and place a hand on my hip, I would ignore the shiver that rocketed down my spine. When I'd accidentally walked in on him in the shower, I'd ignored that the foggy glass didn't hide the straining cock he was squeezing in his hand. And I was especially ignoring the tension that kept coiling tighter and tighter between us.

He hadn't tried to kiss me again since that first morning, and I was starting to wonder if maybe I'd done something wrong. Or maybe he was waiting for me to make a move. Or maybe—

Fingers snapped in front of my face. "Hey, earth to Maddie," Bex teased.

I blinked and refocused on Bex, who was standing in front of me. I'd completely missed whatever she'd been saying.

"Sorry," I mumbled, ducking my head so my loose hair fell in front of my eyes like a curtain.

Bex snorted a laugh and moved to my open closet. She flipped through the racks, back to her quest to find me an outfit for the game tonight. I was used to being in my cheer uniform, not figuring out what to wear.

Instead, I was sitting on my bed while Bex picked something out for me.

"Maybe you should stay home and take a nap," Bex suggested, pulling out a black sweater dress and then replacing it. She glanced over her shoulder and flashed me a smug grin. "I'll tell Ryan he should've let you sleep last night if he wanted you to be awake and coherent for the game."

I frowned and then sighed. "Actually? That's what I was thinking about."

"The sexy details of your nighttime escapades with PC's semi-reformed bad boy?" She rolled her eyes.

"More like my chaste, PG-rated nights with a guy I'm wondering if I pushed too far away?" I spread my hands out helplessly.

Bex made a face. "Ouch. Really?"

I groaned and fell back on my bed. "I even left the door open when I took a shower this morning." And Ryan, ever the freaking gentleman now, ignored it and kept getting ready for his morning classes.

"Look, if Ryan's turning down sex, that could mean one of two things," she began. "Either he's decided to become a monk—"

I snorted.

"—or," she went on, talking over the noise I'd made, "he's really serious about you."

"How can he be serious about me when he's not even kissing me?" I demanded, pushing myself up to my elbows and glaring at her.

She gave me a look that said I was an idiot. "Maddie, he's trying to show you that he wants more than sex. Besides, I thought you were still very anti-forgiveness."

"I was. I mean, I am."

She stared at me until I relented.

"Okay, so maybe all of this close proximity to him has my hormones going crazy. Or maybe I've got Stockholm Syndrome—that's a thing, right?"

"It is," she agreed, "but I don't think it applies. There could be a little bit of a savior thing going on here."

"Because of Adam?" I picked at a thread on the comforter. I'd told Bex what had happened that night and that I'd asked Ryan to stay with me. She also knew Adam was dead, but I hadn't shared my mostly unconfirmed suspicions about how and why he'd really died.

She came over and sat beside me. "Maddie, it's okay to change your mind. Yes, Ryan broke your heart. But if you want to forgive him, that doesn't make you a bad person. It makes you human."

"Can't we keep emotions out of it? I'd rather focus on the physical. Ryan and I are great at that." Or, we had been.

She chuckled and slapped my thigh before getting up and resuming the task of finding me an outfit. "That's my point, Mads. He's trying to show you he wants more than that. He wants all of you."

I'd opened my mouth to argue when the floor shook.

No, the whole goddamn *building* shook.

Just as fast as it started, it stopped.

"What the hell was that?" I breathed, bracing for whatever came next.

Bex barely hid a smile. "That was your first California earthquake."

"Holy shit." I looked around, wondering if there was any damage. "Should we leave the building? Does it need to be cleared for safety?"

"Mads, it was barely a blip, and all these buildings are earthquake proof. It's really okay."

"It's really *not*," I insisted. "The ground isn't supposed to do that."

"Do what? Get more action than you?" she teased.

I groaned because dammit, she was right. And that wasn't fair.

"But can't he at least want *some* sex?" I groused, my lips turning down. "It's not like I can even get myself off when he's in bed next to me." My cheeks burned with mortification at the thought.

Bex, however, cracked up. "I mean, that might be the tipping point. If he sees your fingers in his cookie jar? He'd probably take some action."

I scowled. "It's *my* cookie jar. And that is a weird metaphor."

She shrugged. "Well, you're a weird girl."

I threw a pillow at her head and missed. "I need a new friend."

"No you don't," she sing-songed, finally pausing her perusal of my closet on a blue halter dress with an open back and slightly flared skirt.

My eyes widened. "No."

She grinned back. "Yes."

"That dress belongs in a club," I protested, "not on the bleachers."

Now it was her turn to scoff at me. "Okay, I know you're usually on the field in cheer uniform for games, but you'll see tonight that

199

these games are basically a fashion show. Besides, this is blue. You'd be showing school spirit."

A slow idea started to form in my head. "School spirit, huh?"

"You know, when you smile like that, I get scared." Bex began to shake her head and back away.

I grinned at her. "Let's go. We have a stop to make before the game."

"We do?"

"We do," I assured her before whirling away.

It was time to show Ryan I meant business.

I was fully aware of the eyes on me as I walked through the crowds packing into the stadium an hour later.

"Explain how this is less revealing than the blue dress?" Bex whisper-hissed at me, staying close so we wouldn't be separated. Ryan had given me tickets on the fifty-yard line behind where the team would be, but getting to the seats required walking down a set of concrete stairs that might literally be the death of me.

The black stiletto heels with the red soles I'd selected were shiny under the stadium lights. One wrong roll of my ankle, and I could see my head cracking against a step.

I glanced down at my outfit and grinned. The skinny jeans, a pair of Madelaine's that I hadn't been able to fit into at the beginning of the term, were molded to my legs like a second skin, but it was the top that had people's mouths dropping open.

Using the key Ryan had given me, I'd slipped into his room and snagged one of his extra jerseys. I was swimming in it, but had tied it in a knot on one side and put on a flesh-toned strapless bra under it so it looked like I was naked beneath the jersey with a million holes. The V-neck hung off my bare shoulder, and I'd pulled my hair into a high, sleek ponytail to show off the column of my throat—a feature I knew firsthand drove Ryan crazy.

I checked the seat number on our tickets and started down the stairs, moving slowly until I reached our row and slipped inside. When I sat down, I realized I knew the girl sitting to my right.

"Imani, isn't it?" I asked hesitantly. We'd never really spoken, except at one of the first games of the season when she'd given me the cold shoulder, but it felt rude not to say something now.

She turned, arching a perfectly shaped dark eyebrow. "Am I supposed to be impressed that you remembered the little people, Queen Cabot?"

Okay, so she still hated me—or, rather, *Madelaine*—as much as the last time we'd met.

"You changed your hair," I tried, nodding to where her previous black and gold braids had been replaced by a shiny curtain of waist-length hair with blunt ends. "I like it."

"I don't care," she replied with a fake smile to match her tone. Her gaze moved past me and softened. "Hey, Rebecca."

"Imani," Bex greeted softly. "How's Eddie?"

The smile that lit up Imani's face was breathtaking. Seriously, this girl belonged on a runway. "He's great. Looks like he'll be one of the first-round draft picks, if his season holds up."

Okay, she couldn't be all bitch if she was being nice to Bex.

Bex smiled. "That's amazing! Congrats."

Imani's eyes went cold and flat as she turned to me. "Kind of surprised to see you hanging out with the ice princess again, Rebecca. Unless this is some new form of torture?"

"Maddie and I are friends," Bex told her firmly. The slight growl in her tone made me smile inwardly. My bestie was a kitten with claws, and it was kind of adorable when she used them.

Imani looked confused. "Seriously?"

"Yes," I cut in. "Seriously. Just like I'm seriously with Ryan."

Her amber colored eyes narrowed.

"I get it," I said, recalling that Ryan told me he'd grown up with Imani in the same circles when he'd told me about the teammates and some of their girlfriends. "I was a bitch. Worse than a bitch, but I'm trying to make up for it."

"You think you can?" Imani's brows lifted in challenge.

I met her gaze. "I think I'm trying. If that works for you, awesome. If it doesn't…"

"If it doesn't, *what?*"

I shrugged. "Then I guess we'll sit here in silence for the rest of the season, because I'm not going anywhere. Either way? Get used to it."

She watched me for a moment. "You know, this is the first conversation I've had with you where I didn't completely want to claw your eyes out."

A ghost of a smirk touched my lips. "Oh, goodie. We're making progress."

"We're making something," she muttered. "Look, my mama taught me that forgiveness is divine, but my daddy taught me that second chances are earned. If Rebecca and Ryan see something in you, then I'm willing to let bygones be bygones."

"Okay," I agreed.

"But," she added, holding up a finger with a glittery blue nail that had been filed to a point as sharp as my stiletto, "if you hurt either of them? I'll bury your skinny ass. And if you fuck with my man's chances at going pro? They'll need dental records to identify you when I'm done. Got it, princess?"

"Whatever you say, sunshine," I agreed with an easy smile.

Her eyes narrowed. "I swear, it's like you had a fucking lobotomy."

"You're not entirely wrong," I murmured, turning to smile at Bex, who flashed me an adorable thumbs up as the guys ran onto the field. Energy swelled in the stands as people started cheering.

My gaze moved through the players until I landed on number ten.

Ryan ran in front of his team, leading them to the sidelines where they gathered. As the announcer had us stand for the singing of the national anthem, he removed his helmet, and his eyes searched the crowd until he found me.

The way his jaw dropped a little when he saw his jersey on me confirmed I'd made the right call. I grinned back and gave him a small wave. His shoulders shook with laughter as he turned away, shaking his head.

"I think you got his attention," Bex told me as the song ended and we sat down.

Imani snorted "Honey, I think you've got *everyone's* attention. Seriously, are you even wearing underwear?" She held up her hand. "Never mind. I don't wanna know."

I gave her an odd look.

Sighing, she explained, "Two seasons ago, I made the mistake of telling Eddiethat I hadn't worn any underwear to the first playoff game. They *won.*"

I started laughing, knowing where this was going as Bex leaned around me with a frown.

"What does that matter?"

"Players are superstitious," I replied, and Imani nodded. "If they think it'll lead to a win, they'll keep it up. Some players don't change underwear or socks."

"*I* didn't get to wear panties for weeks." A devilish smile stole across her face. "Not that it was *all* bad. My boy is hella creative when he's given open access."

I choked on a laugh as Bex's cheeks turned pink and she sat back in her seat with a weak, "Oh."

My attention went back to the field as Ryan and two of the Knights players stepped up for the coin toss against the Copper Field Vipers. Their black-and-gold jerseys made them look like devils compared to the Knights' royal blue and white, and I knew from the way Ryan talked that this would be a hard game.

The Vipers and the Knights had been rivals for years, and last year the Vipers had won because Madelaine had hand-fed them information about the Knights' plays.

By the end of the first quarter, both teams looked exhausted, and I'd bitten off most of my nails. The score was still at zero for both sides, and the Knights were within field goal range.

"Come on, baby," Imani whispered, watching her boyfriend step onto the field.

Without thinking, I reached over and squeezed her hand. "He won't miss." Eddie Jones was one of the best kickers in the division.

Last season he'd made a sixty-yard field goal to clinch a victory. This forty-four-yard field goal would be a breeze by comparison.

Surprise lit her face, then determination as she nodded and clutched my fingers.

As soon as the play was set in motion, Eddie ran forward with the grace and speed of a cheetah. His foot connected with the ball, and it tumbled through the air. Everyone in the stands held a collective breath as we waited.

It sailed through the goalpost with room to spare.

Imani screamed and leapt to her feet. "Way to go, baby!"

Bex and I shot up, too, celebrating with the rest of the fans as the teams reset.

I staggered back in surprise when Imani threw her arms around me. Her infectious smile made me giggle.

"I'm going to grab a drink," Bex called over the shouting and cheering.

"Want me to come?" I offered, even though I really wanted to stay and watch the game.

She shook her head. "Want something?"

"Celery stalks?" I deadpanned, cursing Gary and his goddamn diet.

Bex made a face and took off up the stands. Ignoring the craving for junk food, I turned my focus to the game—the Vipers had thrown a ball that was intercepted by the Knights—when Ryan jogged back onto the field. I was too busy admiring his ass in those tight pants and didn't realize someone was sitting next to me again until I turned.

"Bex, did—oh." I stopped when I realized Charles was sitting in Bex's seat. "You're not Bex."

"I'm not," he agreed with a smile. "I just popped over to say hello to a friend."

"Thanks," I started, when Imani let out a squeal and launched herself over me and wrapped her arms around Charles.

"Charlie! What the hell, man? I thought you moving across the pond meant I'd see you *more*, not less." Imani let him go and returned to her seat. She glanced between us. "You know Madelaine?"

"I do," Charles replied with a smile.

"And you two know each other," I deduced with a small, confused smile.

Imani grinned. "Our families go way back. I thought they'd never agree to let him leave that stuffy old boarding school in Oxford."

"It definitely helped that your stellar academic career paved the way," he told her. "Imani is going to be the best neurosurgeon on the West Coast."

"He's being ridiculous." Imani rolled her eyes, but then grinned devilishly. "I plan to be the best neurosurgeon on the *continent*."

"Well you're on your way," Charles confirmed before glancing at me. "Are we being horribly rude?"

"Not at all," I assured him.

"I should get back to my seat," he said, pointing a few rows up where I recognized some members of the soccer team. "I only wanted to say hello."

"There's a party tonight. You should come," Imani suggested.

Charles glanced at me. "Will your fiancée be in attendance?"

"Probably," I replied with a laugh. "He's part of the team, so…"

"I swear, I don't know what you see in him," Charles mused, shaking his head.

"Hey, Ryan's cool," Imani argued.

"If you insist." Charles stood to go, but Imani jumped up for one last hug.

"It's good to see you, Charlie," she told him as he kissed her cheeks.

"Likewise. Maddie," he said with a smile before ducking to hug me like an afterthought.

Laughing, I gave him an awkward, one-armed hug so I could keep watching the game.

Which was why I saw the Vipers' cornerback tear through a hole the defense opened and slam into Ryan's side, bringing him down with enough force to make his helmet bounce off the turf.

When the players cleared, everything in me went cold. Ryan didn't get up.

He didn't move.

And I stopped breathing.

CHAPTER 26

MADDIE

"Holy shit," Imani whispered as the medics raced onto the field. As soon as they knelt down, I jerked into action.

"Move!" I ordered Charles, pushing by him and racing down the stairs as fast as my heels would allow. By the time I made it to the bottom, Ryan was already being carried off the field on a backboard and in a neck brace.

My heart sank at the idea of a spinal injury. Football was a violent sport at the best of times, but both teams had been foaming at the mouth for this match up.

"Maddie!" A sharp voice called to me, and I glanced over to see Ash running toward me from the sidelines, helmet tucked under his arm.

"Where would they take him?" I demanded, needing to see if Ryan was okay for myself. "What's the closest hospital?"

"We have a full medical suite in the locker room." He pointed a finger in the direction of the stadium hallway that led to the locker rooms and press area.

I nodded and hurried to the hall, ignoring the people who tried to stop me to ask if Ryan was okay.

What—because I was his fiancée, I had a psychic link to his well being? I fucking wished.

It took forever to navigate my way through the crowd and down the hallways.

There was usually an attendant at the front of the hall to keep fans out, but he was nowhere to be seen. I kept going until I found the door for the home team locker room and pushed my way inside.

It was quiet here. Abandoned clothes were strewn about, like the team had begun partying before they'd made it onto the field. But an energy still lingered in the air.

Or maybe it was the smell of stale man-sweat.

A man wiping down the benches jumped when I stormed through the space like a woman on a mission.

"Who are you?" he demanded. "How did you—"

"I'm Ryan Cain's fiancée," I cut him off. "I need to see him."

"Uh, he's being checked out right now. They're in the middle of a scan," the man told me. "I don't think you're supposed to be in here."

I arched a brow. "Okay, you can be the one to tell Ryan you kicked me out when he needed me."

The man paled and straightened, and I kinda felt like a bitch for playing that card.

"Look, I just need to make sure he's all right," I assured him. "I swear I'm not a crazy stalker or something."

He sighed. "I have to finish up in the other locker room before halftime. I guess you can wait here for them to be done." He gestured to the half-closed door on the far side of the room. "They're in there."

"Thank you," I breathed, clasping my hands over my heart and smiling as he left me alone.

I slowly sank onto the bench and waited.

And waited.

Finally, I heard voices toward the back and stood up. I moved forward, gently nudging open the door until I saw several people crowded around an exam table. I could make out dirty cleats hanging off the end facing me.

"You've got to lie down," one voice insisted.

"No, I've got to get back out there." That sounded like Ryan. A very pissed off Ryan.

An aggrieved voice barked out, "You know you can't do that until you're cleared."

"*If* he's cleared," a third, more subdued voice added.

"I'm fucking *fine.*"

"Until I've cleared you for a potential concussion, you aren't, so lie the fuck down, Cain!"

Standing in the doorway, I watched Ryan glower at the three men trying to hold him back. But then his eyes moved to me and widened, causing everyone else to turn.

"Are you okay?" It seemed stupid to ask, but it's all my brain could think up.

His dark-blonde hair was sweaty and sticking up in places, but his face was pale. He was probably in a lot of pain but trying to hide it.

"Miss, you can't be in here," the more timid of the three men said, glancing up from his clipboard to squint at me.

"She's my fiancée," Ryan replied in a voice that left zero room for argument.

"Is he okay?" I repeated my question to the men around him.

"I'm fine, Maddie," Ryan began.

I held up a hand to stop him. "Thanks, but I think I'll listen to what the doctors have to say."

"It doesn't look like a concussion," the oldest man with silver hair and a stethoscope around his neck told me. "I'm Dr. Travers."

"Maddie," I murmured in response as I edged closer to Ryan's side. "And are you sure? I mean, concussions and football can be catastrophic, even if it's minor now."

Dr. Travers's mouth hitched up. "Pretty certain. But I only graduated top of my class at med school. We can find another opinion if needed."

"Sorry." I didn't mean to step on any toes. But I'd seen a lot of nasty concussions, and back in Michigan, they usually hadn't been monitored.

Dr. Travers just smiled. "Don't be." He tapped a hand on Ryan's shin. "She's a keeper."

"Yeah," Ryan agreed softly, his dark blue eyes drawing me closer still. "What are you doing here?"

I leaned a hip against the edge of the exam table while the others stepped away to discuss his condition. "If you're not sure why I'm here, you definitely hit your head harder than you thought."

"Aw, honey, you care." The teasing in his voice almost hid the small note of vulnerability that slipped through a crack in his armor.

I trailed a finger down his bare arm. "Of course I care."

His hand shot out and grabbed the bottom of my shirt. "Did you steal this from my room?"

"Borrowed," I corrected. "I wanted to show my school spirit."

"My spirit definitely feels... moved." Ryan gave me a dazzling smile, and I almost forgot that there were other people in the room.

"Okay, Cain," Dr. Travers announced, coming back over. "No concussion."

Ryan smirked at him. "I told you."

"But," the doctor continued, "I want you to take it easy. Finish out the rest of the quarter in here. You can play the last half."

"Not fucking happening." The glare Ryan shot him would've folded lesser men.

"Listen, kid, that CT scan we did is clearing you, but you lost consciousness out there."

"For a second," Ryan argued.

"I don't give a shit. The last thing I want is your coach to have my balls in a blender because I let you push yourself." Dr. Travers shook his head. "It's bad enough I'm married to his sister. You think Coach is a hardass? It's genetic, and she actually has access to my balls on a daily basis."

I couldn't help the snorting laugh that slipped out.

"Quarter's almost done," the doctor added, softening his voice. "Score's still the same. Rest up, and then get the win when you're back on the field." He glanced at me. "I need to get back out there. Can you make him stay put?"

"Yes, sir," I agreed.

As soon as the three men left, Ryan was already swinging his legs over the side of the table.

"What the hell!" I planted my hands on his shoulders and pushed him back. "You have to stay here."

"I'm not leaving my guys out there, Maddie," he snapped, his eyes flashing. "I can at least stand on the sidelines."

"God, sometimes you are so freaking infuriating!" I snarled, giving him another shove as I moved between his spread thighs to block him from standing. "Just stay here and relax. You'll get your chance to go kick some more Viper ass."

His eyes blazed as he stared at me. Slowly, one corner of his mouth hooked up. "Maybe I want a different kind of ass."

"What?" The confused question was barely past my lips before his hands settled on my hips and he picked me up to straddle his thighs.

"Ryan!" I squeaked in alarm and tried to wiggle free. It was useless; his iron grip held me tight against his chest, and all my struggling did was help raise another kind of thing. This one was decidedly more corporeal than spirit.

"Ryan." His name tumbled out in a breathless whisper.

His gaze darkened. "Fuck, I love when you say my name like that." He leaned forward and grazed his lips across my exposed shoulder. "Again."

My head tipped back, giving him more access. "Ryan."

He groaned softly, lifting his hips to press his hard-on against my center.

I cried out, looping my arms around his neck so I wouldn't tumble backward.

His teeth nipped at my collarbone. "Do you know how many times I've dreamed of fucking you in here?" A hand slid up my ribs to knead my breast.

I arched into his touch, dizzy and overwhelmed while craving more. When his fingers twisted my nipple, my hips jerked against him like there was a direct line between my tits and pussy.

"We don't have much time," I murmured, knowing there was a literal clock ticking down somewhere.

He lifted his head, the impish look in his eyes sending a thrill down my spine. "You know, there's an old wives' tale that athletes shouldn't get off before a game or big match. Apparently the idea is to focus all that pent up aggression on the field." His hand moved aside the collar of my—*his*—shirt and slipped under the cup of my bra to pluck at my sensitive bud.

I whimpered, screwing my eyes shut as I rocked into him.

All at once, he stopped. He pulled his hand out and moved me off his lap.

My eyes snapped open, and disappointment swelled in me.

He shot me a wry smile. "What can I say? I'm superstitious." He slipped off the edge of the table, his front brushing against me.

I moved to step back, trying to ignore the way my pulse thundered in my ears, but his hands shot out and held me still. In one sweeping motion, he spun us and positioned me on the table.

"But that doesn't mean I can't get my girl off," he added with a throaty chuckle that made my lower belly clench.

"Ry—"

"We've gotta be fast, baby," he whispered, cupping the side of my face in his hand and kissing me slowly. The languid, unhurried drag of his kiss was in direct opposition to his words, but I didn't care.

I sank into his kiss, loving the way he moved his lips across mine to coax them open and slip his tongue inside. The sheer rightness of his kiss resonated on a bone-deep level that had me forgetting all the problems in our past.

When his other hand moved between us and cupped me between my thighs, I gasped. He dragged his knuckles up and down my denim-covered slit, adding just enough pressure to drive me crazy but not send me over the edge.

My nails dug into his shoulders as I silently begged for more.

"Hang on, baby," he whispered against my jaw before deftly undoing my pants with his long fingers. He let me go long enough to peel the jeans from my body, my shoes clattering against the floor below.

Sitting on the exam table in a thong with the open and empty locker room at Ryan's back felt all kinds of wicked. A shiver of excitement rippled across my flesh as he moved my panties to the side and sank a finger inside of me.

I groaned at the intrusion, and that broke off into a desperate whine of need when he added a second finger.

"Shhh," he reminded me with a chuckle. "There's probably a guard outside, and the last thing I want is him coming in here." Lust filled his eyes as he glanced down at where his fingers were slowly fucking me. "The only thing coming in here is you, Mads."

I nodded, wanting that, too. I'd been aching for this for days, and it didn't take long to push me over the edge. Ryan's fingers curled, rubbing some magic spot inside of me while his thumb ground down on the bundle of nerves between my legs and I was *gone*.

He kissed me quickly, swallowing my cries as I spasmed around his fingers. When I drooped, boneless and spent, he wound one arm around me to keep me upright while lifting his fingers and sucking them into his mouth.

"You taste fucking incredible," he groaned, his hazy eyes drifting closed to savor my flavor on his tongue.

A long beep signaled the end of the first half beyond the locker room, and I knew our time was almost up. Without a word, Ryan helped me get dressed, knocking my hands aside and zipping up my jeans for me, which worked out well, since I was still trying to remember how to breathe.

I wanted to laugh, but all I could do was moan a little and wrap my arms around him as my legs tried to give out again.

"Maddie."

I glanced up at him and saw a myriad of emotions in his eyes.

"I know," I whispered, my heart reading the look. "Me, too."

Relief shone in his eyes, and he kissed me once more before escorting me through the locker room and into the hallway, where the team was charging in. Most of them ignored me, happy to see Ryan on his feet.

Ash, Court, and Linc paused as they passed me, each smiling and nodding as if giving their blessing on whatever might have just happened. It shouldn't have mattered, but it did.

I returned to my seat feeling more hope than I'd ever thought possible.

CHAPTER 27

MADDIE

As the massive digital numbers overhead counted down the final seconds of the fourth quarter, I couldn't help but grin. The energy in the stadium was electrifying, and it was all because of the man on the sidelines who already had his helmet off and was grinning while he talked to his coach.

Ryan had stormed back onto the field after halftime and hadn't stopped leading an unstoppable offense down the field. The score was a humiliating 47-3. The Knights hadn't just won; they'd crushed the Vipers. The coach had pulled Ryan and most of the first-string guys off the field a few minutes ago, since the Vipers had zero shot at catching them.

As if he knew I was looking, Ryan turned, and his gaze locked with mine. The sexy smile that spread on his lips made me blush.

"Damn," Imani breathed, fanning herself. "I think *I* got pregnant from the way he just looked at you."

I giggled. Freaking *giggled*.

"So, what happened in the locker room again?" Bex teased from my other side, playfully elbowing me.

"Absolutely nothing," I lied, still grinning.

Imani snorted. "Sure. We totally believe you." She gave a low whistle. "Whatever you did, I hope you're ready to do it again before every game if this is how he plays after."

My body throbbed in response. I could definitely get on board with that plan.

The crowd shot to their feet in celebration as the clock zeroed out. I jumped to my feet with them, hugging Bex and Imani as "We Are the Champions" by Queen started to blast over the speakers.

Ryan's teammates swarmed him, but he turned, his gaze once again finding mine. He shrugged them off and charged to the access stairs at the bottom of the stands. Without hesitating, he jogged up the steps until he was at our row. I shimmied past Bex and a few other people, ignoring the fans who were freaking out that Ryan was in their midst.

"What are you doing?" I demanded with a laugh as he reached out and grabbed me around the waist.

"Kissing my girl," he replied before doing just that. His mouth crushed mine, devouring me, as I wrapped my arms around his sweaty neck. There was nothing soft or tentative about this kiss; he used it to claim me in front of thousands of witnesses.

The roaring in my ears turned deafening as fans went crazy. When I pulled back, breathless and amazed, I saw the giant screens over the field were now showing us.

"Meet me outside the locker room," Ryan told me, his blue eyes blazing as his hands tightened on my hips.

I nodded, my lips tingling from his kiss. The feeling spread down to my toes when he flashed me another panty-melting grin before letting me go and running back down the stairs. He was halted a few times by fans desperate for a photo or autograph, and I watched him until he made it back onto the field and was swallowed up by a sea of royal blue.

I mani and I brought Bex with us to the waiting room next to the locker room. Unlike the other times I had walked in there, the eyes staring at me were filled with curiosity as they bounced from me to Imani and back.

"Hey, Imani," one of the girls said from her seat. Her navy blue eyes narrowed as she took in the sight of us together. "Everything cool?"

"Definitely," Imani replied, nothing but confidence in her tone. "Maddie and I were just talking about how we think the guys will go all the way this year."

We hadn't been, but Imani's lie seemed to open whatever social doors had been closed to me.

The girl with navy eyes smiled and toyed with the ends of her auburn hair. "Of course they will. Ryan was okay, wasn't he Lai—I mean, Maddie."

I nodded slowly, feeling like I'd stepped into an alternate universe. A few weeks ago, these women had barely given me the time of day. Now, with one little word from Imani, I was one of them.

"He's great. No concussion or anything," I confirmed when I realized she was waiting for an answer.

The girl beside her turned her wide brown eyes to me. "That kiss at the end of the game? *Damn*, girl." She shook out her blonde hair as the others broke into giggles.

"So fucking *hot*," another girl added.

"You should've seen it from where I was," Imani chimed in, winking at me. "Do you all know Bex?" She introduced my bestie, giving me a chance to retreat farther into the room. I sat down on the three-seater leather couch pushed into one corner.

There were scattered chairs and couches in the room, along with a table full of snacks with the cooler at the end. The room was painted the same royal blue as the guys' jerseys, with the Knights logo in white taking up the far wall. TVs hung in the room, muted with the captions on, while announcers discussed highlights from the game.

Bex and Imani joined me a minute later.

"Thanks for that," I said to Imani as she slid into the seat across from me while Bex sat on the couch. "You didn't have to."

"I know. And as long as you don't regress, we're cool," she replied, shrugging one shoulder. "But if you hop back on the train to Bitch-town..." She let the threat hang between us.

"I have zero intentions of going back to being that girl," I responded as firmly as I could.

Bex leaned against me. "She's different. Really."

"I hope so," Imani murmured, eyeing Bex. "I mean, if *you're* willing to sit next to her? That says some shit."

I smiled at Bex as the door connecting this room to the locker room opened and players started coming in. The noise level instantly ratcheted up several decibels.

Imani was on her feet before Eddie was even through the door. He was just over six feet tall, not the biggest guy on the team, but he was all lean muscles and built for speed and power. When he saw his girl, his white teeth flashed against dark skin, and the smile he gave her was everything. He crossed the room and pulled her to his chest, kissing her soundly. He broke off and looked at me over her shoulder with dark eyes.

"Hey, Maddie," he greeted with a nod. "Ryan's finishing up with the press, so he might be a few more minutes."

"That was an amazing kick in the first half," I replied. "Close to the collegiate record."

Surprise lit his face for a second before he grinned. "Hell yeah, it was."

Imani leaned her head against his chest, her golden eyes staring up at him adoringly. "You'll smash that record, babe."

He smirked down at her. "Right now the only thing I want to smash is—"

She clapped a hand over his mouth and shot us an apologetic smile. "Sorry. He was raised by wolves."

He snorted and moved his face from her hand. "I was going to say my bed, baby. I'm tired." He gave her a knowing look. "What did you *think* I meant?"

217

"Aaand we're leaving," Imani announced. "See you two at the party tonight?"

"Definitely," I agreed.

"Maybe," Bex added.

I turned to her as they left. "*Maybe?*"

She shrugged. "Look, I'm glad that you and Ryan are back to being... well, you and Ryan. But I'm not sure where I fit in with those guys right now."

"Screw them," I told her. "You fit in with *me*."

"Who are we screwing?" Linc asked as he came up behind me.

I whirled around to see him standing there with Court and Ash. No sign of Ryan, which disappointed me more than I'd thought it would.

"No one," Bex answered for me, her tone frosty. "Absolutely *no one*."

Court scoffed and pulled his phone out of his pocket, focusing on the screen.

"Okay," Linc drawled. His gaze drifted over us both. "Ladies. You both look amazing."

I grinned at him, but Bex gave a soft *humph* and pulled out her phone. A second later, she was playing a game and ignoring us.

Ash cleared his throat and gave me a look. "We're going to head back to the house. Do you want to ride with us? Or wait for Ry?"

"I'll wait." The need to see him again was almost overwhelming.

"Thought you'd say that," he replied with an easygoing smile. "Bex? You coming with us?"

Court snorted. "The ice princess probably has better things to do."

She glared at him for a second before turning to Ash with a sweet smile that set off warning bells in my head.

"That depends," she began slowly, "can I sleep in your bed again tonight?"

Linc choked on his own saliva and turned away before he could start outright laughing. Court's face flushed red, his dark eyes fixed on Ash like he was going to murder his friend.

Ash sighed and threw up his hands. "You know what? Sure."

Court hissed out a breath as he turned and stalked away. He slammed against the door with a loud *bang as he went through it.*

"You're playing with fire," Linc taunted, wagging his finger at Bex.

"Put that away before I break it off," she ordered him coolly.

Looking like a puppy who'd been spanked, he withdrew his hand and curled it protectively against his chest. "I think I liked it better when you were quiet."

"I *know* I liked it better when you guys weren't assholes," she shot back.

Linc tilted his head as he studied her. "Bex, we've always been assholes."

"Not to me," she snapped. She ran a hand through her dark hair. "You know what? I think I'll walk back to my dorm. I'm not in a partying mood."

"Bex," I protested. The stadium was still part of the Pacific Cross grounds, but the dorms were a good two-mile walk, and it was getting dark.

She stepped away before I could grab her hand. "Seriously, Maddie. I have a headache, and I just want to go to bed."

"I'll come with you," I told her, wanting to be a supportive friend. If that meant forgoing a night in Ryan's bed with a lot more orgasms...

Damn.

"You're going to Ryan's house tomorrow anyway," she reminded me. "I'm good. I want to be alone."

"Text me later? I mean it, if you need me..."

"I know." She hugged me quickly before stepping back.

"We'll drop you off on our way," Ash told her.

She frowned at him. "It's not on your way." It wasn't; their frat house was in the opposite direction.

"Then we'll make it on our way." Ash shook his head. "No way are you walking home alone in the dark, Bex. We'll drive you."

"You don't have to."

"It wasn't an offer," he said with a thin smile. "You can either get in the car on your own, or I'll have Linc throw you in the backseat."

"And they say chivalry's dead," she deadpanned.

"So, are we kidnapping you or what?" Linc asked, rubbing his hands together and looking at her expectantly.

I pointed a finger at him. "You're way too excited about the idea of kidnapping my best friend."

He shrugged. "It's been a while since we've kidnapped anyone."

I stared at him as Ash slapped the back of his head.

Linc yelped and rubbed his scalp. "I was kidding."

Somehow I didn't think he was.

"Can we go?" Bex snapped. "My headache is getting worse."

"I can rub your head in the car if you want," Linc offered.

"And I can cut your balls off with a rusty spoon if *you* want," Bex returned.

Linc froze. "Somehow threatening, sassy Bex is even hotter than quiet, timid Bex."

"Dude, shut the fuck up," Ash groaned, pushing him toward the door. "Maddie, we'll see you at the house, deal?"

I nodded and watched them leave as I shook my head. When the door swung shut, I glanced around.

Now I was the only one left. Everyone else had already headed out, so I sat back down and pulled out my phone. I killed time waiting for Ryan by playing a mindless game where I shot dozens of tiny balls at bricks to break them apart. I'd crushed eleven levels before the door between this room and the locker room opened once again.

Glancing up, I saw Ryan was standing there, watching me with hungry eyes. I turned off my phone and set it aside.

"Everyone else leave?" he asked in a low, rumbling voice that made my insides tumble.

I nodded and stood up. "Press done?"

He snorted and nodded, his blonde hair a mess and still damp in places. "I hate answering all their questions. Fucking annoying. Especially when I'd rather be doing other things."

My pulse kicked up a notch. "Like what things?"

He smiled and walked slowly toward me, letting the door to the locker room swing shut behind him. "I misspoke."

"Oh?" I arched a brow.

"There's a *person* I'd rather be doing." The smirk playing on his full lips as his gaze devoured me was enough to make my insides start to tremble.

"Do I know this person?" I asked lightly, playing along as he kept stalking toward me, ever the predator hunting his prey.

He chuckled and reached up to stroke his bottom lip with his thumb.

Why was that so fucking sexy?

When he was close enough, his hands shot out and grabbed my hips to pull me against his hard body. A shiver drizzled down my spine when I felt his hard length press against my stomach.

He dropped his head to press his lips to my bare shoulder. He laved open-mouthed kisses across my collarbone and up the side of my throat until he found my mouth.

I groaned as he kissed me, teasing my mouth open with his tongue before stroking inside me with languid thrusts. A whimper slipped out of me as he nipped at my bottom lip.

"Fuck," he murmured, burying his face against the side of my neck as his hips jerked against me. "I feel like a horny thirteen-year-old. This drive home is going to suck ass."

"It's a mile," I said with a laugh, angling my head so he could keep kissing my skin.

His hand slipped under the jersey I'd stolen from him and snaked up my ribcage to palm my breast. His head came up to capture my lips as he pinched my nipple hard. I jerked against him, heat flaring from the pebbled tip and spreading across my chest. He swallowed the moan that tore free when he tweaked my other nipple.

He tore his mouth from mine, his chest heaving. "You have no idea how much I want to strip these jeans off you and fuck you right here."

My tongue darted out to wet my swollen lips. "Sounds good to me."

He smirked down at me, tucking a lock of hair behind my ear as his hand slid back down my hip, and then lower. He cupped me between my legs, grinding the heel of his hand into the denim covering my pussy.

"Shit," I whispered, my eyes screwing shut as arousal saturated my panties. At this point, I'd be lucky to leave without a wet spot on my jeans.

"The next time I'm balls deep in this pussy," he started, rubbing me again and sending shockwaves rippling from my center, "I'm not planning on leaving for a long fucking time."

My breaths came in ragged pants as I looked into his eyes. It was unreal how easily his touch could unravel me.

"Any idea *when* that will be?" I managed to get out.

"As soon as I get you back to my room. In my bed." He pressed down on the bundle of nerves between my thighs once more and I swore I saw stars.

I gripped his shoulders as my knees started to shake.

His free arm wrapped around my back to support me while pinning his hand between us. He left himself enough room to maneuver his hand as he gave me the pressure I needed to feel my orgasm starting to build.

"Ryan," I whispered, my head dropping against his chest as I let the sensations swell inside of me.

He chuckled, the warm sound rumbling between us. "I can feel how wet you are through your jeans, baby. I can't wait to get you in my bed so I can lick you clean."

I cried out, jerked against him as I came hard enough for my legs to give out. He held me up until I found my legs again, then he patted the front of me like my vagina had behaved exactly the way she was supposed to.

Which, fuck it, she had. She was trained to come on command for him at this point.

I lifted my head, breathless and dizzy, and very much aware of the erection nudging insistently on my side.

"Let's go," he murmured, dropping a soft kiss to my lips.

I held him still when he started to move back. "You didn't..."

Another smirk. "I told you. I'm not leaving your pussy once I get back in there, Mads. And the cleanup crew will be through here soon."

I glanced at the doors—one to the locker room, the other to the hallway. Both were closed and everything around us was quiet. "How soon?"

A wrinkle creased his forehead. "What?"

"How soon until they come to clean up?" I clarified.

"Maybe an hour? Definitely not enough time for me to do all the things I want to you," he added.

"But enough for me to do what I want with *you*," I countered, moving out of his arms.

"Maddie—"

He stopped speaking when I lowered myself to my knees. I peered up at him through my lashes, reaching out to slowly open the front of his jeans and tug them down along with the black boxer briefs.

His cock sprang free, hard and heavy. A pearly drop of fluid seeped from the tip. I smeared my thumb across it before bringing my thumb to my lips and sucking it into my mouth.

Ryan's throat worked as he stared down at me. The dark look in his eyes sent a new wave of arousal to my center.

Yeah, there was no saving my panties or my jeans at this point. They were as gone for this man as I was.

Still keeping my eyes on him, I moved closer until I could lick the velvet steel of his tip. His cock jerked in response, and he hissed out a breath, his hands clenched at his sides.

Smiling to myself, I turned my attention to the task literally in front of me. Bracing my hands on his thighs, I sucked him into the wet heat of my mouth until he touched the back of my throat. I gagged a little but forced myself to be still.

"Fuck, Maddie." His voice, raspy and harsh, was all the encouragement I needed to keep going.

I hummed around his length as I lifted my hand to tease the heavy balls between his legs. The grunt of approval from him was accompanied by a hand fisting in my hair.

Typical Ryan. He'd tried to let me take the lead, but it wasn't in his nature to sit back and let anyone else take control.

He angled my head where he wanted me and thrust into my mouth hard enough to make me gag again only to quickly retreat. He fucked my mouth almost lovingly, not pushing me to the limits we both knew he was capable of. He was almost sweet.

And I was almost over it.

I mean, I loved sweet Ryan. But the guy I had fallen for was, as Linc had so eloquently put, an asshole. He didn't handle me like some fragile little doll. Not until recently.

I missed that. I missed the way he would take control and dominate me.

As he pulled back out of me, I let my teeth graze the underside of his cock. He jerked and hissed, stopping immediately. I stared up at him, wondering how I looked from his view—on my knees, spit smeared on my chin, and eyes daring him to do something about it.

The smile he gave me would have terrified the devil.

"Okay," he whispered, his hand stroking the side of my face. "Message received, baby." That was the only warning I got before he thrust back into my mouth, holding himself against the back of my throat until I choked and tears crowded in my eyes.

He pulled out, hands on either side of my head, only to shove right back in, taking from me what he wanted.

I pressed my legs together to try to remove the ache stirring between them. I was seconds away from slipping my hand into my pants when Ryan lightly kicked my knee.

"Uh uh," he grunted, his blue eyes glittering. "You've already come twice today. You don't get to again until later when I say so, and only if you're a good girl."

What the fuck? That was a shitty rule, but I didn't really have time to think about it before he was pushing his dick to the back of my throat.

Again and again and again.

My nails dug into the backs of his thighs as I held on while he used me the way he wanted. It felt good to let go and be his again. I'd missed this; I'd missed *us*.

"Fuck, Maddie," he hissed as his cock jerked in my mouth. "You better swallow every fucking drop." He pressed all the way inside my mouth and came with a guttural groan that I felt down to my toes.

I swallowed him down, taking as much as I could. When he pulled out of my mouth, his hand caught my chin. His eyes narrowed as he gathered the sticky, slick mess around my lips on his thumb and pushed it into my mouth.

I sucked his thumb clean, blinking away the last of the tears in my eyes. My makeup was probably trashed, but I didn't care. I felt alive for the first time in weeks as I kneeled at Ryan's feet.

He grinned at me while tracing my swollen lips with his finger. "Good girl."

CHAPTER 28

MADDIE

When Ryan parked his car in the designated presidential spot at the frat house, I should've known that he and I wouldn't be picking up where we left off. People were everywhere, the celebration of the Knights victory in full swing. A crowd greeted Ryan as soon as he opened the car door, and a beer was pressed into his hands.

And then a pretty girl with a perky set of double Ds propped up and on display in a low-cut shirt laid a hand on his chest.

I practically growled, a little on the feral side since being left hung out to dry in the locker room. Except not much drying had occurred on the short ride over. At this rate, I was going to have a major chafing issue from the soaked panties and wet denim rubbing me raw.

Not that I really cared too much; I could still taste Ryan on my tongue, and my body ached to finish what we'd started. Which was why seeing another girl throw herself at my guy, only a few feet in front of me, was making me feel all kinds of territorial.

I was seconds away from rounding the car and tearing the girl off him when he did it for me. He knocked her hand aside with a glare.

"Don't fucking touch me," he ordered in a cold voice that made her stumble backward in her five-inch stilettos. His lip curled up in disgust as he brushed away whatever imaginary cooties she'd left on his shirt.

The girl tried to slink away, but Ryan apparently wasn't done.

"Leave," he snapped, and the crowd around him fell silent. The bass pumping through the speakers in the houses vibrated around us, like some ominous soundtrack to this girl's humiliation.

I almost felt bad for her as I came around to Ryan's side. He wound an arm around my waist and anchored me to his side, but his gaze was still fixed on the girl who was now desperately looking for an ally in the crowd.

Everyone stared at Ryan, me, or the ground.

"Do you need me to provide you with an escort?" Ryan added in a clipped tone.

She shook her head, her face pale. "No. I mean—I didn't... I'll leave you alone."

"Too late," he retorted. "You've annoyed me, and you've insulted my fiancée. Get the fuck out of here before I have you thrown out like the trash you are."

I winced inwardly because *damn*.

She turned and fled down the driveway on wobbly legs.

"Wasn't that a little harsh?" I whispered.

He shot me a look. "Let me ask you a question. If a guy came up to you or Bex and grabbed you without permission, would you be cool with it?"

"Absolutely not," I replied immediately.

"Then why should a woman be able to touch *me*?" he countered.

He had a good point.

"You're right," I admitted.

His lips curved into a smug smile as he lifted the beer in his hand to his mouth while the hand on my back dipped to the swell of my ass.

Yeah, I was painfully aware of the wet spot between my legs, the damp fabric almost cold now as I moved.

I raised myself up to my tiptoes to whisper in his ear, "I'm going to go change."

His gaze snapped to mine. "No."

My brows slowly climbed. "No?" I repeated, a little dumbstruck.

He grinned and leaned in, his lips brushing my ear. "I like the idea of you thinking about me every time you move."

I wrinkled my nose. "Ryan—"

His teeth bit on my earlobe hard enough to sting. "No, Maddie. Do as I say."

Fuck. That growly tone wasn't helping the situation in my pants.

"I'm not your property," I snapped, keeping my voice quiet because people were still around us. "You can't just order me around."

He pulled back and smirked. "Can't I?"

I scowled at him. "No."

"Let's test that theory, shall we?" The teasing glint in his eyes, coupled with the knowledge that Ryan pretty much owned this school, should've made me rethink what I was saying.

But honestly? Part of me craved this. I loved pushing his buttons and getting him worked up.

His expression softened unexpectedly. "You're right, baby. Let's go upstairs and you can change."

I deflated a little at his sudden change. Even though I was getting what I wanted, I'd been enjoying our game.

Now it looked like sweet Ryan had returned.

He kissed the side of my head. "I'll be back," he told the people still lingering around before threading his fingers with mine and leading me into the house and up the stairs to his bedroom.

I hesitated a minute when we passed Dean's old room. It still creeped me out to be anywhere near a single thing associated with that douche canoe, but Ryan kept going until he'd unlocked his door and ushered me inside.

"Did you want to take a shower?" he offered with a wry smile. He turned away and went over to the nightstand on the side of the bed where he slept and pulled open the drawer.

"No. I just need to change," I replied, frowning a little. I spotted my overnight bag on the chair by his desk and gave myself a mental reminder to thank Ash for bringing it for me when he'd dropped off Bex.

Speaking of, I needed to check in with her at some point. I pulled my phone out and set it on the desk as a visual reminder to check on her once I'd changed.

I unzipped the bag and pulled out new underwear and a pair of skintight pants that cost as much as the down payment on a new Honda.

"Maddie."

"Shit!" My heart leapt into my throat as I whirled around, stunned to see Ryan *right there*. I hadn't even heard him cross the room. "You scared me."

An odd smile played on his lips. "Do you remember when we first met?"

"What?" My nose scrunched up. "When you thought I was Lainey? Yeah. I can't really forget that. I thought you were a psycho." He'd pinned me to Madelaine's bed and threatened me. It had scared the crap out of me.

He chuckled. "I mean, you weren't wrong." His hands landed on my hips, and he whirled me around before shoving me backward. My legs hit the edge of the bed, and I toppled over.

Ryan chased me onto the mattress, straddling my hips as he pinned me with his weight. Before I could fully comprehend what was going on, something hard, but soft, snapped around one wrist and then the other.

I glanced up, stunned to see I was secured to the freaking headboard with leather bands. The asshole had pinned my arms above my head, leaving enough slack for me to wiggle around so my joints weren't stretched to the point of pain, but I was still *handcuffed to the bed*.

"What the hell?" I practically screeched, tugging at the restraints.

Ryan smiled and lifted off of me. "Still think I'm not in control?"

"I still think you're a psycho," I spat. I yanked at the bands again and hissed when they didn't give. At least they were lined with something soft and padded. "Seriously, Ryan, this isn't funny."

He glanced down at me from where he stood at the foot of the bed. "It's a little funny."

I mustered every ounce of annoyance heating my blood and channeled it into a glare. "Let me go."

He rolled his eyes. "I will. Eventually." He turned away and fished his wallet out of his back pocket before tossing it onto his dresser, completely uncaring that I was flopping around like a fish out of water.

I huffed and dropped my head when I realized I wasn't going anywhere unless he uncuffed me.

Motherfucker.

"Okay," I muttered. "Ha-freaking-ha. We'll go party first."

He turned back to me. "No, *I'm* going down to the party. You're staying up here."

I opened my mouth to argue, but he stopped me.

"How about I make it worth your while?" He meandered back to the foot of the bed. He reached down and slowly pulled off my shoes.

I arched a brow, waiting.

"I have to put in an appearance. Have a drink with the team. But for every minute I spend down there, I'll owe you an orgasm this weekend."

It was like my stomach took a header off a thousand-foot cliff.

"Thirty minutes, thirty orgasms," he mused, dragging his teeth across his bottom lip as he watched me with hooded eyes.

Holy shit. Could my body even handle that? I mean, the two orgasms I'd had today had left me wanting a nap. Thirty in three days might actually kill me.

He tapped the top of my foot. "I need an answer, baby."

I swallowed, my mouth suddenly parched. "So, we spend—"

"Uh uh." He shook his head. "You're staying up here. That's the deal."

"Why?" I demanded.

"Because I like knowing you're waiting for me in my bed," he admitted honestly, his gaze caressing my body. "And I can't wait to fuck you while you're wearing my number."

My pussy spasmed, clenching around nothing. His smile grew wider, like he knew the exact reaction I would have to his words.

"Fine," I breathed, wondering if I'd truly lost my mind. I mean… what the hell was I even thinking?

He grinned and held up my phone, then opened the timer app. "You really need to set a password on this thing, baby. But here. Now you can keep track of what I owe you." He moved around the bed to position the phone against the lamp on the bedside table near my head. Then he leaned over and kissed me.

It ended way too fast for my liking, and I sighed unhappily as he walked toward the door.

I glanced up at my bound arms. "Don't I need a safe word or something?"

He laughed. "No. You just have to trust me."

My heart seized in my chest, and I swallowed the impulse to say, *I do.*

For the second time tonight, his expression gentled. "If you really want me to stop this game right now, I will. But I'm hoping you'll give me a chance. I'm not going to let you down again, Maddie. I promise. Are you in?"

Trying to regroup, I glanced at the timer. I sighed softly, letting go and praying this was the right call. "One minute down. You really want to keep racking up time?"

The slow grin that spread across his face was all the confirmation I needed in my gut to know I'd made the right call.

He snapped his fingers, as if something had just occurred to him. "Shit, you know what? I forgot." He went to the bed and quickly undid the button of my jeans, peeling them *and* my panties down my legs so I was completely nude from the waist down.

I let out a wholly undignified squeal and pressed my legs together.

His dark chuckle was the stuff nightmares and dreams were spun from. "What? You said you were uncomfortable. We can't have that."

"Ryan," I hissed, embarrassed and a little turned on. "Pants! I need them!"

"You really don't," he drawled, his hungry gaze studying between my legs. His tongue darted out to lick his lips. "God, I love your pussy. So fucking pink and wet and perfect."

A groan worked its way out of my throat, and I felt it get a whole lot wetter.

He ran his thumb across his bottom lip. "Have I mentioned how good you taste? I wonder how many times you can come on my tongue before you black out. That could be fun, right?"

And now I was panting, my chest heaving as my nipples tingled and tightened at his filthy words.

"Maddie?"

My gaze snapped to his.

"Do you trust me?" He touched my ankles and slowly spread my legs until he'd created a space to kneel between them.

"Ask me something else," I whispered, shaking my head.

He grimaced a bit, crawling over my body until his hands were on either side of my head. "Do you trust me?"

Tears pricked my eyes. "It's not that easy."

"It can be," he murmured, reaching up to adjust my head so his pillow was under it. The scent of him filled my nostrils, and it smelled like home.

"Trust. Me." He was asking, his blue eyes searching mine for the answers he needed.

The walls around my heart started to crumble. When I blinked, a tear fell free. He dipped his head, catching it with his lips as he kissed it away. "Madison, trust me and I'll give you everything."

"And if I say no?"

His lips twitched, almost sadly. "Then I'll still give you everything. I love you, Mads. I didn't even know what that word meant until you came into my life."

"If you break my heart again, it'll destroy me," I told him, barely able to speak around the lump of emotion lodged in my throat.

He didn't flinch as he met my gaze. "If I break your heart again, it'll break *me*, Maddie. Please. *Trust me.*" This was as close to begging as Ryan Cain would ever come, and he was doing it for me.

"I trust you." The words detonated between us, and I felt the shift in the atmosphere. A weight I hadn't known I was carrying lifted from my shoulders, freeing some of my burdens.

I was hopelessly, utterly screwed, because there wasn't a part of me that didn't still love this man. I wanted to trust him; I *needed* to trust him. I'd been so alone for most of my life, and then I'd been given a taste of what it felt like to be the center of someone's world.

A beautiful smile crawled across his face, and then he was kissing me. His tongue licked at the seam of my mouth, coaxing my lips open so he could take everything I had left to give. His kisses were my own personal drug; addictive and heady.

He pulled back, shifting his weight to one hand as he reached back into the nightstand.

Hopefully for a key, because I wanted to wrap my arms around him.

But, when he moved back over me with a wicked smirk on his face, I had a feeling I wasn't about to be uncuffed. His hand slipped between my legs, a blunt finger circling my clit twice before sinking into my heat with ease.

"So fucking perfect," he whispered, kissing my lips softly. He withdrew his finger, and I felt something slightly bigger than his finger slip into me.

"What are you doing?" I asked, my eyes wide as he removed his hand and licked his finger clean.

"Playing with my girl," he answered, grinning. He looked at the clock. "We're already up to eight minutes, and I haven't even gotten downstairs yet."

"You could just stay here with me," I tried, moving to hook a leg around his waist.

Ryan chuckled and got off the bed. I felt his absence like a physical blow, and my body wanted him back.

"Still trust me?" he pressed, arching a brow.

I gave him an unamused look. "I'm having second thoughts, actually." I squeezed my legs together, feeling whatever was between them refusing to give. What the hell had he put inside me?

"It's a vibrator," he informed me, likely noticing me trying to work it out. He pulled his phone out of his pocket and unlocked it. "There's an app, so while I'm downstairs, you can start knocking off some of those orgasms I owe you."

My jaw dropped. "You... *What?*" *Oh shit.* With my hands bound, I wouldn't be able to take it out or... "Did I somehow miss your kinky side before?"

He tilted his head, amused. "I like control, Maddie. More specifically, I like controlling *you.*"

Those words really shouldn't have turned me on the way they did. Dammit. I was going to have to burn my feminist card.

"And yeah, maybe I played it a little on the safe side with you when we first got together, but if we're really going to do this, I'm done hiding pieces of myself from you. Starting with the fact that I like having you tied up and helpless while I drive your body crazy."

Heat flashed through me, and I felt my nipples pebble at his words.

He turned the phone so I could see the app, his thumb poised over a button. "What do you say?"

I looked at the door. "What if someone comes in?"

"No one will," he assured me. "Trust, remember?"

My hands curled into useless fists. "Trust, right. Fuck me."

"Soon," he added, his gaze electric as it moved over me. "You good here?"

"Will you let me go if I say no?" I challenged, rolling my eyes.

He grimaced. "Yes. Say *no* and this ends now. I won't try anything like it again."

I glanced at the clock and clicked my tongue against my teeth. "Thirteen minutes. You better move your ass."

"See you soon, baby." He winked at me before he left the bedroom. I heard the sound of the door lock.

I stared at the ceiling for a beat before glancing at the timer.

I squeezed my eyes shut and tried to drown out the party happening two floors below, but the bass seemed to sync up with my thundering pulse. My skin prickled with awareness, and I huffed out an annoyed breath.

The sudden vibration in my pussy made me cry out, my back arching off the bed. In less than a minute, I was panting and writhing, desperate for release.

And then, just as fast as it had started, it stopped.

I was going to kill Ryan.

CHAPTER 29

RYAN

If it wasn't for the fact that I knew my team needed me, I'd be balls deep inside the best pussy I'd ever had. Instead, I was standing outside as the party raged on around me, sporting a fucking epic woody while trying not to look at my phone too much.

Between this season and last, team morale was a roller coaster. Tonight's win had us on an uphill swing, but I knew it was crucial for us to be a united group.

Even if all I wanted was my girl.

Unable to resist, I pulled out my phone and bypassed the app I'd been using to drive Maddie crazy since I'd left her. I logged in to the secure footage link that Ash had set up in my room last year and tapped the icon for the live feed. I was immediately greeted by the sight of Maddie, handcuffed and sprawled across my bed as her legs trembled with the force of the orgasm I'd let her have a minute earlier.

She was perfect. And completely fucking *mine*.

I finished the rest of my beer before pocketing my phone and turning to make an excuse to leave.

Ash smirked at me, the fucker.

"What?" I demanded, trying to play it cool.

"Haven't seen Maddie all night," he commented with a nonchalant shrug. He tipped his own beer to his lips. "I thought she was coming over with you."

"She did. She's in my room."

His gaze sharpened. "Doing what?"

I met his gaze evenly. "Whatever the fuck I want her to do."

A begrudging smile inched across his face. "Does that mean you two have sorted your shit out?"

"It means she's accepted I'm not letting her go," I admitted, remembering the way she'd teared up when she'd finally admitted she could trust me again. She was breaking down as she built me up. I would spend the rest of my life proving I was worthy of her—her love, her trust, just fucking *her*.

Ash's bemused expression turned serious. "Don't fuck this up, Ry."

I almost bristled, but some deep part of me knew he was trying to give me solid advice. "Maddie's it for me," I admitted softly, letting the truth be known between us. "I don't fucking deserve her, but I can't let her go. I won't. She's mine, and she has been since that night I realized who she was."

He clapped a hand on my shoulder. "You're going to have to let her in. All the way, man. Your dad, Phoenix... You're going to have to lay it all on the table."

"I plan to," I replied. Tonight was the last piece of the puzzle I'd needed to fall into place. Maddie was where she belonged, and this was the first time in a long time that I felt absolutely sure about us. Sure that we could handle anything. "Once I get through this weekend at home with our dads, I'm telling her everything."

"Good. It's about fucking time." Ash shoved me away with a smirk.

I glanced around, ready to wrap this up. The team was celebrating —some by finding a willing girl or two and hooking up, others by drinking, and a few by just chilling. The party was a success, and I could make my exit. Fucking finally.

Unlocking my phone once more, I turned the vibrator up to one of the higher settings and went to get my girl.

W hen I'd first moved into my room, I'd spent a weekend with the guys making sure it was soundproof. Not that I had a problem with the guys' hearing a new girl scream my name, but because these fuckers were nosier than an old folks' home of church matrons.

In our world, knowledge was power, and finding out secrets was the ultimate currency. It was why I kept my room locked and had security cameras installed after Madelaine's betrayal last year. I guarded my privacy as closely as possible.

Even still, as I unlocked the door, I could hear Maddie's muffled curses as she moaned. My dick was practically punching its way out of my jeans as I stepped inside. I turned off the vibe with a swipe of my finger.

"Motherfucking fucker," Maddie panted, her eyes screwed shut as I cut off her ascent up the hill toward another orgasm. "I swear, I'm going to—"

"Going to what?" I asked, cutting her off as I closed the door and locked it.

Her eyes popped open, and she turned to glare at me, her cheeks flushed and strands of hair stuck to her sweaty forehead.

"You're an asshole," she spat. "Do you know how many times I've been *right there*, and you stopped the damn thing?"

I smirked, because of course I knew. It had been intentional. I'd let her have one in the beginning, but for the last ten minutes, I'd been intentionally dragging my girl along a razor's edge of pleasure and denying her because I wanted all of her orgasms. I wanted her strangling my dick as she convulsed around me. I wanted her flavor exploding on my tongue as I licked her into oblivion.

I wanted every fucking thing from this girl, and tonight, I was going to start taking it.

I reached behind me and fisted the material of my shirt, then pulled it over my head. The smirk that crept across my face when Maddie's hungry gaze devoured me was impossible to suppress. This girl was fucking dangerous for my ego.

238

She rolled her eyes and let out a little huff. "Yes, you're gorgeous. You know it, I know it... Everyone knows it." Her lips puckered in a sour expression. "Including that girl who was all over you when we got here."

"Jealous?" The idea of her jealousy shouldn't have made me as happy as it did.

She shot me a droll look before glancing up at her bound hands. "Honestly? I'm not sure which one of us made out better tonight. I'm kind of doubting *she's* tied up like a criminal."

With a chuckle, I grabbed her ankles and pulled her down the bed so her hands, still bound, stretched above her head in a way that pushed her full tits up to strain against the front of my jersey. My dick jerked, aching to be inside her.

"You look good enough to eat," I murmured, brushing my thumb against my lower lip as I watched her.

Her cheeks flushed an addictive shade of pink that I wanted to see on her face every single day for the rest of our lives. I moved to stand at the foot of the bed, my gaze traveling up her insanely long legs, which felt like heaven wrapped around my waist when I was pounding into her. But the glistening skin between her legs, swollen and red and soaked, was my own personal nirvana.

Something that sounded like a half-moan, half-whimper slipped from her lips and she pressed her legs together. I reached out and shoved them apart, not done looking at her.

"Ryan." My name was a breathless gasp as her hips lifted off the bed, seeking what I'd been denying her for the past twenty minutes.

I knelt on the edge of the bed and lifted one leg to balance her foot on my shoulder. Turning, I kissed the inside of her ankle. Goosebumps broke out across her calf, and she shivered under me.

I took my time, moving down the sweet length of her leg, peppering kisses across her flesh until a breath separated my mouth from her pussy. She seemed to freeze, even her breathing silenced as she waited for what came next.

I lowered her leg and started the same treatment up her other leg. When she huffed out a frustrated breath, I reached into my back pocket and pulled out my phone. Opening the app I'd been using all night, I turned the vibrator inside her onto a medium setting. Her body jolted, a curse flying from her mouth that morphed into a groan I felt in my bones.

She was practically twitching under me when I reached her center once more. Instead of backing away, I swiped the flat of my tongue up her slit before suckling her clit into my mouth as hard as I could.

A loud cry pierced the room as she came. I kept sucking on the bundle of nerves between her legs, dragging out her orgasm. Her body spasmed and bowed off the bed, her legs shaking uncontrollably.

Reaching up, I plucked the vibrator from her soaked pussy and replaced it with two of my fingers as I lapped up all of her honey. God, she tasted fucking divine. I curled my fingers inside her, rubbing at the spot I knew would send her flying again.

"No!" she practically shrieked, trying to twist her hips away as her head thrashed back and forth. "Ryan—I can't. It's too... *fuck*. It's too much."

I chuckled and worked a third finger into her, stretching her, as I grazed my teeth across her clit. She came again with a fresh gush of arousal that coated my lips and hand.

Aftershocks rippled through her as I slowly relented and eased my fingers out of her. She clamped around me briefly, her body not wanting to let me go. I kissed the top of her pussy before moving up her body.

Her chest heaved between us, and the dazed look in her eyes made my chest swell with pride because I'd rocked her fucking world.

And I wasn't close to done.

I kissed her, pushing my tongue into her mouth and forcing her to taste herself on my lips. My hips ground against her, the denim causing enough friction to make her flinch a second before her eyes rolled back in her head and she groaned.

"You're so fucking perfect," I whispered, kissing the underside of her jaw.

"I think you killed me," she mumbled, shaking her head slowly.

I grinned against her neck. "We're just getting started, baby. By my count, I still owe you another thirty-nine."

"Maybe we need to work out some kind of payment plan," she joked.

I pulled back and studied her. "Need a break?"

Her eyes narrowed for a brief second, some of that fire I loved in her coming back. "I can handle whatever you're giving, Cain."

She was so perfect for me.

"I need to ask you something first," I said reluctantly, needing an answer to a question that had been plaguing me since she'd returned. Now, seeing her here like this, I couldn't ignore the obvious.

She cocked an eyebrow.

My hand settled on her hip and I schooled my features so I wouldn't wince at the sharp angle of her hip bone digging into my palm. "We need to talk about *this*."

She stilled, her gaze shuttering before my eyes. "That's not a question."

"Fine," I corrected, swallowing down my urge to say something sarcastic. "What's with the sudden weight loss? And the weird as fuck diet? Since when do you care what you eat?"

Her lips flattened into a mulish line. "What's that supposed to mean? I can't care about the way I look?"

"You absolutely can," I shot back, some of the heat I'd been trying to rein in filtering through. She was trying to deflect, and that was insulting as hell. "But *you* don't. I fucking love

That you didn't worry about every calorie that passes your lips, like ninety-nine percent of the other chicks around here. And I loved that I didn't have to feel like I was going to snap you in half if I wanted to pound into you as hard as I wanted."

Her eyes flashed. "I won't break because I lost a few pounds." She looked away from me like she was... ashamed?

I forced myself to stay calm, knowing she was trying to pick a fight. We both had a tendency to jump into *fight mode* when cornered. "Maddie, stop twisting what I'm saying. I'm worried, baby."

She glanced away and stared at the wall. "Did it ever occur to you that maybe I haven't had much of an appetite since you blew my world apart?"

Fuck, that hurt so goddamn much.

She squirmed, and not in the way I'd been craving. A look of doubt crossed her face, and it damn near broke my heart when she whispered, "Can you let me go, please?"

From the handcuffs? Sure. From my life? Never.

"I'm sorry, baby," I whispered, reaching up and unlocking her hands, because I needed to wrap my arms around her and feel her hold me back. I pulled her onto my lap so her legs straddled me, her bare ass balanced on my thighs as I hugged her to my chest. After a beat, a shudder rippled through her, and she wound her arms around my neck, clinging to me.

I smoothed a hand down her back, before massaging her shoulders in case there was any lingering ache. I felt like an asshole when she shivered. I shouldn't have pushed her tonight. I'd come so fucking close to losing her for good, and I still probably needed to take it slow.

The problem was, slow wasn't in my nature. And after what had happened in the locker room and then tonight... I'd thought Maddie wanted more. It had felt like we were moving past the nightmare of the last few weeks.

I cleared my throat. "Why don't you take the bed tonight? I can sleep on the couch, or crash downstairs so you can be alone."

Her head snapped back, her cornflower blue eyes wide. "What? *No.* That's not what I want."

"Maddie—"

Her hands came up to frame my face. "I want *you*, Ryan. God help me, but I do. I shouldn't. And yeah, there's still a huge part of me that's worried you'll change your mind *again* and this will all come crashing to an end, but..." Her eyes squeezed shut. "I'm so tired of fighting."

The corner of my mouth hooked up. "Are you sure? I'm kind of a handful."

"I want all of you. Every piece. The good and the bad, the light and the dark."

I hesitated. "My dark is pretty fucking black, Madison. I've done shit that if you knew…"

"I can take it," she said fiercely, her eyes narrowed as if daring me to contradict her. My fucking little warrior.

"I'll tell you everything. It's too much to get into tonight," I added, "but as soon as we're done at my dad's tomorrow, I'll tell you whatever you want to know. But once you know, there's no going back."

"Going back stopped being an option the day I took over Madelaine's life," she told me. "But I need to know that we're in this together."

I nodded slowly. "Okay, baby."

She smiled at me for a beat, then tilted her head. "So… is break time over?" She wiggled her hips, pressing against my dick. The little bit it had deflated during our serious talk was gone as it turned to fucking stone.

I barked out a laugh. "Ready for more?"

"I'm ready for everything," she confessed, a little shyly, "as long as you're with me."

I smirked and deposited her on the bed before I got up and went to my dresser. I opened the top drawer and found what I was looking for, then turned and went back to her.

Grabbing her left hand, I tugged off that gaudy rock that cost a fortune and meant nothing. Without thinking, I tossed it into the trash by my desk.

"Ryan!" Her eyes widened.

I pushed my grandmother's ring back onto her finger where it belonged. "I'm with you, Madison. Yesterday, today, and every fucking tomorrow." I kissed the back of her hand reverently, then I pressed my own hand between her tits and pushed her back onto the bed.

She smiled at me, and the trust and innocence in her gaze was like a punch to the dick. How the fuck had I gotten this lucky? I sure as shit hadn't earned it, but I'd hold on to it with everything I had.

I covered my body with hers, capturing her mouth in a searing kiss as her fingers scratched down my abs and fumbled with the button of my jeans. When she worked the front open, her small hand slipped inside and squeezed my cock.

"Fuck," I hissed, breaking the kiss to drop my forehead onto her shoulder.

She helped push my jeans and boxers out of the way, and then guided me inside her. I slammed into her, bottoming out on the first thrust. We both groaned as her pussy pulsed around me, holding me tight in her wet heat.

I pulled out and drove back in with enough force to move her up an inch on the bed. She wrapped her legs around my waist, pulling me in deeper.

"Harder," she begged, her nails scouring my back in a way that was sure to leave marks I'd be wearing tomorrow.

Grunting, I changed the angle, knowing I'd hit the right spot when her pussy convulsed and her gaze grew unfocused. I made it my mission to hit that spot as many times as I could before she exploded.

I managed seven more thrusts before her entire body went rigid and then seized, a sharp cry piercing the space between us as she milked me for everything I had. I groaned as lightning zipped down my spine, and I emptied myself inside of her.

Breathing harder than I had after the game, I collapsed onto her chest, my face pressed against my jersey. Her fingers came up to absently stroke my head.

"Thirty-eight to go," she mumbled. "You really might kill me before the weekend is over."

I lifted my head to look at her. "Want me to stop?"

Her eyes narrowed in a playful way that had my dick starting to get hard again. She licked her lips. "Never."

CHAPTER 30

MADDIE

A shudder rolled down my spine as Ryan turned the car into the long driveway leading to the sprawling Cain Estate. My stomach churned as I stared up at the three-story monstrosity with its manicured lawns and marble statues. On the outside, this house was an architectural dream, but I knew the man who owned it was an asshole of the highest order.

Seeing Beckett Cain wasn't high on the list of activities I wanted to partake in. It fell somewhere between using a stranger's toothbrush and playing tag with a rabid wolf.

Ryan reached across the console and laced his fingers with mine, giving me a reassuring squeeze. My skin prickled with awareness as I reacted to his touch. Last night had been amazing. Freaking amazing.

We'd gone several rounds, and I'd grabbed only a little bit of sleep throughout the night. I'd woken up this morning with one of Ryan's hands curled possessively around my breast, the other nestled between my thighs. As soon as he'd realized I was awake, he'd languidly stroked an orgasm out of me with his fingers before rolling me onto my back and impaling me with his hard cock.

By my count he'd knocked ten orgasms off the tally he owed me. It might have been eleven, but I wasn't entirely sure if that time in the middle of the night when I'd slipped in and out of consciousness, his face buried in my pussy, was actually real or a dream.

But as Ryan parked his car in front of the stairs leading to the house, everything in me shriveled up.

"In and out, baby," he murmured, looking at the house. His gaze cut to me. "At least Cori will be happy to see you."

My spirits lifted at the thought of Ryan's younger sister, Corinne. She was an absolute sweetheart who had a few learning disabilities, giving her this eternal innocence that Beckett was all-too-ready to decimate if Ryan didn't toe the line.

Make that if Ryan and I didn't toe the line. If I didn't marry Ryan and produce a baby so that Ryan could claim some familial inheritance, Beckett had made it clear he wouldn't lose any sleep marrying off Corinne to some asshole with the sole purpose of knocking her up. She was barely eleven.

I fucking hated that prick.

After giving Ryan a small smile, I let go of his hand and climbed out of the low sports car. It took a little maneuvering to make sure I didn't flash anyone who might be standing near a window. As I shut the door, a clap of thunder echoed overhead. Gray clouds swirled ominously, and the palm trees lining the driveway swayed. The uncharacteristic Southern California storm left heavy shadows across the grounds of the Cain Estate.

Ryan came around the car and grabbed my hand in his before leading me up the stairs. As he reached for the bell, the door swung open, and the butler greeted us.

"Mr. Cain, Miss Cabot." He inclined his balding head and stepped back to allow us entry. Once he closed the door, the silence in the large foyer became a living, breathing thing, waiting for whatever was going to happen next.

I glanced around the imposing entrance. A grand, sweeping staircase curved up the right side with gold spindles and a gleaming matching railing. Old and probably pricey artwork that looked hideous to me hung on the white walls, making the space seem more like a museum than a home.

The formal sitting room to the left was closed off behind glass doors, but I could see inside to the pristine white furniture and carpets against a rich dark wood floor. The huge foyer with marble floors extended down a long hallway that I knew from experience led to a kitchen a chef would salivate over.

Everything was so cold and antiseptic. It actually made me miss my tiny little trailer in Michigan. At least that had felt like an actual home.

"Where's my father?" Ryan asked, his indifferent tone at odds with the gentle way he held my hand.

"In his study. Can I get either of you anything?" The man looked bored out of his mind as he spoke. The bushy white mustache over his lip twitched as his small brown eyes studied us.

"No, Thomas," Ryan said with a shake of his head, dismissing him.

"Very well, sir. Lunch will begin at half past one. We're waiting on Mr. Cabot. His plane was delayed."

My spine stiffened. I hadn't spoken to him since the night Adam had paid me a visit, and I wasn't looking forward to our reunion.

Ryan's hand tightened around mine, like he knew the wave of anxiety roiling through my stomach was sending me into freak out territory.. "Where's my sister?"

Before he could barely finish the question, a shrill squeal rang out from the top of the curved staircase. Shoes clomped down the steps at a rapid pace as Cori practically tripped over her feet trying to get to her brother. I managed to step away before the tiny blonde tornado threw herself into his waiting arms.

I smiled, watching them reunited.

"You're here!" Cori cried, her voice echoing in the vast space.

"Hey, kiddo," Ryan greeted, the affection in his voice making my insides gooey.

But that was shattered a second later when an annoyed voice bellowed, "What the fuck is that racket?" A door down the hall slammed open and Beckett stormed into the hallway.

Corinne cringed, letting go of Ryan and ducking her head as her brother maneuvered her behind him. I reached for her hand, feeling the need to shield her as her father glared like she was the root of every problem he'd ever had.

Not even my drugged-out Mom in her coke-induced rage black-outs looked at me with as much hate and contempt as Beckett did his daughter.

"She was just saying hi." Ryan cut off his father coldly.

Beckett didn't spare his son a look. He was still focused on Cori, who was trembling beside me. "What have I told you?"

"To be quiet when you're working," Cori replied in a teeny tiny voice that wobbled with fear. She pressed harder against my side.

"Why is that so difficult for you to understand?" he went on, a vein popping out in his neck. "How stupid can you be?"

"Enough!" Ryan barked, his hands balled into fists at his sides. I tugged Corinne back in case things turned violent.

Honestly? I was kind of hoping Ryan decked his dad. I'd probably even use these pointy as hell shoes to land a kidney shot while he was on the ground.

"I'm sorry," Corinne whispered, tears rolling down her pale cheeks.

"Yes, you are," Beckett sneered before turning away from her in disgust. He turned his ire on Ryan. "Don't tell me how to handle *my* daughter."

"Maybe when you act like a father, I won't give you shit about the way you treat her," Ryan snarled in return.

Still seething, Beckett turned his cold blue eyes to me. His lip curled. "Well, if it isn't the little whore."

It's not like I'd anticipated Beckett would roll out the welcome mat for me, but seriously? Ryan stepped forward and shoved his father back a step. "Watch yourself, old man."

Beckett laughed, the caustic sound bouncing around. "Seriously? You're that pussy whipped already by a tight—"

"It's vital to you keeping all your goddamn teeth that you don't finish that sentence," Ryan spat, his shoulders rising with heavy breaths.

I shot Beckett a glare with as much hate as I could channel and then turned to Cori, smoothing out my expression. "Hey, why don't we go upstairs?" I suggested, wanting to get this sweet little girl as far away from her douchenozzle dad as possible.

She gave a hesitant smile, and I caught Ryan's eye. He gave a subtle nod of approval, and I hurried Corinne upstairs. The shouting began anew before we were halfway up.

I'd been in Corinne's room only one other time, so I let her lead the way and made sure I closed the door tight after we were inside. But then I froze, my puzzled gaze taking in everything I was seeing.

Or *wasn't* seeing.

"Cori," I started slowly, "where's your stuff?" When I'd been here a few weeks ago for her birthday, this room had been full of stuffed animals and everything pink that a princess could want. Now the walls were a pale gray, and there was a gray and lemon chevron striped duvet on her bed.

The only personal touch I spotted was a picture of Ryan and Corinne at the beach from a few years earlier, sitting on the glass nightstand by her bed.

She wandered to the bed and jumped on the edge, swinging her legs. "Daddy said I'm an adult now. I have to act like it. And big girls don't have toys."

Motherfucking Beckett Cain. If Ryan didn't kill him, I would.

Corinne was *eleven*. She should absolutely still have toys and stuffed animals and whatever the hell else normal little girls had in their bedrooms.

"What did it mean?" she asked suddenly, lifting her heart-shaped face with those Cain blue eyes that reminded me so much of her brother.

I frowned and walked over to her. "What did what mean, honey?"

"Whore?" The dirty word in her innocent mouth was just fucking wrong.

I grimaced and crouched in front of her. "It's a mean word."

Her brow wrinkled. "Daddy says it a lot. Sometimes on the phone. Sometimes when he's mad, and sometimes when he has women over to visit and his voice gets all weird, like when I get sick."

I didn't want to think of the pussy parade Beckett probably strolled through this house, and I hated that Cori had to live here.

"It's not a nice word," I said carefully. "We shouldn't say it."

Her eyes rounded. "Okay. I'm sorry."

"You don't have to be sorry," I assured her, pushing to my feet. "Have you been practicing your cartwheels?"

Her face brightened. "Yes! I'm getting better!"

I glanced at the window and saw rain starting to splatter the glass. Next time I came over I hoped we could go outside to practice.

"Want to know a secret?" Corinne whispered.

My gaze shot to her, my lips turning up. "Sure."

"I hid Majesty," she confided, her eyes huge.

It took me a second to remember the white and black dog with strands of sparkly pink tinsel in its synthetic fur. It had been a birthday present, and she'd adored it.

I looked around. "Where?"

Her soft voice lowered. "In Ryan's room."

My brows shot up.

"Daddy never goes there," she said quickly. "And I didn't think Ryan would mind. She's in his closet, in his old football bag."

Thunder rumbled overhead, and she jumped. Panic filled her eyes as she looked at the window.

"It's just a storm," I promised.

Her lower lips trembled. "I hate it. I want my puppy." Her gaze shot to the door. "But Daddy might be out there. If he sees her, he'll get big mad."

My lips twitched. Hearing her say that would've been adorable if not for the obvious fear. "Big mad, huh?"

She nodded.

"What if *I* go get Majesty?" I whispered. "Ryan's room is at the end of the hall, right?" There was no way Beckett and Ryan were done shouting at each other yet, so I'd likely be able to slip in and out.

"You'd do that?"

I nodded, and she sprang off the bed to wrap her arms around my waist. "Thank you, Maddie."

I stroked her soft hair. "Wait here, okay?" I turned and hurried from the room and down the hall to the last door. Pushing it open, I stepped into Ryan's world.

It was a shame I didn't have time to dive into what was clearly teenage Ryan's domain. The room was dark, the navy painted walls and black wood furniture making it seem like a cave. The massive king-size bed stood prominently across from a wall of floor-to-ceiling windows that were covered by heavy drapes that blotted out the sun.

I gave the room a cursory look, taking in the sitting area with a recliner and a sofa in front of a massive TV mounted to a wall. Several gaming consoles and controllers sat on the cube shelving unit beneath it. There was an empty desk and a bookshelf full of old textbooks and framed photos. I spotted an en suite through a door near the bed, which meant the door near the desk was probably the closet.

Pulling it open, I searched for a light switch. Of course it was a massive walk-in closet. And it smelled like Ryan as I entered and started looking around for the old football bag. Finally spotting the beaten-up blue bag, I pulled it out and unzipped it. Tucked under an old PCA playbook was Majesty.

I yanked the dog up and started to stand when I heard someone in the bedroom. Thinking it had to be Ryan, I poked my head out.

My heart dropped when the wrong pair of blue eyes stared back at me.

"What are you doing in here?" I asked Beckett, dropping the stuffed dog and kicking it under a rack of shirts.

Beckett smirked at me. "I own this house, remember?" He nudged the door shut, and my insides clenched.

Not liking how I was backed into the closet, I came out.

"Why are *you* in here?" he asked in a soft tone, a strange sort of smile on his lips.

I lifted my chin. "Where's Ryan?"

"Busy." He glanced around the room. "Looking for something else to use against my son?"

My eyes narrowed. "No."

He chuckled. "Pity. That last stunt…" He slowly walked toward me, pausing when he was inches away. His hand came up and touched the ends of my hair. "That was brilliant."

"B-brilliant?" I stammered, my heart thundering in my chest. I took a step back and hit the door.

His smile grew as he closed the space between us, his hand sliding around to cup the back of my neck in a way that was wildly inappropriate. "And the look on your father's face... Fucking genius, pulling that shit at the engagement party."

I was too stunned by what he was saying, what he was *doing*, to move. Hell, I was barely able to breathe as my hands hung limp at my sides.

His hands had no such issue; the hand not wrapped around the back of my neck settled on my hip and squeezed.

"When you proposed humiliating Gary and Ryan months ago, I never imagined that you would be so creative." His cheek pressed against mine, his teeth nipping my earlobe. "You really are my good little whore, aren't you?"

I shuddered as the words of his initial greeting took on a whole new meaning. Unfortunately, he clearly misunderstood my horror and revulsion for permission. He pressed against me, rubbing himself against my stomach.

"I deposited your part of the money in your account, but I hope that's not the end of our time together." He licked up the column of my throat.

That snapped me out of whatever the hell alternate world I'd stumbled into. My hands flew up, grabbing his arms and trying to push him away. "I'm marrying Ryan."

His eyes glittered with amusement as he lifted his head to look me in the eye. "You know, Laine, I almost bought this reformed-slut routine until that night. But you'll always be the girl who crawled into my bed last year because she knew which Cain had the *real* power."

Oh, fuckity fucking *fuck*. What had my twin done *now*?

"Okay, wait—"

Beckett silenced me by slamming his mouth down on mine. I gasped, in horror, and he used the opportunity to shove his tongue into my mouth. His hips ground into my stomach, pinning me against the door. I couldn't move. I tried shoving at him, but he didn't budge.

"What the fuck?"

I didn't think things could possibly get worse, but hearing Ryan's stunned voice made me realize how wrong I was.

Beckett's head lifted, and Ryan's surprise arrival unbalanced him enough for me to shove him away.

I stared at Ryan, my heart falling to my feet at the fury in his eyes. I'd seen that look before, and I wanted to cry.

"Ryan." Beckett adjusted his shirt and smiled at his son like this was totally normal behavior. "Did you finish your phone call?"

Ryan's face flushed. "Seriously? That's all you're going to say?"

The corner of Beckett's mouth curved. "What? You want an apology? Grow the fuck up. Maybe if you acted like a man, you could hang on to a woman."

Ryan's gaze cut to me. "Get out."

Horror washed over me. No, no. He *had* to understand. "Ryan—"

"Get. *Out*," he hissed, eyes flashing dangerously. He stepped away from the door, clearing a path for me.

I dipped my head to hide my tears as I ran out of the room.

CHAPTER 31

MADDIE

Every part of me wanted to run and hide, but there was nowhere to go. Ryan had driven us here, and even if I could somehow manage to get his keys, I still didn't know how to drive. I didn't even know my way around this damn house to find a private corner to regroup in.

Not that what had happened upstairs was in any way my fault, but before, it had obviously been Madelaine screwing around on Ryan. I couldn't claim that when he'd walked in on his dad shoving his tongue down my throat and grinding on me like a rail at a skateboard park.

But would he understand that I hadn't wanted any of that; that I'd tried to stop it?

"Maddie?" Corinne's soft voice diverted my inner freakout, and I turned to see her door cracked as she peered out. "I heard more yelling."

I quickly went into her room and closed the door. "It's okay."

"Majesty?" Her face fell when she realized I didn't have the dog. Another boom of thunder shook the house, and she let out a soft scream before diving for my waist and hugging me.

"She's still in Ryan's room in the closet. Your dad caught me—"

Her head tipped back, eyes wide. "Did he hurt you?"

My eyes narrowed, concern replacing my panic. "No. Why? Does he hurt *you*?"

Her gaze jerked away, and she gave a small, unconvincing shake of her head.

"Cori, if your dad is hurting you—"

"He just says mean stuff," she mumbled, burying her face against my chest. "But he's my daddy, so he loves me. I make him angry because I'm stupid. I need to be better."

For the second time in less than ten minutes, tears flooded my eyes. "Honey, you're *not* stupid. Your dad shouldn't say those things."

A sharp knock sounded on the door at my back, and a second later, Ryan opened it. His expression gave nothing away, looking like it had been carved from the same stone as the silent statues scattered around the grounds.

"Your father's here," he told me in an even tone that made me want to scream. "We need to get downstairs."

"Cori's scared of the storm," I muttered, still stroking her hair. I was probably ten different kinds of cowardly for hiding behind his sister right then, but I needed space to think.

Some of the ice in his eyes melted. He looked at Corinne. "Ms. Wallace is on her way up. I told her to hang out with you until the storm passes."

His sister lifted her head. "I'm not eating with you?"

His lips pressed into a thin, tight line. "No. It would be boring anyway."

"Can Maddie stay with me?" She peered up at me with guileless eyes. "You're more fun than Ms. Wallace."

"Very *well*," Ryan corrected, shaking his head a little ruefully. "Sorry, Corinne, but Madelaine needs to come downstairs with me."

Madelaine.

The only thing saving Ryan from me tearing into him and demanding he listen to me was the little girl between us.

This was the engagement party all over again, except he'd seen *me* kissing his dad with his own eyes. Sure, he might have spent the last week telling me he trusted me, but even I knew this looked bad.

Corinne reluctantly let me go. "Will I see you later?"

Ryan gave her a soft look. "Yeah. We'll stop by and see you before we head out, okay?"

She sighed softly and nodded. "Okay. I love you."

"I love you, too," he murmured, forcing a sharp smile onto his lips for her benefit before turning to me and opening the door a bit more. "Let's go."

"See you, Cori," I whispered to the little girl who had stolen my heart.

Her sweet, innocent smile was almost my undoing. "See you later. Love you, Maddie!"

Emotions choked me, nearly strangling my words. "I love you, too, sweet girl." Sucking in a wobbly breath, I joined Ryan in the hallway.

He closed Corinne's door and turned away from me sharply, not waiting to see if I was following or not.

By the time we made it to the top steps, I couldn't take it. I reached out and grabbed his wrist. "Ryan."

He froze and glanced back at me before jerking away. "Not now."

"It's not what you think," I hissed, my chest burning with a need to tell him what had really happened.

He whirled and backed me against the wall, his blue eyes blazing with a promise of pain. "Not fucking *now*. We need to get through this lunch with our fathers, so do me a favor? Be quiet and don't leave my side so I can get us out of here without killing someone. Think you can handle that?"

I swallowed, the simple movement like forcing broken glass down my throat. All I could manage was a nod as the glass began shredding my insides. The hate in his eyes, which barely masked the absolute raw pain, was crushing. Agony ripped through me as I realized how much damage Beckett had done to us.

His gaze searched mine briefly, and finding whatever he was looking for, he gave a curt nod before turning and leading me down the stairs by my wrist like a disobedient child.

Dread coiled in my stomach as we descended the stairs. By the time we made it down the hall to the dining room, I was ready to be sick. I couldn't miss the way Gary's gaze sharpened as I entered. He stared curiously as Ryan deposited me into a seat before taking the chair beside me. With Beckett on his other side at the head and Gary directly to Beckett's right, the four of us made for a small group at the table, which easily sat sixteen.

Two massive crystal-and-gold chandeliers hung from the ceiling at either end of the dark walnut table. Matching high-backed chairs with cream-colored cushions lined the table. The glass wall behind Gary showed off the backyard, with its sprawling lawn and sparkling pool and grotto.

Beckett cleared his throat and lifted a tumbler of amber liquid. "Shall we toast to your fallen friend? May Kindell rot in hell." He threw back the drink with a grin.

My hands curled into fists on my lap under the table. I couldn't help looking at Ryan out of the corner of my eye, but he didn't seem phased in the slightest.

The corners of Gary's eyes twitched, but that was the only sign he gave that he gave a shit about Adam's death.

"Good fucking riddance," Ryan muttered, reaching for his water goblet and taking a long drink.

Amen, I agreed silently, not moving.

Gary's gaze flicked to me. "How are you, sweetheart? Sorry I haven't been around as much."

I pasted on a fake smile. "Wonderful."

Beckett snorted in amusement, and I could practically hear Ryan grinding his teeth.

Gary's eyes narrowed. "I heard from the designer. Your dress will be ready for your first fitting over Thanksgiving weekend. I was thinking you could come to Milan with me instead of staying behind by yourself."

To most girls, a trip to Italy with their father would have been a dream come true. But I knew this was just his way of keeping tabs on me while school was officially closed for the week. At least I wouldn't have to deal with Adam, too.

"Actually, we have plans," Ryan informed him.

Beckett's brows lifted. "Oh?"

"Grandfather has requested our presence." Ryan leaned back in his seat as he leveled a glare at his father. "He's also requested Corinne come. You know how the old man can be."

Now it was Beckett's turn to clench his teeth. "Fine. Take your sister. One less headache for me to deal with." He flashed a row of even teeth at his son. "I heard from his nurse. She doesn't think the old bastard will make it to the end of the year."

Father and son stared at each other, locked in some silent battle of wills that eventually ended when Ryan grimaced and gave a small nod of acquiescence. Beckett chuckled, the sound about as comforting as the roar of a ravenous grizzly.

"Should I take that to mean things have been smoothed over between the two of you?" Gary drawled, eyeing us with interest.

"We both know what we have to do," Ryan answered, looking at me. "Don't we, Madelaine?"

I nodded slowly. "Yes."

Beckett laughed and reached over to clap a heavy hand on Ryan's shoulder. "See, son? Just because someone else gets her ready for you, that doesn't mean you still can't enjoy yourself."

Oh, *ew*. Was he talking about Dean, or himself? Either way, I was going to need a barf bag.

Ryan's lips lifted in a cold, almost dead, smirk. "If you say so. Personally I've never been a fan of someone's sloppy seconds. But hey, if that's *your* thing..."

Beckett's smile turned brittle.

I stared at my plate, not sure if my cheeks were heating because I was angry or mortified. Honestly, it might've been both.

Gary hissed a breath between his teeth. "Sounds about right."

Beckett turned his cold glare at Gary. "Something to say, old friend?"

Gary shrugged an indifferent shoulder. "Just that your son seems to have figured it out. I mean, come on. How many women did you fuck after I did? I lost track over the years."

Beckett shot him a mocking look. "What can I say? Pussy's pussy.

And you had a penchant for slumming it. Those sluts will let you do anything. Like... fuck. What was her name? The blonde with the big tits? She lasted a little longer than the others. Amy? Andie?"

Ugh, okay, I needed to be anywhere but here right now. The misogyny was suffocating. These assholes were disgusting. I turned to my own water, trying to wash away the gross taste this conversation was leaving in my mouth.

Beckett snapped his fingers. "Angie. Angela... Porter, wasn't it?"

I choked on my water. My eyes burned as I slammed my glass down. Ryan and Gary eyed me, the first with something that looked like concern and the second with cruelty. Beckett was oblivious as he went on about my *fucking mother.*

"Jesus, that bitch was up for anything. A little coke and... fuck." He shook his head at a fond memory.

Gary watched me, a bemused smile toying on his lips. "She was a greedy cunt. Wanted more than she ever deserved. But her skills ended in the bedroom."

Beckett slapped a hand on the table, sending the cutlery bouncing as he laughed. "Fuck that. Those skills translated pretty well to the kitchen, a coat closet, a bathroom..."

Ryan sighed, the sound coming out like an annoyed rumble. "Seriously? Did Madelaine and I really come here to talk about how much action you two got before your balls started to shrivel?"

Gary didn't pay him any attention. "You know, Beck, you always did love chasing down whatever pussy my dick landed in."

My hands clenched on my lap, impotent fury whipping through me.

Beckett scoffed. "It wasn't her cunt. She had a mouth like a fucking hoover and her ass... If you didn't plow into that a few times, I almost feel sorry for you. Like I said: a hit of whatever and she was into it all." His grin turned feral. "And even if she *wasn't?* The fight was half the fun."

My stomach churned, a cold sweat breaking out on my forehead. I couldn't hear this right now. I couldn't *be here* right now.

Vaguely, I felt Ryan's hand slip over mine. I couldn't even let myself acknowledge that maybe there was still something to salvage between us if he was reaching out to me.

"I wonder what she's up to," Beckett mused, rubbing his jaw. "Probably OD'd or some shit."

Gary let out a soft laugh, his gaze landing squarely on me. "I have an idea where she might be."

I shoved away from the table and ran, barely making it to the hallway powder room and kicking the door shut before I fell to my knees and threw up into the toilet.

CHAPTER 32

MADDIE

We never said goodbye to Corinne.

Ryan told them I'd been fighting a stomach bug that was going around the school. I half expected one of our dads to make a crass joke about how I better not be pregnant, but they didn't.

Probably because if I *was* pregnant? That meant even more money for them. After all, their goal was to get me married and knocked up by the end of summer so they could each cash in on some family trust funds.

Ryan had ushered me out of the house and into his car as quickly as possible before peeling down the driveway with a loud *screech* of the tires.

The rain had stopped, but the clouds were still a turbulent shade of grayish blue as they swirled overhead, blotting out the sun and making it seem later than barely two o'clock in the afternoon.

I was numb as Ryan drove, Gary and Beckett's callous conversation about my mom echoing in my ears as Ryan drove us away in silence. I stared at my hands in my lap until my vision blurred with tears. I gasped as the car made a sharp turn. My seatbelt locked up as I was thrown to the side.

"Sorry," Ryan muttered, his jaw clenched as he stared furiously out the windshield.

I glanced at the unfamiliar road lined with heavy underbrush, and then my gaze skimmed the clock on the dash. I hadn't realized we'd been driving for an hour already. "Where are we?"

"Taking a detour," he answered, his tone clipped.

"Ryan—"

"Just... I need to think," he told me with a shake of his head. The veins of his forearms rolled as he flexed his hands around the steering wheel, gripping it with white knuckles.

I sank back in my seat and turned my face to the window so he wouldn't see when the tears started to leak out of my eyes. I thought I'd known what hopelessness felt like, but I'd just uncovered a whole new layer.

I was utterly, totally alone. There was no one left I could depend on, except for Bex, and doing that put her at risk. If Gary and Beckett could so callously laugh over raping my mother while getting ready to eat lunch, then I knew Gary would easily carry out his threat to hurt Bex. He was a much bigger monster than I'd ever imagined.

And my mom was trapped somewhere with him.

She might've been the world's shittiest mom, but no one deserved what he was doing to her.

The bushes and skinny trees cleared suddenly, and Ryan pulled the car to a stop in front of a vacant stretch of beach. The waves of the Pacific Ocean crashed rhythmically in front of us. With the storm retreating into the horizon, it was a beautiful and deadly sight.

A small blue-and-white house was tucked into the sand reeds a hundred yards or so from the water. The white wraparound porch gave it an inviting feel, but there were no lights on. No one was home.

"Where are we?" I whispered. Maybe I should be worried that he'd brought me somewhere so remote and desolate.

Ryan killed the engine. "My mom used to bring me to this beach when I was a kid. After she died... I would come here to think. To process shit my dad would say and do." His lips turned up slightly. "I came here with the guys after I got engaged to your sister. Drank until I threw up."

"Why bring me here?" I turned and gave him my full attention.

"Because I need to think," he answered honestly, looking at me finally. Regret filled his eyes. "This isn't working, Maddie."

A crack split my heart. "I didn't kiss your dad, Ryan."

"I know," he replied, reaching over to wipe away a tear that tumbled down my cheek. "I knew the second I walked in what that was. I'm so sorry I wasn't there. I should've... Fuck, I should've known he would try something."

I shook my head, confused. "But you were so mad. You told me to be quiet—"

He pressed a finger over my lips, shushing me. "Because it was the only thing I could think of to keep from killing my dad. Not hypothetically, Maddie. I was going to kill him."

I frowned. "Ryan."

He shifted forward in the seat and reached behind his back. When his hand appeared a second later, it was holding a gun.

My heart stopped, my gaze flying to his. "Where did that come from?"

He set the gun on the dash. "My bedroom. If he'd touched you again, I would've shot him. Fuck, I probably should have anyway. The woman they were talking about? That was your mom, wasn't it?"

I nodded slowly. "Yes."

His eyes slid shut as he grimaced. "I'm so fucking sorry, baby. I'm so sorry that you had to hear that."

His apology, and the agony in his voice, ripped through the last of my defenses. My face crumpled as I fell apart, sobs wracking my body. A bell chimed overhead as Ryan shoved open his door. He was ripping my door open and unbuckling my seatbelt before I realized what was going on.

Lifting me effortlessly into his arms, his hands slid under my ass as I wrapped my arms and legs around him. His steps never faltered as he carried me across the sand and grass toward the house. I buried my face against his neck as I cried, too exhausted and overwhelmed to keep pretending everything would be okay.

I was insanely out of my league, and I had no idea how to pull the emergency brake of the crazy train I was on.

Ryan shifted my weight to one arm and used his free hand to reach into his pocket and pull out a set of keys. A second later, he slipped a key into the lock of the front door, and it opened easily.

A loud beeping sound blared from a keypad to the right, and he punched in a code to make it shut up. Then he kicked the door closed and walked us deeper into the house.

I finally lifted my head when he settled us onto a large chair, me straddling his lap as he kept me close.

Sniffling, I looked around at the dove gray walls with white trim. The furniture was functional and comfortable. An overstuffed sectional was a darker shade of gray that picked up some of the darker grains in the wood floor. We were sitting on a matching loveseat, and two black leather recliners filled out the rest of the space with a glass and white wood coffee table in the center. Large windows showed the beach outside, and I spotted a kitchen toward the back of the room.

"What is this place?" I asked, curiosity getting the better of me.

Ryan's lips twitched. "My house."

My brows shot up. "You have a house?"

He nodded slowly, his expression guarded. "Yeah. Built it a few years ago after I bought the land. I wanted a place where I could remember my mom and get away."

I was still stuck on him owning a house. "A few years ago? You're only twenty-one."

A soft, breathy laugh escaped him. *"That's* what you're focused on?"

"Most teenagers don't buy a house, let alone build one. Especially when they have a freaking estate," I pointed out.

His gaze sharpened. "That place is my father's, Mads. It sure as hell isn't my home."

"Okay. So is this your home?"

He glanced around. "I don't know. Maybe one day."

I wiped under my eyes, thankful I'd gone with a waterproof mascara that seemed to be living up to its name. "Ryan—"

"You need to go, Maddie," he cut me off in a gentle tone.

I paused and stared at him in confusion.

His knuckles dragged up the length of my spine as he pressed his lips together. "You can stay here until we figure out how to get you away."

"You want me to leave?" There was no disguising the hurt I was feeling.

"Fuck no. I want you to stay, but what happened back there? Maddie, I don't know that I can protect you. Madelaine was a bitch for setting you up to live her life. You had no idea what you signed up for, and I think it's time you cut your losses." He shook his head sadly. "I love you too much to keep putting you in a position where you're going to get hurt over and over. And that's exactly what our fathers will do."

He lifted his hands to my face and pushed my hair back. "You need to leave, baby. Maybe one day, when all this shit is over, I can find you and..." He let the unspoken idea hang between us.

In another time, another world, this would all be different.

But I wasn't going anywhere. I couldn't, even if I wanted to.

"No," I told him, my hands resting lightly on his shoulders.

His eyes narrowed. "I wasn't asking, Madison, I'm telling. You're leaving as soon as I can figure a way to get you out. You can go back to being Madison Porter, but I'll make sure you and your mom are set up even if I have to hire a fucking army to guard you."

I sucked in a sharp breath. "I'm not going anywhere, Ryan. And there is no Madison Porter."

He stiffened under me, readying for a fight. "Dammit, Maddie—"

"He killed me," I said simply, letting the truth out. When he stared at me in confusion, I elaborated, "The night of the engagement party, Bex tried to help me run. I made a stupid, impulsive decision to say goodbye to my sister on my way out of town. But the name on her grave wasn't hers—it was *mine*."

Understanding dawned in his bright blue eyes.

"When his guards dragged me back, he told me the truth. That he'd made it look like I was the one who died in the fire in Greece. Everything from my old life is gone, Ryan."

A slow smile started to spread across his face. "Even better. Ash can help me set you up with a whole new life. You can start over. We can fake your records easily enough, pick a new name, and move you across the country. Hell, *out* of the country."

God, this man. If I hadn't loved him before, then I absolutely would have now. "You think Gary doesn't have a contingency plan in case I decide to run? I grew up with *nothing*. I could survive on nothing if I wanted to. I did for years."

His large palms fell to my waist and squeezed. "He has something on you."

I nodded. "My mom. He took her out of rehab and is keeping her locked up somewhere. She's drugged out of her mind, which I guess is a good thing so she doesn't know what's really happening. He threatened to hurt her or worse if I didn't obey him."

"Fuck," he breathed. His jaw tightened. "Mads, I know you don't want to hear this, but your mom hasn't done shit for you. Get out, and I'll work on a way of freeing her while you're living your life."

"I considered that," I admitted, shame coloring my cheeks. "She never was much of a mother, and even if I *could* get her out? Odds are she'd be back to her old ways before long. She's done several stints in rehab, and they never took. I was stupid to think this time would be different."

"I'm sorry," he murmured, shaking his head. "But that's all the more reason for you to go."

I met his gaze and held it, needing him to see the genuine fear I was carrying around. "He also threatened Bex."

Everything in Ryan pulled taut as a bow string ready to snap. "He *what?*"

"He mentioned having her taken and shipped off somewhere overseas to be sold." I grimaced as I told him Gary's plan. "I don't think it was an idle threat."

"It wasn't," he replied in a hushed voice. "Fuck." His head dropped back and stared at the ceiling. "This changes things."

My shoulders slumped. "I know."

He sat up straighter, his eyes blazing as he met my gaze. "I'm not going to let anything else hurt you, Maddie."

"You can't promise that." As much as we both wanted what he was saying to be true, it couldn't be. "And what happened today with your dad wasn't some fluke. He made it seem like he and Madelaine had an arrangement."

"What?"

I nodded and added, "He talked about how I'd done my job by humiliating you at the party, and my cut was in my bank account."

Anger slashed his features. "Mother*fucker*. The morality clause they worked into the marriage contract. Your dad paid out ten million when that video went live. Lainey was setting me up again."

I winced. "Sorry about that."

"I don't even know why I'm surprised by this shit anymore," he mumbled, rubbing a hand down his face. "But I'm done playing their game. Dean was the first step, but it's time to stop playing defense."

"Meaning what?" Apprehension trickled into my gut.

"Remember those answers I promised you?" Ryan arched a brow, waiting for me to nod. "Still want them?"

"Yes," I answered automatically.

"Maddie, if you know the truth, that means you're in, and I can't promise things will work out the way I want. We have a plan, but it's not bulletproof. Shit could go sideways fast, and it could mean we end up worse off than where we started." He watched me carefully.

"We?" I questioned.

"Ash, Linc, and Court are as involved in this as I am. I'll call them right now and have them drive up here. We'll tell you everything. Answer any questions you have. No more secrets." He hesitated. "But that means you're part of it, and there's no going back."

I tilted my head and gave him a sad smile. "I love you, Ryan Cain. Going back was never an option."

His eyes lit up before his mouth collided with mine. He kissed me

267

like a man consumed by desire, his hands clutching my hips tight enough to bruise. A shiver worked down my spine as I realized I liked the idea of wearing his marks of possession over me.

"You messed up," he murmured.

I shot him a curious glance.

"You should've run when I gave you the option. Now I'm never fucking letting you go," he vowed against my lips. "You're mine, Madison Porter. Yesterday, today, and every single motherfucking tomorrow."

CHAPTER 33

MADDIE

W ithin an hour of Ryan calling Ash, all the guys showed up at the beach house with Bex. If we were doing this, we were *all* doing this. Bex was my best friend, and she needed to know what was going on, since it could affect her.

Ryan and I had been sitting mostly in silence, both of us trying to absorb what had happened over the last few hours. It felt like everything had shifted, but strangely I felt more in control than I had when I'd woken up.

I stayed curled on Ryan's lap as we waited, his fingers tracing lazy, random patterns up and down my back, across my hip and thigh until we heard a car's tires crunch along the gravel and sand where we'd left his car.

It wasn't a surprise when a key scraped into the lock on the front door and opened it minutes later. Ryan trusted his friends with everything, and I had a feeling that extended out here.

They walked into the living room in silence, each with an expression more grave than the last, until Bex appeared. Her hazel eyes showed she was confused about why she'd been brought here, but that was because of me. When Ryan had called Ash, we'd both agreed that Bex needed to be looped in on everything, too.

I gave them each a sad smile from where I was curled in Ryan's lap, my head resting against his shoulder as exhaustion weighed heavily in my bones.

Ash dropped into one of the recliners, nodding to us both while Linc and Court sat on the sectional. Bex tried walking to the other recliner, but Court snagged her hand and tugged her into the space between him and Linc on the couch. Her cheeks flushed and she looked ready to fight him on the seating arrangements, until she met his eyes. Whatever she saw there had her relaxing back against the sofa without complaint.

"Okay," Ash began, his pale green eyes meeting mine, then Ryan's, "what's up?"

Ryan and I exchanged glances, and I gave a small nod for him to take the lead.

"I wanted you guys to be here when I told Maddie everything," he explained.

Linc's brows rose. "Everything?"

Ryan gave a grim nod. "Everything. No more secrets." His gaze moved to Bex. "And since this involves Bex, too, I thought she should hear it."

"I agree," Court murmured, absently rubbing his thumb across his bottom lip.

Ash didn't look quite as convinced. "No offense, Bex, but this might not be a secret that you want to hear or want to be part of."

"She needs to be," I cut in before Bex could. "Gary threatened her."

"The fuck did you just say?" Court spat, his dark eyes filled with promises of violence and pain as they turned to me.

Linc leaned forward. "What are you talking about? What kind of threat?"

Bex laid a hand on each of their thighs. "Chill, guys. I already knew that."

Court turned his fiery stare to her. "And you didn't think to fucking tell me?"

Her eyes narrowed in return. "Don't you *dare* look at me like that,

Court Woods. You don't get to question a single thing I do. We're *not* friends."

He gave her a dark look. "No, we're not."

Bex jolted like he'd slapped her. Cheeks flushed, she looked down and moved closer to Linc. Court still looked ready to punch something, frustration burning in his gaze as his jaw clenched and he looked away.

"As riveting as this conversation is," Ash began, shaking his head, "can we get back to the actual threat?"

A heavy sigh rumbled out of Ryan. "It's more than that."

I didn't bother sitting up as I explained what had happened with Gary. How he threatened Bex, how he was holding my mother's life over my head. I let myself relax against Ryan's chest, pulling comfort from his touch as I told them every fucked-up thing Gary had done since the engagement party.

"I don't even know what to say," Ash muttered, rubbing his jaw as he stared blankly at the coffee table.

Linc pushed to his feet. "I need a drink. And food. Should we order food?"

Bex's eyes narrowed at me. "You're eating real food, Mads. No more of this fucked-up diet that Gary's punishing you with."

I winced as I felt Ryan's gaze bore into the side of my face.

Okay, so I'd told them *almost* every fucked-up thing.

"It's fine," I mumbled, trying to dismiss it.

"It's not," Ryan replied evenly. "Is that why you've lost weight?"

I squirmed in his lap, and his arms tightened around me like he expected me to bolt.

"Yeah. He put me on this strict diet for the wedding." I rolled my eyes, not sure why I was so embarrassed to be discussing something so trivial. I'd never had an issue with my weight or eating before. I'd been happy with how I looked, but I could definitely see how the pounds I'd lost had nipped in my waist. Sometimes it didn't seem that bad. Plenty of girls dieted. Hell, it was practically a sport at Pacific Cross.

"Fuck that," Ryan spat. He looked at Linc. "Order some pizzas, and make sure they know about her allergy."

Linc nodded and turned away, already pulling his phone out.

"It's *pizza*, Ry. Last time I checked, peanuts weren't a readily available topping," I said with an amused laugh. My stomach growled at the idea of gooey, cheesy pizza. Grease, cheese, and carbs.

Yes.

He shot me a look that said he didn't care how ridiculous he sounded; he wasn't taking any chances with my health.

Linc came back moments later with a bottle of tequila and a stack of glasses. "Pizza will be here in about forty minutes." He started pouring shots and passing them out.

I declined, but Ryan took a glass, balancing it on my knee as he waited for everyone to get settled.

"Forty minutes will give us enough time, I guess," Ash began, looking at his friends. They all turned their attention to Ryan.

His clear blue eyes locked on mine. "Sure you're ready for this?"

I smiled at him. "I'm in. Whatever it is, I'm in."

"Me, too," Bex added.

Ryan exhaled, his cheeks puffing out. "Remember the phoenix tattoo I said we all have?"

I nodded, remembering the fiery red and orange bird that covered a large expanse of Ryan's back.

"Phoenix isn't just a tattoo." He hesitated. "It's *us*."

I blinked. "You're a mythological creature with wings?"

"No, smart-ass," he chided, shaking his head. "Phoenix is a company. *Our* company. We started it three years ago."

"You started your own company," I said slowly, still feeling like I was missing something.

"Were matching tattoos a requirement?" Bex added, amusement coloring her words as she glanced around at the guys. "Or just a team-building exercise?"

"Phoenix is a company we formed when we realized our fathers were monsters," Court answered flatly. "When we realized that each one of our fathers was a self-serving prick who was out of control, we decided that instead of inheriting their kingdoms, we were going to burn their shit to the ground."

Linc raised his glass mockingly. "And rise from the ashes of what we'd destroyed to leave a different legacy."

Ash leaned forward, his forearms braced on his knees. "Beckett and Gary aren't the only assholes running shit in this country." He inclined his head at Court and Linc. "Our fathers are just as culpable. Mostly because they've all thrown their hats into the same fucking ring."

"And what ring would that be?" I asked, dread pooling in my chest as I waited for the answer.

"Human trafficking," Court finally answered. His gaze snapped to Bex. "So, when Gary said he could sell you to some overseas prick, it wasn't an idle threat. He could auction you off in a matter of hours, sweetheart."

Bex's face paled.

"Wait, hold on. I don't understand." I looked at Ryan, needing to know more, but not sure what questions to ask.

He sighed softly. "Let's start at the beginning, okay?"

I nodded, the quick, jerky movement showing how rattled I was.

"We all grew up together," he started. "Our fathers have known each other for... fucking forever. Since before *they* were at PC. Obviously you know our dads went into business together. They merged parts of Cain Global and Cabot Industries to focus on energy resources. Oil and gas, mostly. Offshore drilling rigs and, more locally, fracking in North America. But the biggest money comes from Asian countries where they do the same thing but pay a fraction of the labor costs and can control the market better."

"I thought fracking was illegal." I thought back to when I'd mentioned it in a research paper years ago when I'd been asked to write about sustainable energy sources. Truthfully, I didn't know much, except that it was bad.

"In some places," Ash agreed. "But in countries overseas, Beckett and Gary have made a killing exploiting people who live in shitty conditions. Fracking destroys the land and often contaminates the water tables. People get sick and die. But at the end of the day, they throw money at an official who says they didn't do anything."

Linc gave a dark chuckle. "Yeah, because it's totally normal for a hundred and six people to get the same kind of rare blood cancer in a town of five hundred." He shook his head in disgust.

"But your dads aren't involved in that," Bex pointed out. "I mean, Court's dad is in the military."

"*Ex*-military," Court corrected with a grimace. "The General now has his own army of mercenaries that he's contracted to help them cover up shit that goes wrong internationally. For the right price, of course. Beckett and Gary practically have him on retainer."

"You call your dad the General?" I huffed out a small laugh.

Court met my gaze. "No, I usually call him the fucking cocksucker. But Jasper Woods is proud as fuck of his military career and insists everyone refer to him by his rank. Even my mother. The man is a fucking narcissist."

"Oh," I whispered, my gaze darting away to Ash. "And your dad?"

Ash ticked up a finger. "My dad is an accountant. Howard Newhouse. He helps them all move their money around in different shell companies and offshore accounts to skirt tax and labor laws."

I glanced at Linc without thinking.

The corner of his mouth hitched up in a rueful smile. "My family operates a chain of hotels. My dad is Kent Westford."

I gave him a blank stare. Was that name supposed to mean something?

Ryan rubbed a hand up my back and leaned in to explain, "The Westford Group is worth billions. They have luxury and boutique hotels across the globe, baby."

"That doesn't sound very criminal," I admitted.

"It is when several of them have secret sex dungeons where they cater to whatever your sickest whim might be." Linc's cold eyes met my gaze and held. The demons I saw in his eyes made me shudder. "That's where this whole thing started. A fucking club where they..." He trailed off, a muscle popping in his jaw. He reached for the bottle of tequila on the table and bypassed his glass as he tipped the contents into his mouth.

"And your moms don't care?" I asked in a hushed voice, stunned.

"It's amazing what you can ignore as long as your black card bill gets paid," Ash told me. "Welcome to the world of the rich and the depraved. Aren't you glad you came to join us?"

"I don't remember any of that," Bex murmured, a frown pulling her brows together. "I mean, I remember us all going on vacations together as kids. Your parents weren't around as much as mine, but they never seemed *evil*. But then again..."

"Then again *what?*" Court prompted, his brown eyes narrowed with concentration as he watched her.

She glanced at him. "Then you guys dropped me. Our parents stopped doing stuff together, and then Madelaine hated me. Then it was just me."

"You really don't remember?" Linc asked from her other side.

"Linc," Court snapped, a hard edge of warning to his tone.

Bex's head swung back and forth as she watched them have a silent conversation. "What? What am I missing?"

"Nothing, Becca," Court finally said, forcing a grim smile.

She bristled at the attempted brush off. "No, explain what you're talking about. What don't I remember?"

Linc cleared his throat, looking tense. "Our dads were doing business together, but things fell apart when you got sick."

Her lips smashed together. "That's it? Really?"

Court nodded slowly. "That's the core of it, yeah."

Her forehead wrinkled, not quite ready to let it go. "Court—"

He reached over and covered her hand with his. "I'm sorry we just dropped out of your life before, Becca. There was a lot of bad blood between our dads, and I... I'm just sorry. For a lot of shit."

She didn't look convinced, but I could see her backing down. For the moment, at least.

I cleared my throat. "Okay, so, your fathers are all into some shady business shit, but how does that translate to human trafficking and you guys creating a company?"

Ash let out a heavy breath and pinched the bridge of his nose. "It started with my cousin, Victoria. My *adopted* cousin, I should say. My aunt and uncle adopted her when I was twelve. She was, like, eight at the time? I didn't see her much, and honestly, I didn't really care about her. She was this weird, scrawny girl who couldn't speak a word of English, and I barely saw her. Not until the night I had to stop by and pick up some tax shit from my uncle's home office when I was eighteen."

His expression went flat and cold. "No one was supposed to be home. When I was leaving, I heard this sneeze from the hall closet. I figured someone had broken in and was hiding, so I yanked open the door, ready to kick their ass. Instead, I found Victoria. She was living in a fucking closet. She wasn't their daughter—she was their servant. They treated her like shit. I hadn't seen Victoria in years, and the girl was so fucking skinny and had all these scars. My aunt drank a lot and would get violent. Victoria's hair had been shaved off." He scoffed under his breath, the noise one of pain and loathing. "My aunt apparently got jealous that her hair was turning gray and Victoria's was still pretty, so she hacked it off."

Disgust curdled like sour milk in my stomach. "Oh, my God."

"Turned out that they'd bought her for two hundred dollars when she was a kid. It was cheaper than hiring someone, and it gave my aunt someone to take out her rage on."

"Is she still there?"

Ash's eyes blazed as he looked at me. "Fuck no. I got her out that night. She was scared as shit, still could barely speak a word of English. Luckily Linc took a few years of Russian in high school and was able to translate enough for us to know she shouldn't go back home. Her dad was a drunk who'd sold her to pay off a gambling debt. We got her out of the country and helped set her up with a place and funds to live off."

"And your aunt and uncle?"

His lips twisted into a smirk. "What were they gonna do? File a police report to track down the daughter they'd purchased to be their slave? No way in hell did they want that shit going public. But it opened my eyes, and that's how I started noticing a pattern."

"A pattern?" I echoed, sitting up a little straighter.

He nodded. "I've always been good with numbers and computers. My dad convinced me to spend some of the tax season interning with him, and I noticed payments to an account simply marked *X3*. My uncle had it, as did a bunch of others."

"It's the name of the club inside my dad's hotel in Colombia," Linc supplied. "Ash followed the paper trail, and it turned out there was this entire ring of people buying and trading humans like fucking baseball cards out of my dad's club."

"Jesus," I whispered, my hand flying up to cover my mouth.

"There are a lot of people involved, but all of our fathers are big players. Remember Shutterfield?" Ryan gave me a pointed look.

Ugh, yes. The first time I'd met Beckett had been at the dinner where Ryan had secured some deal with a company called Shutterfield in Indonesia. He'd even referenced that the CEO had a thing for little boys. Ryan had found him with an underage boy and blackmailed him into the deal.

Ryan saw where my mind went and nodded. "Yeah."

My hands balled into fists on my lap as I glared at him. "You told me that it was just another price to be paid. You... Jesus, Ryan, tell me you didn't make a deal to help our goddamn fathers by sacrificing some innocent kid."

"Not exactly," he answered. "Yes, I made the deal because I needed to sell it to Gary and Beckett. But I never looked the other way like I let you think I had."

Court coughed surreptitiously. "If you happened to follow global news coverage, you might've seen that a few days after Ryan left Indonesia, that man had a heart attack. Sadly, he didn't make it." By the twist of his lips, he looked anything but sad.

My breath caught as I studied Ryan's eyes. He'd missed his calling as a poker player, because he gave nothing away. But no way was it a coincidence. Especially not knowing what I did about Adam.

"Don't ask questions unless you want the answers," he reminded me softly.

And *that* was my answer.

Surprisingly, it was one I could live with. The same way I could live with knowing Adam hadn't died in a simple car accident.

I swallowed, letting that information settle and realizing I wasn't upset or bothered in the least. "What is Phoenix?"

"Phoenix International is a company that has quietly been selling bogus foreign and domestic assets to our fathers for the last two years," Ryan replied, his calm, even tone utterly confident and controlled.

"Shell companies," Ash explained when I shot him a confused look. "We create fake everything—websites, emails. The patents we've filed for some of the devices are real, in theory, but don't exist."

I tried to keep up. "That sounds complicated and expensive."

"Not really," Ash added. "My dad is supposed to oversee the finances, but he's let me step in more, since I'm planning to go into the family business. I've just... guided them toward the companies I think are the most influential."

Linc laughed and shook his head. "If he only knew the truth."

Ash grinned at him, his white teeth flashing against his dark skin.

I couldn't even imagine how much money they would've invested in getting their company started, let alone buying out holdings and companies their parents controlled. "How did you even get this set up?"

The corner of Ryan's mouth hitched. "We pooled all the money we could, and when that wasn't enough, my grandfather provided funding."

My mouth fell open.

Ryan took it as an opportunity to kiss me, his tongue sweeping into my mouth. He pulled back just as fast, smug satisfaction glinting in his gaze. "What have I told you about open mouths?"

I snapped my mouth shut, feeling my cheeks burn as they turned red. My brain took a second to kick back into thinking mode. "So, your grandfather's in on this?"

Ryan nodded. "He hates my father. Always has. He was against my mom marrying him from the start, hence why he set up his inheritance to go to his grandchildren. He and my Nana didn't want Beckett anywhere near it. When we told him what we'd found out and wanted to do, he offered to help. Liquidated a bunch of assets and helped us set up Phoenix."

"And none of your parents know about it?" Bex's concerned gaze flicked around at each of them.

Court chuckled. "Fuck no. They're too blinded by greed to see what we've been doing. Ash is able to manipulate the paperwork enough to sell it. Cain Global and Cabot Industries are the core of the entire infrastructure. They fall apart, and their entire plan goes to shit. They're controlling all the money, all the investments needed to make everyone's plans a reality."

"Everyone meaning Gary, Beckett, Jasper, Howard, and Kent?" Bex confirmed. "They're all in on this together?"

Court nodded. "But Gary and Beckett are the key. They've controlled the bulk of the finances they need to get everything set up."

I frowned, feeling kind of dumb. "I still don't get it."

Ryan touched my chin with his index finger. "It's a house of cards, baby. Our fathers have been buying into companies that don't exist. We've been stringing them along with promises of ideas and patents that'll never amount to a damn thing."

I sat back, stunned. "This is why Gary wants my inheritance. Why Beckett wants a grandchild. They need that money."

"More than ever," Ash agreed. "They've already stretched their resources thin, Beckett more so than Gary."

"He's obsessed with one upping Gary and Ryan." My gaze flicked to Ash. "But you knew that."

He nodded. "Gary and Beckett have been best friends as long as they've been rivals, but now they're realizing that if they can cut the other out, they get all the money. The final nail in the coffin was your engagement party where, thanks to Madelaine's stunt, Beckett got an extra ten million."

"Less," I murmured. "He gave some to Madeine, remember?"

"It was less about him getting ten million and more about making Gary *lose* ten million dollars."

I rubbed my forehead. "Jesus, this is exhausting."

Ryan's hand cupped the back of my neck, his fingers digging into my tense muscles. "I know."

"How long can you keep this up?" Bex asked. "I mean, this can't last forever, right?"

Linc snorted and looked at Ryan. "We had a plan, but that shit got blown to hell a few weeks ago. Taking out O'Shea was sort of the catalyst for going public."

"How so?" Bex stiffened in alarm.

Ryan shifted us a little to reposition his arm around my back, pulling me up a bit. "O'Shea's father has been my dad's lead attorney for years. It bought Dean some latitude that he seriously fucking misjudged. Turning him in meant we needed to sever the connection between my dad and his." Ryan reached for the tumbler of tequila and downed it like a shot. "After we had Dean arrested, we knew we needed to also take his father out of commission before he could find a legal loophole to get Dean out. Peter O'Shea is one of the best attorneys in the country. He's on the fast track to become the US Attorney General. Or, he *was*."

Ash smirked. "Until we released some of his dirty little secrets to the world, right after his son got arrested. Rumor has it he'll be disbarred by the end of the month, if not arrested."

"How?" I gaped at him.

His green eyes glittered. "It's amazing the dirt people will share in emails, especially when they're bragging about it to their friends."

"You hacked his account?"

Ash shrugged, the feigned innocence utter bullshit. "Hacking is illegal, Maddie, remember? Besides, it's not hacking if he sent pictures of some of his wilder exploits to my dad's account. I technically have access, since I intern for the firm."

I pointed at Ash. "I get how *your* dad plays into this, and obviously Gary and Beckett," I looked at the guys on the couch, "but what about your dads? A hotel mogul and an ex-military guy don't exactly scream criminal enterprise."

Ryan toyed with a lock of my hair. "Did you know human trafficking is a business that makes more than one hundred fifty *billion* dollars a year?"

"Are you fucking kidding me?" The words exploded out of me in surprise.

He shook his head. "Gary and Beckett realized they were missing out on something that's mostly been run by overseas cartels from piss-poor small towns. They pull the right connections and grease the right wheels? They could double that. Easy."

"Beckett and Gary provide the financial capital, my dad makes sure it's funneled the right way," Ash went on, "Court's dad provides the muscle to move the people from country to country, and Linc's dad finds the buyers or arranges a fucking auction at his clubs. Our fathers, and O'Shea, had it set up."

Bex toed off her shoes and pulled her knees to her chest, her heels digging into the edge of the sofa. "But why does hurting the O'Sheas mean you have to bring Phoenix out now? You said you've been working to dismantle your fathers' businesses for years. How does getting Dean arrested mess things up?"

Court draped an arm along the back of the couch, his fingers brushing her shoulder. "O'Shea was working the political angle. He knew which judges and people to pay off to make sure no one looked twice when a shipment of televisions was actually a cargo ship of women and children. But now there's going to be too many eyes on him."

I shuddered and tucked myself closer into Ryan's chest, remembering the callous way that Gary and Beckett had talked about my mother. Hell, I'd seen the way they regarded all women and children. I could absolutely see them being heartless enough to view human beings with dollar signs.

Ryan rested his chin on top of my head, quiet and contemplative. "We have a little time to figure out our next move. They'll need to stop and regroup, but it won't take them long to find someone else with enough connections to help them start their side project."

I scoffed. "Really? I'd love to see the job posting on Craigslist for *that* position."

"Who the fuck is Craig?" Ryan's brows slammed down in confusion.

I sighed. "Wow. I need to find some friends who live in the real world. It's a website where people can post anything from job offers to free furniture."

Linc's head cocked to the side, an amused smile on his lips. "Huh. What a cute idea."

"There's a line of people waiting for the chance to get in good with our fathers," Ryan said, rolling his eyes at his friend. "As soon as O'Shea's shit blew up, there was a queue of men vying for his position. They all know each other through *X3*. They'll have their shit together soon, and we need to be ready."

Ash shook his head. "They're not there financially. My dad was bitching about it last night when he had me dig into O'Shea's financials to triple check nothing could come back to bite them in the ass."

"Do they *know* that you all know what they're doing?" Bex questioned.

Linc's expression darkened. "They think we're on board with it all. Anything to make sure our families remain at the top of the food chain."

"We were raised to think this was normal," Court supplied, his tone softer as he watched Bex. "And we're not the only ones."

"It's why no one blinked when you stepped in and handled the Shutterfield thing," I mumbled, glancing up at Ryan.

He looked down at me and nodded. "Yeah. But it's also why they'll never see us coming until it's too late. They think we're all on board with their plans. That we'll fall in line when the time comes."

I glanced at each of them, amazed that they'd put this all together to stop their fathers. My gaze finally settled on Ryan. "What happens after you stop your dads? Phoenix closes shop?"

"Our dads aren't the only bad guys out there," Ryan told me softly with a grim shake of his head. "Beyond what we're doing financially, we're also working to help people like Victoria who have been hurt. Relocation, therapy, and everything in between to make sure they're taken care of once they're free."

I stared at him, amazed. I'd pegged him so wrong when I'd first met him. I'd thought he was in on everything his dad was. That he'd protected Dean because it was what guys like them did for each other.

My hand came up and cradled his jaw. "You're incredible."

His eyes warmed a split second before he turned his mouth to kiss my palm. Then his arms tightened around me, fierce and protective. "I'm not letting anyone else get hurt, Mads."

"None of us are," Court added, his tone finite, and I noticed that Bex had moved closer to him. Maybe there was hope for them.

Maybe there was hope for us all.

CHAPTER 34

MADDIE

Our problems were too convoluted to be fixed in a day, but I felt infinitely better about facing them with a stomach full of cheese, pepperoni, and soda.

I pushed my plate away with a groan as I leaned back in my seat at the dining room table. Unlike the pretentious rooms at Gary's and Beckett's, Ryan's dining room was bright and airy with more floor-to-ceiling windows showcasing the oceanfront. The pale wood table sat eight, but it was a tight fit with the six of us. These guys weren't small, and I wasn't even surprised when Linc opened the front door to reveal a delivery man with five pizzas and two boxes of breadsticks.

Across from me, Bex lifted a hand a moment too late to conceal a massive yawn. She shot me a sheepish look. "Sorry. I didn't sleep that great last night."

I glanced at Ryan and felt my cheeks redden when he smirked back at me. We hadn't done much sleeping ourselves.

Ash looked down at his watch. "It's barely five. We can head back in a few minutes."

Bex gave a slow nod, looking like she was in a carb coma. From her right, Court reached over and smoothed a hand up and down her back. She seemed to melt a little more as she leaned into his touch.

When I arched a questioning brow in her direction, she gave me a half-shrug in response. With everything we were up against, I guess her anger toward him had fizzled.

"Can we stay here tonight?" I asked softly, looking to my left at Ryan.

Surprise lit his face. "You want to stay?"

I nodded, resting my elbow on the table and dropping my chin into my hand. "I like it here. I mean, I know we have to go back eventually, but..." Here I could just be *me*. I didn't have to pretend everything was okay in case Gary had his spies watching me.

"We can stay here tonight," he replied, his eyes soft. "We'll head back to school tomorrow afternoon."

Relief saturated my bones as I grinned at him.

Shaking his head, he tapped the tip of my nose. "Fuck. There isn't much I won't do if you keep smiling like that."

Heat pooled low in my belly as Linc let out a loud groan and stared at Ryan. "Are your balls even still attached?"

"I can assure you they are," I answered for him, my tone full of saccharine. "And unlike yours, they get regular action."

Linc's jaw dropped as everyone started laughing. Eventually, he laughed, too.

When we started to settle, Ryan added, "You're all welcome to stay."

"Plenty of guest rooms?" I assumed, my gaze lifting to the ceiling as I wondered how many bedrooms this place had.

"They each have their own room here," he replied. He gave Bex an apologetic look. "But you'll have to take the couch or double up with someone."

"She can have my room," Court announced. He folded the last piece of his crust and shoved it into his mouth.

"No," Bex argued, shaking her head. "I'm not taking your bed."

"Fine." He grinned at her. "Then I guess we're sharing. Glad that's settled."

Her jaw dropped open. "That's not... I didn't mean..."

He reached over and closed her gaping mouth. "Not like it would be the first time."

"Oh, really?" I shot them a curious look.

"We were *kids*," she shot back, glaring at me. "I thought you were on *my* side."

"Always am, babe," I instantly quipped, meaning every word.

Ryan leaned around me, looking at Ash. "You seem quiet. Everything okay?"

Ash glanced up, his gaze unfocused, like we'd interrupted him plotting world domination. Which, it was Ash, so that was entirely possible. I didn't even want to think of all the things the man could do with a computer.

Speaking of, maybe it was time to pull out Madelaine's phone and check what else had been unlocked. My stomach soured as I wondered what other secrets she'd kept buried. I highly doubted it was a hidden talent for singing the ABCs backward.

"Just thinking," Ash answered, pulling me from that train of thought.

"About?" Linc prompted.

Ash looked around the table before his gaze settled on me. "Victoria."

My brows rose in confusion.

"We got her out. She's safe. And she isn't the only one. We could do the same with Maddie and Bex."

"No." I couldn't shoot the idea down fast enough.

"Hold on," Linc murmured, "he might be onto something. It doesn't have to be permanent. We could get you *and* Bex out of the line of fire."

Bex snorted. "And which one of you is going to sell that to my parents?" She made eye contact with each of them. "If I go missing, they'll go ballistic."

"But if they can't find you—"

She slapped a hand over Court's mouth before he could finish. "It's a complication no one needs."

"It doesn't matter, because I'm not going," I told them with as much decisiveness as I could manage to infuse into my tone. I met Ryan's stare and held it, challenged it.

He sighed. "She's staying."

Ash let out a stunned noise. "Excuse me?"

Ryan's eyes found mine again. "Maddie and I are better together, not apart."

Court gave a low whistle. "Damn."

Linc sighed. "I still think you should both consider leaving."

"Would *you* leave any of us?" I demanded.

"Fuck no."

I lifted my chin. "Are you suggesting any of the guys leave? Because it would be safer for them, too."

His brow wrinkled. "What? No. Mads, I'm just saying—"

"Don't give me the *women and children* speech. This isn't the fucking *Titanic*, and I'm not going to be coddled and protected because I have a vagina. Period, end of story." I gave him a pointed look. "I'm *not* leaving you guys, so fucking deal with it."

"Well, when you put it so sweetly, I can't imagine sending you away," Linc replied wryly, barely hiding a smirk. "But noted."

Somewhat mollified, I looked across at Bex. "But if you—"

"Do you really want me to come over there and slap you?" Bex interrupted. "No. We're all in this together."

"Okay," Court agreed as Linc started humming under his breath.

Bex turned and stared at him. "Really? *High School Musical?*"

He shrugged. "What? It's a good fucking song."

W e cleaned up and went to the back of the house where Ryan had a large media room with a giant sectional that we all climbed on to watch movies from a flat screen that came down from a panel in the ceiling. Using a remote that worked everything electronic in the room, Ryan hit a button and shuttered all the windows to eliminate the glare.

I curled against his side and forced myself to watch the Vin Diesel action movie they'd put on. The explosions rattled the windows and walls thanks to the surround sound system. I let myself get lost in the plot, ignoring the way Linc needed to comment about every stunt until Ash and Court hurled pillows at his face.

Bex dozed off during the movie, her head on Court's shoulder and her feet in Linc's lap. Ash quit paying attention as he focused on his phone. I managed to make it through the movie, but as the credits rolled and Linc moved to put on a second, I tapped out.

It had been a long day, and I just needed a bed—preferably one with Ryan in it—to sleep away what was left of today.

Tipping my head back, I peered up at Ryan. "Is it okay if I go to bed?" It had been a long, emotional day and I just wanted to close my eyes and try to forget it.

He looked down at me, a crease forming between his brows. "Sure. We can go up now."

"You can stay," I started to protest, but he was already slipping out from under me and getting up. When he held out a hand, I took it without argument.

"Sleep well, kids," Linc called, his gaze still riveted to the screen.

I leaned over to see Bex. "She's out."

Court smiled softly as he watched her, his fingers stroking her hair. "Yeah. I'll take her up in a bit. If I move her now, she'll wake up." There was something intimate about the way he watched her, how he touched her. I eased back, feeling like an intruder in a private moment.

As soon as I was within reach, Ryan snaked an arm around my waist and tugged me to his side. "Bed, baby." The deep rumble of his voice woke up parts of me that were interested in a lot more than just sleeping.

His gaze darkened as he caught my reaction, but he didn't say anything. He took my hand and guided me toward the stairs in the front foyer. When we reached the landing, there was a singular hallway with three doors on the right and two on the left.

Ryan pointed to the three doors. "Linc's room, Court's, and the upstairs laundry. My and Ash's rooms are on the other side, each with its own bathroom. Linc and Court share a bath between their rooms."

I nodded and followed him to the end of the hall. He pushed open the door and waited for me to come inside before closing it. He hit a light switch on the wall, bathing the room in a golden glow.

"Wow," I breathed, my gaze taking in gorgeous French doors that led to a balcony overlooking the beach. A door on the other side of the room was half-open, and I could make out the interior of a spacious bathroom.

A massive bed took up the entire wall across from the balcony. Unlike the dark colors of Ryan's room at the frat and the Cain Estate, this room was all light grays and white. It was clean and uncluttered.

I moved to the balcony and pushed the doors open to see the last remnants of sunset bruising the horizon in a wash of purples, pinks, and yellows. There was something calming about the end of a day, knowing that time would carry me away from all that had happened earlier. Tomorrow would be a new start.

Bracing my hands on the wooden rail, I leaned forward and inhaled the salty air. The last dregs of the storm whipped around me in the wind, tousling my hair.

Ryan moved behind me, sliding his arms around my waist and anchoring me to his chest. He propped his chin on my shoulder to watch the finale of the sunset.

"I love it here," I whispered, afraid to lift my voice in case the serene moment shattered like a daydream. "Can we stay here forever?"

"One day," he replied, turning his face to kiss the side of my throat.

"Promise?" I needed to hear him say the words so I could believe that one day we wouldn't be controlled by our fathers and what everyone else wanted.

"I promise, Madison," he vowed, his arms tightening around me.

I leaned against him and fell silent as night crept across the ocean. We didn't move until the stars had begun twinkling overhead and the sea disappeared from view, swallowed by the darkness. The sounds of the waves churning and crashing against the beach filled the air.

When I yawned hard enough for my jaw to pop, Ryan straightened and tugged me back inside.

I glanced down at my dress. "I didn't plan for a sleepover."

"There're extra toothbrushes in the bathroom," he told me while walking to a distressed white wood dresser. He opened the middle drawer and pulled out a black By the Edge concert tour shirt. "Second drawer in the vanity." He tossed me the shirt with a smirk. "You can sleep in that."

"Mind if I take a shower?" I held the shirt to my chest, feeling oddly vulnerable.

He waved a hand at the door. "Go for it."

I slipped into the bathroom but didn't bother closing the door. After stripping out of my clothes, I tossed them aside and turned on the shower. Glancing around the bathroom, done in more shades of gray and white, I caught my reflection in the large mirror over the his-and-hers sinks.

On the surface, I still looked like me. My hair was blonde and longer, thanks to bleach and extensions. My eyes were still the same shade of cornflower blue, but they held a lingering sadness that I couldn't seem to blink away.

I could see the outline of my ribs and the sharp angles of my shoulders and hips. My stomach had a soft swell from all the pizza I'd eaten. My belly wasn't used to that much food anymore, and it actually showed.

I never thought I'd be a girl who cared about how she looked, but I couldn't stop picking apart the ways my body had changed the past few weeks. I'd thought Gary's asshole diet was just his way of being a dick, but I was seeing it for what it was—he was proving he could control every aspect of me, including my body.

Nothing was mine. He'd stripped it all away, taking more and more. And now, standing in the stark white lighting of the vanity, I saw the proof.

Disgusted, I turned and caught Ryan watching me from the door. I froze and waited for him to say something as steam started to fill the room.

"Want me to wash your stuff so you have it for tomorrow?" he offered.

I nodded, grateful I wouldn't have to wear dirty underwear. "Thanks."

He came in and paused in front of my discarded clothes. His gaze swept across my naked body, heating as it lingered on places that started to tingle in anticipation of his touch.

"You're fucking gorgeous, Maddie," he told me as his eyes met mine.

A brittle laugh slipped from my lips. "Am I? Because I barely see the girl I used to be."

"I see you," he replied, his tone fierce. "I see the woman I love, and nothing will change that."

The smile that tugged on the corners of my mouth was genuine and buoyed my heart. Ryan Cain was amazing for a girl's confidence.

He gathered my clothes and left me to shower in peace. I hurried through washing my hair and body, using his products and low-key loving that I smelled like him when I got out and dried off enough to pull on the shirt.

Ryan was sitting in bed, his shirt gone and a whole lot of skin and muscle on display, as he scrolled through his phone. He turned it off and set it aside when I came in.

I pulled back the sheets and dropped into the bed, another yawn stretching across my face.

With a chuckle, Ryan turned off the light with a remote and pulled me across the bed to his side. He tucked me against his chest, sniffing my wet hair.

"Is it weird I like that you smell like me?"

I laughed quietly. "I think it just proves you really are in love with yourself."

He pinched my ass. "Fucking brat."

"You love it," I teased, smiling into the dark.

"I love *you*," he countered.

Still grinning, I snuggled into the pillow while he traced a lazy pattern along my bare thigh. I half expected his hand to drift higher, but it never did. I relaxed, my bones melting as I started to fall asleep.

I was almost out when he said, "My mom wasn't like the others."

Ryan spoke so softly that I almost thought I'd dreamed it. The admission was quiet, almost reverent, and I realized this was the first time he'd really told me anything about his mom.

More awake now, and curious, I rolled over, situating myself on my back as he propped himself up on one arm and looked down at me.

"She didn't give a shit about the money, and she didn't want to look the other way. My parents argued a lot, but my mom wouldn't leave him." Regret filled his crystalline eyes as he lifted a hand, his fingers sweeping across my cheek.

"Why not?"

"My dad played her," Ryan answered. "He said and did all the right things. The Cain family was loaded, but not like my mom's. Honestly, I think the reason my mom got pregnant was because he messed with her birth control. They got married, had me. There were complications, and the doctors told her that she shouldn't have another kid. But she had Cori and..."

And died.

I winced, my heart breaking for the guy who clearly adored his mom. "I'm sorry."

He glanced down at me and smiled. "She would've liked you."

"Trailer trash masquerading as an heiress?" I snorted. "What's not to admire?"

He rolled his eyes. "You don't quit, Maddie. No matter what shit gets thrown at you, you keep getting up. I don't know if I could do that."

"It's easy to get up when you don't have a choice," I murmured.

"You're wrong. You had a choice. You could've bailed on your mom, on Bex, on *me*. No one would've blamed you." His hand moved to splay across my chest, his palm above my beating heart. "This is what makes you different."

Playing up the brat aspect, I arched a teasing brow. "Great tits?"

He tweaked my nipple with a sharp pinch that made me gasp. "No, smart-ass. Your heart." His eyes smoldered as he glanced down. "But you do have amazing tits."

A laugh rolled out of me, and I shoved at his shoulder. "Oh, my God. Stop."

"I don't think I will," he replied with a dark chuckle, palming my breast in his hand and squeezing. "Do you really want me to?"

I shook my head as I squeezed my thighs together. "No."

Fire lit his eyes, and a slow smirk spread over his mouth as his hand drifted between my legs. "Great fucking answer."

CHAPTER 35

MADDIE

I woke alone the next morning as light filtered into the room. The rhythmic sounds of the waves breaking pulled me out of a dream I couldn't quite remember.

Pushing myself up, I ran a hand through my messy hair. It had dried in loose waves that wouldn't be tamed with the single comb Ryan had in his bathroom. But my clothes were clean and folded on a chair by the balcony doors, so there was that.

I pulled on my underwear and paused at the dress. Leaving it, I rummaged through Ryan's drawers to pull out another shirt and a pair of sweatpants with a drawstring, which I pulled as tight as possible.

Catching my reflection in the mirror over his dresser, I chuckled. I looked like a little kid playing dress up in oversized clothing, but it was comfortable.

Barefoot, I padded into the hall and smelled something divine cooking downstairs. I was about to start down when I heard two voices laughing from behind a cracked door. Curious, I wandered to it, and surprise jolted through my body when I spotted Linc and Bex in bed together. They were both fully clothed, or at least had shirts on, so that was something.

Linc noticed me first, his easygoing smile putting me at ease, even if I was confused as heck. "Hey, Maddie."

Bex's head snapped up, her mouth falling open. "This isn't what it looks like."

I leaned against the doorframe. "Funny, because it looks like you're in bed with Linc."

She winced. "Okay, it's exactly what it looks like. But I was cold, and Court was getting up to make breakfast..."

My brows rose as I connected those dots. "So, you're saying you jumped into Linc's bed when you left Court's?"

Linc grinned, loving her discomfort as she squirmed.

"It was only sleeping," she muttered, her gaze skirting away as pink splotches bloomed across her cheeks.

I held up my hands. "No judgment from me. I'm just looking for Ryan and heard you two."

"Sorry," Linc apologized, a wicked glint in his eyes. "We didn't mean to be so loud, did we, honey?"

Bex slapped his chest. "You're the worst."

He caught her fingers and held them. "You know I love it when you get rough."

With a squeak, Bex jerked away and practically tumbled from the bed. Clearly she'd swiped one of their shirts to sleep in. The oversized top fell to her knees as she moved away from the bed.

"I'm just gonna... go." Bex turned and ducked into the bathroom, slamming the door shut and locking it for good measure.

I turned my amused look to Linc. "Do I even want to know your intentions toward my best friend?"

Linc sat up, the sheets pooling around his lap as he rubbed a hand through his dark hair. "Can I get coffee before the inquisition?"

"No inquisition," I replied, shrugging a shoulder. "But I *will* tear your balls off and make you watch as I feed them through a wood-chipper if you hurt her again."

His hands instinctively covered his crotch. "Jesus, Maddie."

"I mean it," I added, my tone serious. "Don't hurt her."

All the teasing from earlier vanished. "I don't plan to. I know we fucked up before, and I'm sorry." He met my gaze and held it. "I apologize for not believing either of you. I should've given you a chance to explain."

"Thank you." I shifted my weight on my feet. "But seriously, what is going on with you three?"

The corners of his mouth tipped up, but I didn't see any happiness in his smile. "Court and Bex have been dancing around each other since they were kids. The timing's always been shit, but maybe they'll get it right for once."

"And you?" I watched him closely, seeing the man beneath the playboy exterior he showed the world. Linc wore his sarcasm and jokes like armor, and this was one of the few times I'd seen what he kept hidden from the public.

He shook his head. "I just want my friends to be happy."

My head tilted. "You deserve to be happy, too, Linc."

He turned to me, and the haunted look in his eyes almost made me step back. "I've done a lot of stuff you don't know about, Maddie. You keep looking at me like I'm one of the good guys, and I haven't been. Not for a long fucking time."

"Good is relative," I said, forcing my tone to be mild and unaffected. "And I know you've all made some choices that I'll never understand, but you're trying to be better. That counts."

His shoulders rose and fell with a heavy sigh. "Maybe. But even if I were a fucking saint, I can't balance the scales of what my father has done. None of us can."

I shook my head resolutely. "That's not on you any more than Gary's shit is on *me*. All we can do is try."

"Maybe." He looked away, not convinced and trying to shut me down.

"I'm going to go see what's for breakfast."

His smile slipped easily back into place. "Make sure Ryan doesn't eat everything before we get down there."

I rolled my eyes. "Sure, because we all know how controllable Ryan is."

"He is with you," Linc pointed out. "I don't think there's a thing you could ask that he wouldn't do, Maddie."

Clearly he'd never seen me ask Ryan to uncuff me from a bed before he went downstairs to party. Smirking, I held back that tidbit and turned from the doorway.

I walked down the stairs and into the kitchen, spotting Ryan on a stool at the island beside Ash. Court was on the other side, cooking on three different burners.

Ash saw me first and tipped his head in a greeting as he met my gaze over Ryan's shoulder. Ryan glanced back as I sidled up next to him and slipped an arm around his shoulders.

"Morning," I told them, leaning against Ryan. I reached for his mug of coffee and took a sip, grimacing when I tasted the bitter liquid. "Yuck."

He took the cup back. "Get your own then."

"You're my fiancée," I pointed out. "Aren't you supposed to do things for me like getting my morning coffee?"

He stared at me but didn't move.

"I got it," Ash told me, going over to the coffee pot.

I stole his seat and tossed Ryan a look. "Clearly I'm engaged to the wrong man."

"If you think Ash can make you scream like I did last night..." He shot a wicked grin at me.

Ash wandered over and handed me a steaming mug before nudging the sugar and creamer closer to me as he sat on the stool to my left. He braced a forearm on the island. "Maddie, I have no doubt I could make you forget his name by lunch."

I turned, acting intrigued at the proposition. "*Really?* Because Ryan does this thing with his tongue—"

Ash chuckled. "Who do you think taught him that trick?"

With a growl, Ryan snatched the mug from my hands and dumped it in the sink on the other side of the counter from us. He shoved back and stomped to the coffee pot, repouring the liquid into the mug before giving it back to me. "Happy?" He glared at Ash. "Fucker. And you didn't even know what a G-spot was until I schooled your ass."

I giggled and reached for the sugar.

Court turned and pointed a spatula at Ash. "He's right." Then he looked at Ryan. "But to be fair, neither of you knew how to properly *take* an ass until I stepped in. Seriously, Maddie, you have me to thank for the lube lesson."

I choked on my coffee, my eyes watering as I managed to snort some of it into my nose. "Oh, my God."

"How about *both* of you stop telling my girl about sex before I knock your asses out?" Ryan snapped.

"Afraid she'll realize she can do better, Cain?" Ash taunted while Court turned back to the stove with a laugh.

I turned and leaned over to kiss his pissed-off mouth. "You know we're kidding."

"Fucking better be," he grumbled, grabbing one of the legs of my stool and yanking me closer. He moved his lips to my ear and whispered, "I'm well aware that you can do better. But you also need to know that I'll kill anyone who tries to take you away from me. Including these assholes."

Court flipped him off while Ash chuckled. Neither seemed concerned by the threat.

I shivered more from the growly tone in his words than the way his breath tickled my skin. Turning my head put my lips less than an inch from his. "Do you honestly think I could love anyone as much as I love you?"

His eyes flared wide for a split second before he closed the distance and crashed his mouth to mine in a desperate kiss.

"Hey, hey!" Court slapped something on the counter to grab our attention. When we broke apart he was scowling. "This isn't breakfast and a show. I cook, you two act like you're *not* horny teenagers for thirty fucking minutes."

"I *am* a teenager," I pointed out. And Ryan was only twenty-one, so not exactly that far from one either.

I watched Court as he turned around. "Besides, you sound like someone who's pissed he left the girl he has a thing for in another man's bed."

Ash gave a low whistle as Ryan chuckled.

Court slowly looked back at me. "Do you want to starve?"

"I'll go buy you whatever you want to eat," Ryan murmured. "Give him hell, baby."

I splayed my hands flat on the island counter. "I'm just giving you the same warning I gave Linc. Hurt my bestie and I'll use that blender —" I pointed to the fancy one with a shit ton of buttons on his right "—to puree your dick and serve it to you with a straw."

"Jesus," Ryan hissed, angling his own dick away from me like it might be in danger.

Please.

I loved his dick way too much to ever puree it.

Court blinked once. "Noted. And for the record? I have zero intentions of hurting Bex."

I arched a brow.

"*Again*," he added with a wince. He went back to cooking, pulling a large skillet of scrambled eggs off the burner.

"Need help?" Bex asked as she and Linc came into the kitchen. Her hair hung wet over her shoulders and she'd opted for the same borrowed-clothes look as me. But, judging by the way Court's eyes narrowed on her attire, it wasn't *his* clothes she'd put on.

Court looked at Linc and narrowed his eyes. "Dick."

Linc smirked and walked to the coffee.

Bex might have been wearing Linc's clothes, but she moved next to Court and helped him finish cooking like they'd been doing it for years. I sipped my coffee as Linc joined us, taking the last bar stool on Ryan's other side. They started discussing something related to Phoenix, and I zoned out until Ash dropped his phone onto the counter by my arm.

I frowned as I looked at the black rectangle. "Where's my purse?"

Ryan paused what he was saying to Linc. "Probably still in the car. Why?"

"The phone is in there."

He reached into his pocket and handed me his phone. "You can use mine."

"No. Madelaine's phone is in there," I clarified. I looked around, making eye contact with each of them. "I want to see what else Ash unlocked."

"You haven't yet?" Ash sounded shocked.

I shook my head. "With everything going on, I couldn't take any more surprises. But I think I need to. Maybe there's something on there that could help us. Or at least give us some leverage?"

"Or it could be more videos of..." Ryan's lips pulled tight as he trailed off.

Yeah. Or it could be more videos of Adam assaulting my underage twin.

"Maybe," I agreed, shoving aside the sick feeling that washed over me, "but I still think I need to know. And I think I'd rather do that with you guys than alone."

Ryan took my hand. "Okay, babe. After we eat, we'll see what's in the videos."

I forced myself to smile, wondering if I'd made the right call. There was a certain bliss that came with my ignorance, but there was also a lot of danger to not knowing all the facts.

And I was done being in the dark.

CHAPTER 36

MADDIE

R yan covered my knee with his wide palm to stop it from bouncing. I'd been nervous since breakfast, but I'd been able to mask it until we all went back to the TV room and Ash hooked up Madelaine's phone to the flat screen.

Bex flashed me a tight, encouraging smile from where she sat between Linc and Court. I tried to return it and failed miserably.

"We don't have to do this," Ryan murmured, his bright eyes locked on my face as he looked for any signs that I wasn't okay.

I placed my hand over his. "Yes, we do. If there is something that can help us…"

"And if it's more of the same?"

I flinched.

Ryan grimaced and started to shake his head. "See? I don't want her shit to hurt you any more than it has."

Ash stood and cleared his throat, watching me. "It's ready, Mads."

I drew in a shaky breath. "Do it."

Ryan hissed out a breath at my side but didn't fight me on it. He just turned his hand over and laced our fingers together as the first video started on the screen.

Bex squinted and leaned forward. "Is that…"

A smile stole across my face as I watched a preteen Madelaine sing to herself in the mirror of her bedroom. She was good, but her voice cracked on the higher notes.

"I'm Madelaine Cabot," she announced with a smirk I recognized from when I'd first met her. She blew a kiss to the mirror and turned to the camera.

"I forgot she used to sing like that," Bex admitted, her voice soft. "She made me watch every singing competition show with her. She was obsessed with them."

Lainey picked up the camera, and it wobbled as she walked. A door opened, and I noticed the floor of the hallway outside her bedroom. Then the camera was bouncing down the stairs before it stopped abruptly.

The camera lifted, and her wide eyes filled the screen. "Shhh," she warned, a mischievous smile starting as she crept forward. She flipped the camera, and a large door came into view. It was barely open, but as she moved closer, I could make out voices.

"It's a fucking relief."

A shudder rolled down my spine at Gary's cold voice.

A snort echoed in the room a second later, and then Adam spoke. "You've always been a lucky bastard."

"Don't I know it." Gary huffed out a laugh and set down what sounded like a glass. "The stupid cunt was getting greedy, too, so that's over with."

I frowned.

"She might've been stupid, but she had a great cunt, and an even better mouth." Adam's knowing chuckle made my skin crawl.

But it's what Gary said next that made me gasp aloud.

"Angie wasn't good for shit except for the gash between her thighs."

Angie.

Mom.

"Fuck," Ryan muttered, shooting me a worried look.

"You would've thought her pussy would've been all stretched out, but it was still so fucking tight every time," Adam added with a snicker that had my stomach flipping violently.

"I still think you're crazy for letting her wet your dick for the last five years, but whatever gets your rocks off." I could hear the smirk in Gary's words.

A wave of nausea rolled through me.

"She sucked like a fucking hoover and was down for anything as long as I threw in an extra hundred to the check you wrote," Adam answered in response.

Hold up. Huh?

Check? What check?

"At least I can stop sending her a grand every month."

My eyes rounded. *A thousand dollars?*

Gary had been sending Mom a thousand fucking dollars every month?

Adam howled with laughter. "That's fucking spare change for you, Gary. I bet I could find double that in your couch cushions. Besides, the money was for your kid. Not the bitch who birthed her."

"*Madelaine* is my daughter," Gary snapped coldly. "And only because I need her. The other one… We both know that Lainey is a means to an end. All I need is one kid to make the will stick. I sure as shit don't need two of them running around here."

"An heir and a spare," Adam taunted. "You know, I've seen her around that trailer. She's already got a perky little set of tits. She's cuter than Madelaine. You might want to consider bringing her to Peter's clubs. You'd make a fucking fortune. Especially if you can get to her before someone pops that cherry."

"My dad," Linc whispered, his wide-eyed gaze jerking to me.

Ryan's hand squeezed mine almost to the point of pain. I didn't think he was aware he was doing it, rage rolling off him in waves as he listened to their conversation.

Gary scoffed. "They're identical, you halfwit. And I'm not doing shit until I get what I need from Madelaine. That spare might come in handy one day."

"I wouldn't mind her in my hands," Adam commented.

"One of these days your predilections are going to get you in trouble. Again."

Adam laughed. "That's what I have you and your army of attorneys for."

"Motherfucker," Court hissed, his dark eyes blazing.

"I could always break her in, you know," Adam added. "Next time I see Angie—"

"Fucking hell," Gary huffed. "One of these days your addiction to underage pussy is going to land you in a cell."

"Fine, I'll leave her tight little cunt alone. But her mouth could be fun," Adam pointed out. "Next time Angie's passed out, I might see who's better. The mother? Or the daughter? I can just picture the little bitch's face if I woke her up choking on my dick."

"He didn't," I said quickly, turning to Ryan, who looked seconds away from finding someone to resurrect Adam just to kill him again. "I didn't know who Adam was until I came to California." I framed Ryan's face with my hands so he had to look at me. "Ryan, no one touched me."

The fury in his eyes was a terrible sort of beauty that sent a forbidden thrill through my chest. It vowed pain and retribution to any and all who would have even considered harming me.

There was something breathtaking about watching the man you loved want to kill for you.

The video on the screen stopped, and silence hung in the room.

"That must have been when she found out about you," Bex offered. "She probably overheard them and went looking for the birth certificates."

I nodded, my gaze moving from her to Ash. "Is there anything else?"

"You want to keep going?" He seemed a little surprised.

"Yeah." I shored up my resolve before looking at Ryan.

He still looked pissed, but a little less murderous. He turned and gave Ash a jerky nod. As soon as Ash queued the next video, Ryan moved me from the couch onto his lap and wrapped his arms around me like he needed to make sure I was still safe and whole.

The start to the next video was grainy and the camera seemed to bounce along in the dark as the person holding it ran. The screen jerked as if someone tripped and hissed, "*Shit!*"

A split second later, the movement stopped and the camera lifted. It took a second for everything to come into focus, but when it did, the camera showed four people standing in front of a brick building. It looked like an old, industrial warehouse with a cracked parking lot and dark windows. The only light came from a streetlamp overhead that cast long shadows on the ground.

"Holy fuck," Ash breathed, his eyes wide as he gaped at the screen.

"Christ," Linc swore, rubbing a hand down his face.

"What?" I demanded.

"It's us," Ryan answered, his tone cold and detached.

As if prompted by my confusion, the camera zoomed in to show Ash, Linc, Court, and Ryan gathered. Ash gestured at the building and the others nodded.

"Where are you?" Bex asked, just as confused as I was.

Court's mouth flattened. "It's Phoenix. This was… shit, three years ago? We reno'd the entire place shortly after."

"How the *hell* would she have known about this?" Linc wondered.

If there was one thing I'd learned about my twin, it was that she was sneaky as hell. I had a feeling she'd known more before her death than any of us could imagine.

"You guys have an office building?" I questioned. That seemed oddly normal.

Court scoffed. "No, we have a facility that we've kept as off the grid as possible as a base of operations. It has everything we could need from setting ops to interrogations."

Okay, *that* sounded more like my guys.

A chill trickled down my spine. "Interrogations?"

Ryan's arms tightened around me. "It's necessary, Mads."

"Sure," I agreed, not sure I wanted more details.

After a few more minutes of talking, the guys walked to their cars and drove off and the video cut out.

But it wasn't the last one.

There were several short videos, snippets of the guys talking, and even one of construction at Phoenix. Madelaine never spoke in them, but occasionally long blonde hair would fall across the screen.

Ash paused the videos and opened up a photo album with more candid shots of the guys spanning a few years. Madelaine almost seemed to have a stalker-like obsession with them, and when she somehow managed to get a picture of Linc looking like he'd just stepped out of the shower, we took a break.

Linc pushed away from the couch and rolled his wide shoulders. "That was creepy as fuck. How long was she spying on us?"

"And what did she find out?" Ash added, rubbing his jaw.

Court leaned forward, his head bowed as he braced his forearms on his knees. "Jesus Christ. How did we not notice she was following us?" Bex moved to her knees and rubbed a soothing hand over his back, her hazel eyes locking on mine.

"Because we were watching our backs for our fathers, not a spoiled princess," Ryan muttered, shifting me off his lap so he could get up and storm out of the room.

Ash looked ready to follow him, but I waved him off and chased after Ryan myself. I caught up with him outside where he'd claimed one of the Adirondack chairs on the wraparound front porch and was watching the ocean.

I leaned against the railing across from him and waited for him to speak first.

"How did I miss this?" He stared at the horizon, like he was desperately trying to make sense of things.

"You said it before," I reminded him. "You expected to have to worry about your dad. Not Lainey."

"How could she have possibly known what we were doing? I mean, Ash buried Phoenix's location." His eyes lifted to my face, and I could see the confusion in them clear as day.

I tilted my head. "When it comes to Madelaine? Who knows how she knew. But we might be able to find out more if we go back and see what else is in those files."

He nodded and got up, then paused in front of me. "You sure you want to keep going?"

I looked up at him and wrapped my arms around his back. "Yeah. I need to know what she knew. Maybe something *will* help us."

He leaned forward and kissed me softly, slowly. I sank into the feel of his mouth on mine as he licked at my lips until I opened for him. His tongue stroked into my mouth, unhurried and almost reverent.

"I love you," he said against my lips when he drew back for a breath.

I smiled. "You keep saying that."

The corner of his mouth hooked up. "I plan on saying it a lot for the rest of our lives."

"Who knew you were such a marshmallow?" I teased.

He leaned against me, his hard dick pressing against my stomach. "Does that feel like a marshmallow?"

A bolt of lust shot through my limbs. "Definitely not."

He groaned and dipped his lips to kiss the underside of my jaw. "How about I kick these fuckers out and we christen every fucking room?"

I gave a throaty hum of approval. "You *do* owe me six more orgasms this weekend."

He grinned, his hands slipping around to grab my ass. "I can't renege on a deal."

The front door slammed open and Linc's head appeared, his face pale. "You two need to get in here. *Now.*" He vanished as fast as he'd appeared.

Ryan took my hand, and we hurried back inside. Bex was back on the couch, watching as Court and Ash seemed to be arguing. Linc dropped onto the seat beside her.

"What happened?" Ryan demanded.

"There's more shit on here," Ash practically snarled, stabbing a finger at the phone.

"Of Phoenix?"

Court snorted. "Oh, no. It's worse than that."

"There's a whole other file," Linc added, shaking his head as though in disbelief. "She got into the clubs. There're pictures, a few videos…"

"What clubs?" I asked.

Linc shot me a look. "My *dad's* clubs. Shit, the stuff she has…"

"How the fuck could she have gotten in there, let alone taken pictures and videos?"

"I'm less concerned with how she got the pictures than knowing if there are more because the people on the videos are *us*." Ash looked around the room until his gaze landed on Ryan. "She has videos of your and Court's initiations."

I had no idea what that meant, but judging by the way Ryan jerked away from me and Linc looked sick, I had a feeling it wasn't a good thing. Court was staring hard at the ground, refusing to look up even as Bex edged closer to him.

"That's impossible," Ryan managed to get out.

Court laughed, the sound utterly void of emotion. "You would think so, but somehow Madelaine got a hold of them. Ours are here, so there's a chance she got Linc's too."

A heaviness settled in the room, and I sensed that whatever had happened with Linc was worse than the others.

"What's an initiation?" I couldn't stop myself from asking, even as I braced for the worst possible answer.

Linc glanced at me, his blue eyes almost lifeless. "Remember when I said I wasn't one of the good guys?"

I gave a slow nod.

"Yeah. Watch that if you need proof. I'm sure mine is on there, too." He got up and walked away.

"Linc." Court reached out for his friend, but Linc shoved by him and left the room.

Bex made a soft sound in her throat and started to go after him, but Court caught her. "No, Becca. Not now. Let him go."

I turned to Ryan, rocked at seeing cracks in their friendship. These four seemed impossibly tight. "What's the initiation, Ryan?"

Ryan looked past me at his friends, his expression more serious than I'd ever seen. "Give us a minute?"

Oh, hell. This *really* wasn't good.

He waited for Ash, Court, and Bex to leave before leading me to the couch. He sat me down and perched on the edge of the coffee table across from me.

"Shit. How do I even start to explain this?" He rubbed the back of his neck, looking lost and more than a little distraught.

I grabbed his other hand. "Hey, it's me. Whatever it is, it's going to be okay."

A nervous laugh slipped from him. "Promise?"

That was a no-brainer. "Yeah. I promise. I'm right here, Ry. Talk to me."

He blew out a long breath. "Okay. You know about the clubs Linc's dad has? There's a... price for membership." He met my eyes. "The four of us all paid it. It was expected, and we weren't given a choice. It's also why we decided to stop our dads once and for all. It was the catalyst."

"Okay, I got it. You had to do something bad, I'm assuming?" My breath caught, wondering how bad it could really be.

He nodded and looked down at the space between us, his throat moving as he tried to control his emotions. "It differs, but it's determined by our father when we turned sixteen. It's a pretty incestuous, fucked-up secret club when you think about it."

I could only imagine what sick thing Beckett had coerced his son into.

"The point is, to make sure no one talks about what goes on in the club, there's insurance. A video. My dad was supposed to keep my tape and use it if I ever tried to betray the group."

My brow furrowed. "So Beckett will release it if you take him down?"

He shook his head. "No. I made the tape part of my deal with him when I agreed to marry Madelaine. He destroyed it. I watched it burn, Maddie."

"He could've made copies," I pointed out.

"No. He couldn't. Trust me."

"Someone did."

"I don't know how," he replied, frustration lacing his words. "I guess it doesn't matter now. But if it gets out..."

"What's on the tape?"

He met my eyes and didn't flinch. "I killed someone."

I absorbed the announcement like a blow, bowing my head and hissing a breath. "Who?"

"It doesn't matter."

"It does to *me*," I insisted, lifting my head and searching his eyes.

His jaw clenched and glanced away resolutely. "I'm not making you an accessory after the fact. There's no statute of limitations on murder, Madison."

I swallowed roughly. "Did he at least deserve it?" I needed to justify this somehow.

He gave a slow nod. "Yes, *she* did."

I clenched my teeth. "Ryan—"

"Beckett wanted to put her husband in his place after he fucked up a big deal. He told me to kill the guy's wife. I considered not doing it. I watched her for weeks to learn her routine, and that's when I saw her beating the shit out of her son. He was born with Down's Syndrome. He would do something she didn't like, and she'd lose it. Even broke his arm once. That's how I justified it, baby. I thought of Cori and..."

I squeezed his hands, understanding. Maybe that made me border-line psychotic, but I couldn't be bothered to care about people who preyed on the vulnerable. Especially when they were supposed to be loving and protecting them.

"If you hadn't seen her do that, would you have still done it?"

He hesitated. "I honestly don't know."

"Is that what the others did? Kill someone?" I sucked in a deep breath.

"Court did. Ash... He had to hack into a political server and get dirt on a politician running for Vice President. When there was nothing to find, because he was actually a decent guy, he had to plant evidence that eventually got him arrested and put in prison."

I gasped. "There's an innocent man sitting in prison because of Ash?"

Ryan grimaced. "Not anymore. He was murdered a month into his sentence." His eyes met mine. "That part wasn't Ash, baby."

"Jesus," I swore, hanging my head. "And Linc? He seemed pretty upset."

Ryan winced. "His was the worst. His dad runs the clubs, Mads, so the shit Kent had Linc do... I can't talk about that. It's Linc's story."

"It's that bad?"

He nodded once, paling a little. "It's *that* bad. It had to do with his sister."

I winced, remembering Linc's sister had been killed by an abusive ex. "Shit," I muttered, running a hand through my hair as Bex appeared in the doorway, a guilty expression on her face.

"Uh, Maddie?" She held up my phone, which was ringing. "It's Gary. It's the second time he's called."

I reached for the phone, missing the chance to answer before it went to voicemail. Before I could unlock it and see if he left a message, it started ringing again. I swiped the answer button. "Hello?"

"Where the *fuck* have you been?" Gary snarled, his booming voice hurting my ear. "When I call, you fucking answer, unless—"

Ryan's face turned thunderous and he started to reach for the phone. I twisted away.

"I've been with Ryan," I cut him off coldly. "Isn't that what you wanted?"

He huffed a breath. "I'm sure you were."

I gritted my teeth. "Did you need something?"

"Watch your tone," he snapped. "Do you need another lesson to remember who's in charge?"

I gripped the phone and swallowed the comment I really wanted to make. "What can I do for you, Gary?"

"Better." He sniffed. "I'm sending a car for you at five. We need to talk."

A frown pulled down my lips. "And we can't do that on the phone?"

"You're right. Perhaps I'll just spend the evening with your mother instead. I was thinking of inviting a few friends over. Perhaps Beckett is free."

"Fine," I replied, turning back to look at Ryan. "I'll come to your house."

Ryan's eyes went wide, then his expression turned pissed. He definitely wasn't on board with that plan.

"Alone," Gary clarified. "Leave Cain behind. We have things to discuss. And Madison?"

I swallowed. "Yes?"

"You really don't want to fucking test me tonight."

CHAPTER 37

MADDIE

"You're *not* going."

I turned slowly and blinked at Ryan, bristling at his command. "I wasn't asking your permission."

His eyes narrowed. Even his chest seemed to get bigger as he breathed harder. "Goddamn it, Maddie."

Bex eased away from us with wide, concerned eyes. The only person she should have been concerned for was Ryan, because he was out of his mind if he thought I would just go along with whatever he decided.

"You don't get to order me around, Ryan. That's *not* something I agreed to, and Gary didn't give me a choice." I glanced at the digital clock near the TV. "It's going to take us, what? An hour to get back to campus from here? He's picking me up at five, so we have to leave soon."

"No, we don't, because you aren't fucking going," he snapped.

"Yes, I *am*," I insisted, closing the distance between us. He might've had several inches and a lot more muscle on me, but no way was I backing down. "You clearly heard what he said. He threatened my mom. I'm going." I whirled away, my long hair slapping his chest. I barely made it a step before his hand clamped down on my arm and spun me back.

"You're out of your damn mind if you think I'm letting you anywhere near him alone after what he did to you last time," Ryan seethed, his teeth clenched and jaw tight.

My brows arched. "You mean after you tossed me aside and left me alone with him?"

Ryan stared at me for a beat before letting me go and pacing away. He paused by the window and looked back as Bex slipped from the room.

"Is this how it's always going to be?" he finally demanded, glaring at me with burning eyes. "You constantly throwing history in my face? I've apologized, Maddie. I'm doing everything I can to make up for what happened before."

I huffed out a low breath, feeling a smidge bad. "I sure as hell don't want to keep bringing this up. Don't you think I wish I could forget what you did?"

A muscle in his jaw popped as he clenched his teeth. "Maddie... Dammit."

"You hurt me," I added, holding up a hand when he started to interrupt. "No, you betrayed me. And yes, I've forgiven you, but..."

"But *what?*" he demanded, blue eyes flashing dangerously. "You *said* that you trusted me, Mads. I thought we'd moved past this."

Shit, I'd kind of backed myself into a corner here, but I couldn't just roll over. Yes, I'd forgiven him, and I was *trying* to move on, but the way he was acting, like I couldn't make my own decisions was really freaking irritating and totally uncool. We were supposed to be in this together.

I looked away as I wrapped my arms around my torso as vulnerability crept in. "Look, the last time I felt this way about you? The last time I *trusted* you? You abandoned me when I needed you most. You didn't trust me."

He flinched. "Baby, I can't tell you how sorry I am for that."

"I know you're sorry. But sorry doesn't erase the pit in my stomach or keep me from habitually wondering when you're going to jerk the rug out from under me again." My chest ached as I told him my biggest fear.

"I will *never* do that to you again. Mads, we're past that," he said, his voice trembling with the effort to convey his point. He crossed to me in two long strides, sliding his hands up my neck to cradle my face. "Jesus, how much longer are you going to hold that shit against me?"

"That *shit?*" I echoed, resisting the urge to step out of his touch, but *damn.* My body craved it like a drug, even if my brain was shooting off *don't be a dumbass* warning bells. "That *shit,*" I clarified, meeting his gaze and legit proud of myself for holding it steady, "damn near ruined everything. I think we can both agree I paid a much higher price than you did."

Fire lit his eyes as his whole body tensed, except his hands. The hands resting on me were infinitely gentle, like he was holding delicate glass between them. "That's exactly my point. You can't go near Gary, Maddie. Not alone."

"The only way I'm going to survive this is by doing exactly what he wants, Ry. If I don't go, he's going to hurt my mother. You know that."

"I know he isn't going to win," he retorted coldly. "I know that I'll snap his neck with my bare hands if he hurts you again."

I leaned my cheek into his palm and smiled sadly. "You say the sweetest things."

A smile ghosted across his features. "I know I fucked up, Maddie. Royally. Epically. But I'm not going to let you down again."

"That's good," I whispered, "because I don't think my heart can take it again if you do."

He rested his forehead against mine and exhaled.

"I need *you* to trust *me*, Ryan," I added, my hands gripping the soft fabric of his shirt.

He let out an aggrieved sigh. "Fine. But I'll be there, too."

"Ryan—"

He silenced me with a fast kiss, and it was freaking unfair how good he was at that.

"I won't come *with* you," he explained, "but I'll follow and be nearby in case you need me. Call me as soon as you leave, and I'll follow you back to PC. That's the best I can do."

"What if he sees you?" But I really liked the idea of having him close.

"He won't," Ryan assured me. "I'll have Court drive. Trust me, no one will notice."

"You mean the way no one noticed you guys planning a secret company to take down your dads?" I snapped my fingers. "Oh, but wait."

His eyes narrowed. "I still want to know how she knew about Phoenix."

"We don't actually know what she knew," Ash pointed out as he came into the room. Court and Bex followed.

I glanced past them. "Where's Linc?"

Court grimaced as he sat down again, kicking his feet up on the coffee table. "Outside. He needs space right now. And where am I driving?"

"Maddie has to go see her dad," Ryan replied, clearly still hating the idea. "We're going to follow her to make sure she's safe."

Ash unhooked the phone from the television. "Do you mind if I hang on to this? I might be able to open more files, and I need to see if mine or Linc's initiations are on here. There are definitely more videos—"

I held up a hand. "I've had enough of Lainey's version of *Candid Camera*. Take it. Do whatever you want."

"You're sure?" Ash pressed.

I nodded. "Tell me if there's anything on there I need to know. One day I might want to go through all of it, but it sounds like whatever's on there now affects you guys more than me."

"Thanks," he murmured, tucking the phone into his jeans.

Bex sighed before stepping over Court's legs and dropping onto the couch beside him. "It's a shame we can't get to her diaries. Madelaine was neurotic about writing in one every single day."

"Seriously?" I frowned. I hadn't taken my twin for the introspective type.

Bex smirked and nodded. "Oh, yeah. She always said one day she'd be infamous and people would want to know all her secrets. She had freaking volumes of them. One for each year. But we were kids. I doubt she kept doing that."

"Where would her diaries be?" I asked carefully.

She gave me a strange look. "Probably in her bedroom."

"The one in Gary's house?" An idea started to form in my brain.

Ryan hissed out a breath, clearly picking up where I was going. "Are you determined to give me a heart attack before I'm twenty-two? No, Maddie. You aren't going on some random scavenger hunt in Gary's house to find something that probably doesn't even exist."

I cocked my head. "I'm sorry, are you telling me what to do again?"

He threw up his hands and stalked away from me. "It's like you're trying to find an excuse to get yourself hurt."

"I'm trying to find us some leverage," I shot back.

"We *have* leverage," he snapped. "That's what Phoenix is. We're bankrupting them into a corner, and when we have them, we'll strike."

"And when will that be, Ry?" I challenged. "Next week? Next year? After we get married? Or should we wait longer and hope Beckett doesn't decide to do something to Cori?"

He sucked in a sharp breath, looking like I'd slapped him. "Don't do that. Don't you fucking dare use my sister as a weapon."

I forced myself to take a steadying breath and held up my hands in surrender. "I didn't mean it like that. I know you're doing everything you can to protect Corinne. I want that, too. But maybe I can find *something* that will help."

Ash clicked his tongue against his teeth. "Maddie, even if you do, the diary of a ten-year-old isn't something that will hold up in court. Their attorneys will have it dismissed as the fantastical musings of a child's imagination, and that's *if* it's not just dismissed outright as a fabrication. Even the videos that were on the phone are mostly circumstantial at best."

317

"The ones of the initiation aren't," I pointed out.

"They're copies of originals. With technology being what it is today, it would be easy to say they're fake, and without the original for comparison, there's no basis," Court chimed in, waving a dismissive hand. "They might cause some social blowback, but nothing we couldn't explain away or get dismissed legally."

I stared at him, amazed and a little horrified. "Must be nice."

He flashed me a benign smile. "It's not the worst thing."

I turned away and looked at Ryan. "I still need to get back to Pac Cross. I have to show up tonight looking like Madelaine, and that takes work."

He scowled at me. "You're ten times more beautiful than she ever was."

"We're identical," I reminded him with a chuckle, even as warmth blossomed in my chest.

He shook his head slowly, his eyes on mine. "Bullshit. Even if she was standing here right now, I would know who you were. No way would I ever mistake you for her."

"Okay, Romeo," Ash drawled, "we get it. You love the girl. But Juliet's right. If she wants to be ready for a car to pick her up in a couple hours, we need to get back."

Bex wrinkled her nose. "Can we pick a metaphor where the main characters didn't die in tragic and pointless ways?"

I suppressed a shudder, because she was right. It was terrifying to think that my love story might turn into a tragedy just as fast as theirs had.

Halfway back to Pacific Cross, Ryan got a text saying he was needed at the frat house. He dropped me off in front of my dorm, and I went inside with Bex to get ready for whatever Gary had planned. Ryan promised to be back before the car came to get me.

After taking a quick shower and blow-drying my hair, Bex helped me pick out a Madelaine-appropriate outfit, and I was glad to have her alone for a minute.

"Where do you think Madelaine would've hidden her diaries?" I asked as Bex finished curling my hair.

She frowned at me in the vanity mirror, pausing before picking up the last section of hair. "I thought the guys said it was pointless."

I shrugged, careful to avoid moving my head too close to the burning hot wand. "I know, but maybe there's something there that might give us a clue. If Lainey was this obsessed with what Ryan and the guys were doing, I can't believe she just turned a blind eye to whatever Gary had planned."

She made a soft sound of agreement. "She hated him, so you're probably right. She loved spying on people when we were little, and it seems like that never changed."

I watched my friend carefully as she turned off the curling iron and set it on my vanity. In the mirror, I watched her brow furrow and pressed, "What?"

She met my eyes in the reflection. "When we were kids, Lainey had this secret hiding spot she liked to put stuff in. It's probably a long shot..."

"I'll take it," I said, spinning around on the seat to look at her. "Where is it?"

"There's an air vent in her closet," she replied. "It's near the ceiling. She would unscrew it and hide stuff in there. She kept her diaries there. But it might be pointless, so please don't risk Gary flipping out to go after something that probably won't even help."

Yeah, I wasn't planning on pinging Gary's radar, but if I could slip away and find it...

Maybe it *was* a long shot, but I needed to do something. I needed to find a way to contribute or feel useful. As long as my mom and Bex were at risk, Gary still had me by the throat.

Granted, Court seemed pretty determined to keep Bex safe, but my mom was on her own. I didn't even have an idea of where Gary had stashed her.

Glancing at the clock, I saw I had a few minutes before Gary's car would arrive. I'd use them to grill my bestie on her love life.

"So," I started, pinning her with a curious stare, "Court and Linc, huh?"

Bex blushed. "We're friends."

"Right. I mean, I wake up in bed with all my friends, too."

"Shut it," she muttered, rolling her eyes.

"Does this mean they're forgiven?" I asked.

"Is Ryan forgiven?" she shot back.

"Yes," I answered without hesitating. "I mean, I'm human, so the doubts creep in, but I do trust him again. Maybe even more than before since now everything's on the table between us."

She nodded. "That's how I feel about Court and Linc. It's scary how quickly I fall back into old habits with them. We were close when we were little, and I felt so blindsided when they stopped talking to me. It was a lot like when Madelaine abandoned me, although the guys never went out of their way to hurt me like she did. They just… seemed to forget I existed."

"And you have no idea why?"

She sighed and shook her head. "No. I mean, I remember so much about when we were little, but also things are kind of muddled, too. It didn't help that I was sick back then."

"Sick?" I tilted my head.

She flashed me a wan smile. "Yeah. Sorry, I forget that you didn't grow up with us. I had cancer when I was ten."

"Holy shit." I gaped at her. "Are you okay?"

"Yeah. I've been in remission for years now. That's why I had the doctor's appointment a few weeks ago? They were checking my blood." She gave me a thumbs up. "Good news I'm still healthy."

I threw my arms around her. "You damn well better be."

She hugged me back with a laugh. "Honestly, I don't even need the scans anymore, but Mom is a worrier, so I humor her."

"And Madelaine *still* made your life hell?"

She wrinkled her nose and nodded. "Yeah."

"That's insane," I murmured, still reeling that she'd survived such a serious illness. I'd always assumed that being rich was the answer to a lot of problems, but the deeper I got into this world, the more I realized that money was often just another issue. Another complication.

And the balance of your bank account definitely didn't seem to matter to things like cancer.

She laughed and tried to dismiss the severity of the situation. "Seriously, I'm good."

I didn't stop staring at her until my phone went off. A text alerted me that my car had arrived. A second later, Ryan texted that he could see the car from where he and Court were waiting.

"Guess it's time to see what Gary wants," I said, standing up.

Bex hugged me. "Be safe, okay? Don't take any stupid risks. Just get in and get out."

"That's the plan," I assured her, my stomach tightening as I wondered why Gary would be calling me to his house. I doubted it was to tell me he'd changed his mind.

I opened my front door and jerked back, surprised to see Linc on the other side. I hadn't seen him since he'd stormed out of the beach house. But now he was all smiles, his darkness held in check.

"Hey, Maddie," he greeted before nodding over my shoulder at Bex and grinning. "Ready for dinner?"

"Sure," she agreed.

Relief surged through my veins as I realized Bex wouldn't be alone. We headed down the hall and into the elevator. Once inside, Linc turned to me and pulled something from his pocket.

"Ash said to give you this." He quickly looped a chain with a silver pendant around my neck.

I lifted the silver circular pendant. "Uh, thanks?"

"It has a tracker in it," he explained. "And if you get into trouble, squeeze the circle. It'll send off an alert. Ryan and Court will come get you, no matter what."

"Smart," Bex remarked as I nodded and let the pendant fall against my chest.

The elevator doors opened, and we walked outside. A sleek black town car idled at the curb, a man in a suit waiting by the back door.

"Be safe," Linc murmured. "The guys won't be far behind. Use the panic button if you need it, Maddie."

"Got it," I whispered before walking to the car. I felt their eyes on me as the driver wordlessly opened the door and I slid into the back seat.

Here goes nothing.

CHAPTER 38

MADDIE

A two hour ride in silence to Gary's house did nothing to calm the butterflies rioting in my stomach. As the car turned onto the long drive that led to the Spanish-style mansion on top of the bluff overlooking the Pacific Ocean, my insides cramped with anxiety.

The driver stopped in front of the main doors. The last time I'd been here, I'd been dragged through those large front doors.

I stared at the front of the house as the driver waited by my now open door.

"Miss Cabot?" he finally asked in a quiet voice.

I blinked, shaking myself out of my funk, and stepped out of the car without a word.

He cleared his throat and blocked me. "Mr. Cabot requested you leave your purse in the car."

My fingers tightened reflexively on the small bag that held my keys, lip gloss, and phone. Odds were it was the phone he didn't want me having access to, and that sent a new wave of nauseating anxiety rippling across my nerves. With a grimace, I tossed the bag onto the back seat.

I fingered the chain around my neck, trying to calm myself as I walked up the stairs. When I ascended to the landing, the front door opened, and Mrs. Delancey appeared.

She gave me a tight-lipped smile and moved back to let me in.

"Any idea what's going on?" I asked softly as she closed the door. I didn't see Gary in the wide foyer, but his office was off the hallway to the left. He could easily be in there.

"No," Mrs. Delancey replied, her voice just as hushed, "but he's been in a mood since he returned home from lunch with the Cains. Tread carefully, dear. He's asked that you go to his office."

"Great," I muttered, starting down the hallway. I paused at the closed door, took a deep breath, and knocked.

I waited almost thirty seconds before the door opened and Gary appeared. His expression unreadable, he stepped back to allow me in. As soon as I crossed the threshold, his hand was around my throat as he shoved me into the wall.

A shocked squeak of alarm was all I managed before his grip tightened. I clawed at his forearm, panic spiraling through me.

After a second, he released me as abruptly as he'd grabbed me. My legs gave out and I slid down the wall, coughing and gasping as I covered my raw throat. I looked up at him through tearful, blurry eyes.

"What the hell?" I hissed, my voice cracking.

He glared down at me as he slammed the door with enough force to rattle the pictures on the walls. "Did you really think I wouldn't find out?"

My mind spun with possibilities. "Find out *what?*" I wasn't sure what he was talking about, and I sure as hell wasn't going to fess up to something until I knew exactly what he was fishing for.

"Ryan knows who you are."

Oh, shit.

"Don't even think about lying," he warned, tugging at the neck of his starched blue shirt while glaring down at me. "I should have seen it from the start. The way he calls you *Maddie*, the way you two seemed to have such a fast relationship. How long has he known? Since the beginning?"

I stared up at him for a heartbeat and tried to figure out how to handle this. "Since a few days after I went to Pacific Cross."

Gary seemed surprised that I'd given up the information so quickly, but he masked it with a scowl. "How?"

I swallowed, carefully trying to select my words. "He bugged Madelaine's room. He didn't trust her after what happened with his coach last year."

His scrutiny only intensified. "And what exactly did he hear? More specifically, who did you say it to?"

Shit. I'd been talking to Bex. No way was I giving her up.

I met Gary's gaze. "I was talking to myself."

He scoffed.

"I spent the majority of my life alone. Sometimes I talk to hear another voice." Not a lie. Mom was frequently in a comatose state, and I'd learned early on that talking to myself would sometimes curb the loneliness when I was by myself at three in the morning.

I shrugged, trying to play it off. "Had I known Ryan was planning on spying on me, I might've kept quiet." I narrowed my eyes at him. "But I didn't realize how much he hated my sister."

"So, he's the only one who knows?"

"Yes," I answered, my heart thudding in my chest. I wouldn't put the guys or Bex at risk, no matter what.

His jaw tightened, and I decided to test a theory. Maybe if there was a common goal, Gary would relent a bit and give me an opening.

The enemy of my enemy is my friend.

"But it's a good thing he knows," I added, watching Gary for any signs he'd take the bait.

Sure enough, he scowled, but curiosity glittered in his eyes. "Oh?"

I let myself exhale slowly.

Gary hated the Cains as much as he needed them. Maybe I could work that angle.

"It's why he's already forgiven me."

His gaze snapped to me.

"He got his feelings hurt, but he realized that the girl in the video was Madelaine, not me." I held up my hand, flashing the engagement ring. "He even gave me his grandmother's ring because he loves me."

He barked out a surprised laugh, his expression cooling from rage to interest. "He's that enamored?"

"Seems to be," I replied. "He really hated Madelaine, but poor, little innocent Madison? He gets to play the white knight and eats that shit up."

"And you?" Gary sneered at me. "You're in love?"

"I was," I admitted, keeping my tone frosty. "But that was before he left me here to get my ass kicked."

Gary didn't even blink at the scorn in my tone. "And now?"

I didn't flinch as I held his gaze. "And now I'm trying to survive. Ryan can kiss my ass."

He smirked at me and then, surprising me, he held out a hand. I took it and allowed him to pull me up.

"Have a seat," he told me, waving a hand at one of the two chairs across from his desk.

I settled into a brown leather wingback chair as he sat across from me.

"Perhaps you can learn better than your sister," he mused, assessing me coolly. "The Cains have been a thorn in my side for years, and unfortunately, my business is intrinsically linked with theirs."

I crossed my legs and leaned back, trying to keep my emotions locked down. "They're playing you, you know. And Madelaine was helping them."

"What does that mean?" he demanded.

I flashed him a thin smile. "It means that Beckett and Madelaine outsmarted you. I didn't know about it until yesterday," I clarified when his face started to turn red. "When I was at the Cain Estate, Beckett came on to me. Kissed me because he thought I was *her*. Then he told me that my share of the money was waiting in my bank account."

His brows slammed down. "What money?"

"I can only assume he was talking about the ten million you had to pay out when that video went public at the party." I tried to make it seem like that night was nothing but a distant memory. "Beckett thought it was Lainey's way of helping him humiliate Ryan. They'd set it up so Ryan would look like an ass and you'd lose. Win-win for them."

With a roar, Gary jumped up and swiped a hand across his desk, sending papers and a laptop crashing to the floor. It was only years of not reacting to Mom's chaotic outbursts that kept me from jumping.

Gary slammed a fist onto the desk. "That backstabbing cock-sucker. I'm going to destroy him."

I smiled. "I was hoping you'd say that."

He stared at me, chest heaving. "What does *that* mean?"

"It means," I began, standing slowly, "that I'm sick of Ryan and Beckett Cain. If you're planning to take them down, I want in."

"What the fuck would you know about it?" He scoffed, looking me up and down with derision.

"I know Ryan loves me," I replied with a mocking edge. I held up the pendant. "Fun fact, if I press a button, he'll come riding in like the fucking cavalry to save me. Apparently he thinks you might hurt me again."

Gary's eyes widened for a second before he locked down his emotions. "Really?"

"He *loves* me," I explained, disdain dripping from my words. "He wants to save me."

"And what do *you* want?" Gary pressed, a curious glint in his eyes.

I dragged a nail across the edge of the desk. "I want my freedom." I lifted my eyes. "You want me to be Madelaine? Fine. I'll play the part. I'll inherit the money. I'll help you stop the Cains."

"To save your mother?" He smirked.

"To save myself," I corrected, folding my arms across my chest. "You know, had you just been up front with me, things could've been different, *Daddy.*"

His eyes narrowed.

"You lied to me," I pointed out. "Made me think you and Made-laine had this amazing connection because you thought I would want that. Some magical daddy-daughter relationship that would save me. I never needed that, but I could've helped you."

"And why would you have done that?"

"Because money talks," I said plainly. "That's why I'm telling you what I know now. You want me to help you stop the Cains? I'm in. You want to make them suffer? I want that, too."

"And your mother?" His brows rose dramatically.

I took a deep breath and shrugged. "What about her?"

"You seemed pretty upset about the way Beckett and I were discussing her yesterday."

My stomach twisted, but I kept going. "No, I'd let Ryan talk me into sushi the night before and it didn't agree with me."

He didn't look convinced.

"You think I didn't know my mother's a slut?" I added with a snort. "Please. I learned that lesson before I had my first period."

"And all that righteous indignation when I dragged you back here a few weeks ago and you saw her?"

Oh, right. *That.* "Look, that night sucked. You want the truth? I loved Ryan. I would've given everything to be with him, and I was a fucking idiot. I bought into his white knight routine, and thought maybe I'd finally get everything I wanted. I've learned my lesson. My mother hasn't done shit for me, and I'm sick of looking out for everyone else only to get bitch slapped for my troubles."

He made a soft, noncommittal sound, but I could see the wheels turning.

I braced my hands on the desk and leaned forward. "If you don't want my help, fine. Don't take it. But I can give you an in with Ryan *and* Beckett. Ryan's tripping all over himself to make it up to me, and Beckett made it perfectly clear yesterday that he's been working with Madelaine."

"Why would you help me?"

"Because the only person I hate more than you is Ryan," I replied, the lie slipping easily from my lips. "I want to see him broken, and you can help me with that."

He rubbed his jaw. "You know, I never wanted to be a father."

"You're a pretty shitty one," I replied, unable to help myself.

He chuckled, agreeing with me. "True. But it was a necessity. Then again, maybe I took the wrong sister. Madelaine could never see what I was trying to do."

"My sister never had to work for a thing her whole life," I retorted. "Try living with nothing, eating moldy bread and washing it down with sour milk when your mother is too high to remember what a grocery store is. You learn a lot about yourself."

He smiled slowly. "Fair enough. But if you think I'm just going to take your word for everything, you're as stupid as that cunt who birthed you. You want to be my partner? Prove it. Find me something useful."

I stared at him in disbelief. "I told you that Beckett played you. That he and Madelaine set you up so they'd get paid."

He shrugged and sat down. "And?"

I glanced down, wondering what I could share that would prove I was loyal to him without actually selling out my friends.

Maybe a lie with a little bit of truth.

Finally, I looked up. "Ryan told me about his initiation. That he killed someone."

Gary's eyes widened. "He told you that?"

I nodded slowly. "He also told me the real reason for the Shutterfield deal. What you're all planning, but more importantly, what *they're* planning." I lowered my voice as I twisted my engagement ring around my finger, trying to sell the next part. "He and Beckett are planning to cut you out of the deal. He told me not to worry—they'll take care of me when they destroy you."

He froze, fury turning his face and neck red.

"Believe me now?" I asked with a smile.

"We're going to end them," he hissed.

"Yes, *we* are," I agreed, satisfaction curling in my chest. "I need to get back soon, or Ryan will get worried."

He nodded. "Yes, you do. I need to know more about what they're planning, Madison. You want your freedom? You'll have it when they're rotting in the ground." He leaned back in his chair. "I'll have Bernard drive you back to school."

"Mind if I stop upstairs first? I think I'm getting my period, and I know there's some extra tampons in Lainey's bathroom."

He wrinkled his nose in disgust and waved me away. "Go. I'll call you later. And Madison?"

I paused in the doorway and glanced back.

"If you betray me, the Cains aren't the only bodies I'll be burying." He gave me a cold, brittle smile.

Unable to stomach any more time with him, I nodded and walked calmly from the room and down the hall before hurrying up the stairs and into Madelaine's old room.

I closed the door and scanned the room to be sure it was empty before I hurried to the closet and turned on the light. The only air vent was nearly three feet above my head. Thankfully there were shelves full of designer purses under it.

I prayed the wood would hold as I quickly scaled them and used my nails to pry open the grate. Silently begging that there not be something furry or creepy-crawly living in the vent, I shoved my hand in and felt around.

At first, I didn't feel anything. But when I lifted onto my tiptoes and reached a little deeper, my hand brushed something metal. Grunting and straining to reach just a little further, I managed to grab the edge and tug it out.

A key.

The small, silver piece caught the light enough for me to make out a number.

I squinted.

No, a number and a few letters.

It was covered in a layer of dust and grime that I managed to wipe mostly away with my thumb.

Why would my sister have hidden a key inside an air vent?

Knowing I was running out of time, I tucked the key into my bra before I wedged the grate back into place and climbed down, careful to arrange the purses that I'd moved. Once I was sure they looked just as they had when I entered, I spun to turn off the light and ran to the bathroom on the other side of the bedroom.

I'd just closed the door to the bathroom when the door to the bedroom opened. I quickly flushed the toilet and turned on the water to wash my hands, my heart pounding.

Locating the stash of tampons under the sink, I grabbed the box and purposefully looked down as I exited the bathroom.

I looked up, not surprised to see Gary on the other side. I lifted my brows as I held the purple and pink cardboard box in my fingers. I smiled curiously at Gary. "Everything okay?"

"Seems to be," he murmured, eyeing my box and then dismissing it.

"Okay then," I said, still smiling. "I'll text you if I learn anything, okay?"

He nodded and watched me leave the room. I held my breath until I was down the stairs, out the front door, and safely tucked inside the car. Then I let out a slow, shaky exhale and resisted every urge to pull the key out of my bra.

I started to open my purse to text Ryan, but almost immediately changed my mind. I wouldn't have put it past Gary to have had one of his goons bug my phone while I was inside so he could make sure I was actually doing his bidding.

Instead, I closed my eyes and laid back against the headrest while I tried to get my heart to stop racing.

CHAPTER 39

MADDIE

Going toe-to-toe with Gary had caused a massive adrenaline surge, and as we rolled to a stop outside my dorm two hours later, I was exhausted and trembling. I didn't bother speaking to the driver as I exited the car. Once inside the elevator in the girls' dormitory, I leaned against the wall and closed my eyes until it arrived at the top floor.

I pulled my keys out of my small purse and unlocked my door. I'd barely made it over the threshold before a hand pressed across my mouth and I was dragged into the living room as the door was kicked shut behind me.

"Shh," a soft, familiar voice breathed against my ear.

Instantly, I melted against Ryan's chest until he turned me around in his arms. He dropped his hand and made a shushing motion across his lips. Ash, standing at his side, reached for my purse and pulled out my phone before running a wand across it.

Looked like I wasn't the only one paranoid about Gary planting a listening device on my stuff.

"It's clean," Ash finally announced, giving Ryan a firm nod.

I whirled around. "How did you beat me back here? I thought you were following me."

Ryan smirked, his hand sliding up to cradle my face. "Court followed you back. I took my car and passed you a few miles miles from the exit to PC." He jerked a head at Ash. "We needed to make sure you didn't say anything in case Gary bugged your phone or something."

"Oh," I managed, my heart still pounding from the surprise of him grabbing me and Gary being freaking Gary.

Ryan wasted no time, stepping forward and hauling me back into his arms. "Are you okay?"

The shaking that I'd been able to mostly control came back in full force as soon as my cheek rested against his chest. I couldn't even lift my arms to wrap them around him.

"Jesus," he swore, pulling back to look me in the eye. Whatever he saw made his jaw clench as a hand slid up to cradle my face. "Baby, what happened?"

"I can get Bex," Ash offered.

I shook my head. "No, I'm okay. I think. It's just... Holy shit. I think I might've messed up."

"Messed up how?" Ryan asked, urgency in his voice even as he ran his hands up and down my arms like he was checking for injuries.

"Gary knows that you know who I am," I muttered, raking a hand through my hair.

Ryan's eyes narrowed. "How?"

I shrugged. "He put it together? You always call me Maddie, we became close so fast, and you forgave me pretty quickly after the engagement party. You even went out of your way to get Dean kicked out. I mean, I think he had suspicions before, but when he confronted me, I couldn't lie about it."

Not unless I wanted a whole new set of bruises decorating my body.

Instinctively, my hand fluttered up to touch my throat. I hadn't seen a bruise in the mirror of the bathroom, but that didn't stop Ryan from going deathly still as his eyes tracked my movement.

"What did he do to you?" He spoke the words so softly I almost missed them. The darkness churning in his eyes threatened to suck me under.

"Nothing. I'm fine."

"Madison," he snapped, framing my face in his hands. His touch was infinitely gentle, but I felt the barely leashed power behind it.

I lifted my hands to touch his forearms. "He didn't hurt me."

"Then tell me what happened," he demanded.

I sighed, my gaze drifting to Ash like he might be an ally. He looked slightly less murderous but just as concerned as Ryan.

Swallowing roughly, I could almost feel the phantom fingers around my throat. "He grabbed my throat, but I'm *fine*," I rushed to add, tightening my hands when he began to step away.

"Ryan," I snapped when his gaze started to drift, "look at me. He didn't hurt me."

His gaze probed mine for a long moment before turning to Ash, who now stood behind me.

"It would be a mess, but you know we have your back," Ash commented. His ominous tone sent a chill down my spine. "You might need to give me a few hours to get everything in place for you two—"

"Get *what* in place?" I demanded, looking back at him.

Ryan rubbed his jaw, looking torn. "What about the rest of you?"

Ash shrugged as they both completely ignored me standing between them. "We made a deal. If it was Bex, none of us would blink at whatever choice Court made."

I clapped my hands together loudly to stop the crazy train they were riding. "I swear to God, if one of you doesn't start talking—"

"We're talking about killing Gary," Ryan informed me flatly, his gaze almost void of any emotion as he turned his eyes to me. "I could kill him tonight and we could be out of the country before the sun comes up."

My jaw dropped with my stomach. "You're not killing Gary."

His brows raised. "He touched you, Mads. I told you what would happen if he touched you again."

A dark thrill shot through me, and I wasn't going to lie. Hearing him admit that? In that rough, dangerous tone? Was seriously hot.

Yeah, I was officially finding a psychiatrist tomorrow to work out why an alpha asshole turned me on.

"It wasn't a big deal," I protested, trying to keep my brain focused on making sure Ryan stayed here and didn't run off to kill my father. Gary might've scared me, but I also proved I could handle him.

"So, he what? Put his hands around your throat because he was measuring you for a necklace?"

Okay, when he put it like that, I understood his anger.

"We're not killing anyone," I told him. "Not right now. Besides, I think I might've found something that can help us." I reached into my shirt and felt around for the key I'd stashed in my bra.

Ryan coughed a little. "Babe, I'm all about your tits, but I don't see them solving our current problems."

Triumphantly, I pulled out the key and held it up. "You're hysterical." I turned to Ash. "I found this in Madelaine's room. She had it hidden—"

"Why were you in her room?" Ryan cut in sharply.

I bit the inside of my cheek. "I needed to use the bathroom."

"Fucking hell, Madison," he barked, turning away and pacing to the balcony doors. "Forget Gary, *I'm* going to throttle your ass. We talked about you not taking unnecessary risks!"

"*You* talked," I agreed, handing the key to Ash. "I never agreed to anything. Besides, Gary didn't care. In fact, I think I even got him believing we're on the same side."

"How the hell did you do that?" Ash asked in bewilderment.

I relayed the conversation I'd had with Gary. How I'd convinced him that I wanted to hurt Ryan and that we were better allies than enemies. Nervous energy bubbled in my veins when I told them how I'd used Ryan's initiation as proof. I also admitted that Bex had clued me in on where my twin's favorite hiding spot was.

"Please don't be mad," I whispered, looking at Ryan, who was still on the other side of the room.

He sighed. "I'm not mad. Impressed, yeah, and maybe a little worried at how easily you can lie your ass off at the drop of a hat."

"I was kind of banking on the fact that Gary would know about the initiations."

Ash nodded. "You're right. Gary's part of it, so he knows what we've all done. But there's no way *you* should have known unless Ryan trusted you enough to tell you, so you made the right call. The info you gave him wasn't damning, but it *did* prove that you can manipulate Ryan."

Ryan's middle finger shot up at his best friend, but Ash just laughed. "Dude, this girl's got you by the balls and we all know it." He glanced at the key in his hand. "There wasn't anything else with this?"

I shook my head and went to sit on the sofa. I kicked off my shoes before tucking my legs under me. "No. Just that key in the vent."

"It might be to a safety deposit box or a storage locker," Ash mused, running his thumb over the ridges. "But there's no logo or identifying markers. I'll see what I can figure out, but it's kind of a long shot."

"Beckett mentioned paying Madelaine for her part in the engagement party disaster," I added. "Maybe there's a financial trail there?"

"Not a bad idea. I'll check it out." Ash wrapped his fist around the key and gave me a tight smile.

"Did you look at the rest of Madelaine's video files?" I asked, curious to know if there had been more.

Ash nodded. "Yeah. Neither my nor Linc's initiations were on there."

"Thank fuck," Ryan breathed.

"She did record a few more of Gary's conversations. One of which he admitted to defrauding investors in a side project that went south a few years ago." He gave a small shrug. "It's not a lot, but I'll take whatever dirt we can get."

Pleased, I settled back against the couch, my gaze darting to the guy who had been quiet the last few minutes. "Ry?"

He glanced up and blinked, like he hadn't been paying attention. He looked at me and then Ash. "See what you can find out, man. I'm staying with Maddie."

Ash snorted and shook his head. "Right. Because if Maddie hadn't dealt with Gary's bullshit tonight, you planned on sleeping alone."

"No, I didn't." Ryan smirked at him. "The only guy sleeping alone tonight is... you. Now get out so I can finish talking to Maddie before I finish paying up on our arrangement."

My cheeks instantly turned red, and Ash started to smile.

"What kind of arrangement?"

"The kind where—"

I vaulted over the back of the couch and launched myself at Ryan, slapping a hand over his mouth. "Goodnight, Ash!"

He was still laughing as he left us, and I didn't remove my hand until he'd closed the door. The second I dropped it, Ryan invaded my space. He pressed his chest to mine, peering into my eyes for a heartbeat before his mouth slammed onto mine.

I gasped in surprise at the force of his kiss, my back bending over as he dominated me and took what he wanted. I stumbled back a step, and he chased me until my butt hit the edge of the sofa. My fingers clutched at his shoulders to keep from toppling over.

His hand slipped between us and came to my neck, his fingers laying dangerously close to where Gary's had hours earlier. He applied enough pressure to break our kiss and left me panting as I blinked up at him.

The heat in his gaze was like a soldering iron to my heart as he branded me as his with nothing more than a look.

His fingers tightened, not enough to hurt or scare me. Unlike the way Gary had grabbed me, there was control in Ryan's grip. The fire in his eyes didn't terrify me; it *consumed* me.

His thumb swept across the curve of my jaw, his touch demanding and gentle at the same time, erasing the memory of the way Gary had manhandled me earlier. Longing replaced fear, want eclipsed panic.

A soft whimper slipped from my lips as I squeezed my thighs together, desperate for friction to relieve the needy ache that was spiraling tighter and tighter in my core.

His eyes narrowed and his other hand dipped under my dress to delve between my legs. His fingers stroked me over the lace of my panties, not pressing hard enough to give me any sort of relief. I rolled my hips, ready to take it for myself when he snatched his hand away with a hiss.

"Ryan—"

"If you want me to stop, tell me now," he whispered, his voice a rough, guttural vibration humming in the air between us. His thumb stroked almost lovingly over my pulse as it beat a crazy rhythm in my neck. "We can sit down and talk, and I'll take you to bed and make love to you."

The fact that he was holding my throat in his hand almost in the same way Gary had wasn't lost on me. But Gary had grabbed me out of anger and violence with the intent to do harm.

When Ryan touched me like this, I knew he could hurt me just as easily, and in worse ways, than Gary would have. But I trusted Ryan, and knew he was trying to wrest back some of the control he thought he was losing. He was replacing a memory of fear with a new one just for us.

I could stop this, if I wanted. I could step back, and I knew he would let me go. Go back to a softer, gentler Ryan.

But, if I was being totally honest with myself, I loved it when he got this way. When his alpha tendencies pushed past the socially regulated borders of proper and made my stomach clench as heat flooded my core.

Seeing this man come undone, especially because of me, was intoxicating. I'd never get enough of it.

My mouth went dry. "And if I say don't stop?"

The edges of his full mouth curved up. "Then I'm going to fuck you against the couch until the only word you can scream is my name. But I'm not going to be gentle, baby. You'll take what I give."

Oh, shit.

My knees started to tremble as desire coiled under my skin.

He leaned forward and nipped at my bottom lip. "Every. Fucking. Inch." His lips moved to my ear. "What's it going to be, Madison?"

I could barely breathe, let alone think. But one truth would always remain and would always be on my lips.

338

"I'm yours, Ryan. I've always been *yours.*" Heat suffused in my chest as I looked up at him through my lashes. "Do your worst."

The pressure on my neck increased as he pushed me down. "On your knees, baby."

I sank to the floor, a little grateful I didn't have to focus on keeping my knees locked to stay upright. His hands moved to his jeans, undoing the belt and then the button. I could already see the outline of his cock through his jeans, and my mouth watered as I anticipated his taste on my tongue.

He shoved his jeans and boxers over his hips, his cock springing free. He gave me a pointed look before his gaze dropped to his pants, and I helped ease them the rest of the way off while he stripped his shirt over his head before tossing it aside.

I didn't have time to look at all the tan skin and hard muscles before he was tapping the underside of my jaw.

"Open," he ordered.

Obediently, I opened my mouth and gagged as he instantly surged inside and hit the back of my throat. My eyes watered as he withdrew only to push back in as his hands gripped my hair and held me just where he wanted me.

I lifted a hand, wanting to fist the base of his cock and hopefully give myself a little breathing room, but he growled at me and pulled my hair tighter.

"I want your mouth, not your hand," he told me.

Well, okay then. I clasped my hands on my lap, not sure what else to do with them as he drove in and out of my mouth, using me for his own pleasure.

God, why was it so freaking hot?

My hands started to drift under my dress, but I froze on instinct, my watery eyes lifting to see him.

Approval shone in his eyes as he watched me. One hand on my hair eased, and he nodded. "Touch yourself, Maddie."

Not needing any more permission, I pushed my panties aside and circled a finger around my aching clit before sliding two fingers into my soaked pussy.

"Let me see how wet you are," Ryan demanded, his blue eyes bright and hungry.

Almost shyly, I lifted my hand so he could see my arousal glistening on my fingers.

With a groan, he pulled out of my mouth and grabbed my wrist to pull me up. He spun me around to face the couch and pushed me down over the back of it.

"I have to taste you for myself," he murmured as he dropped to his knees. He slid my panties down my legs, and then he pushed my legs wider apart so I was balanced on my tiptoes when he grazed his nose along the inside of my leg.

"Ryan." His name was a breathless plea on my lips that turned into a cry when the flat of his tongue swept up my slit. My fingers curled into the cushion of the sofa.

He ate me like a man starved; sucking on my clit and plunging his tongue in and out of my drenched core. He sank a finger inside me as deep as it would go and rubbed some fantastical spot that had a kaleidoscope of lights bursting behind my eyelids.

I writhed as he worked me over with his mouth and fingers, but when he dragged one finger from my pussy and circled the untouched hole of my ass, I flinched in surprise.

"Ry—"

Oh, fuck.

Forbidden sensations rippled out from the virgin skin as he slowly worked his finger in to the first knuckle. When his lips suctioned to my clit and he pumped the finger in my ass, I exploded with a scream that left my throat raw.

My orgasm hadn't totally stopped when he stood up and pushed inside me with a low groan. His hands clasped my hips in a way that I knew would leave marks.

God, I wanted that. Something primal in me craved seeing his touch imprinted on my body the next day. There was something so deliciously forbidden about the act that it sent a fresh wave of arousal pulsing through my needy body.

"Fuck, Maddie," he hissed in my ear, punctuated by the snap of his hips. "So fucking tight. So fucking mine."

I nodded, wordless and dizzy, as he moved a hand around my front to my clit. His blunt fingers circled it in firm strokes that made my legs start to shake.

Ryan chased me to the top of my orgasm, and for one beautiful, heart-stopping second, everything in my world was right and perfect, suspending in a crystal-clear moment I knew I'd never forget.

Then his fingers pinched my clit, and I surged over the edge in a ball of fire, happy to let myself burn alive if it meant we were together. Ryan came with me, a low groan on his lips that I felt in my soul.

His chest pressed against my back as he collapsed against me, and he pressed a kiss to my shoulder over my dress.

"I love you, Madison Porter," he whispered.

I closed my eyes against the burn of tears. "I love you, Ryan Cain."

CHAPTER 40

MADDIE

The next morning, I woke up sated and alone.
At least, that's what I thought until I heard voices in the
other room.

I sat up and swung my legs over the side of the bed with a wince.
Holy shit, the muscles in my legs freaking *ached*. Ryan had lived up to
his promise and wrung the last orgasm, and then some, out of me just
before midnight. My body was feeling it today.

Honestly, I kind of loved the achy pull of my muscles that
reminded me of everything we'd done.

Except for the mess between my legs because, when I'd finally
fallen asleep, I'd freaking passed out. I hadn't even stirred when Ryan
got out of bed, which was unusual. But now I was really aware of how
much I needed a shower, even if moving was going to be a Herculean
effort.

I was halfway to convincing myself that it wouldn't hurt as much
once I actually got out of the bed when Ryan came back. Noticing my
discomfort, the asshole smirked.

"Everything okay, Mads?"

I flipped him off and stood up, proud when I barely flinched.

He sighed heavily and glanced toward the living room before

closing the door. "All right. I thought you'd had enough last night, but if you really need me to fuck you one more time…"

I pointed at his crotch. "Keep that thing away from me. My vagina is on a mandatory twenty-four-hour hiatus."

He chuckled, his eyes glittering with mischief. "What about your mouth?"

I lifted my brows. "You really want my teeth near your junk when I'm in pain?"

He hissed a breath and moved back a step. "Fair point. The guys are here. They brought breakfast."

I glanced at the clock on my bedside table. We still had almost an hour before classes started. "Why exactly are the guys here?" Excitement thrummed in my blood. "Did Ash find out something about the key?"

"No," he answered with a shake of his head, "but we need to come up with a plan moving forward. This is the safest place we can talk without being overheard, and we have practice tonight."

"What about Bex?"

"On her way up as we speak," he assured me.

"Awesome. Do I have time to shower?" I asked, shooting a wistful look at the bathroom.

The corner of his mouth hooked up. "Depends. Am I joining you?"

"Depends," I countered with a saccharine smile as I propped a hand on my hip. "Do you feel like ever having children?"

He eyed me. "I'll tell the guys you'll be out in a few minutes," he replied, turning for the door. "Take your time, Mads."

"Good call," I said to his retreating back.

I hurried through my shower routine and made a mental note to use the giant soaker tub tonight with some of the insanely expensive bubble bath.

When I came out of the bedroom, dressed and starving, my stomach growled at the smell of bacon, pancakes, and orange juice.

The guys and Bex were using most of the living room, but I loaded up a plate and sat in the empty space between Ryan and Ash on the couch.

"What did I miss?" I asked, popping a piece of greasy bacon into my mouth. I almost moaned in appreciation because it had the perfect chewy-to-crispy ratio.

"Ash filled us in on last night," Bex replied, sitting cross-legged on the floor in front of the armchair Court had taken. "The air vent worked, huh?"

"You're a freaking genius," I replied with a smile.

Ash made a small noise in his throat. "Seriously, what you did was take a big risk, Maddie." He eyed Bex. "And *you* helped her."

Bex scowled at him even as Court tugged a lock of her hair. "I make no apologies for helping my bestie."

"Helping is fine, but you two need to try and stay out of the way where our fathers are involved," Court reminded her.

She tilted her head to look up at him. "Don't tell me what to do."

When he glared at her and opened his mouth to say more, I cut him off. "I can't stay out of it now. Gary expects me to give him info on whatever the Cains are planning."

"Not the worst position for us to be in," Ash added. "We can lead him right into whatever trap we're planning."

"See? I did good." I shot Ryan a smug smirk.

He frowned at me. "No, you did *reckless*. Good just happened to be a lucky as hell byproduct."

"Fun sucker," I muttered, rolling my eyes.

"Aw, baby, you like it when I suck," he reminded me in a deeply decadent tone that made my insides a little melty and my cheeks heat with embarrassment.

Linc set his plate on the coffee table with a groan. "Seriously, I can't handle you two being this fucking cute in the morning. It's nauseating. Can we please stay on topic?"

"Agreed," Ash grumbled.

"Spoken like a guy who went to bed with his hand," Ryan interjected.

Ash scoffed. "And what if I did?" He flashed a feral smile. "My hand knows exactly what I like."

"Mine, too," Bex added innocently, licking a dollop of frosting from her finger as she finished her cinnamon roll.

Everyone stopped and stared at her.

She snorted and rolled her eyes. "What? Guys are the only ones allowed to get off without judgment?"

"Not at all," Linc agreed quickly, his dark blue eyes sparkling as he leaned forward. "But I'm having a hard time picturing the visual. Are we talking left or right hand?"

Court lobbed a biscuit at his head and, with more dexterity than a human should possess, Linc caught it and took a big bite with a wolfish grin.

Sighing, I turned my attention to Ash. "Is there a way to narrow down what the key is for?"

"I'm working on it, but honestly, Mads, it's going to take time." He frowned. "And there's a big chance we won't ever know."

My shoulders slumped a little. "Dammit. I wonder if her CryptDuo app will have anything else in it."

"Maybe? Again, it's going to take time." His lips pulled down in a grimace. "There's a reason the government uses that app for communication."

Bex's head tilted to the side. "What if it doesn't?"

Ash smiled indulgently at her. "Despite what you see on TV, there's not a fast fix for this. The app your dad designed is a fucking fortress."

"Exactly. My *dad* designed it. I'm sure if there's a way to unlock it, he would know. I could ask him," she suggested, her wide eyes looking around at each of us.

"No," Court said almost as soon as she'd gotten the idea out.

She turned and scowled at him. "I want to help, and I bet my dad would, too."

Court's jaw clenched. "No. We'll find another way."

"Why are you being so stubborn about this? My dad could be the key," she argued.

"Your dad can't be the key if he's part of the problem, sweetheart," Linc said softly. The look in his eyes was bordering on pitying, but it hardened when he met Court's gaze. "She needs to know the truth, man. You're not doing her any favors by protecting her."

"Protecting me from what?" Bex asked in a small voice. Her head swung back and forth as she looked between them before finally settling on Court. "Court?"

He wouldn't meet her eyes. He just hung his head and blew out a hard breath.

"Someone better tell me," Bex demanded, turning to Linc.

Linc gave her a steady look. "Bex, your dad is part of it, too. The club, the girls... All of it."

She jerked back like he'd slapped her, bumping into Court's knees. "No way. My dad wouldn't do that."

Oh, hell. My heart broke for her as she tried to fight the truth. As if sensing my pain, Ryan's hand settled on my back.

"Babe, your dad is one of the smartest men in the country, and he's come up with technology that every government agency is dying to get their hands on. You think he wasn't one of the first people my dad approached to help hide his clubs and move his product?" The disgust in Linc's voice left little room to what product he was refer-ring to.

"He wouldn't *do* that," Bex whispered, her gaze begging for him to be lying. When he didn't back down, she turned to Court. "Tell me he's lying."

"He's not, Becca," Court whispered, his dark eyes fathomless as he lifted them to watch her. "I'm so sorry, sweetheart."

She lurched to her feet. "No. No *fucking* way. You're a liar, Court Woods."

He looked up at her and shook his head. "I've never lied to you, Becca. You know that." He grimaced. "Why do you think your parents barely speak to each other? Your mom knows. She found out years ago, but they have a prenup. If she divorces him, she loses everything, including custody and rights to *you*. And it's not like she'd out him—it would blow up your life."

She stumbled back and I started to stand up to go to her. She held up a hand, her wild gaze darting around the room. "You all knew? And none of you said anything?" Betrayal glittered with tears in her eyes as her lower lip trembled.

Ash and Ryan stared at the ground, not speaking and complicit in their silence.

"Maybe you guys should go," I suggested, trying to keep my voice even.

"No," Bex said sharply. "I should go, since I'm clearly the outsider here."

I winced. "No, you aren't."

"Maddie, I love you," Bex told me, tears falling down her face, "but I'm also *well* aware that I wouldn't even be talking to these guys again without you being with Ryan."

"That's not true," Court replied, shaking his head desperately.

"None of you spoke a single word to me for the last eight years. Not until Maddie came here and forced you to let me tag along."

Ryan stiffened. "Bex, that's not how it was."

"Really?" She stared at him, pain etched into her features. "Because where were all of you when I needed you, huh? You were supposed to be my friends, and then just decided I wasn't worth the fucking effort."

"We never—"

"Oh, shut up, Linc!" Bex whirled and glared at him. "You all did. I get it. I wasn't as cool as you guys were. I was just the annoying little sister none of you wanted."

"You're wrong," Court snapped, getting up with fire in his eyes. "There's *so* much you don't know, Becca."

"And why is that, Court? Oh, right. Because none of you tell me *shit*." Her gaze found me. "I need to go."

"I'll come with you," I offered, taking a step forward.

Ryan grabbed my hand and shook his head. "Maddie."

I pulled away and shot him a warning look. "You really don't want both of us pissed at you right now, Ryan."

"Actually, I want to be alone," Bex announced, walking to the door.

"Dammit, Becca," Court snarled, starting to follow her.

"Don't!" She shoved at his chest when he got within range. "I don't want you anywhere near me. Not now, not ever. We're not friends, Court. We're not anything, and I was so fucking stupid to think you cared about me."

"I *do* care about you!" He stepped into her space and didn't move when she pushed him again. "Becca, I was trying to protect you."

"I didn't need you to protect me." A sob ripped from her chest, heartbreak in her eyes. "I just needed you to *want* me."

Court staggered back, and Bex used the moment to slip out the door.

"Let her go," Linc ordered when Court started to go after her.

Court spun, furious. "I can't believe you fucking did that."

Linc looked away, his jaw tight. "She needed to know."

"Not like *that!*" Court roared and punched the wall, putting a nice, fist-sized hole in the drywall. His hand came away covered in white dust and blood.

"Jesus," I hissed, getting up to grab a towel from the kitchenette. I tossed it at him with a frown. "You guys are assholes, seriously. Bex didn't deserve any of that shit, and she *did* deserve the truth."

"I get that she's your friend," Court started, wrapping the towel around his knuckles, "but I've cared about her a hell of a lot longer. You don't know what the fuck you're talking about."

"Watch it," Ryan warned from where he still sat on the sofa. "I get that you're upset, bro, but do not take it out on Maddie."

Court rolled his eyes. "Right. God forbid Maddie gets upset, but Bex is fair fucking game."

"That's not what he meant," Ash countered, trying to diffuse the tension. "And fighting right now is the last thing we need. We need a plan."

Court held up his hands. "You know what? You two plan. It's what you do. I'm just the muscle, right? I'm gonna take a walk." He ripped the door open and slammed it hard enough to make me jump.

After a beat, Linc sighed and stood to follow him. "I'll make sure he doesn't get into too much trouble."

"I have shit to do before my econ class," Ash muttered, getting off the couch. He glanced back at me. "None of this is your fault, Maddie."

Sure didn't feel that way, but I forced a smile as he left. As soon as he closed the door, it disappeared.

"Fuck," Ryan muttered, dropping his head in his hands.

I slowly walked around the couch and sat across from him at the other end. "You realize the moral to the story, right?"

He looked at me with a frown.

"Keeping things from people you love often does more harm than good," I pointed out.

He grimaced. "Do you want me to tell you the whole truth? Because I will."

"There's more?"

He nodded slowly, looking conflicted as my stomach plummeted.

"No," I admitted at last. "I can't know before she does, it wouldn't be right. And if you asked me to keep it from her, I don't think I could."

"Fair enough." He rubbed a hand over his face and looked at the clock under the television. "Why don't I walk you to class?"

I wrinkled my nose. "It feels weird to think about sitting through a class on the limits of algebraic inequalities when our lives are imploding around us."

"Yeah, maybe," he relented, "but at the end of this, I'm assuming you still want to go to college?"

I nodded. "Of course I do."

"Then you need to use that gorgeous head of yours and get good grades." He leaned over and tapped the tip of my nose.

"Ugh." I fell back against the couch. "Can't I just have someone pay my way in?"

He barked out a laugh. "Like you'd let anyone pay your way. I don't think you're capable of letting someone else make a bribe on your behalf."

"True." I smiled at him. "But some days I can't even imagine what the future will look like. Where I'll be, what I'll be doing."

"Me," he answered swiftly with a knowing grin as he pointed a finger at his chest. "You'll be doing *me* in every variation of every possible future. It's probably best if you just accept that now."

I glanced at my engagement ring. "Maybe I can coerce Gary into finding me a less ego-centric fiancé."

With a playful grumble, Ryan grabbed my wrist and pulled me across the sofa until I was half sprawled over his lap. "You love my ego."

I arched a brow. "I love your dick. Your ego is still in question."

His eyes narrowed. "Just my dick, huh?"

My bottom lip rolled between my teeth as I felt his dick swell against my ribs. "You've also got a great ass."

He tipped his head back and laughed, the sound warm and soothing. God, I loved that sound. I loved this man.

And I realized in that moment that there wasn't a lot I wouldn't do, too many lines I wouldn't cross, to keep him.

CHAPTER 41

MADDIE

A week later, and the cracks in our group seemed to only be growing. As I sat at the lunch table in our usual spot, I looked around.

On the surface, everything looked normal.

Well, except for the kiddie table in the middle of the room where Brylee and her friends still sat. They mostly picked at their salads and scrolled through their phones while trying to look elegant perched on plastic chairs meant for six-year-olds.

Honestly, it was hilarious.

But glancing at the faces around our table, I could see the strain.

Bex still sat with us, but she pointedly ignored everyone except me. It had taken Court a few days before he'd finally quit trying. Even Linc seemed disinclined to try and draw her into conversation.

Ash sat on Bex's other side and rarely spoke. He was constantly on his phone.

Ryan was my constant, day and night. He walked me to class without fail, somehow always managing to meet me when my last class of the day ended. Charles had given me shit for it the first few days, but yesterday he'd begrudgingly admitted that he was happy for me if I was happy.

Then he flipped Ryan off before walking away.

Nights with Ryan were my favorite for obvious reasons. I felt safest when I was tucked in his arms as I slipped into sleep. Having him near was as close to normal as I could get, and it was scary how easily we slipped into domesticity with each other.

But the biggest question that loomed in my brain was Gary and what he had planned.

He hadn't reached out to me since the night he'd confronted me at his house, and there was a part of me that wanted to try texting him to instigate *something*.

Ryan was vehemently opposed to me having any contact with Gary.

The chimes signaling the end of the lunch period sounded, and the football players started leaving.

"Wait," Ryan ordered when Linc and Bex started to gather their things. I shot Ryan a curious look, but he didn't speak until the table was mostly gone.

"I need a final headcount for this week," Ryan said, looking at Court.

"This week?" I wrinkled my nose, confused.

He smiled at me. "Thanksgiving. We're all going to my grandfather's. It's tradition." He glared at his friends. "And whatever shit we have going on between us, we're putting it aside for him."

Damn. I'd been so focused on surviving midterms this week that I'd forgotten tomorrow was our last day of classes. And it wasn't like Mom and I had ever made a point to celebrate Thanksgiving, or any holiday really. It was just another day.

Court sighed and pinched the bridge of his nose. "I'll reach out to my brothers and see who's planning on being there."

I reared back in surprise. "I thought you were an only child."

His gaze flicked to me. "My father has another family. I have five half-brothers."

"Another *family*?" I gaped at him.

"Jasper Woods had an obsession with the daughter of the family cook growing up. But Holly Ellis wasn't exactly approved marriage material, so he set her up across town and had seven kids with her." Court grimaced. "One of my brothers died when he was a kid, and my sister was stillborn."

"I'm so sorry," I murmured.

Court shrugged a bit. "It's okay. I'm close with my brothers now that we're all older. They hate the General more than I do."

"So, there's another five Woods brothers running around out there?" I chuckled.

"Ellis," Court amended with a scowl. "They took their mom's last name since they're bastards."

"Oh." I shot Ryan an uncertain look, not sure if I'd just stepped in some family drama.

Ryan leaned in close to me. "They know about Phoenix. They're actually a big part of what makes it work."

"How?" I whispered.

He shook his head. "Not the time or place, baby. You can meet them this weekend."

"Well, some of them. Castle is in basic training and Rook is currently finishing his last tour with the SEALs," Court added, his expression lighter. "Knight, Bishop, and Royal should be there, but I'll confirm to make sure they're back from their last... trip."

Linc snorted and took a drink of his water.

I nudged Bex. "Think you can get away for a vacation so I'm not drowning in testosterone?"

She looked around the table with a bleak expression before meeting my eyes. "And, what? Ask my mom if she'd be cool with me blowing off my grandparents to hang out with the guys of the families she hates and the girl who made my life hell for five years?"

I flinched back and her look softened. "Sorry, Maddie. I didn't mean... I don't think so."

Linc drummed his fingers against the table and glanced at Ryan. "You know I'll be there."

Ash nodded. "Same."

"And Cori's coming, right?" I asked, not wanting her anywhere near Beckett.

Ryan grinned at me. "She'll be there. She loves Grandpa. Probably more than she loves me."

That seemed doubtful; Corinne adored her brother beyond words.

"You should come if you can, Bex," Court said in a soft voice.

She stiffened beside me. "Whatever. I need to get to class. We still on for our study date tonight, Maddie?"

I nodded and watched her gather her things and leave. A second later, Court shoved back from the table and stormed off in the opposite direction.

Linc let out a harsh breath. "Think those two will ever get their shit together?"

"Not if he keeps hiding things from her," I shot back, giving him a pointed look.

"Sometimes secrets are the best thing." His blue eyes focused on me with a dark intensity. "The truth can be more brutal than the lie."

"I disagree."

He grimaced. "That's because you're too naive to know any different."

I bristled. After the last few weeks, the *last* thing I felt was naive. I actually felt pretty freaking jaded.

"Linc," Ryan growled, glaring across the table at him.

Linc held up his hands. "I'm not saying it's a bad thing, Ry. This world we live in is twisted and fucked up, and it's usually women who pay the highest price. Your mom, my sister, Maddie, Bex, Corinne… I'm glad Maddie and Bex don't know how sick shit can get."

"It's hard to protect yourself without all the facts," I mused, shaking my head.

"I'll protect you," Ryan replied instantly.

Ash cleared his throat. "We all will. The same way we've protected Bex. She might not like it, but the lie is easier than the truth."

"I don't agree," I argued, shaking my head.

Ryan's hand covered mine. "I hate to say it, but Linc's right, baby. There's so much fucked up shit in our world I hope you never have to see."

I scoffed in disbelief. "You think I haven't seen the worst?"

Linc's expression turned cold enough to freeze the fires of hell. "I know you haven't, and I'm praying you never do."

～

I knocked on Bex's door later that night and waited for her to open it. When she did, she'd changed out of her school clothes and into pink joggers and an oversized black shirt with the By the Edge band logo on it.

I grinned and pointed to my own white shirt with the same logo. "Look at us matching."

That earned me a grin as she stepped back to let me inside. She waved a hand at her roommate's bed. "She's out. Again. I think she's back together with her boyfriend."

I'd met Bex's roommate only once. She'd seemed nice enough, if a little ditzy. Bex said she was more interested in landing a future husband at Pacific Cross than actually getting an education.

"So, how are you really doing?" I asked as I settled in on Bex's bed while she sat at her desk.

She didn't meet my gaze as she answered, "I'm fine."

I stretched my leg and kicked her chair with my toe. "Liar."

She scowled at me. "I'm surprised Ryan let you out of your cage without an escort."

I smirked, dismissing the barb because I knew she was still hurting over the guys hiding things from her. "My phone has a tracking app so he can see exactly where I am. Besides, he's busy playing frat president tonight. Sometimes we take a break from each other."

"Sorry," she muttered. "That was bitchy of me."

"Considering the shit week you've had, I'm inclined to forgive you," I offered with a wicked smile. "Provided you do me a favor."

"I'm afraid to ask."

"See if you can come to Ryan's grandfather's for Thanksgiving with us?" I gave her my most pitiful look. "Please?"

"We get a whole week for Thanksgiving break," Bex began. "I don't want to spend an entire week with *them*."

"You're not. You're spending it with *me*."

She gave me a look that said I wasn't fooling her, and she was about to start explaining why my argument was invalid when my phone rang. My heart sank, because I knew that sound.

"Ryan checking up on you?" she smirked.

"Ha ha," I deadpanned, fishing my phone out of my backpack. "It's Gary."

Her eyes widened. "Shit. Are you going to answer it?"

"I don't really have a choice." I slid the button. "Hello?"

"What are you doing?" Gary's clipped voice sounded annoyed from jump. Not a good sign.

"I'm studying with Bex," I answered slowly.

"And Ryan?"

"Is at the frat. He has a meeting, but he'll be back in a few hours," I replied, not planning to lie. Not yet. Besides, him knowing Ryan was sticking close to me was a good thing.

He chuckled. "Got him wrapped around your finger, eh?"

"Something like that," I muttered.

"I have some things I need to discuss with you, in private. I'm on my way to the school. Meet me out front of your dorm in five minutes."

My gaze shot to the clock. "Um, okay."

He hung up without a word.

"Call Ryan," Bex ordered, her hazel eyes big.

"And tell him *what?*" I demanded. "He's across campus, and we want Gary to think I'm on his side."

"He's going to lose his shit," she warned me. "Even *I* know we need backup."

I bit my lower lip and checked the clock. Four minutes.

Shit.

"Okay, can you call Ryan? I need to meet Gary." I scrambled off her bed.

"Maddie…"

I paused at the door and looked at her before forcing a smile. "It's going to be fine, Bex. He just wants to talk."

"He's a sociopath!" Bex whisper-shouted at me, standing up. "Maddie, come *on*."

"What do you want me to do? If I don't show up downstairs in three minutes, he'll probably come up here and drag me out. And while I'd love to tell Gary to fuck off, I don't want to blow the progress I've made *or* get kidnapped again."

She huffed as she wrung her hands. "Fine. Go. I'm calling Ryan right now."

"Thank you." I quickly left her room and hurried down the stairs instead of waiting for the elevator. I made it outside and down the steps as a black town car pulled up in front of the dorm.

The driver stepped out and rounded the car to me, his expression almost bored. "I need your phone."

I slowly handed it to him and watched curiously as he tucked it into his pocket.

"Arms up."

I stepped back in surprise, which quickly turned into suspicion when he pulled a thin wand out of his back pocket. "Seriously?"

He simply stared at me until I lifted my arms, then he waved the wand across my body. When nothing beeped, he opened the back door and leaned in. "She's clean, sir." Then he stepped back and gestured for me to get into the car.

Here goes nothing.

I slid into the back seat, where Gary was waiting. His cool gaze swept over me, his mouth pulling down with disdain.

"What the fuck are you wearing?" he demanded.

"Clothes," I snapped without thinking. When his brows slammed down, I quickly added, "I'm sorry. I'm on my period and bloating is a bitch, you know? I wasn't expecting to go anywhere other than Bex's room and my bed."

He seemed slightly mollified at the answer. "You're on birth control?"

I nodded slowly.

"Pill?"

"IUD," I answered, feeling heat rise in my cheeks.

He hummed, the sound almost disapproving. "I'll make an appointment for you to have it removed."

My brows shot up to my hairline. "Excuse me?"

He glowered at me like I was an idiot. "If Ryan knocks you up, we can use it."

It.

My potential baby was an *it* he could use as a pawn.

No. Fucking. Way.

"You know, high school pregnancy wasn't on my list of things to do," I replied mildly, swallowing back my rage. Yeah, Ryan and I had discussed the need to have a baby so his father wouldn't force Corinne into some farce of a marriage to get ahold of their grandfather's inheritance. But that wasn't supposed to happen until *after* we got married this summer, and that was only if we couldn't figure out a way to stop our fathers before then.

Gary waved a hand. "We can pass it off to a nanny when you're done. You'll never have to deal with it again. Although, if you could make it a boy, that would be more beneficial. I'm so sick of girls and their emotions." He smiled coldly at me. "You understand."

I gritted my teeth. "You're aware that women don't actually have a say in the sex of their baby, right? That myth was debunked decades ago."

He simply stared at me, not giving a shit that I had about as much control over the sex of my nonexistent child as I did the weather.

"A baby would entitle us to a share of the Cain estate, but more importantly give us access to the trust Ryan's grandfather put in place to keep Beckett away from it. And I'd love to see Beckett lose everything I can possibly rip from his grubby hands. It would be best if you became pregnant before the wedding. The sooner the better, in fact."

"Uh..."

"I'll see if Dr. Runner can fit you in this week."

"You have a gynecologist on speed-dial?" I frowned and suppressed a shudder.

"I have a physician on call for whatever I need, whenever I need it," he corrected with a withering look.

"It's Thanksgiving, and you know we're going to visit Ryan's grandfather. Plus, I have midterms. I can't miss either of those things," I said quickly, thankful for the excuses. "Besides, I have to be on my period to have it removed, and I'm almost done with mine. It will have to be next month."

His eyes narrowed, and I had a feeling if he thought he could get away with ripping it out of my body tonight, he would.

I crossed my legs on instinct and looked away when he smirked like he knew my thoughts.

"Fine. Next month we'll make an appointment," he agreed. "Now, the trip is actually the reason I'm here." He reached into the inside pocket of his suit and pulled out something small and flat, barely the size of my pinkie nail.

"I know Beckett and Ryan are planning something. I have no doubt that they plan to get you to sign over your shares of Cabot Industries before the ink is dry on your marriage license." His jaw clenched. "Ryan has likely been trying to return to your good side so their coercion is less obvious. I wouldn't be surprised if they tried to turn you against me outright."

I cleared my throat and forced myself to stay calm, flashing him a thin smile. "I think you're right. Ryan's already been making these grand gestures at school, trying to prove he's sorry for the engagement party."

Gary laughed. "Pathetic. For now, let him think he's done just that."

I met his gaze evenly. "Why do you think I let him back into my bed? Hell, he's practically moved in with me."

The approval in Gary's eyes was undeniable. "Well done. Maybe I picked the wrong daughter after all."

I shrugged, trying to feign indifference. "Maybe you did. Again, if you would've just been up front with me, we could've been working together from the beginning." I took the tiny piece of silicon and plastic from his palm. "I assume this is a listening device?"

He nodded. "Exactly. Rebecca's father's newest design. Undetectable from almost every type of scanner. Once you plant it, they won't know it's there."

"And where am I planting it?"

"At his grandfather's home." He grinned at me. "That old bastard hates Beckett even more than I do. I'm sure he's up to something I can use to begin dismantling Cain's empire."

I nodded and folded my fist around the device. "No problem. Do I need to do anything to turn it on?"

"It's pressure activated. Remove the backing strip underneath for the adhesive and press it into place. That will trigger it. Hank is enabling your phone with a Bluetooth app that will record it while you're in the house. Under a desk or in an area where most of the men will be talking is best." His gaze locked on mine. "And I don't think I need to remind you not to get caught, Madison."

"No, you don't."

He smiled, the look reminding me of how he'd treated me before I knew he was the devil incarnate. "Perfect. When you've returned, I'll have a car bring you to the house and you can deliver your phone."

"Ryan's getting needy," I remarked. "He'll want to tag along. He doesn't like letting me out of his sight."

"Oh?"

"He tracks my phone." That probably was a fairly innocuous detail. "The only reason he's not coming to find me is you came to the dorms. If you'd driven away, he'd be chasing us down."

He frowned. "Noted. Well, tell him it's a fitting for your wedding dress. It isn't a lie. The seamstress has some follow up questions, and I can't exactly send Adam."

I snorted before I could stop myself, sarcasm dripping from my words. "*So* sorry about that."

He gave me a sharp look. "Yes, I'm sure you're devastated by his loss."

I gave him my full attention, letting my indifferent mask slip because I wasn't going to hide my real feelings about that asshole. "I wish I had thought of cutting the brakes to his car myself."

His brows slammed down in suspicion. "His brakes weren't tampered with. I checked the reports myself."

I froze. "He was drunk, right? That's what the news said."

"Hmm," he agreed, rubbing his jaw. "Was he drunk when he was with you?" Accusation lingered in his eyes.

"I was more focused on him pawing at me to care about if he was drunk or not," I snapped.

His eyes narrowed, his gaze probing as he watched me closely.

I didn't say anything.

Finally, Gary sighed and settled back in his seat. "He was a tool. Sometimes a liability, but I didn't have to question his allegiance. Although he's one less loose end for me to tie up when this is all over, so I suppose whoever killed him did me a favor."

"K-killed him?" My voice shook. There was no way he could know it was Ryan, right?

Gary simply met my eyes, not speaking.

Someone tapped on the glass beside my head, and I jumped to see the driver standing there.

"You should get back to your friend before you're missed. I'll see you next week when you've returned." Gary's hand clamped down on my wrist and squeezed hard, grinding the delicate bones together.

I sucked in a sharp breath and forced myself not to jerk away.

"Don't disappoint me, Madison."

"I won't, *Dad*," I added with a bitterly mocking bite.

A smile ghosted across his face and he released me. I opened the door and got out. The driver handed me my phone without a word and closed the door before spinning on his heel and going to the front of the car.

I moved back and watched the car disappear down the drive and into the night. It wasn't until the taillights faded from view that I let out a shaky breath and my knees started to tremble.

An arm wrapped around my waist, pulling me backward into the shadows of the dorm before I could say anything. Another hand clamped around my mouth, silencing any protests as I was dragged into the night.

CHAPTER 42

MADDIE

F ear spiked through me, saturating my blood until it ran cold. I managed to suck in a breath through my nose and sagged in relief when I inhaled the scent of sandalwood and spice.

"I wouldn't relax if I was you," a very pissed off Ryan growled in my ear. As soon as we were around the side of the building, he let me go.

"You scared the shit out of me!" I hissed, slapping his chest.

He grabbed my wrist, the same one as Gary, and I winced. He froze instantly. "Maddie?"

I tugged free. "I'm fine. Gary grabbed me there, and I bruise easily."

His chest heaved as he backed me against the rough stone side of the building with his presence alone. "This is exactly why I don't want you near him!"

I lifted my hands to his chest, trying to calm him down, but his anger was a palpable thing radiating between us. "Ryan, I'm *fine*. We both know I don't break easily."

His forehead dropped to mine. "Do you know how scared I was when Bex called?" His hands found my hips, and he pulled me to his chest. "Christ, Madison."

I wound my arms around his neck. "I'm okay. He didn't hurt me."

He pulled back enough to glare at me.

"Much," I amended with a small smile. "But we need to talk about what happened."

He nodded and lowered his mouth to kiss me softly, like he needed to reassure himself I was standing in front of him, safe and all right. He laced our fingers together and pulled me back to the front of the building.

"I need to check on Bex," I started as we stepped into the elevator and he hit my floor.

He wrapped an arm around my waist, anchoring me to his side. "She's with the others in your room."

"Everyone's there?"

"Yeah. Ash thinks he might actually have a lead on that damn key."

I perked up. "Really?"

He kissed the side of my head. "Yeah."

"So it was a *good* thing I went looking, huh?" I couldn't help needling him, but the look he threw my way made my smile wane.

His jaw clenched as he reminded me, "It was *reckless*, Maddie. Gary isn't someone to mess with. We've spent *years* quietly creating a way to stop him—to stop all of them. You got lucky. If he caught you…" He shook his head grimly. "We have to play this perfectly, or someone could die."

I swallowed audibly.

His expression gentled and he reached for my face, framing it in his hands. "I won't let them hurt you, Maddie. But I'd rather not spend the rest of my life in prison for killing them if they come after you." His gaze swept down my body. "I can think of so many other things I'd rather be doing."

I rolled my eyes, trying to downplay the wave of heat that rippled through my body, as the elevator doors opened.

Flashing me a grin that made my toes curl, Ryan grabbed my hand again and led me to my room. He opened the door with his own key. I hadn't given it to him, and I'd decided weeks ago I wasn't even going to ask where he'd gotten it.

Typical Ryan.

Bex jumped off the couch where she sat between Linc and Court—huh, looked like things had thawed between them—and threw her arms around me. "Are you okay?"

"I'm fine," I assured her, but met everyone else's gaze, too. When she let me go, I kept my focus on Ash. "Ryan said you figured out the key?"

He nodded. "Yeah, but don't get too excited. It's to a safety deposit box for a facility in Las Vegas called Pandora."

I tilted my head. "Like a bank?"

He snorted. "I fucking wish. More like a fucking black hole for the worst people in the world to hide all their dirty laundry. It's not public knowledge—you need to know someone to even get an interview to have a box there. Who the hell knows how your sister swung that."

Yeah, I was quickly learning not to underestimate anything my sister was involved in.

"Can we access it?"

Ash shot Ryan a look, bypassing me. I turned to my fiancé with an expectant look.

"Maybe," Ryan hedged.

"*Maybe?*" I repeated letting the annoyance in my tone filter through.

His gaze hardened. "You'd have to use the key. But there's also a failsafe measure, and *that* depends on what your sister signed up for."

"Meaning?" I pressed.

"If she opted for a DNA sample, you're good," Ash explained. "Identical twins have the same genetic makeup. But if she selected a biometric scan—fingerprinting—you won't be able to pass yourself off as her. They'll know you're the wrong person."

"It's a gamble," Ryan finished, shoving his hands into the pockets of his jeans. "I don't think it's one worth taking. None of us would be able to go in with you. They take your phone and check you for wires and recording devices before you go in. You'd have to shower and wear clothes they provide so they can make sure you're not going in to record anything, and the location is a veritable black hole. If you get into trouble in there, we'd never know. You'd be completely on your own."

I let that sink in. "Okay. And if I'm willing to take the risk?"

"It's not just Ryan," Linc spoke up. "None of us think you should take the risk. We'll keep going with Phoenix and handle it the way we've been planning. Madelaine's secret changes nothing."

"Or it could change everything," I argued, turning to Ryan. "Do you know what Gary wanted? He gave me *this*." I pulled the bug out of my pocket and held it up. "I'm supposed to record shit between you guys and your grandfather when we go there."

Ryan folded his arms over his chest. "That's not a surprise. We can even use it to feed him the information we need to send him on a wild goose chase."

I planted my hands on my hips and stared at him. "He's also making an appointment to have my IUD removed so you can knock me up."

Bex gasped beside me. "What the hell?"

Ryan, however, didn't blink. "So we use condoms. Or you have another put in when you come back from having it removed. We can find a doctor who won't tell your father."

Like it was that fucking simple. Clearly he didn't know about the pain and process that was associated with having a piece of metal inserted into your cervix. I'd had mine put in last year, and I didn't plan on going through *that* again until it needed to be replaced.

"We're not having this conversation right now," I informed him, and something in my tone must have resonated, because he ducked his head with a short nod.

Bex touched my arm. "I asked my mom if I could go with you guys for Thanksgiving. I don't know what's going on with her, but she said yes."

Relief surged through me. "Really?" I hadn't realized just how much I needed my best friend close by until now.

She nodded. "Yeah. Apparently my grandparents are planning to go to my cousin's in New York, and my mom was just going to do something with us. But since I can go with my friends, she's going to Paris for the week instead to visit friends."

My gaze cut to Court, who was still sitting on the sofa, before darting back to her. "You're good with that?"

She smiled brightly, but I saw the unease lurking in her eyes even as she happily announced, "Absolutely. It's been a while since I've seen Court's brothers. Knight is a riot—you'll love him."

In my periphery, I saw Court's jaw clench.

"I need to finish studying for my midterms tomorrow." She gave me another quick hug and left.

"She's gonna be the fucking death of me," Court muttered, dropping his head back and covering his face with his arms.

I bit the inside of my cheek to keep from telling him—*again*—that this could've been avoided if they'd been honest with her.

"I'm excited to meet your brothers," I said, trying to change the subject.

Court nodded. "Yeah. Knight, Royal, and Bishop all confirmed they'll be there. They just finished a job for us, so it'll be a good chance to catch up. Plus, we love Grandpa."

My eyebrow quirked up.

"They all call him Grandpa," Ryan explained with a shrug. "They have since we were kids."

"Because he's the only decent grandparent we have between us," Linc mumbled.

"I never knew my grandparents," I added. "My mom's parents died in a car accident when she was eighteen, and obviously I didn't know Gary's."

"We'll leave after breakfast on Wednesday," Ryan decided before giving each of his friends a pointed look. "Good night."

Linc smirked and saluted him as he and Court stood up. Ash flashed me a small smile. Within seconds they were gone, and I was alone with Ryan.

"You're not going to Pandora," he informed me.

I rolled my eyes, having already expected his pushback. "It's a weird name for a super-secret facility, right?"

"There's a strip club on the ground level that acts as a front. The rest is underground. Deep underground. Like twenty stories. And it makes sense. Pandora, like the Greek myth with the box that couldn't be opened."

"No, it *shouldn't* have been opened," I corrected with a grin. "But it was."

"Maddie, stop," he snapped, closing the distance between us and grabbing my shoulders. "Baby, you can't keep throwing yourself into every situation. Let us handle this, okay?"

"*Not* okay," I shot back. "I'm not going to sit back and let the menfolk handle the shitstorm we're in just so you can keep me safe."

A begrudging, amused smile twisted his lips to the side. "Menfolk, huh?"

I jabbed a finger in his chest. "I'm serious, Ryan."

He sobered. "So am I. Something happening to you scares the hell out of me, Madison. I can handle a lot, but not *that*."

I sighed and looped my arms around his neck. "And you don't think that something happening to *you* scares the hell out of *me*? You promised you wouldn't keep things from me, but I don't just want the words. I want us to be partners."

His jaw tightened. "You don't know—"

"If you tell me that I don't know one more time, you'll be sleeping on the couch for the foreseeable future," I cut him off with a grim smile. Seriously—I understood the need to protect me; if I had all the facts, I might feel compelled to protect *him*.

A hand slipped up to cradle the side of my face, his eyes the shade and intensity of a turbulent sea during a storm. "I wish there was a way to take you out of this world. I hate how much you've been hurt by it."

Framing his face with my hands, I peered into his eyes and prayed he could see my sincerity. "I know, but you're not responsible for what other people have done. If we're going to be together, and I mean *really* be together, then you need to accept that I'm not the girl who sits on the sidelines when shit blows apart. I want to be next to you, even if the world is burning down around us."

"What your dad said... About removing your birth control?"

I groaned and slipped away from him. "I feel icky even having had that talk with him. He legit wants me to get knocked up as soon as possible."

"Would it scare you if I said I didn't *hate* that idea?" Ryan asked softly at my back.

I spun, surprised. "Uh..."

He grinned wryly. "There's something about the idea of you, pregnant with my child, that's really fucking hot. I want that."

I ticked up a finger. "First? It's *our* child. Our very hypothetical, *theoretical* child."

With a chuckle, he nodded. "Okay."

"Second, I'm not ready to be a mom. Yet," I added, feeling the need to clarify that point. "Honestly? I never really considered kids until I met you, and that's mostly because I think your father's the brother of Satan for suggesting Cori get married and pregnant to get at your grandfather's money." I took a deep breath. "But the idea of the choice being taken from me is beyond disgusting."

"You're right," he agreed. "We'll figure something out, okay?"

"I feel like we say that all the time," I replied with a groan as I wandered to the couch and fell onto it. I glanced at the clock.

Ugh. I still had at least another two hours of cramming to do before my last midterms tomorrow.

Ryan came and sat on the edge of the coffee table in front of me. "We do say that all the time, but it's true. We're going to get through this, Mads."

We'd better.

Because the alternative wasn't an option.

CHAPTER 43

MADDIE

My brain was mush after finishing all my midterms a couple days later. I was exhausted and spent most of the car ride to Ryan's grandfather's house asleep, after shoving aside the feeling of being a jerk since Ryan's sports car sat only two and that meant Bex had to ride along with Court, Linc, and Ash in the car behind us.

The six-hour drive to Napa didn't seem that long, and I was still a little out of it when Ryan turned off the main road and onto a smaller one lined with huge oak trees and thick foliage. We drove through a tunnel of greenery with hints of the sun peeking through above the canopy. Ornate lamps occasionally appeared among the trees, and I realized this wasn't a road; it was a driveway.

Halfway down, we were met with an imposing wrought iron gate with a sign reading *Brookfield Estate & Vineyard*. An actual guardhouse sat to the left. The man inside stepped out, and I watched as he approached the side of the car.

"Hey, Tim," Ryan greeted easily after rolling down his window. He didn't bother taking off his aviator shades.

"Mr. Cain," Tim replied, dipping his head. His gaze swept to me, and Ryan's hand reached over to settle on my hand possessively.

"This is Maddie, my fiancée," he explained, his tone cool and dismissive.

I almost rolled my eyes, because there was no way Ryan could possibly think this security guard with thinning hair and a handlebar mustache could be competition. But really, his jealous streak knew no bounds.

I leaned forward with a grin and gave a small wave. "Hi."

"Miss," Tim greeted stiffly, but I could see the edges of his mouth twisting as he tried not to smile. He quickly turned his attention back to Ryan. "Your grandfather is expecting you, sir."

Ryan nodded, and Tim took that as his cue to walk back to the guardhouse. Moments later, the gates swung open and we were rolling through the opening.

I slapped Ryan's arm. "You didn't have to be an ass."

He scoffed. "He was checking you out."

"Probably to make sure I didn't have a bomb or wasn't holding you at gunpoint to make you drive here," I teased, shaking my head. Feeling amused, I leaned over the center console and pressed my lips against his throat. "Why? Jealous, baby?"

The hand on my thigh slid up suddenly, dipping under my skirt and cupping my pussy like he owned it before giving it a squeeze. I squeaked and tried to close my legs, but it was too late. His hand wasn't moving.

"I don't have to get jealous." His fingers leisurely stroked the lace of my panties. "We both know who this belongs to."

It was hard to think with his fingers feathering across my core, not giving me enough pressure to do much more than send waves of *want* pulsing through my body.

"Ryan." My voice came out thin and almost whiny. I couldn't stop myself from lifting my hips to search out his touch, craving more.

The asshole smirked. "Yeah, babe?"

"Stop." Gritting my teeth, I reached for his wrist and tried to get his hand out of my skirt. I wasn't walking into his grandfather's house horny with soaked panties.

"You sure?" The blunt tip of his finger pressed more firmly where my clit was.

"*Yes*," I hissed, but I wasn't entirely certain if it was because I wanted him to stop or keep going.

With a dark chuckle, he dragged his fingers down the inside of my thigh before settling his hand on my knee.

I shuddered and fisted my hands on my lap as I tried to get my body under control.

The trees and underbrush gave way to a massive circular driveway in front of a three-story English style mansion. The white brick looked softly weathered, with lush green ivy crawling up the corners and creases and curling around some of the black shutters framing gleaming windows. A fountain bubbled in the grassy center of the circular drive, which extended down a hill and disappeared around the back of the house.

"Holy shit," I breathed, sitting up and peering out of the windshield. "This looks like something out of a fairy tale."

The corner of Ryan's mouth kicked up. "I guess."

I smacked his shoulder again, but this time he caught my wrist and held it. "You know, if we're adding slapping each other to the list of things we do, that ass of yours is going to pay the price."

Well, that was one way to get me to shut up. And yet, as he airily tossed the threat out to me, I didn't hate it. In fact... I was kinda turned on.

He must have read something in my eyes, because he really grinned then and murmured, "Interesting."

Blushing, I looked away and pressed my lips together to ignore the way he laughed. A moment later, he opened his car door and got out, so I took that as my cue to do the same, pausing to shove my feet back into the ballet flats I'd kicked off at the start of our road trip.

My legs ached as I stretched them, and I twisted my back to relieve some of the tension as the others got out of Court's Range Rover. Ryan pulled our bags out of the back before jerking his head, indicating that I should follow him up the front steps to a massive set of glass doors.

I glanced back to see Bex yawn, clearly having slept her way through the drive like I had. When she stumbled a little, Court was at her side to steady her. I called it a win that she didn't immediately pull away.

The doors before us opened, and a thin, willowy older woman with white hair pulled back into a severe bun at the base of her skull greeted us. The formal look on her face softened when she saw Ryan, and she surprised me by throwing her arms around his shoulders.

"Oh, my, boy," she cried, hugging him hard before holding him away from her body and taking a long look at him. "Your mother and grandmother would be so proud." Her gaze cut to me. "And this must be your fiancée."

"Maddie," I said, holding out my hand.

She took it in hers. "A pleasure to meet you, dear. I'm Mrs. Beechum, Mr. Harris's house manager. If there's anything you need, please don't hesitate to ask. I've set you up in the western wing in one of the guest—"

Ryan groaned. "Really?"

A twinkle lit her dark eyes as she looked at Ryan, and I realized she was teasing him. "I'll have her things brought to your room, darling." She winked at me, her mischievous expression instantly putting me at ease. "But if he takes untoward liberties with you, dear girl, say the word."

I eyed Ryan. "Duly noted, Mrs. Beechum."

"Come in," she encouraged us, and we'd no sooner crossed the threshold than she was greeting the others with delight. She fussed over Court needing a haircut, asked Ash if he was still on track with his double majors, and teased Linc about a tackle he'd missed in the last game.

She adored all of them, and it soothed something in my soul to see an adult in their world give a damn. They all grinned at her, eating up her questions and praise.

When she turned to Bex, her head tilted. "Little Rebecca Whittier? I don't suppose you remember me, do you?"

Bex blushed and shook her head. "I'm sorry, I don't."

Mrs. Beechum waved away her discomfort with a grin. "No worries, dear. You were a small girl the few times we met, and quite ill, from what I recall. I'm glad to see you healthy and whole."

"Thank you," Bex murmured, clearly embarrassed by the attention.

"All of you must be exhausted," Mrs. Beechum continued, ushering everyone into the foyer. "Set your bags down."

No sooner had the guys dropped our bags and suitcases than people appeared to carry them up the curving staircase.

I looked around the space, taking in the dark hardwood floors, the gold-and-glass chandelier that hung above us, the cream-colored walls, and artwork that looked like it cost a fortune amongst framed family photos. Looking closely, I could make out younger versions of not only Ryan and Cori, but the guys, too.

"This home is beautiful," I said in awe. Unlike the cold and sterile marble entryway of Gary's house, this looked inviting. Like I could turn a corner and find a stone fireplace with an overstuffed armchair to curl up in, surrounded by walls of bookcases.

I already never wanted to leave.

Mrs. Beechum beamed at me before glancing around the space with pride in her eyes. "It *is* lovely. Clara—forgive me, Mrs. Harris—had splendid taste. It has carried throughout the years." She looked at Ryan. "Your grandfather is waiting for you in the sitting room. He's been looking forward to your visit."

"Is Cori here yet?" he asked.

She nodded, a bright smile on her face. "Yes. She's out at the stables. There's a new litter of puppies. I told Brenda to have her in by supper."

Ryan grinned. "Awesome." He grabbed my hand and tugged me forward.

"Supper is at seven!" Mrs. Beechum called. "And make sure you give those girls a proper tour of the house."

"A tour, huh?" I teased softly.

Ryan's gaze turned molten as he looked down at me. "Your tour starts and ends in my bedroom."

I faked a yawn. "I *am* sleepy."

His lips brushed my ear as he whispered, "And your pussy is soaked for me. Somehow I think we'll be up late tonight taking care of that instead of sleeping." He slapped my ass, and I jolted but managed to cover my cry of surprise as we walked into a room with large windows and several leather couches.

Linc chuckled at my back, and I adamantly refused to let myself turn around. Instead I focused on the man in the wheelchair facing one of the windows that overlooked a lavish vineyard.

"Grandpa," Ryan greeted.

Mr. Harris turned, his weathered face instantly brightening as Ryan went over and hugged him.

"My boy," he wheezed, patting Ryan's back. He looked at the guys behind me. "*All* my boys."

"Hey, Grandpa." Ash went over and hugged him, followed by Linc and then Court.

Bex lingered at my side.

"Maddie." Mr. Harris turned his attention to me. "How are you?"

This was the first time I'd seen Ryan's grandfather since the engagement party. Thankfully he'd left before Dean's shitshow surprise and my very public downfall, but he had to have heard about it.

And yet, there wasn't any judgment in his gaze.

"Hi, Mr. Harris," I returned.

"And Rebecca Whittier." His assessing gaze roved over her. "It's been a long time, sweet girl. How are you?"

"Well, thank you," she answered, the picture of politeness. "And you, sir?"

He scoffed and laughed a bit. "So formal. Please don't feel the need to observe social etiquette in my home. I want you all to be comfortable."

Ryan flashed me a smile. "I already told Grandpa that you both know about Phoenix."

"Which makes both of you family in my eyes," Mr. Harris concluded. "If my boys trust you, then so do I. But first, I'd like to speak with Maddie, alone."

Ryan's brow furrowed as his gaze cut to me. "Grandpa—"

Mr. Harris held up a hand. "It wasn't a request, Ryan. I believe Ms. Flounders prepared some snacks for you all in the kitchen."

Ryan still looked at me and relented only when I nodded.

If his grandfather wanted to yell at me in private about making his grandson look like an idiot in front of the world, I could take it.

"Fine," he muttered. "Let's go, guys."

Bex touched my shoulder as she followed the others out of the room.

"Would you mind closing the doors, my dear?" Mr. Harris requested, folding his hands in his lap.

I turned and closed the heavy wooden doors that shut off this room from the rest of the house. When I faced him again, apprehension swirled in my gut.

This man meant the world to Ryan. He meant something to all of the men in my life I actually gave a shit about. He might be the person who could help us stop Gary, Beckett and the others.

But right now, he was studying me in a shrewd way that missed nothing. His age and the sickness slowly stealing his body away hadn't dulled the sharpness of his mind. As he watched me, I couldn't figure out exactly what he was thinking.

Finally, the corners of his mouth tipped up. "I'm afraid the afternoon chill is getting to these old bones. Would you hand me that blanket?"

I retrieved the one he motioned to at the end of one of the couches. The soft fabric felt heavenly against my palms, and I shook it out as I approached to drape it over his front instead of just handing it to him to sort out.

That must have been the right call, because his smile warmed considerably as I tucked it around his legs. After a second I stepped back, but I wasn't entirely sure what to do next.

He gave me the answer by simply saying, "Sit down, Madison. I think we need to talk about a few things."

CHAPTER 44

MADDIE

"You know my name?" My heart hammered in surprise, and I wondered briefly if this was some kind of test.

Mr. Harris chuckled but it quickly turned into a violent, racking cough. I grabbed several tissues from the box on one of the end tables and pressed them into his hands. Spinning, I spotted a wet bar and hurried to pour him some water.

The coughing fit had subsided when I returned to his side, but I still helped him take a few small sips.

"Thank you," he wheezed, leaning back when he'd had enough, the tissues crumpled in his hands.

A woman bustled into the room like she'd been waiting at the door for signs of distress. I squinted as I watched her take his tissues and fuss over him, trying to remember her name from when I'd met her at the engagement party.

Her blonde and silver hair was kept in a short, smooth bob, and she moved around the room with practiced ease to help him.

"Eloise, right?" I kept my voice soft. "Is he all right? Should I get Ryan?"

"He's fine," she assured me, the elegant lilt in her French accent setting me at ease. She shot Mr. Harris a stern look. "But you *are* over-doing it, and we've discussed this."

Mr. Harris grinned at her, looking like an unruly boy. I saw so much of Ryan in his face. He patted her hand. "I'm fine, Lou. And I'll take a rest before dinner, I promise. Would you mind giving us a few more moments?"

She looked dubiously between us but finally relented. "Very well. But I won't be far." She glanced at me. "Please call if there's an issue."

"Of course," I said.

"Just what I needed," Mr. Harris muttered wryly, "two of you ganging up on me. Although with Vera, I suppose that's three."

"Vera?"

"Mrs. Beechum," he elaborated, then waved a hand at the couch behind me. "Please sit. And yes, I'm fully aware of who you truly are. I had my suspicions when I met you at the engagement party, and Ryan confirmed it when we spoke a week or so ago."

I folded myself onto the seat at my back. "What kind of suspicions?"

Mr. Harris sighed and leaned back slightly, his face twisting into a scowl. "Beckett Cain has been the bane of my existence for nearly twenty-two years. I keep tabs on him and all of his so-called friends. I was also on the board at the hospital in Los Angeles where you and your sister were born. Your father might have paid people to look the other direction when it came to filing the paperwork, but I was well aware that there were two Cabot heirs."

He gave me a pitying look. "Although, I truly believed you'd escaped the dour fate that awaited your sister. I'd never considered that you might eventually be brought back into this madness. That was a miscalculation on my part."

I clasped my hands in my lap. "I mean, why would you have ever thought about me again? If Gary'd had it his way, I'd have never existed."

He snorted in derision. "I highly doubt that. Gary Cabot may be vile and despicable, but he isn't an idiot. He knew your worth, and I'd be willing to wager every bottle in my wine cellar that he knew exactly what he was doing, bringing you here."

"Madelaine brought me here," I corrected.

"My dear, if you believe that, then we have even more work ahead of us than I thought," he replied, his tone grave and serious.

I flinched back. "I was *there*, Mr. Harris. She came to Michigan and made me an offer."

"I'm sure she did," he agreed, "but if you think your father was ignorant of it, you're grossly underestimating him. Your sister was reckless, and it would stand to reason that she ran out of chances with your father."

"He isn't my anything," I replied, coldness seeping into my words. "Gary Cabot is a monster, and he needs to be stopped. And you're not the first person to suggest my sister's death wasn't an accident."

He shook his head grimly. "It wasn't. I saw the medical report. She died of smoke inhalation before the fire ever reached her body, and there was a toxic amount of sleep medication in her system."

My hand drifted up to cover my mouth. "He killed her."

"That would be my guess," he answered gently. "After her stunts last year, Madelaine was proving too much of a liability. When Gary could no longer control her, he took her out of the game."

"This isn't a game," I hissed, tears gathering in my eyes. "This was my sister's *life*. Now it's *my* life, and because I'm with Ryan, it's his, too."

"My grandson is well aware of the risks, but I'm not entirely sure you are." His blue eyes studied me intently. "He loves you. I often wondered if Beckett had taken Ryan's ability to give his heart to another away, and then you came along." His gaze drifted to my hand, where the engagement ring Ryan had given me rested. "Losing you might be the thing that breaks him, Madison. I need you to be aware of that when you're making your decisions moving forward."

"It goes both ways," I replied. "Losing Ryan would destroy me. I love him, Mr. Harris. More than I've ever loved anyone in my life."

Approval gleamed in his eyes. "Good. That's good. I wanted that for my daughter, but she wound up with a nightmare instead. I know she would have loved you, as would my Clara."

"Thank you." I ducked my head, humbled at the praise.

"Now," he started, clearing his throat, "I understand Ryan has informed you about Phoenix."

I nodded slowly. "He has. And I have to be honest with you, Mr. Harris, my father sent me here to spy on you. He thinks I'm working with him."

"I highly doubt that," he rebutted. "He's too skeptical to immediately accept your change of heart. But I would guess sending you here as a spy is a test. One you'll need to pass. I'm certain we can come up with a few conversations he can overhear that will help establish you as a potential ally."

I rubbed my forehead, suddenly exhausted. "I don't know how you all have done this for so long. I've only been in this world for a few months, and I feel like I'm drowning half the time."

"Unfortunately you've been thrown into shark-infested waters in the middle of a hurricane with no life jacket."

"That's a pretty spectacular way of putting it," I agreed with a small giggle. "Have a spare life jacket?"

"My dear, sharks don't need them." He grinned at me, and I couldn't help smiling back.

"Fair enough. But I do want to help, however I can. And if Gary did kill my sister, he has to pay for that."

"One monster at a time, Maddie," he told me. "But our first course of action needs to be somehow minimizing the power that Beckett and Gary have over you and Ryan."

"Gary wants to destroy Beckett." I bunched my lips to one side as I considered how to pull that off.

"We need a way to neutralize them both, or at least cripple them a bit. We'll work on that this week while you're here. I want you as involved as you're comfortable."

"You might want to tell Ryan that. He's the one who wants to put me on a shelf in a glass case." I crossed my legs and gave him a pointed look.

He barked out a laugh. "I'm sure he does. Men can be a bit bull-headed when it comes to protecting the ones they love most."

"I don't think that instinct is gender specific," I added wryly, shaking my head. "If there was a way that I could lock him up and keep him safe, I might be tempted to."

"And that's why I couldn't be more happy he found you," he replied, sagging a bit in his chair like the wind had been knocked out of his sails.

I stood up and touched his arm, worried. "Mr. Harris? Are you all right?"

He laid a rough, cool hand over mine. "Just a tired old man, Maddie. I do think I'll take a rest and leave some of the plotting to the younger generation."

"Should I get Eloise?" I bit my lower lip and cast a furtive glance at the door.

The woman must have the hearing of a bat, because the door opened and she strode in with a slight glower to her angular face.

"I really must insist you rest now," she informed Mr. Harris. She went behind his chair and settled her palms on the handles as she used her foot to unlatch the brake.

He nodded and patted my hand. "Maddie, I've been Mr. Harris most of my life. You can call me Michael." His eyes glittered. "Or Grandpa, like the others."

"Stop embarrassing the girl, Michael," Eloise chided, wheeling him from the room.

"Um, where's the kitchen?" I called as they left.

Eloise paused and pointed down the hall adjacent from her. "Follow that hallway to the end."

That sounded simple enough, but three hallways and four wrong turns later, I finally heard the sounds of people shouting and laughing. I followed *that* hallway to where it opened up into a kitchen a chef would die for.

There was a wall of stainless-steel doors that I could only assume were refrigerators and freezers which matched the three ovens I counted, and two gas ranges. In the center of the room was a massive island with seating for five. Each seat was taken, and a few other people stood around talking.

Five people I knew, three I didn't. But considering how they easily seemed to laugh and joke around with the others, I could tell these were Court's brothers.

It didn't take a genius to guess that Knight was the one seated to Bex's right while Court glared from across the island.

"Maddie!" Ryan waved me over, an easygoing smile on his face that only increased when I walked toward him. He was seated at the end of the row of barstools with Ash to his right and someone I didn't know standing to his left.

Three new sets of eyes locked on me, watching with interest as I moved to Ryan's side and he hooked an arm around my waist to pull me between his legs.

"Guys, this is Maddie," he introduced, kissing the side of my neck as he wrapped both arms around my waist and pulled my back to his front. "Mads, that's Knight—" the guy whose name I'd already guessed, sitting beside Bex "—Bishop—" the guy across from me chugging an energy drink "—and Royal." He motioned to the guy directly at my left.

Royal narrowed his eyes at me. "Nice to meet you." The cool tone of his voice said otherwise.

All of Court's brothers resembled him in some way, so Jasper Woods must have some strong genes. They were huge, and I couldn't spot an ounce of fat on their bodies.

Weapons.

They looked like human weapons with varying shades of dark hair and eyes, except Royal's, which were an icy shade of gray that seemed way too intense.

"Ignore his cranky old ass," Knight chimed in, bracing heavily tattooed forearms on the edge of the island and leaning over to face me with a grin that showcased two insanely deep dimples. He shook his longish dark hair out of his eyes. "Royal's face would break if he smiled."

"How about I break my foot off in your ass instead?" Royal

growled, the ominous threat sending shivers down my spine. He glared at his brother, and I caught a flash of shiny white skin that disappeared under the collar of his shirt. The scar went almost to his jaw. His gaze snapped back to me with a scowl. "Problem, princess?"

I bristled. "Only if you keep looking at me like that."

Bishop laughed, tipping his head back. His dark hair was buzzed short, the look having made him seem like a threatening giant until he'd laughed. *That* sound was rich and throaty. "Fuck, I like her, Cain."

Royal muttered something and turned away to go to one of the steel doors. He yanked it open and grabbed a bottle of beer from the top shelf before sauntering back over and planting himself in the same spot. He twisted off the cap, but before he could take a drink, I snagged the bottle and lifted it to my lips.

"Oh, shit," Bishop hissed, pressing his fist to his mouth as he barely held back a chuckle.

I set the drink down in front of Royal with a saccharine grin. "Thanks for the drink, buddy."

Ryan's body shook with laughter behind me, but Royal let out a noise that sounded like a pissed-off bear. He stalked back to the fridge, grabbed another beer, and this time opened it and chugged half of it on his way back.

"Chill, big brother," Knight commented, shaking his head. He glanced at me. "Seriously, Maddie, ignore his surly ass. He's a bitch unless he's on a mission and can boss us around."

Royal tipped the drink to his full lips again. "Maybe I wouldn't have to boss your asses around if you followed basic directions the first fucking time." He leveled a stare at Bishop.

Instead of crawling under the table and hiding from the anger in Royal's expression—the way most normal humans would have—Bishop smirked and flipped him off.

Royal grabbed his bottle and looked at Ash. "Let me know what you find out, okay? I'm going upstairs."

"Don't be late for dinner," Ryan ordered. "Cori's expecting to see you."

Shockingly, Royal's face softened, and the tiniest of smiles hitched up one corner of his mouth enough for me to see he had at least one dimple, like his brother. "I'll be there. I've missed the little squirt."

"Actually, resting up a bit before dinner sounds good. I could use a shower," Bex agreed, hiding a yawn behind her hands.

"Need help?" Linc offered, sitting between her and Ash.

"Maybe," she agreed, then turned to Knight. "Can you give me a hand?"

As if not sensing that his life was in danger from his half-brother, who was openly glaring at him, Knight held out a hand and helped Bex off the stool. "I live to serve you, m'lady."

Bex giggled, and I swore Court's face turned purple from the rage he was barely holding in.

Bishop clapped a hand on Court's shoulder as they left the room, and Court waited until they were gone before ripping away from his brother and stabbing a shaking finger at Linc. "I swear to Christ…"

Linc held up his hands innocently. "Dude, it was a *joke*."

"Knight won't do anything," Bishop said evenly, the voice of reason. "They're *both* trying to get under your skin. Calm down."

"Fuck off," Court snarled. He turned and stalked out the back door, slamming it hard enough to shake the walls.

Linc rubbed his jaw. "Shit. Think I went too far?"

Ash scoffed. "Yeah. Those two have enough shit to sort out without you adding to the pile."

Linc's face fell, and he stared down at the counter for a second before getting up. He hesitated by his seat and looked at Ash. "You know, he isn't the only one who cares about her. Just because I'm not acting like an asshole doesn't mean I like this anymore than he does."

Ash blinked in surprise. "I didn't mean—"

"You think I wanted to tell her what an asshole her father is?" Linc went on, shaking his head. "I hated doing that, but she needed to know. We've protected her for *years*, and I'm really trying to remember why we thought the best way to do that was keeping her at arms' length. Maybe if we'd been in her life, Dean wouldn't have drugged her that night."

"She also might be dead," Ryan added quietly, his hands tightening on my hips. "We made the best choice we could."

Linc stared at him for a beat. "Did we?" He left without another word.

Bishop sighed and smiled at me. "You sure know how to clear a room, don't you, Maddie?"

"It's a talent," I mumbled, watching as Ash got up next.

"I have some stuff I need to research before dinner. I'll catch up with you guys later, okay?" He was gone in seconds, too.

"And then there were three," Bishop murmured. He froze suddenly, and I had a feeling Ryan was giving him some kind of look since a moment later he said, "Actually? Then there were two. I'll see you guys later."

When it was just us, I turned and faced Ryan, my lower back resting against the edge of the island counter.

"What'd Grandpa want?" He brushed a lock of hair from my face and tucked it behind my ear.

"Why didn't you tell me you told him who I am?" I tilted my head and watched him.

He pressed his lips together. "I didn't want him thinking you'd hurt me when you didn't."

"He told me that he knew Madelaine had a twin."

His eyes widened in surprise. "He did?"

I nodded. "He's kept tabs on Gary because of Beckett."

Ryan snorted. "God, he hates my dad more than I do."

"Didn't think that was possible," I admitted, tracing a star pattern on his denim-clad thigh.

"My dad ruined my mother's life, and my mom was my grandpa's everything. Nana had a hard time staying pregnant. She had four miscarriages before they had my mom, and Grandpa begged her not to get pregnant again when she almost died having her. They both gave my mom everything they had."

"I'm sorry," I whispered, touching the side of his face.

He pressed a kiss to the inside of my wrist. "She would've liked you. They both would have."

My lips turned up. "Your grandpa said that, too."

"We have time before dinner. Are you tired?" The gentle look in his eyes made me want to curl into his side forever.

Instead, I drew in a deep breath and grinned. "Did someone say there were puppies?"

CHAPTER 45

MADDIE

C ori swung our hands between us as we walked back to the house.

"Red is the biggest, but Lovey is the fastest," she informed me. After playing with the litter of Labrador puppies, Cori and Ryan had taken me on a tour of the rest of the stables. Corinne had made sure to introduce me to the horses; Red and Lovey were her favorites.

Ryan had told Brenda, the horse trainer who had let Corinne follow her around for the afternoon, that we'd take over for her once Cori hugged me and refused to let me go. Brenda, to her credit, had smiled and said she didn't mind, and it was obvious she meant it.

"I'm still too little to ride Lovey, but I can ride Red." She leaned into me and lowered her voice. "You really can't ride a horse?"

"I really can't," I assured her for the fifth time.

"Ryan can," she boasted, grinning at her big brother, who held her other hand.

I met his gaze over her head. "Hmmm, I never really considered a cowboy fantasy…"

He laughed loudly, one of my favorite sounds, but Corinne's face screwed up in confusion. "What's a fantasy?"

I coughed a little when I choked on my own spit. "It's like a dream."

"Huh." She shrugged and hummed a song I didn't recognize under her breath as we finished the trek from the stables to the house.

Ryan opened the back door into the kitchen, and three women all looked up. Their faces lit up when they spotted Corinne.

With a squeal, Cori dropped our hands and ran at the oldest woman, hitting her hard around her midsection and rocking her back a few steps until her back bumped into the counter.

Laughing, she wrapped her arms around Corinne. "And where have you been, my girl?"

Cori looked up with glittering eyes. "I saw the puppies, Ms. Flounders! And the horses. Did you know Juniper is going to have a baby next month?"

Ms. Flounders's eyes rounded dramatically. "Heavens, no. What should we name it?"

Corinne giggled. "We can't name it till we know if it's a boy or a girl."

The older woman slapped her forehead. "Of course we can't." Her gaze moved past Corinne to where Ryan and I lingered by the door. "And who's this?"

"That's Maddie," Corinne spoke up. "She's gonna marry Ryan."

Ms. Flounders's brows lifted. "Is she now?"

"That's the plan," I replied with a smile. "It's a pleasure to meet you."

"Pleasure's mine," Ms. Flounders replied with a warm look. She glanced down at Corinne. "And you, little miss, need to wash up for supper. You smell like horses and puppies."

"The best smells!" Corinne proclaimed, throwing her arms in the air with a flourish.

"Perhaps, but not for dinner. Ms. Wallace is waiting for you in your room." Ms. Flounders leaned in close and added in a stage whisper, "I think there's a new dress waiting for you."

Another squeal and Cori snuggled close to Ms. Flounders for a second before tearing out of the room.

"Corinne!" Ryan shouted after her, shaking his head with a rueful smile.

"Sorry! I'll walk!" she called back, and the sound of her footsteps slowed—barely—as she went from sprinting to power walking.

"Sorry, Ms. Flounders," he apologized, and I gaped at him until he said, "What?"

"You apologized. Like *that*." I snapped my fingers, still stunned. I leaned up to press the inside of my wrist to his forehead. "Are you sick? Do you have a fever?"

He poked my side, and I jumped back with a giggle.

"You're hilarious," he muttered dryly.

"And rude," Ms. Flounders scolded. "Maddie, this is Helena and Nancy." She gestured to the women helping her. "One of us is usually in here, should you need anything."

"Rule number one," Ryan warned, "is no touching Ms. Flounders's kitchen."

Ms. Flounders sniffed and turned away. "I like things a certain way, and I've never heard you complain, young man."

"Nor will you," he vowed, placing a hand over his heart before winking at me. "Dinner at seven, right?"

Ms. Flounders nodded as she stirred something on the stovetop. "Yes."

I glanced at the clock hanging above her. We had less than thirty minutes, and I was hoping I could clean up a bit. I could smell the scent of horses and hay clinging to me.

Ryan's hand found the small of my back and nudged me forward. "We'll be back in time."

"Nice to meet you all," I called as I was ushered down the hallway. We passed several rooms—a library, a formal sitting room, a den with a large television, and a massive dining room. A few doors were closed, and it felt like we'd walked the length of a football field by the time we made it to a staircase I hadn't seen yet.

"I'm gonna need a map," I muttered as I started trudging up.

Ryan chuckled at my back and took the opportunity to slap my ass.

I squeaked and whirled around, two steps above him and finally a smidge taller. I glared down at him.

He flashed me an innocent smile. "What? It was *right there*, Mads."

Huffing, I jogged up the rest of the steps and paused at the landing, not sure where to go. There were three doors, and then the hallway curved to the left.

"This is the east wing," he explained. "The live-in staff are in these rooms."

"How many people live here?" I asked as we kept walking.

"Eloise, Ms. Flounders, and Mrs. Beechum. Mrs. Beechum's husband, too. There's a separate bunkhouse and cabin for the stable hands, and then there's another set of cabins and bunks out by the vineyard and orchard."

We turned the corner. "This is the guest wing," he explained. "The guys and Bex are all sleeping here and here." He pointed to a narrow staircase that went up to the third floor.

Two more turns, and my head was spinning.

"This is where the family stays." He pointed at a door. "Cori's bedroom." He sighed at the next door and pushed it open to peer inside. "This was my mom's room when she was a kid."

I glanced around inside. It looked like the room had been suspended in time.

Delicate floral wallpaper with lavender and pale pink flowers covered the walls. There was a white, four-poster bed against one wall, and a matching white armoire and dresser along with two end tables on either side of the bed. A writing desk was tucked into the far corner with stationary atop it like it was waiting for someone to sit down and write a letter. There were paintings of horses, and two shelves of the bookcase near the desk were full of trophies and ribbons.

There was a large window seat that overlooked the backyard. From across the room I could see the stables, the paddocks, and the vineyard in the distance. Endless rows of greenery crawled across the countryside and disappeared down the hill.

"Wow," I murmured, looking up to see Ryan staring sadly at the space. I touched his hand, drawing his attention back to me. "You miss her."

He nodded and closed the door, then pointed down the hall to a set of double doors. "Grandpa's room." He hooked a thumb at another door. "Our room."

I couldn't help the playful smirk that tugged at my mouth. "Ours, huh? What if I wanted my own room?"

His lips pressed into a firm line as he shook his head. "Sorry, baby, but we're out of rooms. It's either sleep with me or bunk in the stables."

I pretended to think it over. "What about the bunkhouse? I'm sure one of those guys would let me crash in their bed."

"Maddie," he began with a heavy breath, "do you have any idea how hard it is to find and train people to do what ours do so well?"

I frowned. "Uh, no?"

He crowded me against a wall with a growl, bracing his hands on either side of my shoulders. "Extremely difficult, and I'd rather not have to hire and train a whole new group because they touched you."

A laugh exploded from my chest. "You're insane."

He cocked an eyebrow. "Only because you make me that way," he replied before leaning in and kissing me slowly.

That spark of desire I'd managed to contain in the car roared back to life like a bonfire set ablaze. My hands reached out for him, hooking in the belt loops of his jeans and trying to tug him closer.

He didn't budge.

His lips left mine and moved to my jaw. "We don't have time for me to do all the things I want to." A hand lifted and palmed my breast, his thumb sweeping across my nipple.

With a soft moan, I arched into his touch. "We can be fast. Really fast."

I felt him smile as he kissed his way to the scoop-neck collar of my dress. The material was too stiff for him to pull aside. That alone was grounds for me to never wear this dress again.

Except, when his hand dipped between my thighs, his fingers easily skated under the hem and brushed against my center.

"I'm kinda curious to see just how fast I can have you coming on my fingers," Ryan's low voice rumbled between us. A gasp ripped from my chest when he eased a finger into my panties and then inside of me.

My head fell back, hitting the wall with an audible *thunk*.

"Shit," Ryan muttered, quickly pulling his hand away.

I started to whine in protest, but he flattened his hand across my mouth. I could smell my arousal on him, and I darted my tongue out to lick his palm.

He growled again, the sound more animal than man, and then he spun me around and dragged me into the room. He shut the door and locked it quickly.

I backed into the space, nearly tripping over a bag at my feet.

"Bed. *Now.*" Ryan's curt tone practically had me running for the bed. He followed at a slower pace. "Palms on the mattress, ass in the air, baby."

A thrill shot down my spine and curled hotly between my legs as I complied. His hands shoved up my dress to my hips while his feet kicked mine apart. I heard the zipper of his pants a moment before he pushed my underwear aside and slammed into me.

My face dropped to the bed as I groaned long and low, the feel of him deep inside me making my legs tremble as my hips hit the edge of the bed over and over. I didn't even have time to catch my breath as he set a brutal pace, using my body just how he wanted.

A finger reached around to firmly massage my clit. I came with a sharp cry, chanting his name as he groaned behind me, his hips slapping my ass as he came inside me.

I collapsed onto the bed, boneless and wrung out. "I'm dead. Go on without me."

He chuckled, the low, throaty sound making my belly clench. He pulled out of me before dragging my ruined panties down my legs. I reached back to pull my dress down so my bare ass wasn't hanging out, but he stopped me.

I shivered as he ran a finger, still slick from my arousal, down the cleft of my ass. Everything in me tensed when he probed, almost curiously, at my back entrance.

"Ryan," I said, unsure if I liked this or not. When he'd done it before, I'd been so deep in my arousal, it had felt fantastic. But now, laying on the bed while he inspected my asshole, I felt vulnerable.

"One of these days I'm going to take you here," he promised, the dark vow sending shivers down my spine. "But right now we only have ten minutes to get downstairs for dinner." His finger disappeared, and my dress was smoothed over my butt with a gentle pat.

Still weak, I pushed myself up. I was pretty proud when I wobbled only a little on my feet. "I need a shower."

"No time," Ryan informed me with a knowing grin.

I scowled at him. "I'm not sitting through dinner with your sister and grandfather like *this*." I waved a frantic hand over the area of my crotch. I could feel us smeared on the insides of my thighs.

His eyes gleamed. "Yeah, you are. And I'm going to love every fucking second of knowing I'm still dripping out of you while we're down there."

My pussy clenched hard enough to make me flinch. I swear, it was like she had her own brain where Ryan was concerned.

His smirk only grew bigger as he watched my reaction. "Tell you what, Mads. I'll help you wash up after dinner. I'll make sure to clean up every last drop."

"You're evil."

He pulled me to his chest. "No, I'm yours."

I laughed. "Same difference."

CHAPTER 46

MADDIE

"I really hate you right now," I hissed as Ryan led me toward the dining room, where I could already hear people talking and laughing. I'd changed into a pair of jeans and a sweater, but I still *really* needed a shower. And the more I walked, the more I became aware of the messy situation I was currently in.

Ugh. So gross.

Ryan grinned at me, unashamed. "No, you don't."

No, I didn't hate him.

But when we entered the dining room, I *was* annoyed and working on a plan to make him suffer later.

A long, walnut table with room for twelve dominated the space. Mr. Harris was already seated at the head. To his left were Royal, Knight, Bex, and Court. To his right sat Ash, Linc, and Bishop. Ryan pulled out the seat next to Bishop for me to slip into, and he sat at the opposite end from his grandfather.

We'd barely sat down before everyone heard small footsteps running.

Corinne burst into the room with a grin, wearing a freaking gown made for a child. Her hair had been pinned up, and she looked ready for a ball.

With an excited cry, she raced past everyone to the front of the table, where Royal waited. He pushed back and caught her in a hug, a smile completely transforming his face.

"Hey, kid," he greeted, the affection in his voice apparent.

"I've missed you!" Cori squeezed her arms around his thick neck and then pulled back. "Did you see the puppies? I showed them to Ryan and Maddie, but you need to see them, too. Grandpa said I can have one, but it has to live here."

"Did you figure out which one you're gonna pick?" Royal asked, his dark eyes locked on her animated face.

With a chuckle, Knight got up and held out his chair for Corinne to take. "You want my seat, sweetie?"

"Thanks, Knight," she chirped, sitting down and never taking her attention from his older brother. Shaking his head, Knight moved to the other side of the table and grabbed the empty seat between Bishop and Linc.

"Oh, I want a girl puppy," Corinne said, completely serious. "But there's two girls, and I don't know which one to pick."

Mr. Harris cleared his throat, clearly enamored with his granddaughter but also seeing the staff hovering by the connecting door to the kitchen, where they waited with trays. "Rinny, can we maybe talk about puppies after we've said the blessing?"

My surprise must've shown, because Ryan leaned in and explained, "Nana was religious and made us pray before every meal. Grandpa still does it."

That was unexpectedly sweet and touching. I paused as everyone bowed their heads for Mr. Harris to bless the meal and the people around the table. He solemnly asked for protection for those that *weren't* at the table, piquing my curiosity.

Apparently I wasn't the only one, because as soon as he was finished, Corinne asked, "Where's Cas?"

"Working, little bug," Bishop answered before murmuring his thanks to one of the servers who began setting plates of salad in front of us.

Her nose wrinkled. "I'm not a bug."

"Sure you are," he teased. "Cute as a bug in a rug."

She giggled. "Bugs don't have *rugs*, Bishop."

"So, let me see if I have this straight." I pointed at Bishop. "Bishop, Knight, Royal, Castle, and Rook? Does someone have a chess fetish?"

Instead of the smile I expected, Bishop's expression darkened. "Our father. He sees us as his own little pawns to move around the board at will."

I tried to make a joke to lessen the sudden cloud of doom hovering around us. "I'm surprised there isn't a King. Or, wait, is that what your dad calls himself?"

Ryan sucked in a sharp breath. Across from me, Court grimaced. "King died."

Open mouth, insert foot, Maddie. I'd forgotten Court mentioned one of his brothers died as a child along with his stillborn baby sister.

"I'm so sorry," I apologized, wishing the floor would open up and swallow me whole.

Bishop smiled at me, but I could tell it was forced. "It's okay. It was a long time ago."

I shot Ryan a desperate look, not sure how to get out of this conversation. He looked at his sister, who was eyeing the multiple forks beside her plate with interest.

"Cor? Maybe we can help you figure out the best puppy," Ryan suggested, using his sister's energy to swing the topic of conversation in a whole new direction.

Forks abandoned, Corinne brightened and started elaborating on the differences between the two female puppies. It only took a few seconds of her exuberance to lift the mood, and soon everyone was chiming in to ask her questions about her potential dog.

By the end of dessert, Corinne had settled on the chocolate Labrador girl and planned to name her Lady-Princess Delilah Autumn Rose. But we could all call her Lilah since we were family. And, not to be left out, the yellow girl was dubbed Empress Sofia Little Foot.

When Ms. Wallace came to get her after she'd finished her chocolate chip cookie dough ice cream with rainbow sprinkles, Cori had someone new to tell all about her puppy. She was happily chattering as they left the room.

Mr. Harris watched her go, his eyes soft and a little misty. "She's growing up so fast."

Ryan nodded and sipped the beer he'd opted for. "She is."

"And your father? Is he treating her any better?"

Ryan shook his head, and Royal scoffed under his breath.

"The good news is he at least seems to have stopped looking at every investor as potential husband material," Ryan added, a note of murderous rage coloring his words. "Now that Maddie and I are getting married in a few months."

I reached over and covered his hand with mine, lending support.

"Perhaps we should retire to my office and discuss a few things tonight so we can properly focus on celebrating tomorrow." Mr. Harris glanced around the table, his expression tense.

Eloise slipped into the room and set down a small cup full of pills and a glass of water.

Mr. Harris frowned but downed the pills and water without complaint.

Court sighed and leaned forward. "I wish you'd consider the clinical trial in Los Angeles. The compound they've come up with is already having great results. It could buy you—"

"No," Mr. Harris interrupted gently with a shake of his head. "And we both know there's no guarantee I'd even receive the treatment. I'm as likely to get the placebo as the medication."

"There's a neurosurgeon in New York who's been in the papers for some new laser removal treatment," Bishop jumped in. "Her name is Skylar Fischer. You could set up a consultation and see if it's an option."

"I appreciate what you boys are trying to do, but no. I'm an old man, and I'm ready." Mr. Harris gave them a sad smile. "I miss my Clara. I'm ready to see her again." He pushed back from the table and glanced up at Eloise. "If you wouldn't mind, Lou."

She nodded and wheeled him from the room, ending the conversation. Everyone got up to follow them.

"What's wrong with him?" I asked Ryan when the room had mostly emptied.

Ryan grimaced as we got up. "He has an inoperable and fast-growing tumor around his brainstem. It's compressing the parts of his brain that control function, and it's already impaired his motor skills and limbs. Soon it'll start pushing into the parts of the brain that regulate his organs. It won't be long after that."

The sadness in his eyes made my chest ache, and I quickly wrapped my arms around him. He hugged me back fiercely, a small tremor rippling through his massive frame.

"I'm sorry," I whispered. "He's an amazing man. I wish I could've known him longer."

He kissed my forehead. "I wish you could've, too."

When we showed up in Mr. Harris's office, everyone was already gathered. I'd expected some formal looking office with lots of bookshelves and old wood furniture, but the room was full of light. Floor-to-ceiling windows looked out the back of the house with a similar view to upstairs. Rolling hills with horses, stables, and the vineyards beyond.

There were bookshelves, but they were white, and framed pictures blocked a lot of the book spines from view. A fireplace was built into one wall, with a framed photo of Mr. Harris and, presumably, Mrs. Harris with a younger Ryan and toddler Corinne on the mantle.

Several soft-looking gray couches and matching armchairs were arranged around a coffee table. Mr. Harris was still in his wheelchair between the two. Knight, Bex, and Court were already on one couch. Ash, Linc, and Bishop were on another. Royal was in one of the armchairs.

Ryan sat in the other chair, and I went to sit alone on the third sofa, but Ryan hooked an arm around my waist and tugged me onto his lap.

I didn't bother resisting. He seemed to like putting me there as much as I loved being able to cuddle against him.

When Mr. Harris smiled at us, I relaxed even more.

"How did things go in Budapest?" Ash asked, looking at Royal.

"No issues. We got all three relocated. Everything went the way it was supposed to," he reported, all business.

"Three?" I interjected.

Royal's gaze flicked to me with... annoyance? "I thought she was aware of what we were doing."

Ryan stiffened beneath me, but I didn't need him to defend me from this royal jackass.

"*She* is right here and has a name," I snapped. "And I'm so sorry if I don't know all the shorthand jargon yet, but I'm learning."

"Three kids," Bishop explained, shooting his older brother a glare. "They were being moved from Indonesia to Budapest under fake visas as exchange students. We intercepted them before they could be sold off and found stable housing for them where they'll be treated as kids and not indentured servants for the next fifty years."

"Jesus," I murmured, looking at Bex who looked as ill as I felt.

"Couldn't some of them just go back home?" Bex asked.

Court touched her leg, the gesture both comforting and intimate. "Who do you think sold them, sweetheart?"

She recoiled in horror.

"It happens more than you'd think," Linc added. "Especially in rural areas of poor countries. Sometimes the parents think they're giving their kids a chance at a better future, but a lot of times it's just greed."

I sat back as the guys discussed another upcoming mission— apparently there was a new *shipment* going to Linc's father's club in Buenos Aires at the same time as the one in Morocco. The guys were split on which group to save, but both weren't an option.

"This is why we need a second team," Linc fumed, running a hand through his hair. "We need more people so we can spread out more."

"We could try splitting—"

"No," Royal snapped, cutting Knight off with a sharp look of reproach. "There's only three of us as it is. Maybe when Cas finishes his last tour and joins us we can consider breaking into pairs, but even then..." His dark eyes cut to Linc, and he heaved a heavy breath. "Kent's not content moving a couple women or kids around at a time. He and Jasper are talking about moving up to a larger scale. They met with the Russians last week. They're finalizing everything in the next few weeks."

Court sat up, eyes wide. "How the hell did we miss that?"

"Because we've been too preoccupied with Gary and Beckett," Ash muttered, clearly frustrated. "Fuck."

"Russians?" I pressed, looking at Ryan.

His mouth flattened. "They operate one of the biggest trafficking networks in the world. If Linc's and Court's dads start using them, it opens up a huge network that will be damn near impossible to shut down."

"Everything hinges on them being able to buy in," Ash argued. "They don't have that kind of capital."

"Yet," Linc protested. "But Beckett and Gary could, theoretically, decide to play nice with each other again, and then..."

"We need to stop Gary and Beckett now," Ryan mused.

Mr. Harris cleared his throat. "How much is left before we would gain control of Cain Industries?"

Ash sighed. "With all the shares we've bought up, we have forty-three percent. We don't have controlling interest."

"You own forty-three percent of Cain Industries?" Bex gaped at them.

Ash smirked and nodded. "We've been slowly buying them up under different shell companies owned by Phoenix. Beckett thinks he's selling off tiny pieces of his companies to help keep his accounts flush and subsidize the money he's been hemorrhaging from bad investments. When we finally get enough to have controlling interest in CI, we'll merge all the shell companies under Phoenix and *we'll* own Cabot Industries."

"That's diabolical," she murmured.

"And brilliant," I chimed in.

Ryan laced our fingers. "Thanks, baby."

Mr. Harris nodded slowly. "What about Cabot?"

"Technically he still has the higher financial portfolio, but it's a house of cards. He's been shuffling money around, and it's spread thin. He needs an influx of cash *soon*. They both do."

"Sooner than later." Bishop's lips thinned. "The deal with the Russians is going forward. Beckett and Gary need to get the money together, or things will start going bad. You can't just break a deal with the Russian mafia."

"That's why he's determined to have the wedding happen soon." I frowned. He was gambling his future on a payout of the trust fund that had been set aside for me. That money would set him up. "And probably why he wants me to get pregnant."

"Pregnant?" Knight's nose wrinkled in disgust. "Aren't you still in high school?"

"He knows about my will," Mr. Harris murmured, thoughtfully rubbing his jaw.

"Your will?" Knight asked curiously.

Mr. Harris hissed out a breath. "I knew Beckett would be able to manipulate Ryan by threatening Cori, so I rewrote my will. The bulk of my estate goes to their children."

"Smart," Royal mused, nodding slowly as he agreed with the plan.

I nodded. "Yeah, well, Gary's counting on me to get pregnant so we have access to that money too. The plan is for me to get knocked up, and then he generously offered to let me hand off my baby to nannies."

"Fucking hell," Royal hissed, leaning back and crossing his ankle over his knee. He looked offended at the idea, and I kind of liked him at that moment.

Ryan shook his head. "We're fighting wars on too many fronts. We have to figure out a way to minimize it. Royal's right—we're spread too thin."

"How?" Bex asked, her voice hesitant as she looked around.

But no one seemed to have an answer.

My stomach sank as I leaned back against Ryan. Like he sensed my worry, he wrapped an arm around my waist.

Mr. Harris finally let out a shaky breath. "We still have several days. We'll come up with a plan."

"And if we don't?" Royal demanded, his tone biting. "Then all of this is for nothing."

Mr. Harris sat up a little straighter, his eyes sharpening as he looked every single one of us in the eye. "I'm not dying without knowing I've destroyed everything Beckett Cain has built."

CHAPTER 47

MADDIE

Despite the lingering doubt about how we would stop our fathers, the guys seemed able to set it all aside for Thanksgiving. They played touch football out in the yard with Corinne, though half the time it seemed like *she* was the football based on how much they carried her around. Bex and I joined them, and I wasn't sure why Ryan put me on the opposite team from himself until he tackled me and pinned me to the lawn to kiss me senseless while everyone laughed.

Knight tried pulling the same move with Bex, sans kissing. Apparently Court wasn't happy about it, because on the next play, he tackled his half brother with enough force to knock his leg off.

Yes. His *leg*.

Apparently his left leg from the knee down was prosthetic. When Bex and I stopped and stared, He nonchalantly explained he'd lost it when an IED exploded under his humvee the previous year. He grinned at us while strapping it back on, not seeming bothered by the injury at all. Cori, also clearly used to it, even stopped to help him.

Dinner was calm and fun, but I could see the strain on Mr. Harris. His hands shook as he tried to eat dinner, and he left before dessert was finished. He asked Cori to take him upstairs and read him a bedtime story, and she happily scampered off.

The staff started clearing the plates, and I immediately got up to help them. Ryan stopped me with an amused look. "They've got it, Mads."

My eyebrows crawled up my forehead. "Wow. You can't even stop being a douche on a holiday where you're supposed to be thankful for all you've got."

Royal snorted a laugh and grabbed a few of the side dishes. "Finally, someone else who doesn't have a silver spoon shoved up their tight little ass."

Ryan hurled a spoon at his head. "Talk about her ass again."

Royal simply smirked, ducking the flying utensil. "I was talking about *your* ass, pretty boy."

I giggled and sidestepped Ryan's reach as I helped carry the dirty dishes to the kitchen.

Ms. Flounders watched me curiously as I set the plates on the counter near the sink.

"And what do you think you're doing?" she asked me, obviously amused.

"Helping," I replied, stepping aside so Royal and Bishop could set their dishes down. Knight and Bex followed them, and then the rest of the boys. It was adorable how uncertain they looked carrying dirty dishes and bowls of food.

"Lord have mercy," Ms. Flounders murmured, shaking her head. "This is a sight I never expected to see. But you kids go have fun. We can handle the cleanup."

"You're sure?" I pressed.

She smiled and nodded, then looked at Ryan with a scowl. "This one might be too good for you."

He grinned. "She absolutely is, but I licked her, and Cori says if you lick something you get to keep it."

My jaw dropped open as my cheeks flooded with heat.

"Licked her *where*?" Knight asked, a gleam in his eyes.

Ryan turned and started to talk, but I spun around and pointed a finger at him. "If you plan on licking me again, I suggest you not answer."

With a laugh, he shook his head. "We both know you like my tongue too much for that threat to really matter. Take a walk with me?"

"A walk?" I echoed.

"It's a thing you do with your legs," he explained slowly. Then he started to smile again. "And we both know how much you like doing things with your legs. Personally, I like—"

I clapped my palm over his mouth with an outraged cry. "I swear, Ryan Cain…"

His eyes were practically sparkling with mirth as he dared me to do something.

"Fine," I groused, lowering my hand. "Let's go for a walk."

The early evening air was still cool when we stepped outside, and I was glad I'd brought a jacket with me. Even still, I gripped Ryan's hand and leaned against his arm for warmth as we headed toward the stables.

"Cori seems happy," I murmured as we walked past the barn.

He nodded. "She loves it here. So do I."

"I hadn't noticed," I teased. In fact, I loved the more playful, relaxed Ryan I got to see here. All the guys seemed more at ease. Hell, even Royal had laughed a few times.

"I don't know if it will be the same when Grandpa's gone," he sighed a few moments later.

My hand squeezed his. "What happens to Brookfield when he's gone?"

"It goes into a trust until his great-grandchildren come of age." Ryan's lips quirked into a rueful smile. "He knew my dad would convince me to sell it off."

I glanced back at the house. "Yeah, I'd imagine the house is worth a lot."

He snorted. "The house is only worth a couple million, it's the vineyard that's worth eight figures, easy."

"You say two million dollars like it's *nothing*." I glared at him, irrationally irritated at his indifference to that amount. "That's a freaking fortune."

"I guess."

I nudged his side. "No guessing. It is."

"Fine. But the land is where the value is. The winery is worth exponentially more. My great-great-grandfather started it. Planted the first crops with his own hands. It was a small farm, and then things took off. Now their wine is sold and distributed across six continents." A look of pride entered his gaze as he led me to the edge of the fence that separated the empty field where the horses grazed and the first rows of the vineyard. Across the field I could make out a training arena for the horses.

He led me up a small hill, and I gasped when I saw the valley below. It was filled with row after row of fences that would hold and grow countless grapes when the next season began. I could only imagine how beautiful it would be to see the land before me lush with potential. To the left was a large, stone building that butted up against a copse of trees. Beyond that was a row of small cabins and one larger cottage.

"Holy crap," I breathed, taking in the scope of the operation. It was so massive, I couldn't even see where it ended.

"The winery is in that building." He pointed to the largest. "The manager lives in the bigger house, and the rest of the team live in the smaller ones. There's a set of barracks toward the back part of the farm where we have bunks for use during picking seasons. Sometimes we hire five hundred people for the season, if it's a good year."

"Does your grandfather still run things?" I turned to him, curious about how involved his family was.

He shook his head. "No. Not anymore. He's technically the CEO, but it's a title on paper only. The manager runs the day-to-day operations."

"And they'll be CEO when your grandfather…" I couldn't finish the question.

"No, I will be. I'm the executor of the estate until one of my children, or Cori's, comes of age to take over." He looked around, surveying what would eventually be his kingdom. "The guidelines of the executorship maintain that I can't sell off or break up the company. It's protected for the next generation."

I pulled him to a slow stop. "So, you're running Phoenix, finishing college, starting quarterback for a D-1 school, *and* going to be running a winery?"

"And getting married." He winked at me, but I saw the stress lines pulled tight around his eyes.

Unable to help myself, I reached up to try and smooth them away with my fingertips. "That's a lot, Ry."

"There's no other choice," he replied, his hand molding to my hip. "Besides, the manager will stay on to help. Kevin has been with the company since before I was born. He loves it as much as Grandpa."

"Not for the foreseeable future," I muttered, shaking my head. Being at Brookfield was a nice break from the chaos of our lives, but I also knew we were living in a bubble that would eventually burst.

In a few days, we would be back to our reality where lives literally hung in the balance. It was exhausting. Sometimes I wondered if it would ever end.

My shoulders slumped, but Ryan was quick to bend at the knees and meet my eyes. He gently lifted my chin up with his knuckles.

"Maddie, we—"

"Will get through this," I finished for him. "How are you not *exhausted*? It doesn't seem like we'll ever be on the other side."

"We will," he promised, wrapping an arm around my shoulders and pulling me against the hard wall of his chest. "One of these days, we'll be standing here with our kids running around playing."

I dropped my head back with a half-laugh, half-groan. "Oh, yeah? And how many kids are we having in this future?"

"Seven?"

I pulled back immediately, like I could get pregnant from a hug. "Are you birthing five of those?"

He grinned at me. "Split the difference at five?"

Smiling, I patted his cheek. "Sure, babe. As soon as you figure out how to get pregnant three times on your own."

He rolled his eyes. "Fine, we'll talk about it another time."

I snorted but didn't argue with him. Last I checked, it was my uterus, so that entitled me to the majority vote in what happened with it.

Speaking of majority...

I leaned against Ryan's shoulder and inhaled deeply, the warm scents of fall and earth filling my nostrils. "We just need a way to take down Gary and Beckett. They're the money behind it all. If we can back them into a corner, we might get an advantage."

"They're the first domino," he agreed, frown lines appearing between his eyes. "Taking them down is the first step, but..."

I let out a long breath. "But *how?*"

"We need to let your dad overhear a conversation." He rubbed the back of his neck, and I caught a glimpse of the numbers tattooed on the inside of his bicep. "Maybe we can spin that to help us."

My lips bunched to one side as I thought. "Ash said his money is spread thin."

"Yeah, and he's counting on your money to make him flush again." He gave me a funny look. "Marry me."

"Did you miss the part where we're already engaged?" I laughed and flashed the ring in his face as proof.

"No, marry me now. Tomorrow."

I might have laughed it off as a joke if it wasn't for the fact that he looked dead-ass serious.

"Wait—you're not kidding?" I gaped at him. "Ryan—"

He cut me off. "Mads, think about it. The whole reason we're getting married is to access your money. Gary thinks you'll hand it over to him, and my dad thinks we'll give it to him. What if we don't do either?"

"We take the money and run?" As far as plans went, I didn't totally hate it, but I doubted that's where he was going with the idea.

"No, smart-ass," he retorted, rolling his eyes. "We come clean and tell them we're in love and *we're* keeping the money."

My eyes widened. "They'd lose their shit."

He grinned at me. "Exactly. They'd be so fucking crazy over how to pay off the debt they've been amassing that they'd have to lay low to avoid the investors they've ripped off. If we make it known that our money is *ours*, and we have no plans to share it, then they're fucked. Especially if the Russians get wind that they're not getting paid."

"Cori," I said suddenly, shaking my head. "Your dad could go after Cori."

"No way he could marry her off. No one would take the risk with him being under that much scrutiny." His smile grew calculating. "Especially not if she's hidden away somewhere and we tell people that you're pregnant."

"Now I'm pregnant, too?" I laughed at him, unable to help myself. "Ryan, I'm *not* pregnant."

"They don't know that," he pointed out. "And I'm sure we could use a fake sonogram photo or something to drive the point home. It's not a permanent fix, Maddie, but it could send them into enough of a tailspin that we could do real damage. Beckett might even be desperate enough to sell off the last eight percent of Cain Industries that we need to take control once and for all."

"You really think it would work?"

He nodded. "But it's more than that. I love you. I *want* to marry you. Not for them or some deal, but because there's no rest of my life without you in it. Making you my wife tomorrow or in ten years won't change the fact that you're mine and I'm yours." He laid a hand over my heart, his eyes burning as they searched mine. "Marry me, Madison Porter."

"Are you asking or telling?" I teased, my eyes welling up.

"I'm begging," he whispered. The sincerity in his gaze was staggering and overwhelming. My heart swelled in my chest, ready to burst.

God, I fucking loved him so much. Maybe too much.

But, for better or worse, we were in this together until the end.

I closed my eyes and dropped my forehead to his shoulder. "Yes."

He held me away from him, grinning like a kid at Christmas who'd just opened the one present he'd truly wanted. "Yeah?"

I fisted the material of his shirt in my hands and leaned back to look up at him. "Yeah. I'll marry you, Ryan Cain."

CHAPTER 48

MADDIE

"**M**addie, this is insane," Bex spluttered after I filled her in on my plan to marry Ryan in—I glanced at the clock—sixteen hours. "Are you sure about this?"

I paused where I was scrolling through my phone looking at a dress I could pick up from a local store in the morning. "Bex, the *only* thing I'm sure about anymore is Ryan."

Her expression softened and she came around to sit beside me on the couch. "Okay, then let's find you a dress."

Ryan and I had gone back to the house and announced our plans to the group. He'd gone off with Mrs. Beechum to plan everything we'd need for a quickie wedding. I insisted I'd be fine wearing jeans, but he'd refused and said just because the wedding was happening fast didn't mean it was going to be anything less than I deserved.

He'd ordered me to find a dress, even saying he'd have it flown in tonight by personal courier from wherever I wanted. I was fine with looking at dresses from the stores in the town a few miles away from Brookfield. Bex and I could get it in the morning.

But the dress was my only responsibility. Ryan said he would handle everything else. I honestly wasn't sure if I was terrified or even more in love with him for that.

Bex and I were debating the merits of strapless or off the shoulder when Linc appeared in the doorway of the sitting room.

"Do you have a preference for cake flavors?" he asked suddenly.

"Are you planning on baking it?" I returned, tilting my head.

He rolled his eyes. "No. Ms. Flounders is planning the menu and needs to know what kind of cake. I was sent to find out, since everyone else is busy."

"Busy doing what?"

He started ticking off fingers. "Ash is handling the last-minute marriage license and tracking down the local pastor. Court, Bishop, and Knight are making sure the grounds are prepared for the ceremony—flowers and an altar and shit like that."

"Of course," I said with a serious nod even though I was beyond amused. "That shit is very important."

Bex giggled while he just grinned and continued, "Royal is on Cori duty. He took her to the stables to see the puppies again. Ms. Wallace will take Cori out in the morning so she isn't here."

"Cori won't be here for the ceremony?" My face fell. I'd kind of hoped she'd be my flower girl.

Ryan appeared at Linc's back. "I wish, but we can't risk my dad finding out about what we're doing. Cori wouldn't mean to, but she could slip and blow up our plans."

"We can trust Ms. Wallace?"

He nodded. "Absolutely. I was actually the one who hired her to work with Corinne. Her parents worked at Brookfield, and she helped take care of my mom. She's loyal to my grandfather's side of the family."

"Okay," I agreed reluctantly. "But I demand a vow renewal at some point where she's part of the wedding party."

"Deal." He flashed me a smile that heated my insides. "Did you decide on the cake?"

"It's *cake*," I whined. "Chocolate, vanilla, red velvet... I'm good with whatever."

"Aren't brides supposed to be super demanding and have had this shit planned since they were five?" Linc grumbled.

"When I was five, I was throwing away my mom's dirty needles and trying to find something edible in the fridge. Not a lot of time to daydream about a wedding," I pointed out.

Ryan's eyes flashed, pissed at the mention of how I'd grown up. "Your mom is—"

"Sick," I finished for him, a warning edge to my tone as I gave him a pointed look.

He snorted, but wisely didn't say anything else. "Okay. I told Grandpa what we're doing. He asked if he could talk to you."

"Is he up for that?" I asked, concerned because he'd gone to bed less than an hour earlier.

Ryan shrugged, tight-lipped. "He's in his room. Do you remember which one it is? I need to take care of something."

I eyed him suspiciously. "What?"

"A wedding present," he answered vaguely, his expression unreadable.

I stood up, tossing my hands in the air. "No presents. I can't get *you* anything."

His eyes gleamed. "Sure you can. You can—"

"No sex talk!" Bex shouted, cutting him off. "We get it. You two are horny little rabbits, but we don't all want to hear it."

Linc held up a finger. "I don't really mind so much."

Ryan slapped the back of his head and Linc yelped, rubbing the sore spot. "You brought it up, asshole."

"Stop thinking about my girl naked," Ryan snapped.

"Then stop bringing it up! Or find a girl less hot," Linc retorted, sidestepping before Ryan could land another blow.

I folded my arms, wondering if this was how I would spend the rest of my life: watching Ryan and the guys he loved like brothers fighting like children while I stood on the sidelines, ready to jump in if they took it too far.

Truth be told, that version of the future didn't suck.

Bex huffed beside me, but she was fighting a smile. She held out her phone to show me a dress, and everything fell away.

That was it. *That* was the dress I could see myself wearing as I walked down the aisle.

"Maddie?" Bex prompted.

"This one," I whispered, my gaze flying to hers. "It's perfect."

She grinned, triumphant. "I'm ordering it now. We can pick it up in the morning."

"Add it to the list," Linc told her. "Court can pick it up in the morning."

She scoffed. "And let him wrinkle it? Please. Tell him I'll go with him. Dress handling is in the maid of honor manual." She gave me a suspicious look. "I *am* the maid of honor, right?"

I rolled my eyes. "Well, it was you or Ash, and you look better in a dress."

Linc made a disapproving noise. "I don't know. There was a toga party last year, and his legs are pretty spectacular."

A laugh bubbled out of me, and I caught Ryan shaking his head and smiling. I started to walk by him, but he snagged my wrist gently in his rough hand and pulled me in for a quick kiss.

I pulled away with a gasp. "It's the night before my wedding."

His brow furrowed. "Yeah, and?"

I looked back at Bex. "Guess I'm sleeping with Bex tonight." I winked at Ryan's shocked face while our friends laughed. "Bad luck to see the bride before the wedding, you know."

"I didn't fucking agree to that," he spluttered.

"Too bad," I called over my shoulder as I headed for the stairs.

My sense of direction must have been improving, because I found Mr. Harris's bedroom door fairly quickly. I knocked softly on the wood in case he'd fallen asleep.

"Come in, Maddie." His voice sounded muffled and a little weak.

Frowning, I slipped inside and looked around the space. It was done in golden wood tones with cream walls. A few paintings hung on the walls, but mostly it was family pictures. Black and white photos of people I would never meet and colorful ones of Corinne and Ryan.

Mr. Harris was in the large bed, a machine taking the place of what should have been a nightstand. A cannula wrapped around his head, feeding oxygen into his nose, as he sat propped around a mountain of pillows.

I couldn't stop looking around at the room. It was beautifully done, and I could see a balcony with a seating area beyond a set of glass doors loosely covered with a gauzy curtain.

"Feel free to make any changes you like," Mr. Harris offered.

My gaze snapped back to him, confused. "Sorry?"

He smiled, the edges of the action tinged with sadness. "When it's your room, my dear." He looked around, as if seeing the room with new eyes. "I see Clara everywhere in this house. It's why I've never changed a thing, but I don't want you and Ryan to feel like you have to keep the house as a memorial to us. Clara put her own touches on this house to make it a home. I'd always expected my daughter to as well, but…"

He let out a desolate sigh, his shoulders slumping. "I'm sorry. I didn't mean to go off like that."

"It's fine," I assured him, standing near the foot of the bed. "But why would I change anything?"

"Because this will be your home," he replied, like the answer was obvious.

When I couldn't think of anything to say, he gestured to the chair adjacent to the bed. "Please, sit. But first, there's a box in the top drawer of my dresser. Would you please get it for me?"

Nodding, I went to the dresser and opened the top. Sure enough, there was a red box inside sitting beside a stack of photos and old letters wrapped with a rubber band.

I took it out and slid the drawer shut before I went to the chair he'd indicated. Reaching over, I tried to hand him the box, but he waved me off.

"Open it."

Frowning, I tugged the lid up. Inside was a simple silver ring. There wasn't anything fancy about it, and it was definitely way too big for me. I shot him a curious look.

"That was my wedding ring," he explained. "Clara put it on my finger, and I didn't take it off until a few weeks ago." He held up his left hand, looking at it with longing. "The tumor eating away at my brain stole most of my appetite, and with the weight loss, it kept slipping off. I finally put it aside when I nearly lost it last month."

His eyes lifted to mine. "I want you and Ryan to have it. I know you'll likely get your own, but since everything is happening so fast, I thought you might need a ring."

I glanced down at my engagement ring, the same one he'd given his wife when they'd had nothing and his family had disowned him. "You chose love over your family."

He looked surprised. "Ryan told you?"

"When he gave me the ring. The first time." I wrinkled my nose. The beauty of that memory had been tainted by the shitstorm that kicked up later that night.

"I love my grandson, but he can be a fucking idiot."

My jaw dropped.

The twinkle in his eye was something I'd seen in Ryan and Cori. "I know he messed up. I'm glad you gave him another chance. His father is like napalm. Corrodes and corrupts everything he touches. He messed with that boy's head for years."

"Beckett's an asshole," I agreed.

"I can't promise Ryan won't mess up in the future," he warned.

I grinned a little. "Oh, I'm sure he will. Then again, I'm no saint myself." I closed the box and wrapped both hands around it. "Thank you for giving us this. I know it'll mean a lot to Ryan, and it means something to me, too. Family's never really been a thing I had."

"You do now," he assured me. "You have a family and a home."

"Ryan said this place has been in the family for generations," I started, "but your family disowned you, didn't they?"

"For a bit. Until my father died. My mother was always the softer of the two. We reconciled after his death. She never wanted anything to do with business, so Clara and I agreed to take over Brookfield. She loved working the land. She was always in the fields during harvest season."

"I'm sorry I missed it." Seeing the husks that remained from the last season made me want to know what it looked like when the land was full of life and promise.

"And I'm sorry I've seen my last," he admitted. He took a slow, deep breath and began coughing. When he turned away, I jumped up and grabbed the box of tissues on the medical cart by his bed.

"Here." I pressed them into his hand and helped him sit up until the fit passed. With a grimace, I took the used tissues and tossed them into the garbage can, trying my best to ignore the flecks of blood dotting the white napkins.

"Sorry about that." A wheezing rattle echoed in his chest.

"No need to apologize," I assured him, meaning it. I sat on the edge of his bed and wrinkled my nose. "I've cleaned up my mom's projectile vomit more times than I can count. A few used tissues is barely a blip."

He gave a low chuckle and patted my hand. "You're a good girl, Madison. I can see why he loves you. But I need to ask a favor of you."

I cocked my head to the side. "Anything."

"Promise me you won't let Beckett ruin him." The fierce spark in his eyes was at odds with the pale color of his cheeks and the frailty of his body. The weathered hand atop mine squeezed with surprising strength. "I vowed I would get him and Corinne free of their father, but I fear I'm running out of time."

I laid my other hand on top of his and leaned forward. "I promise. Beckett won't hurt either of them while I'm around."

His eyes searched mine for a heavy moment before he nodded and relaxed. "I believe you. Thank you, Maddie."

I squeezed his hand tightly. "I think I should thank *you*."

His brows lifted in surprise.

"Ryan may have a lot of faults, but he also has a lot of good in him, and I think that's because of you and your family. Beckett might've tried to mold him into a psycho clone, but he failed. You were a huge part of shaping the man I fell in love with."

It was the truth. Seeing Ryan here, at ease and smiling, made me realize that whatever goodness had been instilled into him came from this side of his family. Michael and Clara Harris loved their grandchildren unconditionally and had done their best to protect them.

But Clara was gone, and Michael's time was running out.

Swearing to protect Ryan and Corinne from Beckett wasn't a problem. I would spend the rest of my days doing whatever it took to keep that monster away from them.

CHAPTER 49

MADDIE

Adison Cain.

M   The slow smile that had started to spread across my lips was quickly dampened by the realization that at the end of today, that wouldn't be my name.

Madelaine Cain was what the marriage license would say. The name I would have to forge to make this work.

I was starting my marriage on a lie.

A dejected sigh slipped from my lips before I could censor myself.

"Hey," Bex said sharply, pulling my attention back to her. She wielded a makeup brush like a weapon, poised to pluck out my eye, as she arched one of her brows. "What's with the sad? I thought you wanted to marry Ryan." A scowl overtook her. "If you've changed your mind, tell me. I can steal another car, and we'll be gone in minutes."

I looked at my best friend, already dressed in an eggplant-colored gown with her hair pulled back by a jeweled clip. She was ready to stand at my side in less than an hour when I married Ryan.

Sleeping hadn't been a problem last night, which was contradictory to what I'd been told was normal bride behavior. I'd slept soundly, finding relief and surety that becoming Ryan's wife was exactly what I wanted. What we *both* wanted.

But this morning, all I could wonder was if our wedding was even legal.

I'd fallen for Ryan over the span of a few weeks at the start of September. And now I was marrying him at the end of November. Three months.

In three months, I'd experienced my highest highs and my lowest lows.

"Am I crazy?" I whispered, looking into Bex's hazel eyes.

She lowered the brush and crouched in front of me. "Maddie, you're not crazy."

"I can't even sign *my* name to the license," I spluttered, twisting my hands in my lap. "Is this marriage even legal?"

"Mads, it's a piece of paper," she said softly. "What matters is you both know who you are. He loves *you*, not a name." She touched my hands, stilling the way I was cracking my knuckles. "Is this what *you* want?"

"I love him, Bex," I answered, my heart practically aching from how full of love it was. I couldn't love Ryan more if I tried. "I want to be with him forever."

"Are you worried?" Her gaze searched mine.

I shook my head. "No. What happened before... Ryan won't do that to me again." A small smile hitched up the corner of my mouth. "And not just because he's afraid you'll rip his balls off and puree them."

"Damn right I will," she affirmed fiercely. "But, for what it's worth? I don't see him doing that to you either. He's completely in love with you, Maddie. I think he'd walk away from this world tomorrow if he didn't have to worry about his dad or your dad coming after you guys."

"I'm scared," I admitted.

"Of being married?"

"Of losing him." My insides chilled at the thought. "If this doesn't work... I can't lose him, Bex."

She gave me a tight-lipped smile. "I know. These assholes have a way of getting under your skin."

"Did you talk to Court?" I knew she'd gone into town with him this morning to get our dresses, but I wasn't sure where things with them stood.

She shook her head. "No. Court and I aren't you and Ryan, Mads."

"And Linc?" There'd been no denying my best friend had a strong connection to both men, and it wasn't a secret they had a history of sharing women.

"Linc's fun," she answered. "With Linc I can let my guard down because... Because it doesn't hurt as much when *he* lies to me or hides things. Court and I are just... we're too complicated. Maybe in another life, another reality, we'd work."

I sniffled and laughed softly. "Aren't we a freaking mess?"

She rolled her eyes, but I saw the tears shimmering in them before she blinked them away. "We can't be a mess. It's your *wedding* day." She picked up the brush once more. "Now, close your eyes so I can finish."

My eyes closed as I relaxed and let Bex finish my makeup. When she was done, she helped me into the gown that was hanging in a garment bag on the door of the closet.

Smoothing my hands down the bodice, I turned to the full-length mirror on the other side of the room and inhaled sharply. "Oh, my God."

Bex clapped her hands together in front of her face, beaming at me in the mirror. "You look *stunning*."

Objectively, I knew she was right.

The strapless, A-line gown was snow white with a slightly flared skirt and single row of rhinestones around my waist, giving me an hourglass shape. The corset under the gown made my boobs look amazing. The gown wasn't overly ornate and elaborate. It was simple in many ways, a far cry from the monstrosity Gary had commissioned for me by the designer known for her outrageous styles.

I traced the row of crystals on the dress with a smile. They were the same color and shape as my engagement ring.

"Something old," I murmured absently, looking at the ring and knowing it would soon have a companion.

Bex's hands settled on my shoulders. "Your dress is something new. Your something blue..."

I groaned, my head tipping back. Bex had shown up with the blue lace underwear that I was wearing under the gown, and the slit up the center was something Ryan would love.

Crotchless underwear or a chastity belt, it didn't matter. Ryan would always find a way into my panties.

And I'd always let him.

"Something borrowed," Bex added, slipping a diamond solitaire necklace on a platinum chain around my neck. The gem rested at the hollow of my throat like it had been made for me.

I gasped, reaching up to touch it. "This is stunning."

"It's from Mr. Harris," she explained. "It belonged to Ryan's mom. He said it was a gift when she turned sixteen. He's been saving it for Cori, but thought you'd like it for today."

"It's perfect," I breathed as someone knocked on the door.

I half expected it to be Ryan—he'd been angling for a way to see me all morning, but he'd been blocked at every turn by Bex, Ash, and Linc.

It was cute the way everyone was determined to keep with the tradition of him not seeing me, but I was also secretly grateful. Honestly, we could use all the good luck we could scrape together.

"Ryan, I swear—" Bex started.

"It's me," Ash called, amusement infused in his tone.

"Is Ryan with you?" Bex demanded, still suspicious.

He chuckled. "No. He's downstairs waiting, impatiently. I was sent to see if you two were ready. The pastor is here."

I turned and faced Bex. "I guess this is it."

"Or I can grab the car and we make a run for it," she countered, smiling.

"I can *hear* you," Ash drawled from the other side of the door.

Bex giggled and went over to let him in.

Ash stopped in the doorway, his pale green eyes on me as he grinned. He looked gorgeous in black pants and a white button up that contrasted starkly with his dark skin. "Damn. New plan—Bex, get the car. Maddie, we can be in Vegas by nightfall."

"Funny," I deadpanned, slipping my feet into the white ballet flats I'd requested for the day. I didn't need heels and pinched toes on my wedding day.

"I'm not kidding," Ash countered with a devilish smirk. "I'm not nearly as much trouble as Ryan is."

I sighed dramatically. "Yeah, but you already said he has more money than you, and we all know that's all I care about."

He gave a solemn nod. "Of course. What was I thinking?"

I lifted my chin with an indignant huff before my facade cracked and I started laughing. He grinned back at me.

"Bex, can you give us a minute?" I requested. "Tell Ryan we'll be down in a sec."

"No problem," she assured me as she stepped around Ash.

He gave me an expectant look. "What's up, Mads?"

Taking a deep breath, I walked over to him and grabbed his hand. "Thank you."

He tilted his head. "For what?"

"For believing in me when the others didn't," I replied. "If you hadn't looked into things, Ryan and I would still be a mess."

"Truth," he admitted wryly. "But Maddie, I didn't just do it for you. I did it for him, too. Ryan's my best friend, my brother in every way that counts. I've *never* seen him the way he is with you. Actually, that's a lie. He used to act like that when we were kids. Before his mom died. He used to laugh and joke. Hell, he made Linc look like the serious one."

My brows shot up.

"I know, right?" He grinned at me. "You brought back a lot of that light, Mads. You gave Ryan a reason to keep fighting, and you make him a better man."

Tears blurred my vision and I quickly started blinking them back. Bex would kill me if I messed up my makeup.

"Thank you for giving me a part of my brother back," he told me with all sincerity.

"Can you do me a favor?" I asked softly.

He sucked in a breath through his teeth. "Depends. If you really want me to get the car..."

I burst into laughter and shook my head. "No. I'm not running from Ryan. It's the opposite, actually. I'm running *to* him with everything I've got." I squeezed his hand. "But I'd really like it if you were with me when I did."

He frowned, confused.

Shyly, I made my request and prayed he wouldn't say no. "Walk me down the aisle and give me away?"

"Walk you down the aisle, sure," he agreed, pulling me in for a hug, "but I'm not giving you away, Maddie. If Ryan's my brother, you're my sister."

"Thanks, Ash," I whispered around the knot of emotion in my throat.

"But we should really get downstairs before Ryan manages to get past the guys and come find you for himself." He smiled down at me as I stepped back.

"He has zero patience," I chided, shaking my head fondly. I wouldn't change him in any way. I turned to the dresser and grabbed the ring Mr. Harris had given me, slipping the band onto my thumb.

"Shall we?" Ash held out a hand.

I took it with a smile. "We shall."

He led me down the stairs and toward a room at the back of the house. Linc and Bishop stood by the closed doors like sentries, and both smiled wide when they saw us. Both were dressed like Ash in black pants and white shirts.

"You look stunning." Linc greeted me with a kiss to my cheek.

"Ryan doesn't deserve you," Bishop added. "But if you're sure you want to hitch yourself to him for the rest of your life..."

"I've never been more sure of anything," I swore.

"I'll tell them we're ready to start." Bishop slipped inside the room, opening the door only wide enough for his body to fit through.

Nervous butterflies erupted in my stomach. I looked at Linc and

Ash with concern. "You guys are sure we can trust the pastor not to say anything?"

Linc nodded. "He's known the Harrises for decades. He won't breathe a word. Grandpa already made sure."

"Okay." I fidgeted and then froze as the bridal march started playing.

I stared at them both. "Seriously?"

Linc shrugged with an unabashed smirk before turning and picking up a bouquet of roses to hand me. "Ryan wanted your wedding to be as authentic as possible." With those words, he pulled open the door and revealed a completely transformed room.

The few guests we had were standing in front of silver chairs with white padded backs and seats. The sofas and chairs from before were gone. Flowers were everywhere—white and sterling roses. Some of the petals had been dipped in silver paint. A white carpet, lined with silver piping, made an aisle leading to an archway decorated with more flowers. The pastor stood under it, a Bible in his hands, but my eyes were on the man in front of him.

Ryan's cerulean eyes widened for a second before a grin started. He actually licked his lips as his gaze roved down me, taking me in from head to toe. He looked absolutely gorgeous standing there, waiting for me. He wore dark pants, and his white shirt had been rolled up to show off those forearms I loved.

He was every fantasy, every dream, manifested in front of my eyes.

"Ready?" Ash whispered, holding out his arm.

I took it without hesitation. "God, yes."

My fingers tightened around the crook of Ash's arm as he began guiding me down the aisle to Ryan. Bex stood across from him, also waiting for me.

I looked around at the guests with a smile. Court, Royal, and Knight were on one side with Mr. Harris. Mrs. Beechum, Ms. Flounders, Bishop, and Linc on the other. It was small...and it was perfect.

This was all I needed. This man was all I would ever need.

The music, piped in from speakers hidden behind floral arrangements, slowly faded away.

"Fuck, you're gorgeous," Ryan breathed as soon as I was close enough for him to touch. He winced and glanced at the pastor. "Sorry."

The older man smiled, looking bemused at Ryan's slip.

Ash touched the small of my back reassuringly as he stepped around me and went to Ryan's other side as his best man. I passed my flowers to Bex and fully faced Ryan.

His eyes glittered with emotion. "I love you."

"I love you," I repeated, meaning it with every single fiber of my being.

The pastor began the ceremony, speaking words I'd heard so many times on TV and in movies. But now they resonated deep in my bones.

Every promise.

Every vow.

I understood the weight behind the words, the intent that gave them power.

Ryan's eyes never left mine, his hands warmly holding mine as we swore our lives to each other.

The pastor turned to me. "Do you, Madison Porter—"

My breath caught, and Ryan squeezed my hands with a wink.

He'd known. Somehow he'd *known* what I was worried about. Sure, the paper would say Madelaine Cabot, but this moment was for *me*. For us.

"—take Ryan Cain to be your lawfully wedded husband?" the pastor finished.

"I do," I said, barely able to speak around my smile.

"And do you, Ryan Cain, take Madison Porter to be your lawfully wedded wife?"

His expression softened. "I do."

"Do you have rings you wish to exchange?"

Ryan let go of one of my hands to pull a silver band from his pocket.

I stared at the band in wonder, an unasked question in my eyes.

He winked at me. "It was Nana's. But we'll get you your own—"

"I love it," I breathed, cutting him off. It was perfect. Simple and elegant, just like the engagement ring. I didn't need something flashy to prove I belonged to this man.

He took my left hand and slipped the ring on my finger. "I love you, Maddie. Yesterday, today, and every tomorrow until the day I die."

I took the ring off my thumb. His brow furrowed, so I said simply, "Your grandpa."

His eyes shut for a second and he nodded, his throat working.

I pushed the band onto his finger. "I love you, Ryan."

The pastor smiled as he watched us. "It's my honor to pronounce you husband and wife. You may—"

Like Ryan would ever wait for permission to kiss me.

He pulled me into his arms as his lips crashed against mine. Instead of a chaste, simple kiss most couples would exchange in front of people, he teased my mouth open as his hands framed my face to angle my face just where he wanted me.

He licked into my mouth with languid strokes, his tongue curling around mine as he coaxed me into a deeper kiss. I clutched at the front of his shirt until someone started clapping. Then I pulled away with a blush, ducking my head as we turned to face everyone.

My eyes landed on Mr. Harris first, his eyes misty with unshed tears as he applauded. "Welcome to the family, Maddie."

Ryan wrapped an arm around my shoulders and kissed the side of my head. "I'm never letting you go."

I snaked an arm around his waist, snuggling closer. "Same."

CHAPTER 50

MADDIE

By the time Corinne came home a few hours later, the luncheon that Ms. Flounders had set up for us was eaten and the decorations had vanished. I'd changed out of my gown and into another dress Bex had bought me. This one was white with tiny purple flowers dotting it, and I'd kept the underwear, including my matching corset, on, since Ryan hadn't seen them yet.

Somehow I'd managed to sneak away to get changed while he helped tear down all the decorations with the others.

Probably a good call because, once I got my husband into bed, I wasn't letting him out for a while. We couldn't go on an actual honeymoon, but we still had a few days left at Brookfield, so I'd take what I could get.

I walked down the steps as Corinne barreled into the front door with a sparkly pink collar. She triumphantly held it up for me to see. "Look what I got my puppy!" She turned to Ms. Wallace as she came in behind her. The caregiver looked exhausted, but the affection in her eyes set me at ease.

Ryan came down the hallway, still dressed in his clothes from the wedding.

Cori's nose wrinkled. "Why do you look fancy?"

He smiled back at her without a care in the world. "I had something important to do this morning. I was just about to go change."

"Can we ride horses now?" Cori blew past his explanation, not needing details.

Ryan shot me an amused look, and I shook my head. I had zero desire to climb on top of an animal and ride it for hours... unless that animal was the man I'd married.

His gaze turned molten as he watched me, like he knew where my thoughts had gone. I bit the corner of my lip and forced myself to look away before I jumped him in front of his sister.

"Actually, Maddie and I have plans today. Is that okay?"

Her face fell a little.

"I'd like to go horseback riding," Bex volunteered from behind me, brightening the girl's face once more. "But it's been a little while since I've gone, so you might have to show me how." She maneuvered around me on the staircase and came down, holding out a hand for Corinne to take.

"I can show you," Corinne assured her with all the seriousness an eleven year old could muster.

"Congratulations," Ms. Wallace murmured, flashing Ryan and I a secret smile before trailing after Cori and Bex.

Ryan came around the banister, and I paused on the last step as his hands came to my waist.

"Hi, Mrs. Cain," he murmured, his thumb stroking my hip.

I tilted my head to look at him. "What plans do we have?"

"There's apparently this whole law about marriage not being final until it's consummated," he reminded me.

My eyes rounded with feigned horror. "Well, we can't have that."

"Absolutely not." He leaned forward, his lips brushing my collarbone. "But there's still one thing I need to do before I whisk you away and don't let you out of bed for the next day."

I wound my arms around his neck. "God, I love the way your mind works."

"Just my mind?" His breath tickled my throat as he kissed his way up my neck.

I hummed in approval and turned my lips to his ear. "I love the way your cock works, too."

He groaned, his hands tightening to the point of bruising on my waist. "Fuck, Maddie."

I leaned back with a grin. "That's the plan." I gave him a pointed look. "Provided you get dressed and finish whatever pressing task is keeping you from being inside me."

"Tease," he muttered, turning me on the step and cracking the palm of his hand across my ass to get me moving. I yelped and stumbled up a step. "Get this sexy ass upstairs."

With a giggle, I started up the stairs, narrowly avoiding his fingers as they grabbed for my ass and tried to slide up the inside of my thighs. He chased me down the hall to our room, and I wrenched the door open with a breathless laugh only to stop short when I saw someone was already waiting for us inside.

I glanced back at Ryan before settling my eyes on Bishop. "Uh, hey."

"Hey," he greeted, jerking his chin at Ryan. "Ready, man?"

"Ready for what?" I began, but Bishop turned, and I noticed the tattoo gun and machine on the desk.

Ryan stepped around me and stripped off his shirt, tossing it at me with a wink. "Hold that, baby." He sat in a chair beside the desk and laid his arm across the flat surface while Bishop sat in the other chair.

Like he'd done it before, Bishop took a cloth and wiped down the inside of Ryan's bicep where three sets of numbers rested.

10.01

07.18

02.05

He'd memorialized important dates on his arm. The day Cori had been born, the day his grandmother had died, and the day he'd started Phoenix with the guys.

Bishop hit a button and the machine buzzed to life. Ryan didn't flinch as the needle was lowered to his skin.

I watched, fascinated, as Bishop's hand steadily wrote in a new set of numbers.

11.25

Our wedding date.

Bishop wiped Ryan's skin again, smearing some of the ink before cleaning it up and turning off his machine. "You know the drill," he told Ryan, taking off his gloves.

Ryan nodded, his gaze assessing the work. "Thanks, man."

"Anytime, brother." Bishop clapped a hand on his shoulder and started putting his machine back in its case. He paused and glanced at me. "You ever been inked, Maddie?"

I shook my head. "Not yet."

He grinned at my answer. "Call me when you're ready."

"When did you learn how to tattoo?" I edged closer to look at Ryan's arm.

"I bought my first machine in high school. We all need a hobby," Bishop replied with a shrug as he locked the case and straightened. "I like art, and tattooing is an expression of that."

"Did you create the phoenix design?" I asked.

He nodded and held up his wrist. Amongst all the other ink on his forearm was the same design the others had—a fiery orange and red phoenix.

"You all have them?"

Bishop nodded.

"I want one," I announced.

"You do?" Ryan didn't hide the surprise in his tone.

"I'm part of this, aren't I?" I asked, arching a brow.

He nodded and looped an arm around my waist to tug me against his side. "Hell yeah, you are."

"Then I want it all. The tattoo, the secret handshake—"

"There is no secret handshake, baby," Ryan cut me off with a laugh.

Bishop winked at me. "There is. We just haven't taught it to his loser ass."

"How about you *suck* my ass?" Ryan countered.

"Bend over and I will." Bishop lowered the case to the ground and folded his arms, waiting.

Ryan stood up and actually looked like he was contemplating calling Bishop's bluff.

"As hot as that would be," I interrupted, putting my hands on Bishop's shoulders and pushing him back a step, "I have plans for my husband."

Bishop grinned at me. "Yes, ma'am." He gave me a formal salute and grabbed his case before leaving the room.

Ryan's arms came around me from behind, his touch both possessive and gentle. "Say it again."

I feigned ignorance and pretended to think about it. "What? That Bishop's lips on your ass would be hot? I mean, the man's got a mouth made for—"

With a growl, Ryan nipped at the curve where my neck sloped into my shoulder as he pressed his growing arousal on my ass. "Not what I fucking meant. And keep talking about another man's lips. I'll make sure yours are too busy to move."

Still playing dumb, I simply murmured, "Oh?"

Another low snarl slipped past his lips, his arms crushing me to his chest. His lips brushed my ear. "If you want to choke on my cock, you just have to ask." He bit my earlobe gently as my breath caught. "You know *exactly* what I want to hear."

I sighed and turned in his arms to face him. "Husband?"

His eyes flared with something primal. He ground his hard on against my stomach. "Fuck, I love hearing you say that, *wife*."

Electricity shot through my limbs, and I leaned harder against him. "I love the way that sounds." I dropped my gaze to his lips, anticipating him kissing me. Instead, he let me go and stepped away with a reluctant groan.

"Um, hello?" I called to his back, my gaze roving over the hard muscles and the way the phoenix tattoo seemed to come alive with each ripple and movement of his skin. "I demand consummation."

He glanced over his shoulder at me with a smirk. "Patience, Mads." He stripped off his pants, and when he turned toward the closet, I could see the outline of his hard cock.

My mouth actually watered as I clenched my thighs together,

praying my pooling arousal wouldn't actually leak down my legs since I'd opted for the crotchless panties.

These things were a sexy-as-sin idea, but in practice? I would decidedly *not* be wearing them on a daily basis. Especially not around my husband.

I bit my lower lip to keep the giddy laugh that bubbled up firmly inside. I freaking loved that word.

Ryan went into the closet and came back wearing jeans and a gray t-shirt that clung to his chest and biceps.

"Okay, maybe you're confused about how this works," I started, hearing the whining pitch in my voice. "You're supposed to take your clothes *off* to have sex with me."

He grinned and winked. "I'm fully aware of how this works, babe. But we need to go somewhere first."

"We're leaving?"

"Sort of." He held out a hand. "Trust me?"

There was no doubt. No hesitation as I took his hand.

"I trust you," I replied.

Ryan's smile was bright enough to rival the sun. "I think those might be my three favorite words from you."

"I mean it." I touched his jaw. "I love you. I *trust* you."

He closed his eyes and leaned forward, his forehead pressed to mine. "I don't deserve you, Madison Cain."

CHAPTER 51

MADDIE

I t turned out that we didn't have far to go. In fact, we didn't even leave Brookfield.

Ryan stepped around me to unlock the front door of a cottage set apart from the others in the vineyard. He pushed the door open to let me see inside.

I gasped as I took in the vaulted ceilings, the open concept floor plan, and the wood paneled walls. It looked like a cozy, albeit luxurious, log cabin come to life. From the front door, across the living room, and up the stairs was a path of rose petals.

"You did this?" I turned and looked at him in amazement.

He smirked, a little smug. "Of course. I mean, we can't exactly hop on a plane to Fiji for the next two weeks, but I figured you deserved something special for your first night as Mrs. Cain."

I tried to walk by him, but his arm shot out. "What—"

He swept me up in his arms with a grin as I laughed.

"Seriously?" I met his gaze, less than an inch from my face.

He kissed me, holding my weight like it was nothing, and then stepped over the threshold. "Maddie, as much shit as we have stacked against us? I'm doing this tradition right in case we get an ounce of good luck from it."

"Fair enough," I agreed as he set me down. "So, what comes next?"

His gaze slid along the length of my body. "If you have to ask, this marriage is already in trouble."

Smirking, I turned around and looked at him over my shoulder. "Think you can help me with the zipper on this dress?"

He rolled his eyes, but still smiled. "I don't remember being your wardrobe attendant as part of our vows." He reached for the zipper, but I sidestepped him.

"You're absolutely right." It took a little twisting, but I managed to get the zipper down myself. I let the material drop to the floor, leaving me in nothing but the pale blue corset and lace panties.

His eyes flared and he raised a fist to his mouth with a groan that sent arousal spiraling down my chest and straight to my core. "Jesus, you've had that on the whole time?"

I simply grinned and spun with a fake gasp. "I really don't want this dress to wrinkle."

Bending at the waist, I kept my legs straight to grab the dress from the floor. I felt the cool air touch my pussy as the split in the center opened, flashing Ryan. I giggled over my shoulder and ran for the stairs as Ryan cursed behind me.

I barely made it to the first step before he caught me. He ripped the dress from my hands and tossed it aside before spinning me on the steps.

Crying out, my hands grabbed his shoulders while I tried not to fall. "Ry—"

He lifted me over his shoulder and kept going up the stairs.

I slapped at his back, laughing. "Put me down."

His hand came down across my ass, and my squeak of surprise turned into a groan when his fingers slipped beneath the slit in my panties and inside my pussy.

"Fucking soaked," he rumbled, the approval in his tone making me squeeze around his fingers as he walked into the bedroom.

My back hit the mattress with a breathless laugh as he crawled on top of me.

"Fuck, what you do to me," he whispered, almost reverently, before slamming his mouth over mine. He pushed my lips open with his tongue, and I moaned softly as he took control of the kiss.

One hand cradled my jaw while the other held up his upper body. His hips pressed against mine, his already hard cock grinding against me. I opened my legs so he fit between them. The denim of his jeans rubbed against my clit and I cried out, my fingers clawing at his shoulders.

My hips jerked and bucked beneath him, needing friction.

Instead, he pulled his lips from mine and lifted his hips as he began kissing his way down the lacy fabric. He bit my nipples through the padded cups of the corset as a finger slid through the missing part of my underwear and stroked the length of my slit.

He moved lower until his shoulders were wedged between my thighs. He glanced up at me, eyes blazing. "Take your tits out, Maddie. I want to see them."

Awkwardly, I reached into the corset and pulled my breasts over the edge. My nipples, already sensitive from his nipping, tightened even more as he devoured them with his gaze.

"Touch yourself," he ordered.

A blush stole across my cheeks as I lifted my hands and massaged my breasts before rolling my nipples through my fingertips.

He spread my pussy open with one hand and lowered his mouth to suck my clit between his lips as two fingers pushed inside of me.

I arched off the bed, my hands falling to the sheets and clutching them as sweet agony rolled through me.

Ryan's teeth gently caught my clit, and I almost jerked off the bed in shock. Breathing hard, I looked down the length of my body at him.

"Touch yourself," he growled, the demand clear as his fingers stilled inside me. If I stopped, he'd stop.

My fingers shook as I placed my hand back where he wanted. I clumsily ran my palms over my breasts as he curled his fingers, massaging that enigmatic spot that always sent me soaring.

But instead of gliding his fingers in and out of my soaked core, he kept pressure on that spot, never letting up as he sucked my clit between his lips, lashing it with his tongue. I squirmed, the sensations bordering on too much as I tried to get away, but there was nowhere to go.

I exploded with a guttural groan, my toes curling as my body convulsed around him. He never stopped; the pads of his fingertips and his mouth forcing me into another rolling climax.

"S-stop," I gasped, breathless and spinning, as my head thrashed on the mattress.

Ryan glanced up, his thumb stroking the swollen side of my clit. "You really want me to stop?"

"Yes. No. I mean… wait. What was the question?" Seriously, I'd lost the ability to *think*.

He smirked, his eyes hooded and dark as he watched me. "Maddie, look at me."

It took a second to focus, but I finally did. I clenched around his fingers when I saw him smiling at me, my arousal glistening on his lips and chin.

Why was that so freaking *hot*?

"That's what I thought," he murmured, almost to himself. He glanced at my core and kissed the top of it gently, reverently, before climbing back overtop of me. He watched me like I was a puzzle he was trying to figure out.

"What?" I finally asked, unable to stop the small smile from playing across my lips.

"Just trying to figure out how I got so lucky." His voice was oddly hoarse as he studied me with love and need burning in his eyes. "I get to spend the rest of my life with you. It doesn't seem real."

"It's real. *I'm* real," I assured him. My hand moved to the front of his jeans. "And right now, I really need *you*."

He dipped his head, kissing me deeply. I wrapped my arms around his neck as the material of his shirt rubbed against the tips of my breasts, scraping over the already sensitive nubs.

Impatient, my hands delved under his shirt, my nails scratching his rock-hard stomach as I tried to push his shirt off. He stayed firm, not moving as he kissed me like we had all the time in the world.

"Ryan," I whined against his lips, working my fingers under the waistband of his jeans. "I need more."

"Tell me what you need," he whispered, his mouth caressing the underside of my jaw.

"You," I said again, this time with a bit more frustration.

He pulled back enough to grin at me. "You have me. I'm right here."

I glared at him.

"Be specific," he encouraged with a throaty chuckle. His head dropped down to catch a nipple in his lips. "What do you want me to do?"

"I want... Shit," I hissed when his teeth caught the tight peak and tugged. My hands delved into his hair, but I wasn't sure if I was trying to push him away or pull him closer. "I need you inside me."

The corner of his mouth tugged up as he feigned innocence. "Inside where? Your mouth?" He traced a finger around the outside of my lips before pushing it past my teeth. "There. I'm inside you."

I promptly bit his finger.

His brows lifted as he pulled his finger free. "Kinky."

"If you don't..." I huffed, annoyed and frustrated and craving more.

"Don't what?" He was teasing me and loving every minute.

I gritted my teeth and forced a smile as I met his gaze. "If you don't put *your* cock inside *my* pussy in the next thirty seconds, I'm going to file for divorce and find someone who will."

His eyes rounded.

Triumph flared in my chest. "That specific enough for you, baby?"

He lifted off me enough to get his clothes off in record time. "For the record," he began, gliding the tip of his cock through the wetness between my thighs, "you could've had an annulment if we hadn't done this."

His hips jerked, and he slammed into me, filling me completely. My inner walls spasmed with the abrupt intrusion, a low groan crawling from my throat as I worked to stretch around him.

Without giving me a chance to recover, he pulled out and pushed back inside just as fast. I wrapped my legs around his waist, pulling him deeper as I met him thrust for thrust.

Ryan's hand slipped between us, finding my clit with unerring accuracy. His mouth whispered against my ear, "I lied. I'd chain you to our bed before I'd ever let you attempt to end our marriage. I own you, Madison Cain, for the rest of our lives."

I turned my head, catching his lips with mine as I started to break apart in his arms. His tongue invaded my mouth as his cock claimed my center.

All because this man, my husband, had somehow managed to claim my heart while giving me his.

Yes, I was his, but he was also mine. Now and forever, he was *mine*.

CHAPTER 52

MADDIE

When I woke up almost two hours later, Ryan wasn't in bed beside me. I got out of bed and listened, hearing sounds coming from downstairs. I grabbed his discarded shirt off the floor and put it on before going to find him.

He was shirtless—my favorite view—and grabbing a beer from the fridge in the kitchen as I padded down the stairs and came up behind him. I wrapped my arms around his waist and nuzzled his shoulder with a content sigh. "Sorry," I murmured.

A chuckle rumbled out of him. "For what?"

"Falling asleep," I replied through a yawn.

"It's been a long day." He turned and kissed me gently, the soft look in his eyes was one I knew he saved just for me. "We have the rest of our lives together. I don't think napping on our wedding day is grounds for divorce."

"And what are grounds for divorce?" I asked, peering up at him.

He paused, thinking about it. "Nothing. You're stuck with me for life."

"Oh?" Amusement flickered through me. "Even if you spend all your days working, and I get lonely and find someone to... entertain me?"

He nodded with grim determination. "Even then. I'll kill him and fuck every memory you have of him out of your body." He grinned devilishly. "You're mine forever, baby."

I slapped a hand over my mouth to try and hold in my laughter.

His gaze dipped to my bare legs. "But I'm a little concerned that you're already thinking about another hypothetical guy when you just married me." The look in his eyes sharpened to something calculating and dangerous that made my heart pound.

I wrapped my arms around his neck, inhaling his scent. "No hypotheticals. Just you. Always just you."

He let out a breath and kissed the side of my head. "Want a drink? We can hang out on the deck. The sun should be setting soon." He indicated to the rear of the house where glass doors and windows took up an entire wall, painting the room in buttery light.

I nodded and went out there. The deck was large, spanning the back length of the cottage. The little house itself was situated on top of a hill that looked out over the stables and paddocks. From here, I could see horses grazing and running in the afternoon sun. I leaned my forearms on the railing and watched them as I waited.

Ryan stepped onto the deck and handed me a soda, holding a beer in a glass bottle for himself, before leading me to the sitting area.

I sat on the couch, surprised at how soft it was as my body sank into the cushions. Ryan opened a bench and pulled out a blanket to carefully arrange around me. The sun was warm, but the air was still cool.

Sipping my soda, I watched as he sat down beside me, his body close to mine. I snuggled into his side without hesitation, his arm going around my shoulders as he brushed an absent kiss to my hair.

"Pastor Nichols already filed the license. Grandpa and Court are working on setting up something with the lawyers for tomorrow to release your inheritance."

I frowned. "Won't Gary know when the money is touched?"

His fingers slowly stroked my hair as he took a sip of his beer. "No. One of the partners who oversees your family's accounts is working with us."

My brows inched up in surprise. "Out of the goodness of his heart?"

A rueful smile twisted his lips. "No, because we have proof he skimmed money from a few Cabot accounts over the years to support his gambling habits. And I have my own attorneys who worked with Grandpa for years and hate my dad, too. Court mostly deals with them, though."

"He's pre-law, right?"

Ryan nodded. "He handles a lot of the legal contracts for Phoenix. Having him close helps, so at least his mom was good for something."

I looked at him curiously. "Meaning?"

He met my eyes. "Court's dad used to be a general in the army. He left a few years ago and started his own mercenary teams that operate globally. His plan was to create a family of soldiers to do his bidding, hence why all of Court's half brothers are in, or were in, the military."

"Why isn't Court then?" I asked.

"Because of another inheritance stipulation," Ryan answered. "Court's mom comes from old money going back to Napoleon in France. They've all been lawyers, though. Court's mom was one before she was disbarred for showing up high in the courthouse one too many times. Court's the only kid they had, so he's expected to take over her family's stake in the firm when he graduates."

"They never had any other kids together?"

"No. His mom was using for part of the pregnancy, and there were complications. Court was born seven weeks premature , and his mom had a hysterectomy, so no more kids." He grimaced. "Probably for the best. Jasper Woods is a shitty dad. Court and his brothers all paid the price for being one of the General's sons. In a lot of ways he makes Beckett look like father of the year."

I reared back in horror. "That's not possible."

He held my gaze. "Jasper has a thing where he needs to test his kids. He wanted to see what they were made of. It's how King died."

"He *killed* his son?" I covered my mouth in shock.

"Not exactly, but he's the reason King died." He watched me for a second. "We're married, right?"

"Uh, yeah." I gave him a weird look, because we were both at the ceremony a few hours earlier.

"As my wife, I can tell you things and that means you can't tell anyone else," he explained.

"Pretty sure that's how it works, but I wasn't aware we needed a ring and piece of paper for you to trust me to keep a secret," I deadpanned.

He shook his head. "Legally, baby. You can't be compelled to testify in court against me. If I tell you something, there are laws in place to keep us safe."

I stiffened at the implication. "Okay."

His fingertips brushed the back of my neck like he needed to touch me to make sure I was good with the turn this conversation was taking. "When each of his sons turn twelve, Jasper sends them into the woods to survive for a week. They have limited supplies and are left alone. That's how King died."

A shudder rolled down my back. "Oh, my God. Did Court…"

He nodded grimly, but I could see he was holding something back when his gaze cut away from me sharply.

I turned to face him fully, the blanket pooling on my lap. "What?"

Indecision warred on his face. "I can tell you, but Bex is a part of it. And Maddie, she can't know." He grabbed my hand when I started to protest. "It's Court's story to tell her when he's ready."

I was going to lose best friend privileges after this, but I needed to know. I'd been in the dark about so much for too long, and I was rapidly coming to understand that knowledge was power.

"Tell me."

He exhaled hard. "You know Court's and Bex's families were close?"

I nodded.

"Court was always into Bex. I don't think he even knew it, because we were kids and they were just friends, but they were tight. Their families did a lot together—their moms were best friends in high school and sorority sisters in college. I think they were hoping Court and Bex would eventually get married." A sad smile tipped up the corner of his mouth.

I simply waited for him to continue as the pit in my stomach started to open because I knew things had ended badly.

"When Court turned twelve, he was expected to do the same survival week. Even though Court was going to be a lawyer, Jasper expected his son to be strong and to prove it. But King had died a few years earlier, and Court hated his dad, so he refused." Ryan looked away and shook his head slowly. "Jasper couldn't force Court, or just drop him off in the woods like his brothers since he couldn't directly endanger Court."

"Why not?" Not that I was complaining, but it seemed like a weird line in the sand since Jasper didn't give a shit about the others.

"Because he needed Court to access his wife's family money. If Court died like King had, the money reverted to a charity. Every single cent of it. So, instead, he incentivized Court to participate."

Unable to help myself, I reached for Ryan's hand and laced our fingers together. I wasn't sure if I was trying to comfort myself or him.

"Malcolm Whittier was looking for financial backing for his next project. The thing that would become CryptDuo. Jasper agreed to give him all the capital he needed, provided he could... *borrow* Bex for a week."

"I'm sorry. He wanted to *borrow* her?" Anger flared in my chest. It was sick the way these men traded children as currency to get ahead.

Ryan nodded. "To be fair, he made it sound like he wanted to take Bex away for a week for Court's birthday. But in reality, he hid Bex in the middle of the woods and made Court go find her."

I threw my hands up in the air before covering my face, a sick feeling twisting up my insides. "I can't. I can't even fucking deal with this world. What the *hell*?"

He refused to meet my gaze as his head lowered. "There's more. You know Bex was really sick back then. She had been diagnosed with leukemia when she was a toddler and beaten it, but it had recently come back. She was in the middle of chemo treatments when it happened. Court's *mission* was to find Bex so she could get the meds she needed."

All the air left my lungs in a rush. "Why the fuck would her father or mother agree to letting her go anywhere with Jasper?"

"Court and Bex's moms were best friends, and Jasper made it sound like he'd hired a personal nurse to administer Bex's treatments while they were away. He just left out the part that the nurse wouldn't be able to treat Bex until Court found her."

"He found her, obviously." The bitterness in Ryan's tone seeped into my bloodstream. "But it took days, and Bex was unconscious when he found her... She almost died. She was in the hospital for weeks."

"Bex never told me any of this," I whispered.

"She doesn't remember. She was nine, and was so sick... They put her in a medically induced coma to lighten the strain on her heart because she got this horrible infection. When she came out of the hospital, she didn't remember what Jasper had done, or being in the woods." He hunched forward. "Court made us promise to never talk to her, to cut off all contact. He wouldn't let her be used by his father again. He blames himself that she almost died."

"Jesus," I murmured.

He turned and looked at me, the pain in his eyes palpable. "The Whittiers and the Woods stopped being friends. Bex's mom almost divorced her dad, and her dad was so fucked up over being part of her almost dying that he started drinking."

"Bex needs to know this," I insisted.

"Would it change anything?" Ryan's brows lifted. "Would her knowing that her dad almost got her killed *help* her? She's already reeling about him being involved in all this shit, Mads. Is adding more pain on top of what she's already dealing with going to lessen the burden?"

I shook my head, numb. "I don't know, Ry. Bex deserves to know all of this. She's my best friend."

He covered my hands with his. "I know this is a lot, baby. And I know your first instinct is to protect your friend, but telling her isn't protecting her."

"She still needs to know. She thinks you guys just decided you were too cool for her one day and abandoned her." I knew he was right; telling Bex wouldn't change the way their lives had turned out, but it still wasn't fair to keep her in the dark.

"You're right, but Court needs to be the one to tell her. What happened, happened to *them*, Maddie," he told me firmly.

I sighed, my shoulders drooping. "I hate when you're right. Court seriously needs to tell her. And if he doesn't, I will."

He gave me an unreadable look.

"Uh uh," I said, wagging a finger. "I'm not violating girl code to protect Court. We both know how damaging keeping secrets can be, even if you're trying to protect the other person. Like Dean."

His brows slammed down. "What does that asswipe have to do with this?"

"If I had told you that he'd given me a hard time outside your room that day, or about the sweater, we might've been able to avoid the clusterfuck at the engagement party."

"Baby, that's *not* on you. I should've trusted you," he shot back with a sharp shake of his head.

"Oh, I'm not letting you off the hook," I agreed, "but we've all been hurt by secrets. Bex finding out her dad's involved in this was bad enough. You guys can't keep the womenfolk in the dark because you're trying to protect us. This isn't the Dark Ages, Ry. Bex and I aren't just some little flowers that will wilt and fall apart when bad news hits. But it *does* shake our faith in the people we trust when they don't trust us enough to be honest."

He set his bottle aside and picked me up, blanket and all, and settled me on his lap. Burying his face against the side of my neck, he inhaled deeply. "I love you."

I cuddled against his chest, absorbing his warmth and strength. "I know. I love you, too."

CHAPTER 53

RYAN

"You're sure about this?" My wife stared at me from the doorway of Grandpa's office with those wide blue eyes, and all I wanted to do was drag her back to the cottage we'd holed up in for twenty-four hours and fuck her again.

My cock jerked against the zipper of my jeans, because my wife's pussy was my favorite addiction.

I barely tamped down the giddy-as-fuck smile that threatened whenever I thought those words.

My wife.

I'd always been a possessive asshole, but now that I was married to Maddie, it was like a switch had been flipped. I hadn't known how possessive I could be until I slipped that band onto her finger.

Maddie was mine. All fucking mine. And now we were making plans that would keep her safe.

"I'm sure, Mads," I promised, holding out my hand.

Still looking doubtful, she handed me the listening device her father had ordered her to hide. If Gary wanted to hear something, then I'd let him hear the fucking truth. Every single word of it.

Well, mostly.

Grandpa craned his neck to see the device from where he sat on the other side of his desk. "Hard to believe how far technology has come since I was your age. My first computer was half the size of this room."

I shook my head. "And you still use tech from the stone age."

"He might be onto something," Ash muttered, looking up from his laptop. "Grandpa's computer predates the internet. It can't be hacked."

Grandpa smirked at me. "See?"

Maddie stepped back from the doorway to allow Linc and Court to enter. Her eyes found mine, worried and soft. "I'll go hang out with Bex and Cori until you're done."

I nodded. I knew she wanted to be here, but Gary needed to think she was his good little spy. That she'd been able to infiltrate our group, and my trust, so that he didn't see what was right in front of him.

Court and Grandpa had come through; we'd met with the attorneys a few hours ago and set in motion what needed to happen for Maddie's inheritance to be unlocked. It would take a few days, but the money would be in her account by the end of the week. After that, she and Ash would have it moved to an offshore account that Gary wouldn't be able to hack.

I crossed the room and kissed her, loving the way she tasted. "I'll come get you when we're done."

She sighed a little but let me go, and I went back into the office and closed the door.

Grandpa leveled a look at each of us. "We're sure about this?"

"Yes," I answered without hesitation, smiling grimly when my friends nodded in agreement.

Linc leaned forward, rubbing his hands together as he studied Ash. "Everything set up?"

Ash tapped a few keys on the laptop and then smiled. "Yup." His eyes found mine. "Go time."

Taking a deep breath, I peeled the backing from the device and stuck it under the lip of Grandpa's desk.

Court held up a hand for silence, silently counting us down to a believable amount of time that Maddie could have hidden the device and left the office. After nearly two minutes, Court opened the door and then slammed it closed. He nodded at me to start.

"You're out of your fucking mind," Linc started, his tone cold and detached.

Just the way we'd planned it.

"Must be some epic pussy," Court groused, going over to sit next to Linc.

"Shut the fuck up," I growled, genuine heat behind my words because the last thing I wanted to hear, even if we'd agreed, was talk about my wife's pussy coming from my friend's mouth.

Sensing my annoyance, Court grinned and flipped me off.

I took a deep breath. "I love her, okay? You don't know her like I do. She's... changed."

"From a slut to a saint?" Ash snorted a laugh. "Ry, you know you're my best friend, but come on. She's playing you."

"No, she isn't," I insisted. "Grandpa, you get it. You and Nana were in love."

"Your Nana never tried to ruin my life," Grandpa pointed out, a twinkle in his eyes even as he kept his voice harsh. He was loving that we were planning on fooling Gary. "You can't compare Gary Cabot's demon spawn to your Nana. I still can't believe you gave that girl her ring. She would be so disappointed."

"I'm going to offer Gary a deal," I started. "We all know my father is an asshole, but I've had enough. He's threatened Maddie and Corinne. I'm going to sell him my shares of Cain Industries and tell him about the investments my dad's been making."

"Are you out of your fucking mind?" Ash snapped. "You know that's not the plan."

"My new plan is keeping Maddie safe and happy," I vowed, meaning it with every fiber of my twisted soul. "He can have Maddie's money, and then he'll be able to buy out those companies and gain controlling interest of CI. He'll own my dad's company by the end of the year."

"And, what? You and Maddie ride off into the proverbial sunset?" Linc drawled.

"Yes. I *love* her," I replied, forcing myself to sound desperate to sell the point.

Grandpa sighed heavily. "You know, the one thing I hate more than that girl hurting you is your bastard of a father. Gary is the lesser of two evils, I suppose."

"Meaning what?"

"I'm dying," Grandpa said flatly.

It was the truth, but I felt it like a punch to my dick. Pain seared me from the inside out the way it always did when I thought about his impending mortality.

Grandpa rubbed his jaw. "I'll redraw my will to sign everything over to you, provided you agree to take care of your sister."

I grinned at him even as I kept my pitch incredulous. "You *will?*"

He rolled his eyes and shook his head, bemused with the performance we were giving for Gary's effect. "I will. If your father is ruined, he'll have no way to leverage Corinne over you for my money. I'll leave you everything."

I leaned back in my chair with a smirk, because this deal would be too good for Gary to pass up: the chance to fuck over my father *and* get a shit ton of money.

"Maddie and I could live here," I suggested.

Grandpa met my eyes, and suddenly we weren't just playing roles for the recording device. "I think you'd both be very happy here."

I nodded, a knot of emotion twisting around my vocal cords. "We'd love that."

He paused for a beat, nodding at me in understanding before slipping back into the role of reluctant grandfather.

"Then it's settled," Grandpa said with a heavy sigh. "I'll sign everything over to you. I'll have my attorney draw up the new will, but Ryan, I hope you know what you're doing."

I smiled at him, wishing I could be there when Gary heard the recording on Maddie's phone of this conversation. "I do."

CHAPTER 54

MADDIE

The sound of Corinne's giggles was going down as one of my favorite noises ever. It was infectious and exuberant, because the tiny girl with the biggest heart giggled with everything she had.

Peals of belly laughter echoed in the kitchen as Royal picked her up and spun her around. The gauzy yellow princess dress fanned out like she was living every *Beauty and the Beast* fantasy.

Royal set her back down on the floor with a bow. "Princess."

Corinne stifled a laugh. "Beast." She patted his still bowed head. "You're the best beast, Royal."

He grinned at her, dimples flashing. "Well you're the prettiest princess I've ever seen."

Ms. Wallace clucked her tongue from the doorway with an indulgent smile. "This pretty princess needs to get upstairs and take a bath if she still wants to have movie night with her grandfather before bed."

Cori scrambled back, bumping into me where I sat at the island. She spun and gave me a hasty hug before hurtling back into Royal's arms for another hug.

"G'night, Maddie. Love you, Prince Royal!" She danced her way out of the kitchen.

Royal shook his head, the affection in his eyes palpable as he watched her leave.

I cleared my throat. "You're really good with her."

I half-expected the usual walls he wore like armor to snap back into place, but he smiled at me.

"She's an amazing kid," he admitted, surprising me by coming over and sitting beside me. "Has a shithead for a father, but that seems to be on trend around here. But she's still innocent. Still sees the good."

"Not like the rest of us," I murmured.

He nodded slowly. "Yeah. The rest of us are… Well, we never really had a chance, did we?"

I hesitated. "Ryan told me a little bit about your father. About your brother."

His jaw tightened, but he didn't cut me off.

"Anyway, I just wanted to say I was sorry." The words felt lame coming out, the regrets sounding pathetically insignificant to the pain he likely carried.

Again, though, Royal surprised me. "Thanks. King was a good kid. Cori reminds me a lot of him. Same innocence, same way of seeing good in the world."

"How did you get involved with Phoenix?" I asked, putting my arm on the counter and leaning my cheek against my palm.

He frowned, thinking back. "Ry told you about Jasper's plan for having his own little army of militant sons?"

"Yeah. But clearly you're not working for him, since you're *here*."

The tiniest of smiles tipped up a corner of his mouth. "That's thanks to Ash. He found some leverage I could use to get out from under Jasper. I used it to help my brothers, too, but the bastard still has a chokehold on our mom. Even after King and the baby died—"

"Your sister, right?" I interrupted.

"The only girl my mom had. She was between Knight and Castle, but she was stillborn." A dark shadow passed over his face. "Mom was never really right after that. She was never very strong to begin with, but losing the baby killed whatever fight she had left. She does whatever Jasper wants, and he's not above using her to get us to bend to his will. It's why Rook agreed to go play Navy SEAL and why Castle graduated early with his GED so he could enlist at seventeen."

"But not you?"

He met my gaze. "Not me. Not ever again. When I got out of the army, I told Jasper I was done with him. Bishop did the same. Jasper washed his hands of us, called us a disgrace and cut us off financially." He snorted derisively. "As if we need his money. I'd rather live in the gutter and drink sewer water."

I wrinkled my nose. "I've done that. If you can get past the smell, it's not half bad."

He stared at me for a minute before laughing. "You're definitely not like your sister."

I stiffened. "You knew Madelaine?"

"Nah. After I rolled out of Jasper's good graces, Court came to me with a proposition. They were starting Phoenix, told me about the side hustle Linc's daddy has of buying and selling more than stocks and bonds. When I was still in the army, I saw shit that would give your nightmares nightmares. If I could help tip the scales and fuck over Jasper and his friends in the process, I was in."

He gave me a curious look. "I met Ryan through Court a few years ago. They brought Bishop and me here—" he waved a hand around at the room "—and Grandpa invited us to help them. We never looked back, and when Knight was injured in the line of duty, we brought him in, too. Rook and Castle will join Phoenix one day when their tours are done."

"Wow," I murmured, absorbing that info dump.

"Anyway," he went on, "I was helping Ry with something last year. I was picking him up and saw Madelaine. Never met her, but I didn't have to. She screamed spoiled, entitled bitch without opening her mouth."

"She had a hard life." I felt compelled to defend my sister, especially since she couldn't do it herself.

He leveled me with a stare. "Look around, Maddie. Everyone in this house has had a hard life. But none of us let that define us. We rose above it and are trying to be better people. Your sister never did that. She let men like Gary and Adam Kindell and Beckett control her, and she ended up dead for it."

I jerked back, stunned into silence.

He had the decency to appear mildly ashamed. "Look, I'm sorry, but it's the truth. Your sister was—"

"A bitch," I cut him off coldly, pushing back from the island. "I'm well aware. But you also don't know the shit that those men did to her. She never had a chance, and if you think you get some kind of prize for beating your father at his own game when she couldn't, then you're just an asshole."

He shrugged one shoulder, the cold mask of indifference back in place. "I've never claimed to be anything else, but I'm sorry if I hurt your feelings."

I was still staring at him when Ryan appeared in the doorway. The easy smile on his face slipped as he caught the tension in the room.

"What's going on?" His gaze swung from me to Royal and back.

"Nothing," I muttered, running a hand through my hair and turning to give him a tight smile. "Everything go okay?"

"It went fine, and you're upset," he answered, crossing the room to hold my face in his hands. His eyes searched mine, and then he scowled at Royal. "What the fuck did you say to her?"

I lifted my hands to hold his wrists. "We just had a difference of opinion."

Royal got off the stool, his expression still stony.

Ryan let me go and stepped between Royal and me. "Let me clear it up then. She's always right." He hooked a thumb at me. "Got it?"

"Message received," Royal affirmed. His gaze jerked to me. "I'll see you later, Maddie." He exited through the back door.

Ryan's gaze snapped to mine. "What happened?"

"Exactly what I said. We had a difference of opinion." I resisted the urge to rub my head, but I felt a headache building behind my eyes.

"What opinion?" He wasn't letting this go.

"Madelaine."

Ryan's lips pressed together. "I can talk to him—"

"Believe it or not, I can actually handle disagreements with others by myself," I reminded him. "Not everyone has to agree with me, Ryan."

"No, but if they upset you, then I can kick their ass until you feel better," he shot back, only half-kidding.

"Or you can take me back to the cottage and—"

His lips collided with mine. "I wish. Grandpa actually wants to see us."

I shoved aside my disappointment. "Is everything okay?"

He nodded, sliding a hand down my arm and tangling our fingers together.

We walked past the closed door of his grandfather's office. I eyed it suspiciously until we turned a corner to the hallway that led to the back of the house.

"Ash said we should let the device run out of power on its own," he explained when I shot him a questioning glance. "We'll walk in there, say a few things that don't mean shit, just so Gary doesn't get suspicious."

"Sounds good."

He gave me a wry smile. "I could always take you in there and let Gary hear—"

I shuddered, and not in a good way. "No. Absolutely not." My tone came out harsher than I'd anticipated, but he'd stepped a little too hard on the memory of Gary knowing all along that Madelaine was being abused by his lackey for years.

He winced. "I'm sorry, Maddie. I didn't mean that."

I blew out a long breath, still feeling a bit raw from my conversation with Royal. "It's fine."

Ryan pulled me to a stop. "No, it's not. I wasn't thinking."

"I wish our problems were as simple as a disapproving father," I grumbled.

He pushed the hair away from my face with gentle hands. "I know, baby. But we put the plan in motion. Now we need to have faith."

"When did you get all optimistic and positive?" I deadpanned.

He winked and pushed open the door to the sitting room where I'd first met his grandfather while murmuring, "When I married my dream girl."

Heat suffused my cheeks, and I ducked my head so Mr. Harris wouldn't see it as I entered the room in front of Ryan.

"Close the door, please," Mr. Harris requested, waiting for Ryan to do so before continuing. "Ryan, there's a file over there. If you would be so kind? Maddie, please have a seat."

I sank into the chair across from him as Ryan went to get the folder. He handed it to his grandfather before sitting beside me.

Mr. Harris held the file, and a sad smile tipped up the corners of his mouth before he sighed and passed it to me.

I took it, confusion wrinkling my brow. "What's this?"

"Open it," he replied.

Out of the corner of my eye, I looked at Ryan, but he shook his head. He was just as in the dark as I was.

I flipped open the file and looked at the papers in front of me, confused when I saw MADELAINE CABOT listed as... the owner?

Ryan peered over my shoulder, then his head snapped up. "What..."

"Your plan got me thinking," Mr. Harris began, folding his hands in his lap. "This is the way I protect those I love the most. I remove your father's influence entirely from Brookfield if I give it to your wife. And it stays in the family if she owns the land, the stables, and the vineyard."

"You're giving me Brookfield?" I whispered, staring at him.

He inclined his head. "Technically, yes, but I'm anticipating you and Ryan sharing it when Beckett can no longer try to force it from his hands."

"Grandpa." Ryan's voice broke. "I don't..."

Mr. Harris sighed. "I'm dying, my boy. We both know it. When your Nana and I decided to leave the estate to our great-grandchildren, we never expected Beckett to be callous enough to use Corinne, and company bylaws state that the owner must be a relation of the founder, either by blood or marriage. If Madison owns Brookfield, Beckett will never have it."

"I don't know what to say." My fingers tightened around the papers. "This is Ryan and Corinne's legacy."

"And yours," Mr. Harris replied firmly, his eyes flashing with determination. "I know it's in good hands, because your first instinct was to include Ryan and Cori in your argument. You try to protect them without thinking. I wish my Clara was here to see you for herself, but I can't wait to tell her all about the woman who tamed our grandson when I see her again."

"But…" I looked helplessly at Ryan.

"All that's left to do is for you to sign," Mr. Harris interrupted. "I would advise not telling Gary or Beckett about this. Use it as another bullet in your arsenal to take them down. I'm sorry I won't be here to see for myself when they both finally crumble."

Ryan's head bowed, and I couldn't stop myself from reaching out to take his hand. He squeezed mine back so hard it nearly stole my breath. He wasn't a man who would break down and cry, but this might be as close as he got.

He loved his grandfather, one of the few adults who had given him unconditional love and support. And he was going to lose him very, very soon.

I met Mr. Harris's eyes and he smiled softly at me, an understanding passing between us as I promised to do whatever I could to help Ryan and Corinne survive his loss.

Mr. Harris cleared his throat after a silent pause. "Now, I believe Corinne has requested my presence for a movie night. Would you like to join us? It'd be nice to have the whole family together."

My gaze lingered on Ryan before I answered for us both. "We'd love to."

CHAPTER 55

MADDIE

Three days later, I sighed as I watched the Los Angeles skyline pass by the window as Ryan drove us back to Pacific Cross.

His hand found mine across the center console. "I know."

I turned to face him, and my engagement ring and wedding band caught the light. "I guess I need to take this off."

His lips tightened, as did the hand on the steering wheel. His own wedding band flashed when the sun's rays hit it through the windshield. "Yeah."

My phone dinged with an incoming text, and I figured it was Bex. We'd been texting most of the drive back, but I'd started to think she'd fallen asleep.

Looking down, my heart clenched when I saw the message wasn't from my bestie, but from the asshole who'd contributed to half of my DNA.

"Gary," I murmured, squeezing Ryan's hand before I unlocked my phone.

GARY: Car will be at your dorm at 6 pm

"Looks like he isn't wasting any time," I added, relaying to Ryan what the text said.

A muscle in his jaw popped, and the leather on the steering wheel creaked in protest from his tight grip. The engine roared as he hit the gas a little harder.

"We knew he wanted to see me tonight," I reminded him, keeping my voice calm even as I wanted to close my eyes from the way he started weaving in and out of the midafternoon traffic. "This is the plan."

A rough laugh laced with bitterness filled the car. "I can keep going and we'll be in Tijuana before he knows you're missing."

A half smile tugged at my lips. "We could live on the beach. You could run a surf shop, and I'll weave baskets."

Genuine laughter exploded from his chest. "I wasn't aware basket weaving was a skill you possessed."

I shrugged. "I can learn. The other option is five-dollar blow jobs on a corner. I have it on pretty good authority that mine are, how did you put it? *Fucking amazing.*"

At least that was what he'd told me last night as I'd worshiped him on my knees.

He grimaced. "Maddie, come on."

"I know," I sighed with extra drama. "You don't share."

"Actually, I was going to say you're underselling yourself. You're worth at *least* ten dollars."

I tugged my hand free to slap his chest. "Asshole."

He caught my fingers in his again and dragged them to his lips to kiss. "But seriously, I hate sending you there. I could come with—"

"No," I interrupted, my tone firm. "Ry, we've been over this. Gary needs to believe I've got you wrapped around my pinkie."

He snorted. "Not exactly a stretch."

I arched a brow. "Oh? Has the mighty Ryan Cain been tamed at last?"

He scoffed and shot me a look. "Tamed? Not a chance. But you have me doing shit I never thought I would. Like letting *you* take the lead on handling Gary when I should just put a bullet between his eyes and call it a day."

"Great plan," I agreed, my voice thick with sarcasm. "I'm sure Beckett will spend the rest of his day protecting Corinne. And I know

I'd love to spend the rest of my life seeing you from the other side of a piece of glass."

"We'd at least have conjugal visits, babe," he assured me.

"Until you realize the true love of your life is your cellmate, Junior." I rolled my eyes.

He frowned. "Don't cheapen what we have by comparing my need to have my dick sucked on a regular basis. What Junior and I have is strictly a biological release."

"You're beyond twisted," I muttered, barely suppressing a smile.

"I know what we're doing is the best play," he finally relented, "but I also know what Gary's capable of. I'm allowed to worry about my wife going into the viper pit."

I traced his knuckles slowly. "Well, I'm doing this to protect my husband *and* my new little sister. So deal with it."

A frown creased his forehead. "I need to get Cori out of there before shit hits the fan."

I tensed, fear spiraling through me. "I thought that me having Brookfield meant Cori was safe. Beckett can't use her for the inheritance." I'd signed the paperwork over the weekend that made me the owner of Brookfield and the sole heir to the Harris family estate when Mr. Harris passed.

The lawyer, who was older than Mr. Harris, assured us all the paperwork would be filed by Monday. I was kind of amazed at how fast everything had come together, especially over a holiday weekend. But when I'd voiced that thought, Ryan had smiled at me like I was adorable and reminded me that things like holidays stopped being hurdles when you threw enough money at them.

"I still want Cori far, far away," Ryan muttered. "I don't trust Beckett not to lash out at her just to hurt me when things blow up in his face."

"Then we'll make sure she's safe before we make a move," I promised, flashing him a smile full of determination. I quickly shot off a text to Gary to let him know I'd be waiting, then I settled against the seat and enjoyed the time I had left with my husband.

~

My finger felt naked without my wedding band. I'd had one for only a few days, but I loved it. I curled my hands into fists as the car Gary had sent turned up the long driveaway that led to his home.

The sun had just finished melting into the ocean when we stopped in front of the house. I waited for the driver, Bernard, to turn off the ignition and open my door. As soon as he did, I stepped out and squared my shoulders, readying for battle.

"Your father is waiting in his office," Bernard instructed me.

I didn't reply, just gave him a curt nod and headed inside. Mrs. Delancey opened the door when I made it to the top step. Her face showed little emotion, but I thought I saw a flicker of sadness in her eyes.

"Hello, dear," she murmured, closing the door. The sound echoed in the vast entryway.

"Mrs. Delancey." I greeted her with cool indifference. She knew what kind of a monster lived here, and while I knew she was looking out for her son, I still felt like she'd betrayed me. Betrayed my sister.

"Can I get you anything?" she offered, taking my coat when I'd slipped it off my shoulders.

I shook my head, brushing her off as I continued down the hallway. My heels clicked against the marble tiles as I walked deeper into the house. The door to Gary's office was open, but he was on the phone.

Pausing in the doorway, I waited for him to acknowledge me before moving any closer.

He glanced up from behind his desk, his gaze sharpening when he saw me. "Wallace, I'll have to call you back." He hung up the phone and smiled. "Sweetheart, welcome home. I trust your vacation went well?"

I arched a single brow. "Better than well, I'd say."

His lips twitched. "Oh? Did you listen to the recording?"

I scoffed and came into the room, tossing my phone onto the desk as I sat in the chair across from him like I owned it. I crossed my legs. "I might have, if Ryan had given me space to breathe."

His shoulders stiffened, his eyes narrowing. "You think he suspects something?"

"No, more like he's insatiable," I deadpanned, giving him a look. "I swear, the only time he was away from me the entire time was when he met with his grandfather, and even then, it was only a few minutes before he came looking for me."

Gary grinned, and I shoved down the icky feeling that began to fester in my gut. "Sounds like you've got him right where we want him."

I sighed and rolled my eyes. "I hope so, because I'm not sure how much longer I can keep playing the doting fiancée."

"You'll do it for as long as I say," he snapped, and I realized I'd taken my defiant act a little too far.

I smiled serenely. "Whatever you say, Dad."

He watched me, his gaze so probing that I wondered if he knew everything we were hiding. Everything we were planning.

"Then let's listen," he murmured, unlocking my phone and going to the recording app. He hit the play button and let the recording start.

It took everything in me to remain still and placid while I heard them all talking. I wanted to laugh at Linc and Court's outrage. But it was the way Ryan talked about me that echoed in my heart.

The sincerity in his voice couldn't be faked, and Gary's smile grew bigger and bigger as he came to the same realization.

Ryan sounded completely and utterly in love with me, to the point of his own ruin.

When it became clear the recording was over, he pushed my phone across the desk to me.

"Well done, Maddie," he praised, his tone almost warm and caring. Almost.

I huffed a little, playing up my indifference to Ryan's feelings when in reality, I was falling even more in love with him. "Is that what you needed to hear?"

He nodded. "I have a few calls to make. Why don't you go see your mother? She's been asking for you."

My brows shot up. "She has?" My heart started to pound in my chest, worried about how she was doing. "She's *here*?" I had assumed he'd be keeping her locked away somewhere. Not in his own house.

He waved a hand, dismissing me. "Mrs. Delancey will show you where she is."

I rose from the chair and barely stopped myself from curling my hands into fists. "Actually, I should probably be getting back. You see how needy Ryan is."

Gary snorted in amusement. "Clearly, but we're not done. I'll make my calls, then we'll talk."

Suspecting I would piss him off if I stayed, I turned on my heels and stalked out. Sure enough, Mrs. Delancey waited in the front hall. Her tight-lipped smile seemed like it was meant to be an olive branch, but I didn't have the emotional capacity to accept it.

Instead, I walked past her and started up the stairs, leaving her to follow. When I got to the top of the stairs, I realized that I still wasn't sure where in this giant house my mom was being kept.

With a sigh, I turned to Mrs. Delancey, but she was already looking at me like she was gearing up for an apology tour. "Madel—"

I held up a hand, glaring down at her. "Don't."

She flinched. "I'm sorry. *Madison*."

My teeth clicked together as my jaw clenched. "I meant, don't talk to me at all. I don't care what name you call me, as long as you do it in your head. Where's my mom?"

Her cheeks flushed. "I…" Her shoulders slumped. "I'll take you to see your mother. But, I have to warn you, she's…"

"High? Trashed? Unconscious?" I snapped my fingers. "Lounging in a puddle of her own throw up? Trust me, Mrs. Delancey, I've seen my mother in every imaginable state, from fucking a random guy on the floor of our shitty kitchen to semi-normal at the end of rehab."

She gave a silent, tight nod and moved around me to continue lead me down a hallway in the opposite direction of my room. When we reached the last door at the end, she pulled a key from her pocket and unlocked the door.

I let out a strangled laugh. "Wow. Locking her up, huh?"

"It's for her own safety." Mrs. Delancey stepped aside to let me in. As soon as I was through the doorway, she started to close the door. "I'll wait out here."

It took a second for my eyes to adjust from the brightly lit hallway to the dark interior of the room. I was able to make out the shadow of a bed with rumpled sheets, half hanging to the floor. A chair was shoved against a wall, and a coffee table lay on its side in front of it. The room smelled like my childhood—sweat, old cigarette smoke, and hopelessness.

Against my better judgment, I hit the light switch by the door and bathed the room in brightness.

"Maddie!" The sharp squeal was my only warning before my mother came running toward me in her underwear. She was all skin and bones, sharp angles and sallow color. But she was smiling as she pitched forward into my arms.

I grunted as I caught her weight, rolling my eyes to the ceiling to pray for strength.

She was high out of her fucking mind.

Her hands clumsily framed my face, nearly poking me in the eye. "My sweet, sweet baby girl. I told him that I needed to see you or... or..."

I waited, curious what kind of threat she thought she could level at Gary to make him do a damn thing.

She waved a dramatic hand and spun away from me. "Oh, shit. I would've cleaned up if I'd known you were coming." She stumbled to the bed and attempted to straighten the mess of pillows.

The room was hot and stuffy. It reeked of body odor, and I had a feeling Mom hadn't showered in days. Maybe longer.

I swallowed my disgust alongside my worry and the feelings of self-hatred.

She was here because of me.

I should never have agreed to Madelaine's stupid plan.

Heart aching and heavy, I started straightening the bed sheets as Mom flopped into the chair, the strap of her bra slipping down to her elbow.

"Such a good girl," Mom muttered, looking close to tears. "I'm sorry, baby. I'm so sorry. This is all my fault. I'm a mess."

"It's okay, Mom," I assured her softly.

A sob ripped from her chest. "How can you not hate me? Is that why you've been gone for so long?"

I closed my eyes, steeling myself for the shitstorm of her high. We'd gone from elation to sorrow in the span of a minute.

Which meant—

Something hurtled past my head and collided with the wall behind me. I jumped back, eyes wide.

"Where the *fuck* have you been?" She glared at me, her chest heaving so hard I wondered how her tits hadn't fallen out of the flimsy lace bra cups. "Ungrateful bitch. Daddy shows up and you just can't resist everything he has, huh?"

Yup. There was rage. The trifecta of emotions was complete.

"Don't forget where you came from and who was there for you. *I* kept you alive. I made sure you had a home and food and…"

I drowned her out the way I always had.

When I was little, I'd listened to her tirades and done everything in my power to fix whatever I could.

If she called me stupid, I made sure I brought home straight As.

If she called me lazy, I would clean up every mess she made without complaint.

Now… Now I was just over it all.

Frustrated tears burned behind my eyes. I finished making her bed and turned to leave.

"No!" she shrieked. "You don't get to leave!"

I kept my spine straight as I headed for the door.

Desperate hands grabbed me, scratching my arms as she fought to keep me here.

"Maddie, *please.*" Another choked sob as she pulled on my arm hard enough to make my elbow pop. "Don't leave, baby. Please don't leave me again."

I bit my lip to keep from crying. "I'll be back, Mom, okay? But I need to go."

Her face crumpled into tears, and she fell to her knees before I could catch her, heaving sobs echoing in the room.

"Mom, please," I whispered. "You'll make yourself—"

With a choked cough, she threw up on me.

"Sick," I finished grimly, stroking her hair away from her face.

With a groan, she crawled away and collapsed on the floor.

"Mom." My heart broke for the hundredth time in my life as I watched her give up again.

"Just go."

I slowly stood, ignoring the familiar smell of being covered in vomit. "Mom—"

"Go!" she screamed and broke down into more tears.

I forced myself to move to the door. "I'll see you soon, Mom," I promised.

Mrs. Delancey was waiting in the hallway. Her eyes went wide when she saw me. "Mad—"

I held up a hand. "I'm going to go take a shower and change. Can you tell Ga—my *father* that I'll be down in a few minutes?"

She nodded. "Of course, dear."

It was hard to walk away with dignity—bile dripping from my dress didn't exactly scream *classy*—but I kept my head high and shoulders back as I made my way to Madelaine's old room.

I grabbed a change of clothes and locked myself in the bathroom. I didn't let my guard down until I was standing under the shower, the noise drowning out the sound of my sobs.

CHAPTER 56

MADDIE

I could've hidden in the shower for hours, but I needed to finish up with Gary. I was emotionally drained, and all I wanted was to crawl into bed and have Ryan's arms around me.

My body seemed to be on autopilot as I got dressed before going into the bedroom. I sat down at Madelaine's vanity and tried to pull it together. My hands trembled with nervous energy, so I started to braid my hair, some of the ends damp from my impromptu shower.

I rummaged through the top drawer for a hair tie to secure my braid as someone knocked on the door. I jumped to my feet and slammed my knees into the open drawer.

"Shit!" I hissed the word as I reached down to rub my knee.

"Are you all right?" Mrs. Delancey called from the other side of the door.

"I'm fine," I snapped with a little more heat than necessary.

She cleared her throat. "Your father wants to know—"

"I'm on my way now," I replied, cutting her off. I pushed the drawer shut, but of course, it was stuck. I shoved again, harder, but it wouldn't budge.

I ripped it out and muttered, "Motherfucker."

And that was when I saw that part of the drawer had splintered.

No, not *splintered*. A panel of the wood had popped off, and there was something in there.

"What the hell?" I whispered, quickly prying the board back to take a look.

A tiny, flat rectangular SD card. I held it up to the light with a frown. Why would that be hidden in there?

Then again, why *wouldn't* it be hidden there? My sister was the master of secrets.

I glanced around the room, wondering what else she'd hidden in this space.

Another knock on the door, this time more insistent. "Maddie?"

I shoved the card into my bra and stormed across the room as my heart thundered. I yanked the door open, praying I looked calm and composed, if not a little irritated.

Mrs. Delancey jumped back in surprise. "I'm sorry, but you know how he gets."

I gave her a jerky nod while tugging on a pair of Madelaine's ballet flats. Brushing past her, I hurried downstairs. I paused in front of his office door to take a breath and heard voices.

"You did well," Gary's cool voice praised someone.

"Thank you, sir. And thank you for covering my medical bills. That was much appreciated," a masculine voice replied.

I frowned, trying to place the voice. I'd heard it before.

Gary laughed. "Well, next time be more careful. I have plans for those hands and they need to be able to function."

The man chuckled in response. "Of course, sir. I'd underestimated how flammable Egyptian cotton was."

I heard Mrs. Delancey coming down the stairs and quickly made an entrance so Gary wouldn't know I'd been eavesdropping.

After knocking on the partially closed door, I waited for him to tell me to come in. When I stepped inside, I frowned at the man across from him.

He was older than me, but only by a few years, and there was something familiar about his eyes. He watched me with a cold gaze.

"I know you," I said before I could stop myself.

Gary froze, his gaze darting from me to the man with suspicion. Then he suddenly relaxed. "He was Madelaine's driver. You met him in Michigan."

"Evan," I murmured, remembering him. He'd picked me up from the library and brought me to Madelaine that first night. She'd said he was her chauffeur *and* her boyfriend.

"Yes," Gary replied. "He traveled to Greece with Madelaine, as you must know. Evan was injured in the fire that killed your sister. He's been recovering, but now he's back, and not a moment too soon. We have much to do."

Evan smiled at me, the expression doing nothing to put me at ease. "Good to see you again, miss." He turned to Gary. "Did you need anything else, sir?"

"No," Gary replied. "Although, my daughter will need a ride back to the dormitories in a bit. Bernard is on another errand for me."

"Yes, sir." He inclined his head and started to leave.

"And Evan?" Gary called.

He paused in the doorway.

Gary smiled coolly. "Thanks again for handling that... situation."

Evan's mouth curved up, and a shudder rippled down my spine as he replied, "Of course, sir." He closed the door when he left.

Gary's gaze swept over me. "Good visit with your mother?"

I pushed away my unease at seeing Evan and forced myself to slip back into calm, collected Maddie. My lips quirked into a wry smirk. "It was fantastic. I needed another shower today."

Gary laughed. "Yes, well, she's a bit of a mess."

I nodded. "She is, but it's nothing I haven't seen before."

His lips turned down in sympathy. Or whatever his sociopathic ass thought counted as sympathy. "It must have been so hard, growing up with her."

"Well, it wasn't a mansion," I replied tersely as I sat in the same chair as earlier.

"No, but I think your upbringing is exactly what we needed," he mused, rubbing his jaw thoughtfully. "After all, you've been more of an asset to me these last few weeks than your sister was in her entire, pathetic existence."

It took everything in me not to react. "Oh?"

"I just got off the phone with a friend," he informed me. "It would appear that Beckett has been slowly buying up shares in several lucrative pharmaceutical and tech startups. Enough that he's put his own company in jeopardy."

My brows knitted together. "How so?"

Gary waved a dismissive hand. "The details don't matter, but I know the names of those companies, and I've already started proceedings to acquire them outright. But in order for this to work, I'll need you to do something."

"Of course." I was starting to scare myself with how easily I was lying. Thank God I wasn't hooked up to a polygraph, because the thing would've been going nuts.

"We need to encourage Ryan to move up the wedding. It shouldn't be hard, considering how infatuated he is with you. We need access to *your* money and old man Harris's. With those fortunes, we'll have absolute control. The Cains will fall."

"And I'll be stuck with a husband I don't want," I pointed out.

He grinned at me. "Not for long."

Ice flooded my veins.

"Evan is more than just one of my drivers. He handles... delicate matters for me as well," he hedged with a smile that boarded on manically giddy. "In a few months, once all the paperwork is settled, he'll help us remove Ryan Cain from both our lives for good."

My vision swam for a second as I grew lightheaded. He was talking about killing Ryan.

Everything in me screamed against the idea, and I curled my hands around the armrests to keep from jumping up and wrapping my bare hands around his thick neck.

"Madison." Gary's sharp voice cracked through the air, and I jumped. He chuckled. "Already envisioning life as a free woman?"

I forced a thin smile onto my lips as I shrugged. "Obviously."

"First things first," he muttered. "I'll have my lawyers start drawing up paperwork to get us the companies. I can liquidate assets and come up with the funds, but we'll need the wedding to happen by the end of the year so we have access to your trust and Ryan's. Is that doable?"

"Absolutely." If he only knew how doable that really was.

"We'll move fast, and you'll have to keep Ryan focused on you." He eyed me critically. "Do whatever it takes to keep him happy and satisfied. I don't care if you miss every class because you're hiding under the desk at each of his to suck his cock, got it?"

This man had zero boundaries. "Got it."

"Beckett Cain has his end-of-year meeting with his council this week." He rubbed his palms together, looking excited. "I plan on crashing it and letting him know that I'm his new boss."

"Sounds like you have it all planned out," I murmured.

He nodded. "Now go. You need to get back to school and into that boy's bed before his eyes start to wander."

My own eyes narrowed and I got up. "I can do that, but I want you to promise me that you'll tell me before anything happens to Ryan."

He stilled, his gaze turning suspicious.

I giggled and shrugged one shoulder. "I want to be there when he dies. He needs to know I was behind it."

Gary's lips pulled back into a wicked smile. "Of course, sweetheart. Consider it a belated wedding gift."

I winked at him with a bright smile and walked out the door like he hadn't just threatened to destroy my entire world.

Evan was waiting for me outside by the car. He held open the door and I got into the back of the town car, praying he didn't see my hands shaking.

My gaze went to his hands around the steering wheel, and I saw burn scars wrapping around the back of one hand and disappearing under the sleeve of his shirt.

I turned away with a grimace, trying not to think about what those scars meant as I turned over events of tonight in my head. I got lost in my thoughts as we drove, but I couldn't seem to stop glancing at the scars on Evan's hand.

The silvery pink skin seemed to mock me every time we drove

under a street lamp. I couldn't look away, and my stomach was roiling by the time Evan pulled up in front of my dorm.

He met my eyes in the mirror, and I wondered if he could hear the thumping of my heart. "Have a good night, Madison."

I forced a smile to my numb lips, reminding myself that this was still a game. A game that I still had to play.

And *win*.

"It's Miss Cabot," I replied, icicles dripping from my tone as I met his gaze. My breath caught in my chest as we stared at each other in the mirror.

His eyes seemed to gleam at the challenge. "Good night, *Miss Cabot*." He inclined his head, but the action seemed more mocking than respectful.

Whatever.

I shoved it open and slipped out of the car before slamming the door. I kept my steps even and measured as I started toward the front doors of my dorm even as my thoughts started to careen out of control.

Madelaine had gone to Greece with Evan.

Madelaine had died in a fire in Greece.

Evan had burn scars on his hands.

He must have been in the fire, too.

In it... or *started* it. Gary had all but outright admitted Evan would kill Ryan on his orders when the time came.

My hands shook as I opened the door, and I heard the car start to drive away. A wobbly breath rattled from my chest as I exhaled, Gary's words playing on a loop in my mind.

Thanks again for handling that... situation.

My hand slapped the button for the elevator, but I was too out of it to fully recognize when it arrived. Somehow I was inside the car, and my legs gave out as the truth crashed over me.

I'd just been driven home by the man who had killed my sister on my father's orders.

CHAPTER 57

MADDIE

I made it to my door but then paused, unsure what to do next. My mind was a chaotic mess of broken thoughts and damning realizations.

Gary had killed Madelaine.

Mr. Harris had said as much, and I'd even kinda believed it myself, but now I couldn't dismiss it.

I knew in my bones that my father was responsible for my sister's death.

And now he was planning to kill Ryan.

Barbed wire wrapped around my chest, slicing into my lungs and heart until I was ready to scream.

I braced a hand on the doorframe and forced myself to breathe, which was, of course, when the door opened.

Looking up through blurry eyes, I was surprised to see Ash's face.

"Hey, I thought I heard—" His eyes went wide and he quickly pulled me into the dorm. "Jesus, Maddie. Hang on." He swept a device down my body, and I passed my phone over without him needing to ask before he checked for any bugs that might have been planted.

When nothing was triggered, Ash touched the side of my face. "What the fuck happened? Ryan's in the bathroom."

"I just need a second," I whispered, leaning against the door. My head rolled back as I stared up at the ceiling. "Where is everyone?"

"Bex is in her room. Court and Linc are at the house, but I can get everyone over here."

"No, I—" I stopped myself. "Actually? Yeah. I think everyone needs to hear this."

"Ah, shit," he hissed, rubbing a hand over the back of his neck. "That bad, huh?"

I could only nod as I focused on controlling the erratic rhythm of my heart and getting my shit together before Ryan saw me freaking out.

"What the fuck happened?" Ryan's voice boomed across the room.

I winced inwardly. So much for getting it together.

Ryan moved Ash out of the way so he was in front of me, his rough hands framing my face with infinite tenderness.

"Maddie, talk to me," he urged, his tone edging on desperate. "What happened? Shit, why are you wearing different clothes?"

I glanced down at the simple green dress I'd switched into, and the cream ballet flats. "Because my mom threw up on my other clothes."

His brows shot up. "You saw your mom? Is that why—"

"Gary killed Madelaine," I blurted out.

Every muscle in him tensed. "What?"

"Did he tell you that?" Ash demanded over Ryan's shoulder.

"Not exactly." I rubbed my forehead and sighed before looking at Ash. "Did you call the others? Everyone needs to hear this."

Ash nodded and tucked his phone into his back pocket grimly. "Yeah. They're on their way."

"Maddie," Ryan snapped, turning my head so I met his eyes. "Are you okay?"

"He didn't hurt me, I swear. No measuring me for a new choker with his bare hands," I assured him, wrapping my fingers around his wrists.

Ryan hissed out a breath, his eyes flashing. "Not fucking funny, Mads."

I was still shaking, still out of sorts, and my brain was going with

473

seriously dry humor to try and regain some sort of control over the night. I took a deep breath and told him, "Gary bought everything, but maybe a little too well."

Ash crowded against Ryan's back to see me. "How so?"

"Seriously, guys, can we wait for the others so I'm not explaining everything twice? I need a drink and a minute to breathe." I fixed my eyes on Ryan and lowered my voice. "Ryan, I promise no one touched me. My mom threw a glass at my head, but her aim still sucks."

"Christ," he muttered, pulling me into his arms and pressing his lips to my temple. I felt a tremor ripple through his strong frame as his hands smoothed up and down my back, like he needed to prove to himself I was okay.

He held me until someone knocked at the door, and then he pulled me to the couch and onto his lap. I shot him an amused look, but he only scowled back, daring me to try and move away.

Ash opened the door for Bex. Her hazel eyes immediately found me. "What happened?"

"Long story," I muttered. "We're waiting for the others."

It didn't take long for Court and Linc to arrive. Once everyone was settled in a spot, I took a deep breath and confessed everything that had happened with Gary. From him buying that Ryan was head over heels obsessed with me to planning to take over all the shell companies Phoenix had set up, his part in Madelaine's death, and ultimately kill Ryan.

When I was done, no one spoke for a long time.

"Well, fuck," Linc murmured, looking stunned.

"I can't believe he killed his own daughter. I mean, that's beyond psychotic," Bex breathed, looking worried.

I chewed on my lower lip, my stomach in knots even as Ryan wrapped his arms tighter around me.

Court rubbed his jaw. "But does he know all the shit that Madelaine did before she died? About Phoenix and us?"

Ash shook his head. "Doubtful. The shell companies are just that, and I buried Phoenix's involvement in them. All their assets are technically held by Phoenix, but we've kept our identities as private as we can. And I really think if he knew, there'd be no reason for him to keep up the ruse."

"But if Gary wants to buy these companies, he's going to come looking for the owners, and that's us," Court reminded him with a grim smile. "The problem with a shell game is the shells can crack, and we're damn close to the breaking point. We can't keep this up much longer. Someone is going to notice."

"Especially since O'Shea is out of the picture," Ryan muttered. "He was good at his job, but he was also easy to distract. The next attorney my father hires probably won't turn a blind eye. If they dig, we're fucked."

"That's why you were so hesitant to out Dean," I whispered, ducking my head. "Everything is a house of cards, and taking him out of the equation rocked the foundation."

Ryan's eyes blazed as they met mine. "You're worth it." Then his gaze cut to Bex. "Both of you are."

"But it's a problem," Bex murmured, looking unhappy.

"Not necessarily," Ash hedged, his brows pulling together as he thought. "I could set up one last fake company to own them all. Gary would throw all his money in *that* company, and we transfer all the funds to Phoenix before dissolving it."

"That still means Phoenix will go public," Ryan said. "Are we ready for that?"

"No, but we could be." Ash pressed his lips together.

"In a week?" Linc asked, incredulous. "No way. Besides, what about Beckett? He'll still be a threat, and we'll never get the shares of CI that we need to close him down for good."

Bex snorted. "It's a shame you can't make *two* companies."

Ash turned to her slowly. "Why?"

She shrugged a shoulder. "If they're each fighting for controlling interest over a different company, they'll be so busy watching each other that they won't see you guys moving in the background. Give Beckett a heads up that Gary's getting ready to make a move, so he invests everything he's got left into that company while Gary does the same."

"Huh." Ash seemed to consider what she was saying.

"That's a lot of variables at play, none of which we can control," Court began slowly. "We'd have to hope neither Gary nor Beckett decides to really dig into the company profiles, or they'd see the shit they're buying is an idea that doesn't exist."

Ash shook his head reluctantly. "It doesn't really matter anyway. There's not enough time to create a whole new company and concept that Beckett will have time to check out. Even I'm not that good."

"So, we're still screwed?" I sighed.

Ryan's thumb brushed across my arm. "No." But he didn't sound entirely convinced.

"It doesn't matter now," Ash replied, his eyes flashing. "We can use this. I think Bex had the right idea, but the wrong approach."

Bex's eyes widened. "I did?"

"How?" Ryan asked with a snort.

Ash pointed at him. "You need to tell Beckett what Gary's planning."

"Wait, what?" I hissed, my jaw dropping open.

"Why the fuck would I do that?" Ryan stared at Ash like he'd lost his damn mind, which he very well might have.

Ash rolled his eyes, seemingly annoyed that we didn't immediately get what he was thinking. "We have one last shell company we've been holding back for Beckett to buy into, right?"

"Right," Ryan agreed cautiously. "The one *Gary* is going to see holds control over the other bogus companies he's planning to buy out from under Beckett."

"It's Tuesday night, and the Cain board meeting is Friday morning. Gary might be able to scrape the money together to cover the existing stock options for the companies, but he'll never have the capital to get to the parent company. And even if he did? We tie it up with red tape and stall."

"But Beckett—" Court started.

"Ryan goes to Beckett and tells him Gary's plan." Ash's eyes flashed as he looked at his best friend. "You sell that Maddie has turned on her father. We use the same plan that we used with Gary, but reverse it.

You tell your father how Maddie is so in love with you that she's planning to turn over her trust to you alone as soon as you can get married. Maybe even hint she's been talking about eloping and cutting Gary out."

"But Beckett and Madelaine set up Ryan. He'd never buy that she's fallen for him," Bex said, looking uncertain.

"True, but Beckett also knows how much Madelaine hated Gary," I mused thoughtfully. "He'd might buy her playing Ryan to screw over her dad. Hell, Beckett might even think he's still partners with Lainey. They'd cut out Gary *and* Ryan."

Ash smirked knowingly. "We get Beckett to go all in by exposing Gary. He buys into this last company with everything he has left to get ahead of Gary, but what he's really doing is going completely belly up. They each invest in a company they'll own fifty percent of, but all they're buying is a piece of paper. We'll own them *both* in one fell swoop."

"We're counting on Beckett believing Ryan's word," Linc pointed out, his tone dubious. "That's he's utterly and completely in love with Maddie to the point he'd say fuck it to his future."

Ryan smirked and kissed my jaw. "Not a stretch."

Heat curled in my belly as I cuddled closer to him.

Linc rolled his eyes. "We get it, bro. You got the girl and lost your balls in the process."

I smirked at Linc. "I can assure you his balls are firmly intact and functional."

Linc's jaw dropped as Ryan barked out a laugh.

"Can we stop talking about Ryan's balls and get back on track?" Court drawled, rolling his eyes as Bex giggled.

Ash scooted to the edge of the couch and looked at Ryan, all business. "Beckett's hatred of Gary is bigger than anything else. At this point, he has nothing to lose. If he sits on his ass, Gary will outmaneuver him. Do you think you can sell it to him?"

"Yeah." Ryan nodded slowly, and I could see the wheels turning in his head as he figured out how to pitch it to his dad.

"But if Beckett stops to look into what's going on, he'll know he's been played. He could even give Gary a heads up," I argued, shaking my head.

Ash grimaced. "It's a risk, I know. But it's the only real play we have if we want them both taken out now. You two announce your marriage at the meeting. During it, we'll take Phoenix public with all our names listed as owners, and the fact that *we* control every company Beckett and Gary have bought into."

I gaped at him. "You want us to go public at the Cain board meeting? In front of Gary *and* Beckett?"

"Are you fucking insane?" Court stared at him.

"Ash, I don't know..." Ryan hesitated, looking torn.

Ash glowered at the floor as he seemed to take a beat to figure out how to say what he needed to. "Guys, this is it. We're not going to have another shot at taking out Beckett *and* Gary. Gary is leveraging himself to the fucking gills with this deal. If we get Beckett to do the same, they'll fold. They won't have a choice."

Linc sucked in a sharp breath through his teeth. "Okay, so we take out Beckett and Gary, but we still have a problem. Phoenix going public means my father—and Court's—will know. We'll lose all elements of surprise."

"It's not ideal," Ash agreed grimly, "but it *is* the only way to completely stop Gary and Beckett right now. We're out of time."

"Stopping Gary and Beckett is only half the battle," Court argued. "My dad and Linc's—"

"Are counting on being able to strike a deal with the Russians to open up a pipeline to funnel as many women and children through as they can." Ash glared at him. "But the deal hinges on the money Beckett and Gary are supposed to provide. Without those funds, they're all fucked."

"But won't that put Maddie and Ryan right in the line of fire?" Bex asked softly. "If they're at the board meeting, it'll be them against a room full of assholes."

"We could all be there," Ash replied.

"Jesus," Linc hissed, throwing himself back against the couch with a pissed expression. "Then Court and I lose the inside track with *our* fathers, and we're flying blind. Ash won't be working on the books anymore... We'll be fighting a war without the advantage of knowing our opponents' next moves."

Ryan's somber gaze moved to each guy in the room. "We need to vote on it."

"No," Linc said immediately. "Yes, we'd take out Gary *and* Beckett, but Phoenix isn't ready to take on my dad. Not yet. Even if things with the Russians go south, he still has too much pull for us to take him on."

Court looked at his best friend. "I agree."

"I say we go for it," Ash reiterated. "Ry, you know it's the right play."

Ryan looked at me and slowly nodded. "I agree with Ash."

Bex bit her lower lip. "What happens when there's a tie?"

Linc scoffed. "Time to call Grandpa. He's the tie breaker." He looked at Bex and his expression softened a bit. "When we set up Phoenix, we each got twenty-two and a half percent. Grandpa got the residual ten. We needed someone to be able to break a tie, if it ever came to it."

"Okay. I'll call him," Ryan muttered, moving me off his lap to pull out his phone.

"Stop," Court replied stiffly, his gaze moving to... me. "Brookfield wasn't the only asset he signed away in those papers we drafted for him. He also gave Maddie his shares of Phoenix."

My eyes went wide as everyone turned to me except for Ryan, who looked pissed as he glared at Court. "Seriously? You just snuck that in there?"

"It's what Grandpa wanted," Court argued. "Ryan, the man is going to—"

"Don't fucking say it," Ryan roared, shoving to his feet and stalking to the other side of the room.

I watched him, worry for him tangling with disbelief over this new turn of events. Eventually, I focused on Court. "Why didn't either of you tell us?"

Court's lips pressed into a hard line. "Honestly, because no one thought it would matter immediately. It was a last-minute addition. Grandpa wanted to be sure his shares were taken care of. They're actually for Corinne, but the Phoenix bylaws say we all have to maintain an equal share in the company. The only options to put them in trust for Cori were Beckett, a neutral party, or Maddie. Grandpa trusts Maddie."

I buried my face in my hands, overwhelmed and unprepared. Whatever decision I made, I was making it for Corinne. Not me, not Ryan... I needed to do what would help her the most.

"I think Ash's plan is the best," I finally admitted reluctantly.

Linc snorted in derision and shook his head. "Guess I shouldn't be surprised you sided with Ryan."

"What the fuck does that mean?" Ryan exploded, his eyes flashing as he whirled to face his friend.

I quickly stood up and moved between them, but I looked at Linc when I spoke. "The shares he gave me are for Corinne. I picked the option that helps *her*, and that's getting rid of Beckett. He's hurt that little girl enough, don't you think?"

Linc stared at me for a beat before his shoulders slumped. "Yeah, Maddie. I'm sorry."

I nodded once, accepting his apology, before stepping back and giving Ryan another look that said *I've got this.*

Ryan rubbed his jaw. "I need to go see Beckett."

Court grimaced. "If they figure this charade out, we're fucked. And not in the good way."

My stomach plummeted. One way or another, this would all be over soon.

I just prayed we were all still standing at the end.

CHAPTER 58

MADDIE

No one had much to say after that. Ash was in his own head, plotting the next steps. Linc and Court spoke in hushed voices, speculating about how their dads would take things. Ryan had gone into the bedroom to talk to his grandfather about our new plan and figure out a safe place to stash Corinne until we knew Beckett wasn't a threat. At least she was staying with Mr. Harris for the rest of this week.

Bex got off the floor where she'd been sitting and dropped down beside me on the couch. "How are you?"

I faked a bright smile. "Freaking amazing."

"You're a shitty liar." She shook her head.

"I saw my mom," I confessed. I'd left that part out of the conversation with everyone because, in lieu of everything else, it hadn't seemed important.

Bex sighed and took my hand. "That bad?"

My eyes drifted shut. "She's a wreck, Bex. I don't know what to do. Even if we stop Gary, I guess she goes back to rehab? But who the hell knows if it'll take. I'm so tired of worrying about her. It's exhausting."

She wrapped an arm around me and laid her head on my shoulder. "I'm sorry, Maddie."

I glanced at her with a smile that waned when I noticed she was watching Court. Knowing now what I did about how close she'd come to dying, it made sense why he'd thrown up walls between them.

But there was no denying they had unfinished business.

"Talk to him," I whispered, nudging her with my shoulder.

She picked her head up. "No, Mads. That ship has come and gone and sunk. Like the *Titanic*."

"You know what I've realized?"

Her brows lifted, waiting for me to elaborate.

"Everything could change tomorrow. Our lives are in such chaos that there's no telling when the bottom will fall out. Do you really want to take the chance on something happening and never telling him how you feel?" I searched her eyes with mine. "You've both made mistakes, Bex. Him more than you," I added when she looked ready to argue.

She flashed me an impish smile. "Most of the time, when I look at him, all I see is what I lost. But then there are these moments when I see what we could've had. That's what hurts the most."

"So tell him that," I encouraged softly.

She shook her head. "No. Imagining a potential future with him is easier than having that door closed for good. I mean, it sucks, but at least this way I can always think about *what if*, you know?"

"Bex." My heart ached for her.

She smiled thinly. "I'm kinda tired, Mads. I think I'm going to go to bed. Unless you need me to stay?"

All I could do was shake my head and wonder if I'd pushed her too far.

She got up and Court's gaze darted to her. "You leaving?"

Bex nodded. "Yeah. It's been a long day."

Court stepped away from Linc. "I'll walk you to your room."

"No," she said quietly, ducking her head. "I'm good."

He looked like he wanted to argue, but he simply watched her leave.

Ash closed his laptop. "I should go, too. My battery is almost dead, and I didn't bring my charger."

Linc sighed. "We should all go." He looked at me, as if confirming I would be okay when they left. God, I loved my friends.

"I'm good," I replied with a smile that took some effort. "Actually... Are we okay? I know you didn't want this—"

Linc crossed the room and put his hands on my shoulders. "No, I didn't," he admitted, "but we're family, Maddie. We don't always have to agree on everything, and I know you're thinking about Corinne first. But us disagreeing about business doesn't change the fact that I love you, okay?"

"Christ," Ryan muttered from the doorway to the bedroom. "I leave my wife alone for five fucking minutes and you're already pawing at her and declaring your undying love for her?"

Linc glanced over my shoulder. "Never said it was undying." He winked at me before kissing my cheek.

Ryan growled. "Enough, asshole."

Linc shot him an innocent look that was full of shit. "She's practically my sister."

"And my fist is about to be practically in your face," Ryan snarled, coming up behind me and wrapping his arms around my waist to pull me backward into his body.

I smirked at Linc, unable to resist riling up my husband. "Call me later when the ball and chain goes to bed, okay?"

Linc barked out a laugh that Ash and Court joined. Ryan didn't seem so amused as he ground his rapidly hardening dick into my ass.

"Pretty sure you won't be available to talk," he warned me, nipping at my earlobe as he whispered. "I have plans for this mouth."

A shiver of anticipation rolled down my spine.

"And we're leaving," Ash deadpanned, shaking his head but not bothering to hide a smile. "We'll talk more in the morning. Don't forget we have—"

"Practice at nine," Ryan finished. "I'll see you guys there."

"G'night, Maddie," Linc said, miming a phone call with his hand and mouthing, *Call you later.*

Ryan growled behind me, and I giggled as our friends left. As soon as the door was shut, Ryan swept me into his arms and carried me into the bedroom, where he tossed me onto the bed.

I hit the mattress with a squeak as I bounced, but he was already on top of me before I could consider trying to escape.

"Hi," I said breathlessly as his hips pressed to mine, pinning me in place while his massive arms caged me in.

He smirked, the corner of his mouth hooking up in a way that made arousal pool between my legs. "Hey."

I watched him, his crystal blue eyes only inches from my own. My tongue darted out to wet my lips as I anticipated his kiss.

He smoothed some of my hair back from my face. "Are you really okay?"

I wound my arms around him, slipping them under his shirt to slide up his back. "I'm really okay. Or as okay as I can be, considering Gary is threatening to kill you."

"He won't touch me," he promised.

"He better not," I muttered. "I'm too young to be a widow." I tried to make light of the situation, but my voice cracked at the end. The idea of something happening to him was like a rusty spear being shoved into my heart.

"I'm not leaving you, Madison Cain," he whispered, kissing my lips softly. "I have a lot of plans for you."

"Oh?"

He nodded. "I intend on being married to you for a very long time. I figure we'll take down our fathers, make the world a better place, finish school, maybe have a vow renewal ceremony?"

I giggled as he seemed to seriously be planning this out. "And—"

"Shh." He covered my mouth with his finger. "I'm planning our future, baby. Speaking of, babies. We're going to need them."

My brows shot up. "Oh, we are?"

"I'm still thinking at least three or four. I mean, you're a twin, so there's always a chance we'll have a set of those, but I'm good with that."

"Well as long as *you're* good with it," I remarked dryly, rolling my eyes. "I'm still not sure which uterus you're planning on using to carry all these kids."

"Cori will love being an aunt," he pointed out, blowing past my argument with a grin. His eyes glittered. "And I'll love helping you make them."

I raked my nails lightly down his spine, loving the way he shuddered in my arms. "Feel like practicing? For the children's sake, I mean."

He grinned down at me. "I love the way your mind works, Mrs. Cain." His hand slipped under my dress and found the center of my panties already damp.

A low groan worked out of his throat as he slipped two fingers inside me, thrusting deep and curling them. My back arched off the bed as a cry fell from my lips.

"So fucking tight. So fucking perfect." He kissed me slowly. "So fucking mine."

I whimpered, rolling my hips as his thumb brushed my clit.

"That's it," he encouraged, kissing the side of my neck. "Ride my hand, baby."

My cheeks flushed as I ground against him shamelessly. It didn't take long for me to shatter beneath him.

I tried to catch my breath as he pulled my clothes off. When he unsnapped my bra and pulled it away, he paused.

"Uh, Maddie?"

"Yeah?" I frowned, not sure why he was stopping and staring at my tits like I'd grown a third nipple.

His fingers delicately lifted something from my breast. "What's this?"

The sim card.

"Oh, my God." I'd forgotten about finding it and tucking it into my bra. "I found that in Madelaine's room after I showered. It was in this weird compartment inside one of the drawers on her vanity."

"Huh." Ryan studied it with narrowed eyes. "No idea what it is?"

I shook my head. "I grabbed it on impulse. I figured if she'd taken the time to hide it, there must be something important on there."

"Good thinking. I'll call Ash—"

I grabbed him before he could turn to get his phone. "What you *need* to do is finish what you've started, Ryan. Ash can wait until tomorrow."

He grinned and set the sim card aside. "If you insist."

CHAPTER 59

RYAN

The last thing I ever wanted to be doing was driving to my father's house. But combining that with an early practice that had put my body through hell, an offense team meeting that kept me from seeing Maddie at lunch, and leaving from that to drive home... I was in a shit mood.

I missed my wife.

Fuck.

A stupid, sappy smile tugged at my mouth even as I parked my car around the side of the house.

God, I loved that woman. She was the reason I was doing all of this. As long as Maddie was all right at the end of this fucked up shitshow, I'd be good.

I got out of my car and headed inside, knowing Beckett would be at his desk, probably thinking he was on top of the world.

There was no denying I loved that I was about to fuck up his day.

I smothered my smile and put on my game face as I walked into his office without knocking. I came up short, forcing myself not to grimace when I realized he wasn't alone.

Beckett glanced up at me from where he had one of the younger maids bent over his desk, plowing into her ass. "Need something, son? Give us a minute and she's all yours."

Disgust curdled like sour milk in my stomach, but I made myself eye the skinny brunette with big green eyes like I might've been interested. "Pass," I finally replied, dropping into one of the chairs facing his desk like I wasn't totally repulsed by the scene before me. "I like my girls to have more ass."

Baring his teeth, Beckett slammed his hips into the girl with a sneer. Like fucking her harder would make me somehow want a piece of her. When the girl winced as the edge of the desk cut into her hips, I pulled out my phone and absently pretended to scroll on social media until they were done.

Unsurprisingly it didn't take long for Beckett to finish with a wheezing groan. The girl took that as her cue to let out a breathy moan a porn star would've been proud of. I doubted she was getting off, but she knew how important it was to stroke his fragile ego.

Beckett pulled out of her with a wet squelch before slapping a hand on her ass hard enough to make her cry out for real. He pulled off the condom and tied it before handing it to her like a parting gift. "Leave us."

She bent to grab her dress, but he stomped a foot on it with a smirk. "Go on. Let my son see exactly what he's missing by turning you down."

I barely spared her a glance as she sauntered by, completely nude. She had nothing I wanted.

Once Beckett put his limp cock back into his pants, he sat across from me. "Something you needed, Ryan?"

"More like something *you* need," I countered. "I know about the companies you've been buying up."

He didn't look surprised. "And? I sent the preliminary agenda out to the members yesterday. I'm planning on announcing the acquisitions formally at the board meeting in two days."

"You're about to be announcing how you lost the fucking company," I retorted. "Gary also knows. He's currently working to leverage every asset he has to buy you out."

He exploded from his chair with a roar, slamming a fist onto his desk. "How the fuck did he find out?"

"Maybe one of your board members?" I drawled, uncaring when his cheeks turned a mottled shade of purple and the vein above his left eye bulged. Him having a stroke right here and now would actually be kind of perfect.

"There's an ironclad NDA in place," he snapped. He slowed his breathing and straightened his shoulders. "It doesn't matter. Gary can't have enough money left to buy me out."

"Oh, he does," I assured him.

His gaze sharpened. "How would you know that?"

I smiled, folding my hands over my stomach as I leaned back in my chair. "Because my fiancée told me so. Even recorded the conversation they had last night."

"Madelaine told *you* that?" Disbelief and derision dripped from his words.

I shrugged. "She and I have come to an understanding. Mostly her understanding that between me and Gary, I'm by far the lesser of two evils. You know how much she hates him."

"Exactly. So why the fuck would Gary tell her shit?"

A grin stole across my lips. "Because I might've helped her convince him that she's on his side by letting her record a conversation where I confessed I was hopelessly in love with her and was willing to give her everything."

He stared at me for a moment before bursting out into a deep laugh. "Sometimes you manage to surprise me, Ryan. Not often, but sometimes."

"You have one shot to get ahead of him," I advised, laying out the plan I'd gone over with Ash on the drive over until my brain was ready to bleed. "Did you ever stop to wonder why you were getting those companies so cheap?"

Beckett scoffed. "I'd say a ninety-million-dollar investment is a tad more than *cheap*."

"The parent company is divesting their interests, but it isn't enough. They've got someone on their payroll with an idea that will make Malcolm Whittier look like an imbecile. But the project hit delays and they need investors. It's why they've been selling off portions of smaller projects and companies, but they're still short. They're planning to look for investors next month."

Beckett eyed me critically. "How do you know this?"

"Ash," I replied. "He's been keeping an eye on things and found out where all the companies are connected. They're planning on launching technology that will guarantee military defense contracts, but also be available to the public."

His eyes widened, and I knew he was taking the bait.

Bex's dad had created CryptDuo as a secure way to transfer and download files for the military and political heads in our government, but they'd never made the tech public, so they were missing a large chunk of the market.

I met his gaze and went in for the kill. "All of our shit aside, Cain Industries is my birthright. I'm not fucking giving it to Cabot or his whore of a daughter."

"So what are you proposing?" Beckett asked, a slow smile spreading.

"Invest in the parent company before Gary finds out, then it won't matter about the smaller companies. You'll own the rights to the technology. That's where the real money is."

He watched me for a second before looking away. "As much as I hate to admit it, I'm a bit tapped out. I don't know that I can invest that much."

I'd suspected as much. "Then let me help."

His eyes snapped to me.

"I've barely touched my trust fund," I said. The multimillion-dollar trust had been set up by my mother before her death. Her shares of Brookfield's profits were split between myself and Cori, to be unlocked when we turned twenty-one.

I wasn't lying; I'd barely made a dent in the massive fortune that had been left to me and continued to grow as Brookfield was one of the leading wineries in the world. Besides, giving him this money meant it was going straight back into my pocket through Phoenix anyway.

"You'd do that?" Beckett's head tilted as he watched me.

I stood up and smirked. "Absolutely. At the end of the day, we're family. Fuck the Cabots."

"All right, son," he agreed softly, nodding. "Let's end the Cabots once and for all."

CHAPTER 60

MADDIE

"Tell me again we're doing the right thing." My voice came out as a fragile whisper in the space of the car.

Ryan's jaw tightened, and he reached over to grab my fingers. "We're doing the right thing, baby."

I glanced down at our hands, receiving a small measure of comfort from seeing my wedding band back on my finger. In the few days it had been off, I'd missed it. How silly and sappy did that sound?

But there was no point in keeping it hidden now; today was the day we'd confront our fathers. I knew that Gary was planning on crashing Beckett's board meeting. What neither of them knew was that Ryan and I would also be crashing.

At my feet was a briefcase full of all the paperwork we'd need to prove that we'd outsmarted them.

Our marriage license.

Proof that Phoenix International held the full rights to all the bogus companies both Gary and Beckett had sunk all their money into.

A copy of Michael Harris's will that put all of Brookfield and its holdings in my name.

And—the part I loved the most—a statement from an offshore bank account where my inheritance had been deposited hours earlier.

Court and the attorneys had worked endlessly making sure everything was set up and primed for what we needed. All that was left was this meeting, where we showed Gary and Beckett that we'd won.

For now.

Court and Linc were still worried about the blowback that was sure to come once their fathers found out what we'd all done. Bringing Phoenix into the public light was making them nervous, but we'd done what we could to mitigate the fallout.

Corinne was out of the country. Where, I wasn't entirely sure, but Ryan and his grandfather had made sure she was out of the line of fire. I knew for a fact that Court was hovering close to Bex today while Ryan and I made our announcement.

Linc and Ash had offered to come with us, but Court wasn't leaving Bex's side. In the end, they stayed behind. Ryan wanted this moment with his father as a statement that he didn't need his friends at his back to take the asshole down.

"What do you think about London?" Ryan asked suddenly.

I startled as my mind was pulled from running through all the potential worst-case scenarios. "What?"

"London," he repeated, steering the car off the highway and onto a ramp that led into downtown Los Angeles. "I was thinking about our honeymoon. Holiday break is coming up, so I thought you might want to go then."

"You want to go to London for Christmas?"

He shrugged. "Or Rome. Honestly, whatever you're in the mood for. We'll have about a week during the holidays where we can travel. Unless the team loses a game and we're out for the season. Then we could go longer."

"You're going all the way," I assured him.

He turned and flashed me a wicked grin. "Damn right we are." Yeah, he wasn't talking about football.

"Eyes on the road," I laughed, shaking my head.

"I just think we could use the break," he explained, turning onto a street. "And you said you've never traveled..."

"Honestly? I want to spend the holidays at Brookfield." I glanced over at him. "I want to be with our friends and your family."

"*Our* family," he interrupted.

"Our family," I agreed with a grin. "I think spending the holidays there is important." I didn't bother adding because it would likely be his grandfather's last.

Ryan swallowed. "Thanks, baby. I think that's a great idea. Depending on how things go, we can take a trip this summer. Somewhere warm. A private beach, maybe?"

"Don't we *have* a private beach?" I teased, thinking of his house, now *ours*, an hour away from Pacific Cross. "But we're going to need another room, you know. For Cori."

He stilled and shot me an uncertain look. "You'd want Cori to live with us at the beach house?"

My brows slowly climbed. "I mean, yeah. Isn't that the plan?"

He stopped at a red light and turned to give me his full attention, his eyes soft. "It's what I want, yeah. But I also wasn't going to expect—"

I covered his lips with my fingers, silencing him. "Ryan, I love Corinne. I don't know how we'll make it work, with her in school and us in school, but I know you two are a package deal."

"You're fucking amazing, Maddie."

I blushed and inclined my head to where the light had turned green. "Um, drive."

He smirked and switched his attention to the road. "There's a school nearby that would be good for Cori. It has a big art program and state-of-the-art intramural programs she'd love. Horseback riding, cheerleading, tumbling... But she'd live there most of the year."

I frowned. "Like a boarding school?"

"Sort of." He turned down another street. "Repetition and schedules are what Cori needs. She does best when she has a routine. We're still in school, Mads. I have another year left, and you have college.

Neither of us are in a spot where we can give Corinne everything she needs all the time."

Lips pressed together, I considered his words. "I don't want her to think we're abandoning her."

"We won't be," he said fiercely, pulling the car alongside the curb by a massive glass-and-steel building with a geometric silver statue and fountain in front of it where people had paused to sit as others bustled around them. "Cori knows about the school. She *wants* to go."

"I'm surprised Beckett didn't send her to get her out of the house," I remarked.

Ryan grimaced, his jaw tight. "Beckett wanted Cori close because he knew he could use her to hurt me. Besides, sending her there would be admitting she has learning problems and is developmentally delayed. God forbid she looked less than perfect to his country club buddies."

"If you think that's the best move for Corinne, then I'm in. But I do want her to have her own room wherever we live." I hesitated. "I mean, we never even really talked about where we're going to live. You can't crash in my dorm forever, and I'm not crazy about sharing a house with all your frat brothers."

"Do you want to go to PCU next year?"

"I haven't really thought about it." I hadn't. In the almost four months I'd been going to Pacific Cross Academy, I'd been bouncing from one dramatic scandal to the next, trying not to lose control of my life. I'd gotten into this whole mess because Madelaine tempted me with a future at the college of my choice.

I hadn't thought about college in forever. It was hard to think about a future when I was trying to survive the week.

I wasn't sure what I wanted, except a long nap in my husband's arms, when this was all over.

"Our next step is figuring out what you want," he reasoned, unhooking his seatbelt. "Staying on the West Coast would be easier for Phoenix and Cori, but if you want to go to school somewhere else, we'll make it work."

I smiled softly. "So, you're saying you'll follow me wherever I want to go?"

"Damn right," he replied firmly. "I'll follow you into hell if that's what it takes."

"That's convenient," I murmured, looking up at the building. "Is this it?"

Ryan nodded grimly as an attendant from the valet stand began walking over to us. "Ready?"

"No," I admitted, taking a deep breath as the attendant opened my door and extended a hand to help me out of the car. I took it, the tight pencil skirt that came to my knees combined with Ryan's low-to-the-ground car making me need a little assistance unless I wanted to look hella awkward.

"Miss," the man greeted me, his eyes sweeping down me in a quick assessment. He smiled, probably assuming from the car and the outfit that I was someone worth being polite to. He looked at the briefcase in my hand. "Do you need—"

Ryan came around the front of the car with a scowl, all but ripping my hand from the valet's as he tossed the keys at the man's face. He caught them before the keys could poke his eyes.

"Don't scratch it," Ryan remarked, glaring at the man pointedly as he took the briefcase in one hand before wrapping the other arm possessively around my waist.

The man paled a bit at seeing who was holding on to me. "Yes, Mr. Cain."

Ryan looked at me, all smiles. "Ready, baby?"

"You're the worst," I mumbled as we walked toward the front doors. "He was being polite."

"He was eye-fucking you," Ryan retorted, holding the door for me.

I rolled my eyes. "You're biased."

"Tonight when he's jerking off, it'll be *your* face he's picturing," Ryan growled, his hand brushing my lower back as he guided me through the large lobby.

The space was almost cavernous, and my heels echoed as we walked toward the turnstiles separating the lobby from the bank of elevators. Apart from the front desk and security desk, there was no furniture. Not even a potted plant. It was cold and impersonal, and all I could do was try not to shiver.

The white floor had silvery veins marbled through it, and there was a giant CAIN INDUSTRIES logo stamped in the middle, just in case someone forgot where they were.

Ryan didn't hesitate as he walked us forward, not pausing at the desk. He reached into his pocket and pulled out a laminated card, swiping it across the reader on the turnstile. The metal arms folded down, allowing us through. At the elevator, he used the same pass to open one of the doors.

"So, CI owns the entire building?" I murmured after the doors slid shut.

He nodded, his expression tense as we started to ascend. "I'll take you on a tour one of these days."

I shuddered, thinking of walking the same halls Beckett had created and owned. "Pass."

Ryan turned to me. "Mads, when he's gone, we'll make this company everything it should've been."

I faced him, arching a brow and resisting the urge to smooth the front of my royal blue silk top. "I never wanted to be in charge of a Fortune five hundred company, Ry."

"Top ten," he corrected with a half-smile.

My mouth turned dry. "That, either."

He reached for my hands. "You can do whatever you want, Maddie. I'll support whatever goals you have as long as your ass is in my bed at the end of each day."

I tipped my head back. "You say the sweetest things."

The elevator doors opened with a soft chime, and my heart practically stopped. Everything in me froze as I took in the upscale reception area, complete with a receptionist who looked like she'd been plucked off a runway in Milan to work here.

Her big brown eyes were wide and her face pale as she sat with her head angled toward a closed set of doors behind her desk. I could already hear shouting male voices.

"Looks like we're late to the party," Ryan whispered with a smirk. He nodded at the receptionist.

She frantically patted down the front of her dress, her cleavage practically spilling out of the top. "Um, hi. Sorry. How can I—"

Ryan pointed to the doors. "Actually, we're here for the meeting."

Her eyes widened, and the short, dark bob around her ears seemed to tremble as she shook her head and looked worriedly at the calendar in front of her. "I don't see—"

"We don't have an appointment," Ryan interrupted coldly. He flashed her a toothy smile that was more shark than man. "Tell you what, why don't you take the rest of the day off?"

"What?" She gaped at him.

Ryan simply winked at her. "Look—" he glanced at the nameplate on the edge of her desk "—Sandi, not even your dick sucking skills are going to keep your job safe today."

Her cheeks went a shade of ashen that didn't seem possible under that much spray tan.

"I'd get out while you can," Ryan finished, like they were old friends. The only sign that he wasn't playing around was the hard look in his crystal eyes. "Seriously. Get the fuck out of here."

Sandi swallowed, her gaze shooting to me like I could save her.

I gave her a cool smile. "He's not kidding."

She quickly grabbed her purse from the bottom drawer of her desk and stumbled to her feet. She shot us a worried look, but practically ran for the elevators.

Another *ding* echoed in the space, and Ryan pulled his phone out of his pocket. "Looks like everything's in place."

I sucked in a deep breath, feeling a little dizzy.

"Ready?" he asked me.

"No," I answered honestly.

He kissed me quickly. "Me neither. Let's go."

CHAPTER 61

MADDIE

I should've asked Ash for one of those itty bitty cameras I could pin to the front of my outfit. The looks of confusion on Gary's and Beckett's faces would forever be imprinted on my mind.

The board members of Cain Industries were seated around a long wood table with a finish so glossy I could see their reflections in it. Nearly a dozen men were there, each looking somewhere between amused and bored as Gary and Beckett faced off in front of a wall of floor-to-ceiling windows that showcased a breathtaking view of the Los Angeles skyline.

Beckett smiled at Ryan. "Son, I wasn't aware you were joining us, but good timing. I was just about to show Gary how epically he just lost everything."

Ryan nodded. "Don't let me stop you."

Gary looked at me, suspicion in his eyes as he realized something wasn't right. "What's this?" His eyes focused on where Ryan and I were holding hands. Unlike Beckett, he didn't assume I was here to take his side.

Maybe he was the smarter of the two after all.

"This is you finally getting exactly what you deserve," Ryan replied, his smile icy as he stepped away from me and dropped the briefcase onto the table with a bang. He glanced around the room. "Gentlemen, why don't you all take a break? We have some family matters to discuss."

No one moved.

Ryan smirked. "It wasn't a suggestion. Get the fuck out or I'll have security escort you from the building."

A man with thinning white hair and a beer belly for days scoffed at him. "Beckett, your boy is out of line. Handle him."

Beckett's face turned a vibrant shade of red and he stalked toward Ryan, grabbing his arm as if to physically manhandle him out of the room.

"What the fuck—" Beckett's hissed question was abruptly cut off when Ryan spun and decked him. Blood spurted from Beckett's nose as he fell backward onto his ass with a curse. Several men jumped up from the table.

"Get the fuck out!" Ryan roared, and several men practically ran for the door. I quickly stepped away so I wasn't blocking their exit, my eyes on Gary.

I saw the moment it clicked that he knew something was wrong. That he'd messed up.

Triumph surged in my veins, the elation giving me a high so potent I was almost lightheaded.

A few men lingered, unsure about Ryan, who simply cracked his knuckles as Beckett shoved to his feet. Ryan barely spared him a glance. "Don't even think about touching me again."

Beckett's gaze snapped to me, and Ryan snarled. "And don't you fucking dare *look* at her."

The man who had questioned Ryan looked intrigued. "Who the hell do you think you are? This is a board meeting—"

"Considering I now own the majority stock in CI, I'm overruling whatever board decisions you think you're empowered to make." Ryan cut him off with a smirk. Facing off against a room full of assholes—and punching Beckett—was seriously hot.

My husband was so getting laid tonight.

"You don't own shit," Beckett spat, blood still dribbling from his nose. He stumbled around to the other side of the table before slapping a hand on the speaker box. "Get me fucking security."

No one answered.

"Gave your secretary the rest of the day off," Ryan drawled. He pulled out his cellphone and tapped out a message. "But if you want security, I'll have them come up."

It took less than a minute for three security guards to walk into the room, each one bigger than the next. And finally, Royal stepped in behind them and closed the door, his look somehow furious and indifferent at the same time.

Beckett gaped at Royal, clearly recognizing him. "What—"

"I hope you don't mind, but I asked Royal to handle security until I can find someone I trust to do the job," Ryan explained with a feral smile. He glanced at the man who we had asked to come help us literally take out the trash.

He'd been all too happy to help. Bishop and Knight were around here somewhere, too, along with a handful of men they'd selected from their old squads to help us take control of Cain Industries.

I was amazed that these men had dropped whatever they were doing to help us. Or I had been until Ryan told me how much they were being paid.

Yeah, I probably would've jumped at the chance to make six-figures in a month, too.

"These gentlemen were just on their way out," Ryan said in a clipped tone, jerking his chin at the remaining board members, gaping at the new guards.

Beckett slammed a fist on the table. "You can't do this!"

"Watch me," Ryan replied with a dark chuckle.

The security guards stepped toward the men, who quickly threw their hands up and started for the door with disgruntled and disbelieving expressions.

Royal eyed Beckett and Gary with interest. "Want me to stick around?"

"Just make sure we aren't interrupted," Ryan replied, glaring at his father, who was wiping blood on the cuff of his shirt.

Royal nodded. "You're the boss." He went to leave, pausing to smirk at me. "Maddie."

The corner of my mouth hooked up as Gary blanched, realizing I knew Royal.

Once the door was shut, Ryan resumed rifling through the briefcase until he found the file he wanted. He tossed it across the table at our fathers.

"This is all the documentation you need proving that as of midnight, Phoenix International owns the majority share of Cain Industries," Ryan informed them.

"Phoenix International?" Disdain dripped from Beckett's tone.

"The company that Grandpa helped Ash, Linc, Court, and I set up with the sole purpose of ruining all of you," Ryan replied. "We own every company you've invested in for the last year. Every concept, every patent, every stock... It's *us* you've been paying."

Beckett's face paled and he grabbed the file, flipping through it. "How..."

Ryan turned to Gary. "We also own Praxis Tech. I believe you just invested a significant amount to acquire fifty percent of their stocks because you hoped it would destroy my father?" He glanced at me. "That was the plan, right, Mads?"

I nodded slowly. "Sounds about right."

Gary's gaze snapped to me. "What have you done?"

I simply stared back, happy to let Ryan dismantle their world. I was happy enough just to bear witness to Gary and Beckett lose everything.

Ryan folded his arms across his chest. "Let's call it what it is, boys. You're broke. For the last three years, it's been my goal in life to see this moment happen. To see both of you end up with nothing."

Beckett tossed the papers down with a sneer. "Oh, I wouldn't say that. Seems you've forgotten something, *son*."

Ryan held up a hand. "If this is the part where you threaten Corinne to make me fall in line, it won't work. There's no inheritance. Not for me and not for Cori. Grandpa signed Brookfield away."

"He can't do that," Beckett snapped. "The company has to go to—"

"A familial member by birth or marriage," Ryan parroted with a vicious smirk. "I'm aware. Grandpa signed everything over to my wife this weekend."

It was like all the oxygen was sucked out of the room as he dropped that bomb. Gary and Beckett turned their stares to me, the former with fury and the latter with fear.

I stepped up to Ryan's side, curling my fingers around his arm so they could see my wedding band. "Surprise."

"No congratulations?" Ryan taunted them when they didn't speak.

Gary started laughing. "Thank you for doing exactly what I wanted."

I shot him a withering look as Ryan pulled out another file and slid it over to him.

Gary picked it up, his brow furrowing. "What's this?"

"The balance of my accounts in Switzerland and the Caymans," I replied sweetly. "It's where I had my inheritance moved to. My attorneys filed all the paperwork needed for me to collect it at the beginning of the week."

The slight tremor as the papers shook was the only sign Gary was rattled as he hissed, "What?"

I faked innocence. "Well, between that money and the money I'm getting from Brookfield, I was advised—"

Gary's sudden yell made me jump, and a second later he was rounding the table, his eyes murderous.

Ryan stepped between us, intercepting Gary with a punch to his jaw that made him stumble back. Ryan followed it up with a shot to his ribs before pushing him backward onto the boardroom table, his hands around Gary's throat.

"I've been wanting to do that for weeks," he seethed as Gary uselessly clawed at Ryan's wrists. He was no match for Ryan's strength or fury. "You don't *ever* get to touch Maddie again, asshole. Try it, and they'll need dental records to identify you."

Ryan's icy gaze lifted to Beckett as Gary's feet kicked uselessly. "That goes for you, too. You're done. Both of you. I suggest you leave town before the Russians figure out they've been played."

Beckett's hands balled into fists at his sides. "You're going to pay for this."

"Somehow I doubt that," Ryan chuckled. "But feel free to stick around and try. I hear the last guy who reneged on a deal with the Russians got fucked by a cattle prod until he had a heart attack."

My gaze dropped to Gary, who was turning a concerning shade of bluish purple as his attempts to get free started waning. "Ryan, enough."

Like he was my own trained attack dog, he let Gary go and stepped back to my side. "Whatever you say, Maddie."

Gary rolled onto his side, coughing uncontrollably as he wheezed in a sharp breath.

Beckett turned to me with accusing eyes. "You played me, you lying whore."

Ryan took a threatening step forward, but I grabbed his arm. "You played yourself," I replied, shaking my head.

"Ryan, she's going to fuck you over, too," Beckett insisted. "Are you really this stupid? That blinded by mediocre pussy?"

Ryan just smiled, not rising to the bait. "You've lost, old man. Get your shit and get out before I have my security toss you out one of the windows up here." His gaze slid to Gary, who was just getting to his feet. "That goes for both of you."

"This isn't over," Beckett snapped before storming from the room.

Gary was slower, his gaze moving over me. "I underestimated you. Both of you."

I lifted my chin. "You did."

He stumbled to the doorway and paused, meeting my eyes before he left. "I won't make that mistake again."

CHAPTER 62

MADDIE

I needed a nap.

Watching Ryan slip into CEO mode as soon as Beckett and Gary were confirmed off the premises was hot, but also exhausting. I wasn't entirely sure what was going on, but watching him literally roll up his sleeves and flash me some forearm porn while he jumped on no less than a dozen calls while pacing the length of the conference room? Yeah, that was sexy.

By the time everything at CI was under control, the sun was slipping behind the LA skyline.

Ryan finished his call and turned to me. "Ready to go home?"

I perked up and slipped my feet back into the heels I'd kicked off hours ago. "Definitely."

He scrubbed a hand over his face before flashing me a tired smile. "How are you doing?"

"Shouldn't I be asking *you* that?" I countered, walking to him and resting my hands on his chest.

His hands instantly went to my waist, holding me close. "I'm good." He brushed a lock of hair over my shoulder. "This has been a long time coming. It's a relief."

"Good," I replied, lifting up the last few inches to kiss him softly. "I'm proud of you, Ryan."

His eyes practically sparkled. "Thanks, baby. I'm proud of you, too."

My brows lifted. "Me?"

He chuckled. "Yes, you. Most people wouldn't have handled this whole mess with nearly the grace you have."

"I think you're mistaking grace for survival skills," I joked, embarrassed by the praise. I tried to duck my head, but he caught my chin in his hand and forced me to keep my head high.

"I think you're too modest for your own good," he countered, his eyes searching mine. "You're amazing, Madison Cain."

I sighed, my insides flinching a bit. "Madelaine Cain, remember?"

He shrugged. "So we legally change your name. We can have the paperwork filed tomorrow making you officially *Madison* Cain."

It was stupid to be hung up on a name, but hope thrummed in my chest. "Really?"

He laughed again. "Yes, really. Don't you know I'd do anything for you?"

"I'm starting to get that," I answered, smiling up at him. "But for right now? I'll settle for you taking me home so we can officially celebrate taking control of the rest of our lives."

He barely suppressed a smile. "Why, Mrs. Cain, are you propositioning me?"

I smirked, playing it coy even as I resisted the urge to climb him like my own personal jungle gym. "Let me try this again. Apparently I have a habit of being too... *modest.*" I leaned in, pressing my lips against his ear. "I want you to take me home and fuck me."

Ryan groaned, the sound vibrating between us as his hand tightened on my hip. "Hell fucking yes. God, you're perfect."

I didn't bother correcting him because was I perfect? Hell no.

But was I perfect for *him*? Hell yes.

We finished gathering up our papers and things before leaving the building. Both of us ignored the stares from the confused and worried employees as we left and as we waited for the valet to retrieve Ryan's car.

We spent the hour drive back to Pacific Cross chatting about normal things: His upcoming playoffs schedule, which began Sunday. The classes I would take next semester. Christmas gifts for Corinne.

It was blissfully mundane and just what we needed.

"What about the frat?" I asked once he'd parked the car and we were walking hand-in-hand back to my dorm.

His lips pressed together. "I'm going to give it up. Honestly, I joined because I was a legacy and it was expected. It also gave me access to people, like Dean, that I needed to keep an eye on. But the only guys in there who truly are my brothers are Linc, Court, and Ash."

"Think they'll stay?" I glanced at him.

He shook his head. "Nah. We've talked about it. There's nothing really left for us there. Not now. If anything, we'd have to constantly watch our backs, since a lot of those guys would love the chance to get in Linc's dad's good graces."

"Won't you all have to move out?" I frowned, wondering where they'd go.

He nodded. "Yeah."

I was quiet as we walked up the stairs to the building. "We could... all live together," I suggested.

Ryan paused, glancing at me with an unreadable look in his eyes. "You'd want that?"

I shrugged and tried to dismiss it. "It was just a thought."

"No, wait." He tightened his hand around mine when I tried to pull away. "Mads, we just got married. You want three of my friends to live with us?"

"They're my friends, too," I pointed out. "And... I don't know. You guys are a package deal, and I'm assuming whatever house we get won't be a one-bedroom row home."

He frowned. "What's a row home?"

I stared at him for a beat. "Oh, my God."

He smiled at me. "I get what you're saying, and no, our first home won't be a one-bedroom anything. There's a development in Pacific City where we could live. We're not the first students to get married. The houses aren't quite a big as Gary's or Beckett's—"

"Which is *fine*," I insisted. "I don't need a giant house, but if you want the guys nearby—and with CI and Phoenix, it sounds like they need to be—I'm just saying, I don't mind them living with us. I'm sure we can find a place big enough for all of us."

The corners of his mouth twitched. "You're serious."

"Yes." My cheeks heated as he stared at me like I was offering him the moon. "Why are you looking at me like that?"

"Because I love you and I can," he replied.

My head dropped and I groaned. "Do I seriously have to spend the rest of our lives with you making corny statements like that?"

"Yeah," he answered. "But you also get to spend the rest of your life having me in your bed, kissing every fucking delicious inch of you while making you scream."

I gave a soft hum of approval. "And can we do that *now*?"

Ryan glanced around the empty lobby of the dorm. "Kinky, but sure." His hands dropped to my legs and started to lift my skirt.

I jerked away with a laugh. "Upstairs," I said, backing to the elevators and hitting the button.

He prowled closer, the look in his eyes making my pulse jump as I hit the elevator doors. Before Ryan could grab me, the doors opened, and I stumbled into the car with a laugh that abruptly ended when I crashed into someone.

"Shit, sorry—" I started to apologize, turning around and freezing when I saw Brylee.

Her dark eyes looked at me with utter contempt before shifting to Ryan as he closed in behind me, blocking the doors.

"Well, if it isn't the happy couple," she said, rolling her eyes as she skirted around Ryan to get off the elevator. "You know, you two deserve each other."

"And you deserve an incurable case of syphilis," Ryan mocked, pitching his voice to an awful falsetto.

I barely smothered a snort of laughter.

Brylee looked at us with disgust. "You used to be a king around here, Ryan. Now you're marrying the girl who made you look like a fool."

"Married," he corrected her with a dangerous smile.

Her brow furrowed in confusion until Ryan grabbed my left hand with his and held up our wedding bands.

We hadn't discussed going public with our marriage at school, but apparently we weren't hiding anything from anyone anymore.

Brylee's jaw dropped. "You're *married?*"

I nodded as Ryan looped an arm around my chest and held me against him. He rested his chin on my shoulder and fixed Brylee with a look. "What? No congratulations?"

Her shoulders stiffened.

"No, really," Ryan said, his tone hardening. "Tell my wife congratulations."

Her gaze flicked to me. "Congrats. I hope you both get everything you deserve."

"Didn't exactly seem sincere," Ryan mused, studying her. "Maybe if she got on her knees and tried saying it again..."

"No," I said, shaking my head. "I'm done with her."

He turned his gaze from me to Brylee. "You're lucky my wife is nicer than me."

Brylee's lips mashed into a tight line as she held back whatever spiteful comment was begging to be released.

I tugged Ryan out of the doorway while leaning over to tap the button for my floor. I wiggled my fingers at my nemesis as the doors closed on her unhappy face.

Ryan buried his face against the side of my neck, rocking his hips against my ass. "I still think you should let me have her ass expelled so you don't have to see her again."

I turned in his arms. "And I think we should stop thinking about her. I'd much rather focus on other things."

His head lifted. "I might need you to describe, in detail, what those *things* are, babe."

I stepped away as the elevator doors opened on our floor. "If you need me to explain what I need, I'm worried."

He cocked an eyebrow, his gaze liquid fire as he watched me back away. "Maddie."

I spun and ran, not thinking about the fact that I needed a key to get into my damn room. I hit the door a second before Ryan's arms boxed me in against it. He pressed me against the door with a growl, the hard length trapped behind his pants griding against my hip.

"Got ya," he whispered, nipping at my shoulder before kissing it.

I melted against him, loving the way his body felt around mine. "What are you going to do with me?"

"I'm sure I'll think of something," he answered, snaking a hand around me to unlock the door.

We spilled inside the room with a laugh before he kicked the door shut with his foot and spun me around so I was facing the door.

"Hands on the door," he ordered, sending a thrill tripping down my spine.

I obeyed, my palms splayed flat against the wood.

"Good girl," he praised, the rough timbre of his voice making me shiver as he started working the zipper down on my skirt. Cool air teased the heated skin of my back as he exposed it inch by inch.

He guided the skirt past my hips before stripping my shirt away. I felt the fabric pool around my feet, leaving me in heels and my underwear.

Ryan's knuckles dragged down the length of my spine, hovering at the edge of my panties. A single finger traced the edge of the lace to the front as he crowded against my back, the fabric of his shirt brushing my sensitive skin.

"How wet are you right now?" he demanded, his fingers poised to delve inside my panties and find out for himself.

Something in me ached to tease him, to make him crazy. Maybe that was why I glanced over my shoulder and said, "Not very. I guess married sex is boring."

His eyes narrowed, just barely. It was the tiniest twitch in the corners of his eyes that gave him away, and my only warning that I'd waved a red flag in front of a raging bull.

Ryan's hand jerked away from my body, and I braced myself for whatever came next.

Which was his hand cracking across my ass.

I yelped, dancing to my tiptoes as my ass burned and throbbed where he'd spanked me.

"Boring, huh?" he murmured.

I drew in a shaky, steadying breath and went all in. "Practically tedious."

He laughed, the dark sound making me clench my thighs together. Yeah, we both knew I was full of shit. My panties were soaked, probably ruined for good.

Ryan's hand came down again, this time on the other cheek. He massaged the burn into me with strong fingers before repeating the action again.

Again.

Again.

I whimpered, my nails scraping the wood and chipping some of the white paint as I held as still as possible. All I wanted to do was beg him to strip me completely bare and screw me until I couldn't walk straight.

But this was part of the game, and I was curious to see which of us caved first.

Finally, he stepped away from me. "Don't move, Maddie."

My teeth caught my lower lip, and I heard him walk away from me. I wanted to look but forced myself to hold still. It sounded like he'd gone into the bedroom, but seconds later he was coming back.

He kissed my shoulder, almost reverently, as his hands began pushing my underwear down. He helped me step out of them, and then his fingertips were gliding up the inside of my leg. He sank a finger into me with zero resistance.

"I think we can do better than tedious." He added a second finger but kept his thrusts shallow and unhurried.

My back arched as I instinctively angled my hips so he'd go deeper. Instead, he withdrew completely.

A plaintive whine managed to break free from my lips. "Ryan."

Something else nudged at my opening, cold and slick and not his fingers.

Apprehension curled in my chest as whatever toy he was using was pressed inside me. I flinched at the cool metal as he worked it inside of me.

"I was going to use lube," he informed me, "but since you seem to already be soaked, I figured why bother?" He dragged the blunt object through my slit, circling it around my clit with enough pressure to torment but not give me any sort of relief.

"*Ryan*," I begged, needing more.

"Yes, Maddie?"

"Please."

"Since you asked so nicely," he murmured. "Bend over, but keep your hands on the door. And spread those gorgeous legs, baby."

My cheeks flamed as I moved into the position he wanted. A second later, something pressed against my ass. My spine stiffened at the intrusion. "Ry…"

He kissed my spine, and I realized the object he'd been teasing me with was a plug he intended to put in my ass.

"Let me in, Mads," he demanded softly, working the plug past the tight ring of muscle.

I took a deep breath and forced myself to relax, my nerve endings trembling as he seated the plug inside me. The stretch was uncomfortable at first, but the slow burn gave way to something exotic and sensual.

I exhaled hard. There was something deliciously deviant about this act that intrigued me, and I wanted *more*.

He unsnapped the back of my strapless bra, and it fell away, leaving me completely naked and him still fully clothed. I was about to tell him how unfair that was when his hands came up to cover my tits, pinching my nipples at the same time until they formed tight peaks.

I gasped at the sharp sting that seemed to have a direct line to my pussy. A soft, breathy moan escaped my lips as his hands dropped to my hips.

"Hang on," Ryan warned me a second before he lifted me into his arms.

I clenched my butt, wondering if the damn plug would pop out as he carried me into the bedroom and laid me on the bed. He stepped back, his gaze searing into me as he licked his lips.

He began stripping, letting me enjoy my favorite view as his hard chest and abs came into my line of sight, that enticing V that dipped beneath his pants. He toed off his shoes and worked his pants and boxer briefs down before kicking them away.

He grabbed his cock as it bobbed up and tapped his stomach. Fisting it, he gave it several hard strokes, his blue eyes promising me all kinds of dirty things as he jerked off to the image of me naked beneath him.

His brows lifted. "Open those thighs, baby. I want to see my pussy."

I slowly let my legs fall open, my insides tightening at his rough groan.

"Fuck, you're perfection, Maddie," he murmured, covering my body with his and fitting between my legs like we were two pieces of the same whole.

A second later, he started to push inside of me. Between the plug and his sheer size, I wasn't sure he'd fit until he bottomed out with a hiss.

"Oh, fuck," I whispered, my eyes screwed shut in ecstasy as my body stretched to the point of blinding pleasure. I was full and aching and desperately needed him to move.

He withdrew before slamming back into me. "God damn," he grunted, working over me.

"More, Ryan," I pleaded, my nails curling into his shoulders.

He hooked a hand under my thigh and leaned back until he was able to get my knee over his shoulder, sinking in even deeper.

I cried out, unable to do anything but take what he was giving.

"Hang on, Maddie," he murmured, thrusting deeper inside of me.

The orgasm that had been shimmering somewhere out of reach suddenly blazed to the foreground, and when he ground against my clit on the next thrust, I came undone with a keening cry. I spasmed around him, and he simply rode me through my first climax and straight into my second.

My chest heaved as I struggled to catch my breath. Pops of white lights burst behind my eyelids as he kept going, fucking me like our lives depended on it.

When his fingers slipped between us to rub circles around my clit, I almost tapped out. It was too much; the sensations spiraling inside of me were too fucking much.

I was mindless as his hips collided with mine. All I could do was try not to pass out, but when he pinched my clit and surged inside of me, I was done.

I shattered in every sense of the word, barely aware of him roaring my name as he followed me into oblivion.

CHAPTER 63

MADDIE

F inishing my second glass of water, I refused to meet Ryan's gaze. He laughed, the sound one of my favorites, as he plucked the empty cup from my fingers and got back into bed with me. Without hesitation, he pulled me against his naked chest and freaking cuddled me.

I tried to keep my body stiff, but I was melting against him within seconds.

My body had a mind of its own when it came to this man.

But when he started laughing, I huffed and managed to attempt putting space between us.

"Maddie, come on," he began, a smile in his voice.

"You're way too smug," I shot back.

His laughter bounced off the walls of my bedroom. "Baby, you passed out. I fucked you so hard—"

I clapped a hand over his mouth. "Yeah, yeah. You're a freaking sex god."

He was right, though; he'd barely finished when I lost whatever hold on consciousness I'd managed to maintain. But, to be fair, the man had wrung three crazy intense orgasms out of me in less than twenty minutes.

He could have kept going; Ryan had stamina for freaking days. I was the one who usually begged for a break. This time, though, my body hadn't even let me get the words out before I was unconscious.

He grabbed my fingers and brought them to his lips. "Glad you're willing to admit the obvious."

I scowled at him.

"Seriously, making you pass out from my dick is my new daily life goal," he added, grinning at me.

"You're ridiculous," I said, lifting my nose in feigned annoyance.

"What's that?" He wound his arms around me, pulling me back to him once more. "Something about my dick?"

I turned and opened my mouth to say something else, but a knock at the front door cut me off. I frowned and looked at the door.

"You expecting someone?" Ryan asked, only half-teasing as he got up and grabbed his pants from the floor. His phone fell out of his pocket and he picked it up. "Shit."

"What?"

He turned back to me with a guilty look. "It's Ash. He's been calling. I had it on silent mode."

Another knock, this time more insistent. I swung my legs over the side of the bed and started to get up as Ryan left the bedroom, closing the door.

I hurried and grabbed some clothes when I heard Ash's voice as Ryan let him in. Tying my hair into a messy bun, I checked the mirror and wiped the mascara and eyeliner smudges from under my eyes so I looked less like a raccoon before going out and joining them.

I paused in the doorway as they both turned to me. "What's wrong?"

Ash shot Ryan a look before facing me. "The chip you found in Madelaine's room—were there any others?"

I shook my head. "No. Not that I saw. Why?"

Ash sighed loudly, rolling his neck. "Because somehow your sister got ahold of the security tapes inside the clubs. No fucking clue how she did it, but she has footage of some very powerful men doing some very serious shit."

I gaped at him. "What?"

"Fuck," Ash muttered. "Look, this is serious, Maddie. She's got videos of my dad, Beckett, Gary... Hell, there's even shit she has that I didn't know about. But the footage is recent. And there's a number five on the chip."

Ryan blew out a hard breath. "There are other SD cards out there."

"That would be my assumption. Guys, this is what we need. If we can get more proof, it'll blow their whole operation wide fucking open." Ash's green eyes had a touch of desperation in them. "Is there any chance there are more in her room?"

I spread my hands wide. "Maybe? I mean, I found that one by accident. Then again, I don't see her keeping this shit lying around where Gary might find it. She would hide it somewhere safer than her bedroom if they were that valuable, right?"

Ash grimaced. "In a place like Pandora." He looked at Ryan.

"No," Ryan snapped. "Absolutely not. We already said it's too much of a risk."

"I'm well aware," Ash countered, "but Ry, this is exactly what we need, man. We go public with this shit? It's game over for a lot of people. We're talking Interpol involvement that will put these people behind bars for life. Not just shutting the clubs down, and our dads, but a permanent fucking solution."

Ryan glared at him, his muscles tight like he was seconds away from punching Ash for even suggesting it. "Maddie isn't taking that risk."

"Isn't that a decision *Maddie* should make?" I chimed in.

He stared at me. "Did you miss the conversation where if they find out you *aren't* Madelaine, we might never see you again?"

"We're talking about weighing the value of me against hundreds, maybe thousands, of people being trafficked," I argued.

"Exactly," he spat, eyes blazing. "There's no fucking choice."

"Ryan," I whispered, shaking my head. "Think about what you're saying."

He crossed the room in three long strides, taking my face in his calloused hands. "I'd sacrifice every person in this world for you. *You* are what matters to me."

"And what about little girls Cori's age that are being moved through those clubs?"

He flinched, but held fast. "I can't worry about the whole world when you are *my* whole world."

"I love that you want to protect me, Ryan, but you're not changing my mind. I'm doing this," I informed him as gently as I could. I glanced over his shoulder at Ash. "Can you figure out—"

"No!" Ryan roared, the look in his eyes wild. "Maddie—"

"Ryan," I snapped, grabbing his wrists and digging my nails into them. "If you really think I can ride off into the sunset with you at the expense of others, then you don't know me at all."

His eyes closed, as if this was causing him physical pain. "Do you have to be so fucking selfless?"

"I'm not selfless," I retorted. "I'm doing this so we can put this whole shitshow to bed and be together without any regrets. Without wondering if Gary or Beckett or anyone else will come after us."

He pressed his forehead to mine. "I hate this so goddamn much."

"I know," I replied as gently as I could, "but you have to let me do this. It's the only way, and I need you to support my decision."

Ryan sighed and nodded slowly. "Okay. I'm with you, baby." He kissed me slowly before turning to Ash. "You know how to make the arrangements?"

Ash nodded. "Yeah, but Pandora isn't just a bank you pop into. You have to have an appointment to go inside, and those can take weeks. I can reach out with Madelaine's old phone and initiate contact."

"Do it," Ryan replied, resigned.

I wound my arms around his waist and tucked my head against his bare chest, feeling the familiar thump of his heart. "It's going to be okay."

His arms came around me, holding tight, as he kissed the crown of my head. "It sure as hell better be."

"I'll get started on it," Ash said with a tight smile as my phone started ringing from the purse I'd abandoned by the door when Ryan and I came in.

Speaking of which...

My cheeks heated as I ducked forward and grabbed the purse from under the pile of clothes Ash had stepped over to get into the room. I gathered them in my arms and finally answered the phone. "Hello?"

"Madel—Maddie? It's Mrs. Delancey." She cleared her throat, a nervous wobble in her tone.

Fear spiked in my blood, making me dizzy. There was only one reason she would be calling.

We'd discussed every aspect of taking on Gary and Beckett. We'd protected Corinne and Bex, but my mom... There was no way. I had no way to protect her anymore.

I tensed, bracing for the worst. "Is she dead?"

Ryan was instantly at my side.

"No, honey," Mrs. Delancey answered quickly. "At least, I don't think so. Your father... I don't know what happened. He blew in here like a hurricane almost an hour ago and left with her."

"He *took* her?" My brow furrowed in confusion. I'd expected Gary to run, but taking Mom with him? That seemed like a lot of hassle just to mess with me.

"Yes. I'm not... Did something happen? Usually he gives me some sort of instructions, but I'm at a bit of a loss here."

I covered the receiver end of my phone. "Gary took off with my mom."

"*With* her?" Ryan looked just as lost as I felt. "Why would he do that?"

I shrugged and turned to Ash.

"I'll make sure that we keep an eye out at all airports, train, and bus stations for them both," he assured me, already taking out his phone to do whatever the hell it was he did.

"Maddie, is everything all right?" Mrs. Delancey asked.

"Everything's fine. I have to go." I didn't bother waiting for her to reply before hanging up. "Why would he take her?"

"I don't know," Ryan answered honestly. "But we'll find her, okay? We'll find them both, Mads."

CHAPTER 64

MADDIE

Two days later, the roar of the fans packed into the stadium for the Knights first playoff game was deafening. Energy swirled around me, the vibrations of their cries echoing in my bones as I grinned before glancing at the scoreboard.

21-3.

The Knights had just ended the first half of the game with a solid lead, and the cheerleaders ran onto the field as the guys jogged to the locker room.

Imani clutched my arm, all smiles. "They're playing so well!"

I nodded back at her. "They've earned it."

Hell, we'd all earned a break.

The guys had been working tirelessly to get everything settled at Cain Industries as Phoenix officially annexed the company under their helm while balancing a hellish practice schedule in preparation for this game.

But last night we'd finally gotten some good news: Beckett was gone.

Ash had found a trail that indicated he'd fled to somewhere in the Caribbean. Ryan had already filed paperwork to be listed as Corinne's legal guardian, citing Beckett had abandoned her. For the interim, she was living with Mr. Harris at Brookfield, where there were plenty of people who loved her and would watch out for her. Ryan had also gotten her accepted into the school he'd talked about; Corinne would officially be enrolled after the first of the year.

I couldn't help but look at my wedding ring and smile. Ryan and I had already started looking at potential places to live next semester in Pacific City with the guys. They were all on board with our plan. I'd miss living so close to Bex, but she'd already told me her mom would never let her move in with the five of us.

Was it a weird arrangement? Yeah, but we were family. I wanted them all by my side as we started this new chapter.

Hopefully full of a lot less violence and betrayal and heartache.

Now we just needed to figure out where the hell Gary had gone with my mom. Ash hadn't found any hints as to where they could be. No travel tickets, none of Gary's numerous credit cards had been touched... It was like they'd vanished.

Not that I believed I'd seen the last of Gary. Not by a long shot.

But that was a fight for tomorrow.

Today, I was doing what Bex had suggested earlier and counting my wins where I could get them. And, judging by the way the guys were playing, we'd have another win to add to our growing tally.

"Charlie!" Imani shouted, waving a hand at the Brit ambling up the stairs.

He paused at our row with an impish smile. "Ladies. You all look lovely."

"Flattery will get you everywhere," Imani teased, linking her arm through his and flashing us a bright smile. "How about you escort me to the snack bar? I'm craving a pretzel with extra salt."

"Make that two!" Bex chimed in.

My stomach growled at the mention of junk food. "Nachos for me, please."

Charles inclined his head at us, the picture of formality even as his brown eyes sparkled with amusement. "I live to serve."

"We'll be back in a bit!" Imani called with a small wave.

I turned my attention back to the field as the cheerleaders began their halftime routine.

"Do you miss it?" Bex asked.

I shrugged a shoulder. "Sometimes? But it also feels like a lifetime ago. So much has happened, you know?"

She nodded. "I get it." She grabbed her soda from the cupholder and sucked up the last of it. "I should've asked Imani to get me a drink, too."

"I'll get it," I offered, already getting up. "I need to go to the bathroom anyway."

"You sure?" Bex looked doubtful and hopeful at the same time.

"Yeah," I assured her with a grin. I shimmied out of our row and started up the concrete stairs along with another wave of people.

As always, the line for the women's bathroom snaked out the door and around the corner while men came and went from their assigned bathroom without waiting.

"Men have it so easy," a soft voice huffed behind me.

I turned with a laugh. "Definitely." I eyed the petite woman behind me. She was a good eight inches shorter and majorly pregnant.

She rolled her eyes, swaying on her feet as she rested her hands atop her extended belly. "It would be nice if this one wasn't playing kickball with my bladder every fifteen minutes."

"Ouch," I murmured, shaking my head. "How far along are you?"

"Eight and a half months," she replied. "And I'm ready to issue an evacuation order."

I laughed softly, watching as she winced and rubbed her lower back. "You okay?"

"Yeah," she replied, grimacing. "I just—*Shit.*" She sucked in a sharp breath, her eyes going wide.

"Whoa," I said, my hands fluttering up like I wanted to touch her, but I'd just met her. "Are you sure you're okay?"

She pressed her lips together. "I don't... Ow, dammit."

"Do you need me to get someone?" I asked, looking around like a friend or baby daddy might magically appear. "I can grab security—"

Her eyes were wide with panic. "I think I need to sit down. Can you help me? I think I just need a second."

"Of course," I quickly agreed, taking her arm and leading her from the line.

The inside of the stadium was packed with people darting in and out of shops and waiting in lines for the concessions. The sounds echoed off the cavernous ceiling, and I felt the woman tremble as we made our way through the crowd.

I spotted a security guard a few yards away. "Let me ask him for help."

Her hand squeezed my arm. "Please, don't."

I shot her a confused look.

"They'll call an ambulance, and I'd rather not pay the fee they charge," she admitted.

I understood that. "Okay, but—"

She was already pulling her phone out of her purse. "I'm going to text my boyfriend. I think I need to go to the hospital. Something's not right."

I waited as she shot off a text message, scanning the crowd in case I saw one of my friends, but there were people everywhere.

She smiled at me as she waited for her boyfriend to text back. When he answered back with a phone call within seconds, I mentally applauded the guy in question for not ignoring his phone. She quickly told him she wasn't feeling good and where she was.

"He's getting the car," she told me with a thin smile as she tucked the phone back into her purse. "He wants to take me to the hospital himself." She pointed to the nearest exit only sign. "We actually parked in that lot. Do you mind waiting with me until he shows up? I mean, unless you need to go."

"Of course I can wait with you," I assured her, walking beside her as she waddled through the security stanchions toward the parking lot.

It was quieter out here. Someone was smoking a few feet away, but he put out his cigarette and walked around the side of the building so he could get back inside.

"What's your name?" I asked, wanting to keep her mind off whatever was going on.

"Uh, Kasey," she answered.

I smiled, hoping I looked reassuring and not as freaked out as I felt inside. "I'm Maddie."

"Thanks for helping me, Maddie," she murmured. She gave me an odd look. "That was very kind of you."

I shrugged. "Just doing what I can. Shit, let me text my friends and let them know I'm out here so they don't worry." I dug my phone out of my back pocket and unlocked it to text Bex.

Kasey cried out suddenly, her hands shooting forward to grab me and knocking the phone from my hands. "Oh, God."

Icy cold panic flashed through me, and I looked around to see if anyone could help. All I saw was an older SUV pulling alongside the curb.

"That's... That's my boyfriend," Kasey managed through clenched teeth. "Can you help me?"

"Yeah." I took her by the arms and carefully guided her toward the car.

"Backseat," she told me when I started to open the passenger door.

Without thinking, I opened the backdoor and turned to help her into the car. "Okay, Kas—"

Something sharp pinched my arm. Instinctively, I reached a hand up, rubbing it and wondering if I'd been stung by a bee.

Kasey stood behind me, her face perfectly calm as she watched me.

"Are you..." A wave of dizziness damn near knocked me off my feet. I fell into the side of the car.

Kasey rolled her eyes and looked into the vehicle over my shoulder. "A little help? I'm not lifting her into this thing by myself, Ev."

"What?" Confusion muddled my thoughts. My eyes focused, just barely, on a tiny needle in her hand. "Did you..." My tongue became thick and clumsy in my mouth, not forming words.

Drugged.

The bitch had drugged me.

No, no, no.

My vision blurred, darkening at the edges as I heard someone get out of the car and walk around to our side with heavy footsteps.

"I got her," a male voice replied, his tone cold and familiar.

I blinked up, fear plunging into my heart like a dagger when I saw Evan standing in front of me.

He shook his head at me. "You should've just done what he said."

I sagged against the doorframe, my knees turning to jelly as I started to slide down to the ground.

Evan grabbed me under the arms, and I tried to push him away, but my arms wouldn't move. He lifted me into the backseat of the SUV, and everything faded to black before he even closed the door.

CHAPTER 65

MADDIE

My mouth was full of cotton and ash when I started to wake up. The tiniest shafts of light from a small window above my head felt like icepicks being driven into my eyes. A whimper slipped from me, and I turned my head to escape the pain.

What the hell had happened?

I tried to reach a hand up to cover my eyes…but couldn't.

Prying one eye open, I looked down and saw my hand was cuffed by a leather strap to the railing of the bed I was in. I gave it a futile jerk, but it didn't move. I tried my other arm, but it was tethered the same way.

Panic and fear woke me up as adrenaline surged through my veins. I looked around the room, my breathing coming out in desperate, ragged pants.

The room was a sterile beige color. There was a small bathroom area with a sink and toilet, but no door. Other than the twin bed I was cuffed to, there wasn't any furniture.

No pictures, no clock. No way to tell where I was or how long I'd been here.

A door behind my head opened, and I craned my neck to see who was coming in.

"Oh, good, you're awake." A slender woman with graying hair twisted into a knot at the base of her skull stepped into the room with a clipboard. She leaned out the open door, murmuring something I couldn't make out.

Moments later, a man in pale green scrubs brought her a chair and a cup of water with a straw. He set the chair by my bed and left, closing the door.

I cringed when I heard it lock.

"You must be thirsty," the woman went on, like this was freaking normal. She lifted the straw to my lips.

I slowly took a sip, letting the liquid saturate my mouth. I considered spitting it at her, but had a feeling that wouldn't help.

"There. Feel better?" She set the cup down on the floor and settled into the chair. "Madelaine, do you know where you are?"

I shook my head. "I was... I was kidnapped. There was a girl..."

The woman's lips pressed together in an unhappy line. "Madelaine, my name is Dr. Sharon Browne. I'm a doctor here at the Shadyvale Institution."

I frowned, not really caring about that. "You need to call my husband—"

She sighed, shaking her head and jotting a note on her clipboard. "No, Madelaine. You're safe now."

"Safe? No, I'm not safe. I was—"

"Madelaine, you were brought here because you're suffering a psychotic break," she informed me. "It's no wonder, what with the abuse you've been suffering for the last few months, but you're safe. He can't hurt you anymore."

I shook my head and tugged at my restraints. "Can you untie me? Please?"

She glanced down at the straps and buckles holding me in place. "Not yet. These are for your own safety, I'm afraid. Your father—"

I hissed. "My father is a fucking monster. He's the one who had me taken! I was at a game with my friends and there was a woman who needed help, but it was a trick. My *father* is the one who did this to me."

A tiny crease formed in her brow. "Your father is very concerned for you, Madelaine."

A hysterical laugh bubbled out of me. "My name isn't Madelaine—it's Madison. Madison Porter."

She tilted her head. "Oh?"

I sucked in a deep breath, trying to be calm. "Months ago I found out I had a twin sister named Madelaine Cabot. We decided to switch lives for the summer, but she was killed. No, she was murdered by our father, Gary Cabot."

Dr. Browne nodded slowly and made another freaking note.

"I've been living my sister's life for the last few months, and I know that sounds crazy—"

"We don't like to use that word here, Madelaine," she interrupted me gently.

I almost screamed. "My name is *Madison.*"

"No," she said firmly. "Your name is Madelaine Cabot. You did have a twin sister, yes, but Madison Porter-Cabot was killed in a tragic fire nearly five months ago."

"No, she wasn't!" I shouted, jerking again at my restraints. "I'm Madi—"

"Madelaine, you must calm down or we'll have to give you something," Dr. Browne advised.

"Are you fucking insane? *Listen to me!* My name is Madison Porter. Call Ryan Cain, okay? He's my husband."

Dr. Browne's gaze flicked to her notepad. "I do have that you married Ryan Cain a week ago. Your father is very concerned about Mr. Cain. We know about the abuse and the way he's manipulated you."

What fucking parallel universe had I woken up in? "Listen, lady, you're wrong, okay? You're flat fucking *wrong.* Gary is the bad guy here."

Dr. Browne sighed and stood up. "I see we're not going to be able to continue. Perhaps when you're calmer—"

"I'm tied to a fucking bed and I was kidnapped!" I snapped. "How calm am I supposed to be?"

Dr. Browne knocked on the door. It was unlocked and opened, and the same nurse stepped in.

"Manny, I'm going to need a sedative for Madelaine."

"No!" I cried, not wanting to be knocked out again. Frustrated tears gathered in my eyes, and I could only watch as they both ignored me.

"Let's go with one hundred milligrams of haldol," Dr. Browne went on like I didn't exist.

Manny nodded and disappeared.

"Please don't do this," I begged, feeling the skin around my wrists start to rub raw as I pulled against the straps.

Dr. Browne stood over me. "Madelaine, we're doing this for you. You'll see. It will all be all right."

Manny reappeared and passed her a syringe.

"No, no. Please—"

The needle pricked my skin, and I felt the liquid start to spread as Dr. Browne pressed the plunger down.

"No," I whimpered, my eyes already starting to close.

~

E verything was fuzzy and soft.
I glanced at one hand, flexing each of my fingers and marveling at the way they moved. One by one, they curled and unfurled like magic.

A smile slipped across my lips.

Fingers were fun.

I frowned as my gaze traveled up to the bruise around my wrist. Ugly shades of black and purple made it look strange. I opened my mouth to ask what had happened, but I couldn't make my tongue and lips work.

They weren't as good as fingers.

The door in front of me opened, and I blinked as a man walked into the room, a look of disdain on his face.

I knew him. Why did I know him?

"This could have been so much easier," he hissed, leaning over me and grabbing my wrist. He squeezed, and pain arced through my arm. I wanted to cry out, but my mouth still wouldn't work. "You stupid little bitch. I told you not to test me."

I tried to clear the fog around my brain, but it was useless.

The man sneered at me as he let me go. "You truly thought you could beat *me?*"

Gary.

His name was... Gary.

I knew him.

The door behind him opened again, and two men walked in, both in suits. Only one of them bothered looking at me, the other addressed Gary. "We're ready to begin."

Gary dropped a hand to my shoulder. "All right, gentlemen. Let's go, sweetheart, all right?" He came around behind me, and then I was rolling forward, being wheeled through a long hallway with doors as we followed the two men.

One of them opened a door, and Gary pushed me into a large room.

A courtroom.

I smiled to myself because I knew this word.

"Maddie!" A loud voice roared.

I jerked in the chair, my heart slamming against my ribs as I blinked and tried to find the source of the voice.

"Fuck," someone grunted. "Ryan, sit *down.*"

"Get off me!"

Something crashed like it had been knocked over, and I cringed at the noise.

The wheelchair I was in stopped abruptly.

"Your Honor, I beg you to have this man removed," Gary boomed from behind me. "He's already caused my daughter so much pain."

"You motherfucker," a furious voice hissed. "I'm going to—"

"Ryan! Shut the *fuck up.*"

I turned my head and saw four men. One of them was being held back by two of them, his bright blue eyes wild and frantic as he looked at… me.

Ryan.

My pulse sped up as I met his gaze. I wanted to go to him. I needed to—

Gary pushed me away, breaking our eye contact, and I wanted to cry, but nothing worked. Not my eyes, not my tongue, not my legs.

Nothing except my fingers.

I tapped one against the arm rest just to prove I could do *something*.

My eyes felt so heavy, and I was so tired. I would just rest here for a few minutes and then it would all be better.

It had to get better.

CHAPTER 66

RYAN

I was going to *kill* Gary Cabot.

"Ryan, you've got to chill out," Court hissed, getting in my face and cutting off my view as Gary wheeled Maddie to the front of the courtroom.

My gaze snapped to my friend. "Maddie—"

He grimaced. "I know, bro. But you can't lose your shit here, okay? Maddie needs you to hold it together."

My gaze instantly moved to my wife, who looked like she was sleeping. Fury erupted in my chest at seeing her so broken and helpless.

My hands clenched, and I wished like hell it was Gary's windpipe I was crushing. I'd fucked up by letting him live, but I was planning to rectify that oversight as soon as possible.

"Your Honor..." One of Gary's lawyers stood up, his nasally voice carrying through the room. "This is a private family matter. Mr. Cain and his friends have no business—"

"She's my *wife!*" I snapped before I could consider staying calm.

"Because you forced her hand and manipulated her," Gary cried, looking like a desperate father. He turned to the judge, who seemed to be only mildly interested in what was happening. "Your Honor, Ryan

Cain has been abusing and hurting my daughter for months. His presence here will only hurt her more. I beg the court to have him and his companions removed so this matter can remain *private*."

Judge Norris glanced at me, his gaze accusatory.

I gritted my teeth and held his gaze.

This whole shitshow was a fucking disaster.

One week. Gary had kept Maddie from me for an entire fucking *week*, for most of which I hadn't known where she was.

Bex and Imani had been practically hysterical, crying and frantic, when Maddie had gone missing at the game that they'd had my coach pull me from it. I'd run off the field to find her without hesitating. Court, Linc, and Ash were right behind me.

The Knights lost.

But the bigger issue was *we* had lost.

By the time Ash managed to get into the Knights' security camera feeds, they'd been erased. There was no sign of Maddie anywhere except for her phone. Court found that in the parking lot, the screen cracked into a million pieces.

I'd turned the world upside down trying to find her.

Thank God for fucking Ash who had set up some kind of program that alerted us to anything pertaining to Madelaine's name. When it popped up this morning as a hearing in family court at the last minute, we'd barely had time to get to downtown L.A. before it began.

Gary had managed to not only kidnap my wife but also had her placed on a psychiatric hold while petitioning the court to have her rights transferred to him.

"Everyone sit down," Judge Norris finally ordered.

Ash tugged me into a seat beside him, and I finally let my legs fold enough for my ass to hit the wood. But I had eyes only for my girl.

"I let her down," I whispered, gutted at how fragile she looked.

Linc sucked in a sharp breath on my other side. "Maddie's strong, Ryan. She's going to be okay."

"Look at her," I rasped as her father's lawyers called a shrink to the stand. "She's not even there."

Court leaned around Linc's side. "She needs you to be strong, so man the fuck up, Cain."

I nodded stiffly and drew in a steadying breath. He was right; Maddie needed me to be in control right now for both of us.

The doctor was sworn in, and I could only listen in horror as she recounted *Madelaine's* fractured psyche.

She was delusional because she claimed to be her dead twin sister.

She was suffering from PTSD, likely at the hands of an abusive partner who had been controlling her.

Photos were introduced that showed bruises not only on Maddie but also on Gary—the ones I'd given him that day in the boardroom when I'd thought we were invincible.

I scoffed and shook my head in disgust as the doctor concluded that Madelaine needed intense care and was unfit to make her own choices. She *beseeched* the court to let Maddie's father assume control of her care and finances.

"He's going to use this to get her inheritance," I muttered. "Motherfucker found a loophole."

"Bullshit," Ash replied quietly. "He'll never touch it. Other than Maddie, only you have direct access. Even if he gets guardianship of her, I can keep him out of the accounts."

I scrubbed a hand over my face. "Ash, he knows I'll give him every fucking cent if it means I get her back."

My best friend was quiet, because he knew I was right.

I'd give up anything to protect Maddie.

Gary had me by the fucking balls.

I turned to Court. "Is there anything we can do?"

His lips smashed together. "Not today. Technically you're her husband, but Gary's arguing you're the problem and that your marriage is invalid because you coerced her. And I have a feeling the reason he managed to keep things so quiet is because he knows Norris. We'll file an appeal, but odds are? She won't be going home with you today."

It hit me like a kick to the nuts. All the air rushed out of my lungs, and I couldn't get it back.

"Maddie can hang on," Linc reminded me. "Trust your girl."

I did trust my girl, and I knew she was one of the strongest people I'd ever met. She was resilient and fierce, but there wasn't much she could do to protect herself if they kept her drugged up.

The doctor stepped down from the witness stand, and the eye contact she made with Gary as she walked by his table left zero doubts in my mind that she was in on whatever shit he was trying to pull.

"Find out who she is," I growled to Ash.

He nodded. "You know I will."

"Thank you, Dr. Browne," Judge Norris said, straightening a stack of papers. "I've listened to your testimony and read your notes. I must say, I am gravely concerned for the welfare of Miss Cabot."

I bit back a snarl because that wasn't her fucking name. Never had been. Never would be.

"This court finds there is justified cause to put a temporary conservatorship into place until a more formal treatment plan can be established."

I glared at Court. "Can't we do *anything?*"

"It's family court," he replied tersely. "This isn't a situation where we can object. We have to file our own motions—"

With a snort of disgust, I threw myself back in my chair and watched my worst nightmare finish playing out.

Judge Norris cleared his throat. "This court hereby transfers temporary guardianship and conservatorship control to Madelaine Cabot's father, Gary Cabot, effective immediately. We will reconvene in sixty days to reassess Miss Cabot's state of mind and wellbeing."

Gary couldn't resist shooting me a smug smile, and I wondered how he'd handle being Maddie's guardian if he was six feet under.

No, fuck that. I wasn't wasting my time digging that fucker a hole when I could light his body on fire and call it a day.

"It's not over, Ryan," Ash murmured.

"This case is adjourned." Judge Norris clapped his gavel loudly, signaling the end of the session, and I was immediately on my feet.

I had to get to Maddie, to get close to her even for a second. My hands shook with the need to touch her, hold her.

Pushing past Ash, I exited our row and was immediately stopped by two police officers. I groaned, because what the *fuck*.

"Ryan Cain?" One of them asked, having the good sense to look a little uncertain of confronting me with my friends at my back when we were all pissed the fuck off.

"What?" I snapped, grimacing as Gary wheeled Madison out of the side door they'd originally entered.

The other douchebag sneered at me, slapping a piece of paper against my chest. "We have a warrant for your arrest."

"On what grounds?" Court demanded, grabbing the paper before I could.

Douche Number Two smirked at me. "The murder of Adam Kindell."

CHAPTER 67

MADDIE

Time no longer existed, and neither, it seemed, did I.
I floated along, occasionally getting glimpses of the reality
around me, but as soon as my thoughts started to collect into something coherent, they vanished.

Sometimes I woke up and the room was dark. Other times it was
light. Sometimes Dr. Browne was there, but usually she wasn't.

I was so tired. My limbs felt foreign and awkward. They didn't
work right. Not even my fingers.

Whatever they were giving me was strong. Strong enough that I
didn't know how much time had passed when I was suddenly
drenched in icy water.

I gasped, slamming back against the tiles of a shower as people
started pulling off my underwear.

Wait—where the hell were my clothes?

I pushed at their hands, a pathetic attempt to stop people who
were much stronger than I was. Even still, I managed to land a weak
blow on something soft, and someone grunted.

"Bitch punched my fucking tit," a high-pitched voice whined.

Something—or some*one*—shoved me, and my head cracked
against the tiles. Pops of light exploded behind my eyes.

"Calm down or we'll drug you again," a harsh voice warned.

God, anything but that again. I forced myself to be still as they finished stripping me and cold water rained over my head.

A rough washcloth was scrubbed over my body, and then hands were in my hair, washing it. I winced as they caught on a tangle and yanked their fingers free.

Biting the insides of my cheeks, I closed my eyes and let it happen.

The water shut off, but I was still freezing. A thin towel was tossed at me.

"Dry off," the first voice snapped. "Then get dressed."

I opened my eyes and saw a pile of clothes on the floor. Two women stood before me, not seeming to care that I was freezing and naked.

The one with the high voice cocked a brow. "Or we can walk you through the halls naked." She sneered at me down a long nose. "Skank like you probably gets off on that shit."

I forced myself to move and dried my body off with shaking hands. I dropped the towel twice, and it took several attempts to get the clothes on. Finally the second woman yanked my shirt over my head like I was a toddler.

"Let's go," she ordered.

A shudder rippled down my spine as I tried to figure out where I was.

It looked like an old locker room with a few showers, none of them separated by even a curtain for privacy. There were stalls for toilets, but none of them had doors.

"Sh-shoes?" I asked as my feet slipped on the tiles.

The second woman glanced at my bare feet, and she gave a tight shake of her head. "No shoes until we know you aren't a suicide risk."

"I'm not suicidal," I said slowly.

She shot me a *yeah right* look. "They all say that." Using a keycard, she swiped the lock by the door and waited for it to beep and turn green.

Great. So the bathrooms were on lockdown.

The first woman scoffed at me and turned to start cleaning up the wet towels.

"Let's go," Number Two snapped, nudging me out of the bathroom. "You need to get to your room."

I followed her, trying to get an idea of where I was, but there were no windows. Just fluorescent lighting, white walls, and white tiles beneath my feet. There were doors—so many doors—each with a tiny circular window, but that was it.

"Where am I?" I asked quietly as we turned down another hall. I was trying to remember all the turns we'd taken, but I was exhausted and scared.

She glanced back over her shoulder at me. "The Hightwater School."

"What's that?"

She didn't answer. Instead, she stopped at a door and used her keycard to unlock it. "Here's your room. Lights out at nine. Breakfast at seven."

I stepped inside the tiny square room. A twin bed with no bedding on it was bolted to the floor. A toilet and sink were against the wall across from the bed, and I could see the space where a mirror had once hung. Above that, a clock hung on the wall, surrounded by a metal cage. The only other piece of furniture was a silver nightstand, also screwed into the floor.

The woman paused and grabbed a small cup and plastic bottle of water, which she handed to me.

I eyed the tiny cup with several pills inside of it. Dread churned in my gut. "What is it?"

"Your meds," she answered like I was an idiot.

"But what—"

"Swallow them or we'll inject them," she cut me off.

I took a deep breath and swallowed the pills, washing them down with the water. When I was done, she took the bottle and started to leave.

"Good," she muttered.

"I'm freezing," I said softly. "Can I have a blanket?"

She sighed, clearly annoyed. "No, because you might wrap it around your pretty little throat, and I'm not losing my job because the princess is whacked."

I recoiled and shook my head. "I'm not—"

Another loud, aggravated sigh left her, and I abandoned my protests.

Instead I asked, "What do I do now?"

She met my eyes, a flicker of something humane in her gaze for a split second. "Whatever they tell you. And if you're smart? You won't ask questions." She turned and left, locking the door and leaving me with nothing but questions.

I slowly crawled onto the bare bed and pressed my back against the wall. Dragging my knees to my chest, I wrapped my arms around them and waited.

My forehead dropped to my knees as I swallowed the urge to cry. Crying wouldn't help me now. I just needed to hold on, because I knew Ryan would get me out of this.

And if he wouldn't—or couldn't—then I'd do it my damn self.

COMING 2022: MAD LOVE

Available for Preorder now on Amazon!

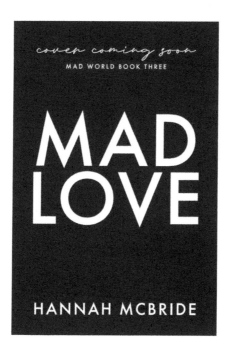

ACKNOWLEDGMENTS

My favorite part has arrived! Time to shout out (or type out) all the people I owe a massive thank you to!

First, I have to start with the epic team who made MAD AS HELL possible: my editor, Natashya Wilson (who may love Ryan more than me); my proofreader, Ricarda Berger; my amazing PA, Tracy Kirby; the cover queen herself, Quirah Casey (Temptation Creations); and Kathy Williams.

I owe my sanity and a lot of this book to a tribe of women who gave me endless encouragement and support: Krista Davis, Nicole Sanchez, Katie Mingolla, Bella Matthews, Elle Christensen, Jenn Wolfel, Jen Grey, Vonetta Young, and Lisa Carina Gaibler.

Endless love and hugs to my Inner Sanctum peeps. I have the best readers EVER. Thanks for being so supportive and excited; your comments give me *life*. Special shoutouts to Courtenay Oros & Kristin Weyrick for helping me out with some names!

If you didn't know, I also have the most incredible, supportive family. Mom, Dad, Micah, Sherry, and Lauren: I love you all so much more than you'll ever know.

Finally to my two littlest cheerleaders with the biggest hearts: Aria & Nora. I love you both more than glitter, makeup, *and* books.

ABOUT THE AUTHOR

Hannah McBride has been many things in her life: a restaurant manager, a clinical research coordinator, a dreamer, a makeup brand ambassador, an event coordinator, a blogger, and more. But at heart, she's always been a writer, and in 2020 she decided to make it official. Good luck stopping her now.

ALSO BY HANNAH MCBRIDE

Blackwater Pack Series:

SANCTUM

BROKEN

PREY

LEGACY

SCARS

REQUIEM (coming Winter 2023)

Mad World Series:

MAD WORLD

MAD AS HELL

MAD LOVE (coming Fall 2022)

Anthologies:

A Bridal Party To Remember

Devour (coming Fall 2022)

Made in the USA
Middletown, DE
29 September 2023

39327689R00311